— THE — BANNERMAN SHORTLIST

Colin Batrouney is the author of
Omar and Enzo in the Big Talking Book (Clouds of Magellan)
and *Creative Writing for Beginners* (Affirm Press).
He lives in Melbourne.

THE BANNERMAN SHORTLIST

— A NOVEL —

COLIN BATROUNEY

CLOUDS OF MAGELLAN

Published by Clouds of Magellan Press, Melbourne, Australia, 2023

ISBN: 978-0-6457328-7-0 (Paperback)
ISBN: 978-0-6457328-5-6 (Hardback)

www.cloudsofmagellanpress.net

For
Catherine, Edwina, Judith, Kaz, Mary & Nicole

I am a man: little do I last
and the night is enormous.
But I look up:
the stars write.
Unknowing I understand:
I too am written,
and at this very moment
someone spells me out.

Octavio Paz
'Brotherhood'

FROM
TROPICS
TO
TABLE

the

GENIUS *of* SUGAR

a history by

JOSEPH E BANNERMAN

AD VITAM AETERNAM

LONDON

4 pm, Harvest Place, Kensington SW7 5

Gideon Bannerman blinked. It was the skeleton clock on the marble mantle that had stopped him. The clock clapped out the hours with a shallow 'ting' that carried with it a tiny reverberant echo. Gideon squinted and noticed the quieter mechanical grind of the little gears whirring in the machinery before each successive ring. After four bells there was nothing.

He kept still and uselessly clasped and unclasped his hands. He clasped them again. For a moment he shut his eyes and saw a darkness vivid with swirling, flashing patterns. Scribbles and blotches seemed to come together and then disperse as quickly. With his eyes still shut, the air around him seemed alive, at once cold and fresh and clear.

He stood motionless on the thready pile of an ancient Aubusson rug. He looked down at his feet. He stood in one grey sock and one blue sock among the woven silk roses and tendrillar leaves worn almost to nothing in patches across the floor.

He stared ahead and saw his troubling reflection in the mirror above the mantle, the mirror's silver mercury backing oxidised into pock-marks leaving Gideon a spotty presence, in a spotty room. The sound of the city around him was muffled in the quiet afternoon. From his upstairs morning room he could hear motorbikes, cars and buses, together with threads of mobile telephone conversations as pedestrians passed on the pavement below.

Harvest Place, the Georgian home he had inherited from his father was built by his family in 1759 from the profits of a trade steeped in blood, human traffic, displacement, tears, enslavement and death: the Bannermans were in sugar.

As a boy, Gideon was fascinated by the origins of his family's wealth. It had in fact, been written up in a slim history of leaden prose penned and self-published by his great uncle, Joseph Edward Bannerman in 1900.

From Tropics to Table – the Genius of Sugar, described the cropping of sugar cane in Guiana and Honduras by 'helpful native workers'. It detailed the refinement of raw sugar into loaves in Whitechapel and the packaging of the product into tightly twilled brown paper cones, emblazoned with the Bannerman Sugar Trading Company insignia, an engraving of a falcon flapping imperiously above the legend, *Ad Vitam Aeternam*. These same sugar loaves were then trundled across the United Kingdom at first by horse, then by train. Thousands of tons of sugar, year after year after year.

This history was mostly a fiction. Joseph had invented a narrative for his family that characterised his ancestors as benevolent waxwork heroes of industry. Titans who had discovered a raw material, and against the odds had bravely hewn it from the ground in foreign lands and carved a lucrative citadel of sugar in the British Isles for the betterment of all.

From Tropics to Table concluded with an odd little meditation on the nature of suffering in what could be described as the book's only acknowledgement of the wholesale misery that sat behind the Bannerman lolly.

'God has granted us good fortune, it is true. Some would say not without a degree of pain and hardship – indeed! But I would ask, dear reader, what great achievements are realised in this world without a measure of pain, of hardship and suffering?'

J.E.B. Covent Garden 1900.

All history now, and little to do with Gideon. The family had not traded in sugar for over a hundred years, and the money generated by sugar that had cost the blood of thousands, was now not his concern. Gideon's main preoccupation at that moment was for one of the last legacies of that fortune, the Bannerman Prize for Literature, and more specifically the shortlist for that prize, which had been announced the night before.

By the mid-fifties, when fortunes made from the profits of enslavement and indentured servitude were frowned upon – even in Tory circles – Gideon's father, Adrian Bannerman, harbouring political aspirations to become the Member for Westminster, decided to set up a trust that would administer a yearly literary prize of 20,000 pounds. The Prize now grown to 50,000, for 'fiction of merit and meaningful value' was open to any novel published in Britain and the Commonwealth in the preceding calendar year. Adrian saw the prize as his entry into a world he little understood and trusted even less; he would be a conservative who would become a champion of the arts. In this way he would distinguish himself from his competitors who promised to do something about transport, housing, or crime. Decades later the Bannerman Prize for Literature was the only thing of enduring value left after that failed push for parliament in 1956.

Under the woolly campaign slogan, 'My England is Your England', Adrian's relaxed campaigning failed to capture the imagination of his potential constituents. When the final results were scrutinised it was determined that Gideon's father had been defeated by over eleven thousand votes. Gideon's mother, Pip, was delighted at her husband's loss. She had hated the idea of public life and was only ever a grudging presence during campaign events and party functions. Indeed, her demeanour only genuinely enlivened on the evening of Adrian's defeat. Moving amongst the glum attendees at campaign headquarters Pip beamed, thanking everyone for their hard work and dedication. She giggled when a volunteer curtsied as she presented Pip with a small bouquet of flowers wrapped in cellophane. For many of the campaign workers this was the first time they had seen Mrs Bannerman sincerely happy, basking in her husband's failure. The lasting memory Gideon had of his mother that cold November evening was of her applauding too enthusiastically during his father's concession speech, snapping the stems of the bunch of carnations she was clutching.

Philippa Bannerman was a woman with an enormous capacity for hatred, and most of it was directed at her husband. Her own family's wealth was derived from shipping, so it was never money that kept the unhappy union of Pip and Adrian outwardly stable. Bound by faith, it was Catholicism that was the glue that adhered every dumb convention and blind propriety to this miserable marriage and sorrowful family.

Gideon was born in 1950 with a twin sister, Diana, afflicted with dual sensory loss – no hearing and little sight. Pip was convinced that her daughter's afflictions were a punishment the Old Testament God she worshipped had meted out to Adrian and herself for his serial infidelities and her tacit acceptance of them. This belief was further compounded one sunny July afternoon when Diana, aged four, choked to death on a glass eye she had torn from the head of a teddy when playing in the nursery. Diana's death propelled Pip into a fierce and unrelenting program of grief and religious observance that she hoped would release her from any future punishments.

For years she enlisted Gideon to accompany her to church, allowing him into her bedroom where he lay in his woollen trousers, cable-knit pullover and shiny black shoes as she readied herself to venerate God and Jesus.

Pip was a thin woman whose perfectly teased and lacquered auburn hair gave her head the appearance of being slightly too large for her modest frame. Gideon loved observing his mother as she 'put her face on' in her lightly perfumed bedroom. She could not leave the house before being inscribed, painted and powdered by Revlon, Max Factor, and Elizabeth Arden. Gideon never tired of the incredible transformation that took place before the tri-fold mirrors of his mother's vanity. He would marvel at her skill in sculpting her eyebrows into determined, intelligent arches, the subtle dusting of her cheekbones and the calligraphic accomplishment of the three broad strokes of crimson that perfectly described her gleaming, expressive mouth – made all the more miraculous as she often affected that last touch in mid-sentence, responding to Gideon's idle questions with cursory, distracted answers.

'Mummy, if God sees everything, can he see us now?'

'Of course.'

'Can he see me in the bath?'

'Stop being stupid.'

'Do you think God likes Diana?'

'He loves Diana.'

'Does God love Daddy?'

'Get your shoes off my bed and stop asking me things.'

Gideon rolled off the bed and walked up to his mother, she turned the full radiance of her freshly made-up face toward him, her eyes glittering sharply in the lights surrounding her mirrors. Pip took both his cheeks into her hands and drew him to her, kissing him on the lips. They both looked back at the mirror and giggled to see Gideon's mouth covered in Revlon's crimson Fire and Ice.

'Aren't you pretty!' She beamed.

She pulled two Kleenex from a box by the mirror, dabbing them on her tongue before roughly wiping Gideon's mouth clean. Folding the tissues lengthwise she dropped them into her black bag, snapping it shut.

'Time to go.'

Gideon would sit quietly in the chilly, roomy interior of the car as they were driven to church. The journey never took more than twenty minutes, but in that time his mother transformed herself from the terrifying woman who stalked the rooms and hallways of Harvest Place in a state of readily available rage, into a vision of glamorous, controlled serenity and generous calm. This version of Pip had a noticeably lower, warmer register to her voice that Gideon always noticed as she greeted acquaintances on the steps of Westminster Cathedral.

Once inside they would make their way past the Chapel of Saint George and the English Martyrs, past the anorexic beauty of Saint John Southworth, his golden head and tiny hands sleeping forever in his glass case. There was never any time to linger as Gideon was tugged along by his mother's black kid grip. At their pew, four rows from the altar, Pip would automatically pause to genuflect, dipping slightly, her head inclined to the cold marble floor and by rote, Gideon would follow. Here they would sit in silence waiting for the service to begin. Pip would always take her rosary from her bag and thread it around her gloved fingers, staring glassily at the altar, while her son's mind would begin to wander.

For Gideon, the church was not a place for prayer and spiritual contemplation. No. The overwhelming impression he took from the theatre of Catholicism was its uninhibited embrace of glamour. From the parishioners turned out in their Sunday best – the hats, veils, the lipstick and the shiny shoes, to the angels, the priests, the cassocked altar boys and the stained-glass depictions of faith and suffering – even the naked, bloodied Christ with his pale, punctured feet, one resting demurely on top of the other – everything was infused with a chaotic sense of sex, violence, and transcendent enchantment. In this heady atmosphere, during the hypnotic liturgy of the sacrament of the Eucharist, Gideon's thoughts would not run to piety but rather drift into a vivid erotica that involved chubby buttocked cherubim, muscular angels, powerful celestial figures overseeing Jesus and his drooping loincloth, his eyes turned upward in an ecstasy of consummate suffering. These distractions inevitably led to hot, commanding erections that would throb and push against his worsted wool trousers, only subsiding once the Mass was concluded.

Afterwards, there would be lunch at Harrods. Gideon would eat sandwiches and drink lemonade. Pip would sit opposite him with a pot of tea as the spell of church would leave her. She would sit smoking, waiting patiently for Gideon to finish, often blowing smoke across his lunch, staring into him in a trance of resigned disappointment that visibly disintegrated her confident beauty.

From the ages of five to thirteen, Pip packed Gideon off to board at All Hallows School in Somerset. It was here that Gideon navigated the drama of puberty in the spooky confines of Cranmore Hall. In those pre-co-ed days the school boarded boys from upper and upper middle-class families from across the country. From the relatively dull routine of Harvest Place with his parents' frosty silences and occasional bouts of domestic and psychological violence, Gideon was pitched into a world of fraternal love, sadism, tribal loyalty and boyish sexual adventurism that formed the basis of his preparation to enter the world.

From All Hallows he was sent to Barlow House at Downside School to prepare him for Oxford. It was here that Gideon was encouraged to find his passion and to pursue that passion into tertiary education. Although he excelled at nothing, Gideon developed a keen interest in history, science and mathematics. He loved the elegance and logic of numbers, and he respected what could be proven in the world – he trusted things that held no ambiguity or mystery. But his passion, pursued with tireless devotion, nurtured at All Hallows and carried over to Downside, was masturbation. In this pursuit of course, he was not distinguished. All his school friends were industriously distracted by the seismic activity that was taking place in their underpants. Where Gideon found himself in the minority was in the area of disguising his same-sex attraction within an enforced same-sex environment. From the moment of his first orgasm and on through the boarding years of strenuous, fervid practice, masturbation reinforced for Gideon that the world could be made breathtakingly and astonishingly vivid in those moments when his body was lifted into climax.

Other boys had shared contraband copies of men's magazines with pictures of beautiful women who cupped their ample breasts as offerings for teenage boys to revere, jutting their buttocks out to form an inviting slide down their backs, their wistful expressions animated by a kind of dreamy, defiant anger that suggested every kind of sexual accommodation. But Gideon would look at these well-thumbed pages of magazines like *Men Only* and *Razzle* unmoved. Instead of *Mandy*, *Cheryl* or *Pam*, the obscure object of desire that aroused the sexual devotion of Gideon Bannerman was the dark haired, doe-eyed beauty of Cliff Richard.

Heartthrob to millions, for Gideon, Richard's smoothly coiffed hair, his determined brow and impossibly perfect features signalled something fundamental and inevitable that went beyond mere adulation. Every time Gideon took out the small portrait of Richard that he had clipped from *Jackie* magazine, staring into the black pools of Richard's eyes, almost willing Cliff to look back at him, to acknowledge his love, he felt the force of a primal destiny. So obsessed was Gideon that he reached a stage where he would only need to hear the reedy tenor of Richard's voice belting out 'Summer Holiday' on the radio to achieve spectacular erections that would demand immediate attention. In this way, over time, Gideon accepted himself as a queer, knowing that if his mother ever learned his secret, she would view his sexual orientation as yet another punishment from her exacting God. But Gideon found a degree of solace in same-sex attraction. As he saw it, in his innocence, it provided him with a way to avoid the treacherous pitfalls of heterosexual union he witnessed in his parents' relationship. Although, he was very soon schooled in the treacherous pitfalls of homosexuality and its own capacity for ambiguity, danger and physical peril.

One wet afternoon after a shivery, muddy game of football where his house, the Downhead Lions had gone down to the Batcombe Tigers seven to zero, he was about to leave the change rooms when Rodney Dalton held him back after the other boys had left, giving Gideon some unsolicited advice about how to defend the goal area against curving balls.

'You can see if he kicks the ball off-centre, then you know the ball is going to curve into the goal, you can see it, do you understand? You can stop it, do you see?'

Gideon wasn't interested in football, or defending the goal against curving balls. He tolerated this tedious advice because he liked Rodney Dalton. Rodney was one year older than Gideon, he was slightly overweight, with a generous spray of acne across his forehead and stubbornly embedded blackheads that peppered his nose. But along with these minor flaws, he had an abundant mop of jet-black curls and black eyebrows that bowed across his brow framing hazel eyes with irises flecked with amber, maroon and black. His eyelids were often slightly drooped, giving Rodney the appearance of confidence, and a lazy sensuality beyond his thirteen years. Gideon found himself powerfully attracted to Rodney's swarthy features and his slightly chubby legs with their fine dusting of black, downy hair.

'You can't wait for the ball – you've got to see it before he kicks it, where he kicks it and how he kicks it – do you know what I mean?' But before Gideon could answer, Rodney added this non-sequitur; 'Have you got any hair?' Rodney's eyes darted from Gideon's face to his muddied shorts. An electric shock pulsed through Gideon's body, his tongue thickened in his mouth.

'Um, er …' Gideon found that he couldn't articulate actual words, but Rodney seemed to understand his non-verbal answer. In a swift move that he was later to realise was well-practised, Rodney scooped his hand inside Gideon's shorts, cupping his penis and scrotum as his other hand pulled the waistband down from behind. He pulled his own shorts down to his knees and took Gideon's hand and wrapped it around his own hardening cock as it waved about in the cold air of the change rooms. Rodney pulled himself close, his hot breath held a memory of aniseed as his lips closed over Gideon's, his tongue pushing into his mouth. For the first time in his life, Gideon felt the crazed rush and heat of another boy's naked body against his own. Within minutes it was over, with hot splashes of ejaculate clamping them together in a rapidly cooling sticky mess. Gideon went to rest his head on Rodney's shoulder in the calming buzz of post-ejaculate bliss but was roughly pushed away. Rodney giggled as he hitched up his shorts.

'That's French kissing, did you know? My sister taught me.' Now he was grinning broadly as he wiped his stomach with his t-shirt. Gideon was left speechless, his pants now around his ankles.

'You're not to tell anyone of this are you?' Rodney said, his brow furrowing as he smoothed down his black curls. 'Do you know why you're not going to say anything Bannerman?' In a dumb sort of way, Gideon shook his head, still unable to speak, his mouth slightly opened.

'Because this will happen.' And with that Rodney suddenly punched Gideon in the face, causing him to stumble backward, his shorts binding his ankles. He needed to steady himself against the lockers as his face reddened in the blinding pain of the punch. Tears flooded into his eyes as a trickle of salty, metallic blood ran down into his open mouth, he hadn't fully lost his erection as he struggled to pull up his underwear.

'Your biggest mistake is that you don't anticipate Bannerman, you've got to get inside the head of the centre forward before he lobs the ball. Think about that.' He shucked on his jacket as he turned to leave. 'Wipe your nose, you've got blood on your vest.' With that he left Gideon sitting on a cold wooden bench, his tears drying on his cheeks in the late afternoon chill.

He sat in the change rooms as the shadows lengthened over the playing fields of Downside School. His head was crowded with pictures and thoughts. Rodney Dalton's thickened belly with the wispy trail of black hair that ran down his stomach from his navel to his groin, the heat of his cock and the way his body shook as he came in a series of short hot spurts of ejaculate that Gideon now traced across his chest and stomach. The sensation of another boy's tongue moving inside his mouth, how that feeling seemed to generate a live current that rode directly to his own cock. The odd detail that Rodney's sister had taught him how to French kiss. When? How? As Gideon collected his things he started to harden again as he recalled Rodney's advice about anticipation and wondered how and when they might do all this again.

Gideon and Rodney quickly became involved in a passionate but brief affair that lasted the remainder of autumn term 1962. Rodney would initiate dangerous trysts in toilets, bathrooms, darkened stairwells and change rooms, and in one spectacular episode where they were almost discovered, under the gabled roof of the library. It was there, during a sleepy afternoon, between stacks of books in the history section where Gideon gently masturbated Rodney as he leaned over a trolley pretending to leaf through an old copy of *A History of Western Philosophy* by Bertrand Russell.

The following spring term, without explanation, Rodney didn't reappear at Downside which plunged Gideon into a deep sadness. This left him to moon about in the places he and Rodney had shared episodes of vigorous adolescent passion. He attempted to reanimate those moments, but his combined effort of memory and imagination failed to conjure Rodney's kaleidoscopically faceted eyes, his kiss, touch or scent. Gideon was left to loiter in darkened stairwells, draughty toilets and among the stacks in the library clutching Russell's *History of Western Philosophy,* mourning his lost love and savouring his first real taste of heartbreak. He was to discover that later in life Rodney Dalton was to become a leading light in the area of 'alternative medicine', fathering five children between two marriages, he championed the notion of massive doses of vitamin C as the key to a long, healthy life. Rodney dropped dead of a heart attack aged forty-four, playing a set of mixed doubles with his then wife Patricia, his son Terry and his fiancé, a student of orthopaedics named Sandra, from Ilford.

That chequered future lay before Rodney as Gideon said goodbye to him in December and journeyed home to London and Harvest Place for a joyless holiday season with his parents. But this Christmas would be different. Gideon felt that he had grown up during this term.

He'd shared his secret with another boy who he felt he could build a life with, even though Rodney never socialised with Gideon at school, openly ridiculing him in front of other boys and would barely look at him when they shared sex. Nonetheless, Gideon was certain that they would be happy together living as adult bachelors in a blurry, abstract future.

He was aware that his sexuality was a mortal sin, that he would suffer in purgatory for eternity, and he had a vague idea that it carried with it all sorts of dangers, prohibitions and sacrifices in this life; but for Gideon, it also carried with it the consolation that whenever he thought of his mother and father, he could assure himself that he was nothing like them.

Glamorous Pip had once been immortalised in 1953 by Angus McBean, the society photographer famous for photographing film stars like Vivien Leigh and Peggy Ashcroft. On that bright, sunny morning, McBean had lit Pip in a way that suggested that she too was an impossibly perfect monochromatic beauty. Dressed in a strapless black Balenciaga organza evening dress, a Bulgari emerald studded dragonfly pinned at her breast, the photographer had posed Pip in the McBean house style. A dramatic shaft of luminescent silver light cut across her face in a portrait that intimated a woman composed of equal parts strength, calm, allure and mystery – in short, none of the things that made up Pip Bannerman.

Once a year, on the occasion of the Bannerman Prize dinner, Pip would attempt to approximate the appearance of the woman in the McBean portrait. Attending the dinner together, Pip and Adrian would also attempt to approximate the appearance of a functional, happily married couple. They would sit, waxen faced during the speeches and smile vacantly when the chair of the prize panel would acknowledge their generosity. Neither Pip nor Adrian ever opened even one of the books that were delivered to Harvest Place which were in contention for the prize. Their only concession to the Bannerman Prize for Literature was to attend the prize dinner each year, but at some point in the early eighties they stopped doing even that. The books would continue to arrive, the staff would unpack them and they would be shelved in the second floor library, to remain forever unopened, unread and forgotten.

In his youth, Gideon was allowed to attend the Bannerman Prize dinner only once. He was fourteen and was outfitted with a new dinner suit for the occasion at Gieves & Hawkes. Pip accompanied him to the fitting where the tailor, a shiny faced Mr Anthony laughed and joked with her about a man called Clive Landry, a jockey of their mutual acquaintance who had experienced a sudden fall from grace due to a scandal involving a steward.

Pip sat smoking in an armchair by a window in the fitting room. She hadn't taken off her tweed coat or her gloves as she sat with her legs crossed, sipping a glass of Don Benigno Amontillado sherry. It was during this time that Gideon realised that his mother's principal afternoon occupation was drinking. She would spend long dull afternoons at her dressing table listening to the weird, saddened clarinet of Acker Bilk's 'Stranger on the Shore', drinking sherry, applying, removing and applying her lipstick again, her glazed eyes staring dreamily ahead. One afternoon Gideon happened upon his mother as she sat at her dresser appearing to be having a very serious conversation with her reflection. Tissues smeared red were littered about the table. Gideon stood watching for a few minutes before Pip realised he was there. She slowly turned from the mirror mouthing quiet words to herself that grew in volume as she stood and faced her son in the doorway, taking a moment to change her focus she straightened her back, speaking directly to him.

'And just who the bloody hell do you think you are?' Gideon stood perfectly still hoping that this strategy would render him invisible to his mother.

'I believe I just asked you a question,' Pip said, slightly swaying.

Gideon swallowed before speaking. 'I don't think I'm anyone. I mean, Mummy, I'm Gideon?'

His mother gave out a little chuckle. 'Oh that's right, so you are.' She said as she sat again, pouring herself another drink.

Gideon stood on a small box as Mr Anthony threaded his tape measure around his waist and across his shoulders to his wrist. Pip sat in a shaft of watery afternoon sunlight as smoke from her cigarette snaked around her shoulders and hung like a solid mass above her head. Since he was being ignored, Gideon allowed their conversation to drift around him as he concentrated on Mr Anthony. Rail thin in pinstriped trousers and waistcoat, standing on his box Gideon could see fine flakes of dandruff nestled in the Brylcreemed rills of his thinning black hair. As he worked with his tape measure, Gideon noticed that his fingernails had been bitten down to the quicks, he could see a spot of blood on the cuticle of his left thumb. From time to time, as he shared jokes with Pip, Mr Anthony's face would crease into a deep grinning smile that pushed his eyes into two fine slits.

'The last time I saw Clive was at Kempton Park, he was on Sea Captain. A great ride. I won eighty guineas.'

'Well done Pip Bannerman!'

'Yes, afterwards he introduced me to that Roger Wallace. A horrible person.'

'Oh yes, perfectly dreadful – we all knew, but you couldn't tell Clive, oh no.'

Mr Anthony knelt on the floor. There was a pause in the conversation as Pip stared at Gideon through a white haze of smoke from her inexhaustible supply of Craven A cork tipped cigarettes. She took a gulp of her sherry as Mr Anthony pulled his tape measure into a straight length.

'Yes, until then Tony, do you know? I had no idea he was a *pansy*.'

As if on cue, Mr Anthony pushed the brass tip of his measure up into Gideon's inner leg, his knuckle gently nudging his scrotum. Looking up at Gideon, he winked lightly, grinning broadly. It was then that Gideon noticed that he was missing an eye tooth. He tapped Gideon's knee.

'You can jump down now, sir.' But Gideon remained on the box, terrified as he felt the twitch of an erection establishing itself in his pants. Mr Anthony briskly turned and walked over to Pip.

'Let me top you up, shall I?'

'Oh would you, Tony? How kind.'

The evening of the Bannerman Prize dinner for 1964, Gideon sat in the back of the car in his new evening clothes as his parents argued over someone his mother referred to variously as, *'That little bitch Vivian … '* or *'That whore … '* or, *'That vulgar tart … '* with his father only occasionally interjecting with a bothered groan, *'Oh Phillipa … really,'* coupled with a dry little laugh that Gideon noticed made the back of his mother's neck flush red. As they passed Charing Cross station the argument finally fell into a lull, but just before the car stopped on John Adam Street, Gideon remembered his mother saying:

'You know Adrian, cheap people carry a smell about them, did you *know* that? You could do me the courtesy of washing Vivian's stink off you before you come home sighing about how very tired you are all the time. You lying cunt.'

Pip had separated the words out in this last insult to give it more punch, but his father just turned to Gideon in the back seat as the car stopped.

'And here we are! Open the door for your mother, Giddy.'

Gideon got out of the car and found himself in the path of a procession of Hare Krishna's, singing and dancing in the evening cold in a fruity waft of patchouli oil and body odour. His mother sat behind the glass of the car window waiting for them to pass, staring at Gideon for a moment before his father joined him at the kerb. As he opened the heavy door Pip swung her feet onto the path, and even standing in the cold night air Gideon could smell the intoxicating scent of tobacco smoke, Chanel No. 5 and sherry that his mother carried after a heavy afternoon with the 'Stranger on the Shore'.

Pip stood by the car a moment, pulling her ermine up around her shoulders, her pale skin prickled by the cold early evening. She stared at Gideon and her husband with a mild squint as if she couldn't quite recognise them. Gideon noticed her toes flexing inside her blue satin shoes as she drew her mouth into a tight, hardened smile, clutching at the edges of her beaded purse, rotating it in her hands the way a blind person might, to reassure herself that it was an object she could trust. Gideon thought she looked small on the street in her blue water-wave taffeta, her fur and her jewels. The coarse language of the woman in the car had been forgotten, Pip was now composed as a glassy beauty, a portrait of drink, anger and shabby disappointments clothed in a skin of glamour.

'Are we ready?' she said as she allowed her husband to take her by the arm and lead her into the Georgian warmth of the Royal Society of Arts.

Once inside the panelled oak of the Great Room, the Bannermans' were led to their table. Gideon was introduced to a number of people who were already seated as his father pulled out a chair for him.

'This would be you, Giddy.'

In front of a white china plate there was a place card with Gideon's name inscribed in black ink. Beside him there was an empty chair with a bunched up pink silk scarf thrown across the seat that appeared to be torn at one end. The place card read, 'Miss Natasha Moubray'.

The room was noisy and crowded with adults in black tie, dinner jackets and evening gowns with the occasional sparkle of necklaces and earrings. Gideon sat looking across the room. He noticed a thin, silvery pall of cigarette smoke sitting barely above the two hundred or so guests at the dinner. There was a small bowl of cashew nuts on the table in front of him and in a matter of minutes, through a kind of nervous boredom, he'd managed to eat the lot. The walls of the Great Room were decorated with six murals depicting Georgian allegories related to human culture and knowledge. The fourteen-year-old Gideon had time to fold his linen table napkin three different ways as he looked up, transfixed by the massive thighs and loincloths of the sons of Diagoras as they bore their father aloft in the panel that depicted the crowning of the victors at Olympia.

'Oh fuckity, fuckity, fuck, fuck, fuck, fuck!'

Gideon turned to see Natasha Moubray take her seat, as she did, she pulled at her dress as it seemed to be caught on the leg of her chair.

'I think I've just torn my bloody tights. Fuck!' She turned to look at Gideon. 'Hello. I'm Tasha.' She picked up his place card. 'And you are, *Gideon Bannerman*. Well, hello. So this is your night?'

'Hello, yes, nice to meet you. Well, er, no, not really, it's, er, my parents, my father is Adrian Bannerman, *technically* it's his night, I mean, I suppose, he's paid for it all.'

'Funny. You don't look like a 'Gideon'. To me you look more like a Neville. Yes, Neville Haddock. That suits you much better.' Neville Haddock? He wondered what a 'Gideon' might look like, if it didn't look like him.

'Neville, Haddock you say? Um … I think I might stick with Gideon tonight if it's all the same to you. It'll be less confusing.'

Tasha looked at him a moment and then laughed, turning to a passing waiter, tapping her glass. Gideon could see that she was no older than he was. She was dressed in a pale apricot gown with thin shoulder straps that kept drooping over her delicate arms, lightly speckled with freckles. It descended from across her chest in a series of ruffles that ended just above her ankles. On her feet she wore a pair of grubby looking champagne-coloured ballet slippers. She had smudges of blue eye-shadow above her eyelids and poorly applied mascara that she appeared to be attempting to blink away. Her ash-blonde hair had the appearance of someone who had hastily taken a hat off and had forgotten to smooth it down. Six diamante encrusted ladybirds sat on two hairclips carelessly pushed up into either side of her head, creating untidy loops of hair that stuck out at odd angles. Overall, she had the appearance of a much younger girl who had unwisely been given permission to dress herself.

'Stop staring at my dress. It's rude.' Tasha said.

'I'm sorry?' Gideon raised his eyebrows.

Tasha pulled at one of the ruffles at her waist. 'I hate this dress. It makes me look like I've escaped from a West Midlands beauty pageant.' Tasha picked up her fork and distractedly turned it over. She looked directly at Gideon.

'Do you know all these people?' Gideon straightened in his chair, his new evening clothes suddenly feeling stiff and uncomfortable.

'I was introduced just now when we arrived, yes? But no, no, I don't actually.'

Tasha sighed. 'Well, they're all dreary. I was so excited to come tonight. My father is *Allan Moubray.*' Her father's name was couched as a pronouncement of sorts. Tasha gestured to a man sitting next to her. He was extremely thin, with a yellowing complexion and a pipe clenched in his jaw. His aged evening jacket was shiny at the elbows and frayed at the cuffs. Allan Moubray was listening intently to a bejewelled woman with ill-fitting false teeth sitting next to him as she discussed the varied nonsensical Saxon inaccuracies of the musical, *Camelot.* Gideon was attempting to look actively engaged in the conversation with Tasha, he wondered if she might be a maniac of some sort.

'My father's novel, *The Flowers of Carnage,* is shortlisted for the prize tonight. Do you know it?'

Gideon took a moment, he was staring at his dinner plate. 'Um … I think I've heard of it, yes?'

'Liar.' Tasha giggled. She leaned forward, her elbow resting on the table, her hand cupping her ear as her fingers toyed with one of her errant loops of hair.

Gideon smiled and shrugged, unsure how to respond. 'So, it's, er, very violent is it? Your father's book? What I suppose I mean is that the title, *The Flowers of Carnage*, suggests that it might be.'

A broad smile crept across Tasha's face as if she had finally understood the punchline to a joke. 'You really are dim, aren't you? How sweet. Sorry. I shouldn't laugh at you, but you are a liar.' She slumped back in her chair, clasping her fingers together and resting them across her stomach. 'I haven't been allowed to read it myself - you guessed right – too violent, apparently. It's about the war – the *Great War*, although why would you call a war 'Great'? It's curious.' Gideon was still considering this question as Tasha continued.

'Yes, can you imagine? My father's so concerned about me being exposed to violence, and he's brought me here!' Her eyes widened for emphasis. Gideon wasn't sure why, but he seemed to understand what she meant by this. Even though, as adolescents he and Tasha had been rendered invisible to the adults in the room, he could sense nonetheless that the occasion was charged with an atmosphere of genteel apprehension and almost palpable hostility.

He looked at the laughing, happy strangers that his parents had become. Others at the table seemed no less artificial to him, just different versions of his mother and father, seen through a haze of cigarette and pipe smoke, in snatches of overheard conversations about politics, an argument over which was the better film, *Zulu* or *Lawrence of Arabia?* The dangers of 'The Bomb'. There was loud talk of the 'full blooded claret' and the 'lovely refreshing riesling', all enacted with a brittle, fabricated gaiety that seemed at once unrelenting and exhausting.

Gideon began to feel defeated by the evening. He wasn't certain he was up to the challenge of sitting beside Tasha Moubray through dinner, the speeches and the prize giving. She seemed jittery and overactive. He noticed her leg was shaking nervously, and in a distracted way, she chewed on a stray frond of hair that drooped at the side of her face in the way a bored child might. Gideon was altogether convinced that she was unhinged, rude and mannerless when she suddenly turned to him and said something that made his misgivings evaporate.

'C'mon Gideon Bannerman, let's get a drink!'

Tasha led the way, taking up her pink scarf and trailing through the rowdy room out onto a crowded landing. Small groups of two or three people stood drinking, smoking and talking, overseen by an oversized portrait of a bored Queen Victoria surrounded by be-ribboned children. A long cushioned bench ran the length of the room in front of a large Palladian window. Tasha led Gideon to sit in a corner by a trestle table loaded with opened bottles of wine and rows of glasses. To their left was a fireplace flanked by two doors leading to a room where waiters would emerge from time to time with plates of food. Gideon caught sight of some grey chicken and blackened steaks.

In a deft move that surprised Gideon, Tasha took one of the bottles of claret from the table and placed it on the floor at her feet, lifting the skirt of her dress daintily to conceal it from the adults surrounding them.

'Don't worry Gideon Bannerman, they think we're children, they don't even see us. Now, your job is to go to the table and get us some glasses – not wine glasses Gideon Bannerman – just get tumblers, that way we won't arouse suspicion.' She finished with a bright smile that suggested to Gideon that he should do what he was told.

He stood. He looked down at Tasha's untidy hair and the sagging spaghetti straps of her ruffled gown.

'I wish you wouldn't call me Gideon Bannerman all the time. It seems like you're blaming me for something, and in any case I'm … ' Tasha looked up at him, sighing as she cut him off.

'Oh, I'm terribly sorry. Go get the glasses Gideon, I'm in desperate need of a drink here. There's a good chap.' She said this tapping him on the side of the leg indicating that he should get a move on.

As instructed, he passed the wine glasses and moved to a silver tray of tumblers and a jug of water. He took two glasses and was about to return to Tasha when a slightly chubby girl with a white shirt and a bow tie set at a careless angle popped up from behind the table.

'Water?' She asked, her eyes rolling to the ceiling.

Gideon felt a rush of panic. 'Um. No. Er, I am … yes, thank you water, yes.' Without shifting her gaze to Gideon, she filled his glasses. He thanked her and made his way carefully through the crowd to Tasha. When she saw him her brow creased, she seemed affronted.

'What's that? I'm not drinking that.' Tasha looked about the crowded landing for a place they might empty the water.

'You're going to have to drink it. *You're hopeless*, Gideon.'

Gideon blinked at Tasha. He felt it was too early in their relationship for her to make such a judgement of him. But it struck a chord. He often felt hopeless. He felt hopeless tonight. He'd only known Tasha Moubray for less than half an hour, but he had the keen sense that she was not to be crossed. He gulped down the water. First one glass, then the other.

'Well done! Now, stand in front of me a moment.' She reached down and took the bottle from the floor and filled both glasses with claret before hiding the wine once again under her skirt.

'Have a seat, Gid,' she said handing him a drink. Tasha raised her head and held her glass aloft. 'Here's to the Bannerman Prize!'

Their glasses clinked and Gideon took a large gulp and was immediately caught in the grip of a hacking cough that pricked his eyes with tears.

'Oh Giddy – full-bodied, eh?' Tasha laughed as she slapped him hard on the back. Once his coughing had subsided, Gideon laughed too. It was probably more wine than he had ever drunk in his life, but he loved the way he could feel its warmth flood his body and cause his face and neck to flush pink. He immediately felt that the claret had shifted a subtle calibration in him that allowed him to feel more at ease, happier, not so hopeless after all. He grinned at Tasha.

'Must have gone down the wrong way,' he said, taking another mouthful.

'Liar!' Tasha giggled.

Gideon thought for a moment. 'Do you know that that is the third time you've called me a liar in the space of half an hour?'

'Is it? Really? Let's drink to that then. Here's to liars!' Tasha raised her glass again.

She looked at him, her eyes narrowed. 'It's funny. You don't look like a liar.'

'No?' Gideon stared at the rim of his glass.

'No. You look kind.' He laughed, embarrassed, he drank some more.

'That furrow in your brow that doesn't go away, it means you care for people. Large green eyes, slightly dull, you need to be careful, you could pass as simple. Your brown hair has the finest suggestion of red in it with that lovely curl at the front, you have tiny ears, they're pretty. You have a handsome mouth, it's full, no chin to speak of but when you can grow a beard that will take care of that, but above all Gideon Bannerman, you have beautiful hands.' And with that she took his hand and kissed it, giggling.

No one had ever spoken to him in that way before. No one had kissed his hand. He reddened.

'Um … thank you, I suppose.' He smiled. They sat in silence for a moment.

 The landing was beginning to clear as Pip Bannerman appeared in the doorway. The wine in Gideon's mouth suddenly tasted sour. She approached Gideon and Tasha beaming; her broad, red smile looked bulletproof.

'Darling, there you are. Your father and I were quite worried, but I see you've met a chum.' Her eyes ran up and down Tasha as she silently itemised her appearance. Gideon stood to greet his mother as his stomach began to churn. Tasha looked up at Pip, smiling.

'Hello, Mrs Bannerman. I'm Tasha Moubray.'

Gideon was familiar with the catalogue of Pip Bannerman's smiles and this one carried with it a shadow of contempt and irritation. He was certain that Tasha would not have noticed, at least he hoped she hadn't. His fingers gripped his glass tightly in an effort to conceal its contents.

'Oh of course, yes, Tasha. I was just speaking to your father about his fascinating book. All about the war. Yes.'

'Oh really? Have you read it Mrs Bannerman?' Tasha asked raising her chin.

There was the smallest pause. Gideon noticed he was holding his breath. He heard his mother make a short snorting noise in response to Tasha's question. Her head made a subtle pivot, inclining it toward the girl.

'Don't you look lovely, dear? What a striking gown.'

Tasha fanned out one of the ruffles of her dress across her lap. 'How kind. Thank you. It's a favourite of mine.' There was another chilly pause.

'Well, don't stay out here too long. You'll miss all the fun.' Without directly looking at Tasha she added, 'I'm delighted to have met you, dear,' – as she turned to walk back into the Great Room. Tasha watched his mother as she moved away in her blue silk, her pale shoulders gliding through the doorway. Tasha's mouth was slightly open, Gideon noticed her scanning the floor with her eyes as if she was searching for the words she needed. She turned to Gideon with a look of empathy, of recognition that she now understood some things about this serial fibber from this brief exchange.

'*Bitch!*' she finally spat out. Patting Gideon's thigh.

'I beg your pardon?' Gideon looked to the doorway where his mother had disappeared.

'What a cow! *Chum?* How horrible, you have to live with that?'

Gideon considered his drink, he could see his dark reflection wobble in the ruby claret. 'Actually, I've never heard her use the word 'chum' before.' Then he added quietly, 'I think she's one of the most unhappy people I know.' They both sat in silence for a moment before he raised his glass.

'Here's to bitches!'

Over the course of the next seventy minutes and two bottles of claret, Tasha and Gideon engaged in a conversation that he was to remember, almost word for word, for the rest of his life. He talked about going to church, life at Downside School, Harvest House, his mother's vacant stares and his father's absences. At one point, Tasha interrupted him with a question.

'Don't you think it's terribly immoral to have all that money? I mean all that money that your father has?'

They were well into their second bottle at this stage, and Gideon had to think to formulate an answer.

'*Immoral?* No, no I don't think so. I mean I've never really thought about it in that way. Actually, I've never really thought about it at all.' He shrugged. Tasha was gently swinging her legs in a distracted way. She adjusted the clip in her hair slightly, to no discernible effect.

'No. Quite. I suppose that's my point really.'

Tasha spoke about her mother, Lucy, who had run off to Bulgaria with a poet called Dimo when Tasha was five, leaving her to be raised by her father in a tiny, gloomy house in Notting Hill. He taught English to newly arrived West Indian migrants and had begun an affair with a black girl called Sophie, who Tasha quite liked, but the relationship was frowned upon in their street. She was not permitted to watch television, but her father allowed her to drink a single glass of wine each night when they sat down to dinner. She spoke about his moodiness and how he could become inexplicably angry, sometimes for days – and then suddenly snap out of it. She thought it was a symptom of his creativity, that perhaps all creative people had these quirks. He encouraged her to read all sorts of novels that Gideon had never heard of, Russian books, German, French and famous English novels that she claimed had changed her life. Here he interrupted her.

'*Changed your life?* But that's hardly possible. You're only fourteen, like me,' he said nudging her shoulder playfully.

'You might understand when you're older,' said Tasha seriously, adding: 'Or perhaps if you ever troubled to *read* a book.'

'Actually, I have read a book,' he said deliberately. She looked at him, raising her eyebrows.

'*Treasure Island.* We all read it at school.' Tasha's mouth gaped open as she laughed out loud.

'Oh. My. God. *Treasure fucking Island!*'

'Gosh, Tasha, you swear an awful lot. I expect you think it sounds clever.' She shook her head, taking another mouthful of wine.

'It's not clever, you idiot. It's *expressive*. More expressive than fucking *'gosh'!'*

Gideon was keen to change the topic. He reached down and emptied the last of the second bottle into their glasses. He noticed that one of the effects of his growing inebriation was that he heard everything that he said back in his head as if someone else was saying it. A bright, cheery stranger.

'Your father sounds interesting,' he said, regarding her with a sideways glance he hoped looked intelligent.

'Whatever do you mean? What a stupid thing to say.'

Gideon held his glass in both hands and took a big gulp of wine. Tasha turned to face him. Her brow was creased, she looked solemn.

'He's sad and confusing and angry and quiet. Sometimes he's quite loving, but it's like a puzzle, living with him. Sometimes I hate it, but there it is.'

They could hear a muffled speech from the Great Room, but the combination of distance and alcohol meant that only very blurry shapes of words reached them. Occasionally there were rounds of applause.

'My father's a lying cunt,' Gideon offered in an offhand sort of way, silently toasting the fact with another mouthful of claret.

'Gideon Bannerman!' Tasha said in genuine shock.

'Sorry.' He smiled, his teeth coated in a thin film of wine. 'Was that too expressive for you?' He laughed at the idea of his father before he turned to Tasha.

'It's true,' he said. 'Yes.' He added quietly to reinforce the point.

There was another round of applause from the Great Room.

'I believe you, Giddy,' Tasha said.

They continued to talk with the empty wine bottles at their feet. They shared their hopes for the future, Gideon said he would go to Oxford to read history and economics, Tasha wanted a scholarship to Cambridge to read English. She was going to write novels and poetry.

Suddenly the landing began to fill up again, but this time people weren't lingering. Many couples were making their way down the tiled stairs to the foyer and out onto the street. Tasha and Gideon sat in silence as people moved past them. For the first time in his recollection, Gideon felt in control of his world. He drained the last of his wine, set his glass on the floor and in an act of spontaneity that felt right to him, he closed his eyes and embraced Tasha Moubray.

He was surprised at how slight she was. She had no shoulders to speak of; folding her into his new dinner jacket, he felt it was like he was hugging a broom. Tasha allowed herself to be embraced, she didn't hug Gideon back, but rather patted him on the side, breathily whispering into his ear, 'Good luck, chum!' and giggled. Her hair and neck carried the fresh scent of soap and powder. With his eyes shut, Gideon's mind was crowded with the memory of Rodney Dalton. Rodney, well-schooled in the art of French kissing by his sister, Rodney's touch, his scent and his trembling body as orgasm shuddered through it with Gideon holding him in his arms. He sighed. He was pulled out of this dream as Tasha was yanked away from him. Gideon opened his eyes to see Allan Moubray gripping Tasha's shoulders tightly and shaking her violently.

'You stupid little girl! What are you playing at?' he shouted, his voice seemed to bounce off the walls of the landing.

Tasha went to look over her shoulder, back at Gideon when her father slapped her face with a loud crack that jolted her head to one side, sending one of her diamante hair clips spinning onto the floor at Gideon's feet. Suddenly the landing was hushed as onlookers moved quietly to the stairs listening to Tasha sobbing. Gideon sat dazed as his mother and father materialised from the crowd. He stood. It was then that the full force of the alcohol hit him. He was unsteady, and he couldn't get a good idea of his parents' features although he was aware that they were in front of him. He could see the orange, blurry glow of his father's cigarette, and somewhere in the distance he could hear his mother.

'Oh, you poor boy – you're unwell.' Was that her hand that was reaching out to him? He was confused by the kind, caring woman he saw speaking to him.

His head felt like a balloon tethered to his spinal column, and he seemed to lose all feeling in his hands. He wobbled toward Allan Moubray where he stood, holding Tasha as she cried into his lapel. Gideon was appalled by him. He was going to do something. He wasn't going to stand by as his new friend was punished by her moody, angry father – and for what? Having a chat? Having a couple of drinks? No. But at that moment a powerful wave of nausea broke over him, filling his mouth with warm saliva, leaving him struggling to orient himself again to his surroundings as they spun uncontrollably around him. Gradually this feeling receded, and he stood a moment as both his mother and father came into focus in front of him. For that moment, he quite forgot about Tasha.

'Oh, hello there, um … who won?' He asked as he struggled to appear normal.

He was about to say something more to his parents when a second wave of nausea overtook him and he bent forward, almost formally, splashing vomit on the floor, speckling his shoes and trousers with what looked like tiny pieces of cashew nut. He straightened, hearing his mother gasp as a hot trickle of piss ran down his leg filling his right shoe and pooling on the floor around him.

He had no recollection of Tasha leaving that night, although she told him when they met again, years later at Oxford that she had screamed at her father all down the stairs. He'd lost the Bannerman Prize that night to a novelist called Janet Tyne for her book, *The Lost Poetry of Josef*, a novella about Stalinist purges. Tasha said that he complained about it for months afterwards, blaming his loss on the fact that his daughter had abandoned him to get pissed with 'that little Bannerman twat'.

Gideon had two clear memories of leaving the Royal Society of Arts that evening. The first thing he remembered was the shock of how cold it was on the street as the wind picked up and flapped his sodden trousers, his breath puffing out of him in hot, solid cones of steam. The second thing was his mother hissing the word, *'Shameful!'* as he was bundled into the chilly backseat of the car. There he lay, curled up, Tasha's ladybirds in the palm of his hand, held to his chest, staring out at the brightly coloured lights of the city as they scribbled past in the night sky. He looked up, smiling broadly in his piss-stained trousers and vomit-speckled shoes as his heart beat out a relentless drum in his head and all through his body in jubilant celebration of his declaration of independence.

For Tasha and Gideon, that night marked the beginning of a friendship that was to last over five decades. They were reunited at Oxford University, where even though Gideon applied himself diligently to history and economics, he only achieved a pass after four years of solid effort. Tasha received scholarship offers from both Oxford and Cambridge but finally decided on St Hilda's at Oxford where her rise was immediate and spectacular.

As an undergraduate, Tasha became known as 'that weird girl in the corduroy frocks' – she had two, one blue and one chocolate brown which she teamed with paisley shirts, sturdy tights and brown brogues. She gathered a reputation for being eccentric, difficult, politically outspoken, and sexually relaxed. She was a fierce debater and made a habit of challenging her tutors and fellow students. She regularly contributed to the student publications *Isis* and *Cherwell*, critical articles on the literature of the day where her eclectic tastes and opinions were often surprising. She championed *Portnoy's Complaint* as a 'liberating satire fuelled by adolescent ejaculate', but thought *The French Lieutenant's Woman* was 'needlessly tricky, reactionary and vaguely dull', and ultimately inferior to *Slaughterhouse-Five*, which she described as 'probably the most important novel of the second half of the twentieth century'.

Although still in her teens, by the time she arrived in Oxford Tasha seemed to already have become an adult. Sure-footed, confident, sharply intelligent and sometimes abrasive, she could immediately disarm others by spontaneous acts of generosity and kindness. At the same time, Gideon stubbornly remained barely out of adolescence. He was a diligent but dull student who fell prey to serial infatuations with unobtainable boys and even in his early twenties remained troubled by the occasional mountainous pimple on his cheek, chin or nose.

Despite their differences, Gideon and Tasha remained close. She sensed his loneliness, she saw his awkwardness and the ways in which his privilege and the wealth of his family, isolated him at Oxford. Unlike many young men in his position, Gideon was acutely aware that he appeared dull to others. He had the debilitating combination of a crushing shyness and a hyper-vigilant sensitivity. Tasha felt sick at the casual cruelties meted out to him by other students who only appeared to tolerate him superficially because of his generous allowance, which they were only too happy to help him spend. She admired in him a kind of accommodating stoicism that helped him withstand the effects of the many subtle social exclusions that occurred in the ruthless caste system at the university. This was a place that valued and rewarded wit, intelligence, beauty and brilliance – in all these areas, Gideon Bannerman was found wanting.

Tasha instinctively understood the social currency of Oxford. She carried with her the cachet of being the daughter of a celebrated author. Her intelligence and eccentricities enclosed her in a kind of protective glamour that drew people to her, they wanted to be part of her life, part of her story. As for Gideon, it was telling that of all the clubs he could have joined at Oxford, from the Arcadian Singers, to the Archaeological Society or the Exploration Club, he decided, along with a fellow student of economics called Paul Buckland, a stocky boy with thick orange frizzy hair and a crippling stutter, to start a club for crossword puzzle enthusiasts called Nine Across. In this way he seemed to be both acknowledging and cementing his own place in the pecking order of the university.

Gideon took a vicarious pride in Tasha's scholarly achievements. She would joke to him that her grades had better be good because unlike him, she was going to have to work for a living. He joked back that she could work for him.

'What a disgusting idea,' she shot back at him immediately. She was not smiling.

Her doctoral thesis, 'Virtue as a Cage; The Politics of Allegory in Spenser's *The Faerie Queene'* created a minor sensation when it was completed as Tasha sought to demonstrate that the values inherent in Edmund Spenser's epic poem of 1590, could be viewed as tools of repression in capitalist structures. In any other doctoral candidate, this kind of idea might have been viewed as little more than academic overreach. But what dazzled Tasha's examiners was the originality of her thought and the breadth of her research. She drew on sources as varied as *The Archers* and *Coronation Street,* comedies like *Steptoe and Son* and *The Rag Trade,* lyrics from The Beatles and The Who, and newspaper copy accompanying Page Three girls in *The News of the World,* sandwiched between Keynesian economic theory and Freudian psychology. The thesis was updated and eventually published to a rapturous critical response. *The Times Literary Supplement* called it, 'a profound insight into the fabric of English cultural life filtered through art, literature, politics and economics. Thrillingly, from Elizabethan England to the emergence of Mrs Thatcher, Natasha Moubray, weaves a tapestry of history, pop culture, social upheaval and politics to startling effect'.

Other books would follow. Twelve in all dealing with subjects as diverse as feminism in the Church of England, subversive Dandies from Lord Byron to Boy George, a tome entitled *Speaking in Tongues* that dealt with the ethics of translating literature with a focus on Russian classics, and *The Chain, The Mill and the Church,* which dealt with the barbarism of the Industrial Revolution, a period Tasha argued that ushered in a second age of state-sanctioned slavery. Her distinguished academic career encompassed a professorship at thirty-two and fellowships at All Souls College at Oxford, the British Academy and the Royal Society of Literature.

By contrast, Gideon's occupations after graduating from university could never have been claimed as a 'career'. He was encouraged by his father to sit on a number of charity boards associated with the Bannerman Trust. This kept Gideon occupied with workshops, planning days, sub-committees and regular interminable meetings in airless rooms chewing dry cheese sandwiches and sipping orange juice or tepid cups of tea.

The eclectic collection of organisations funded by the Trust included: The Babel Council, a charity that worked to preserve antique brick structures that fell between the regulatory cracks of the National Trust and the developer's wrecking ball; The Cantus Society, an organisation whose mission was to catalogue and protect the song of English native birds with patrons that included Prince Charles and Sir David Attenborough; The Arabesque Association, a group that sought to support 'handicapped' children, as they were then known, up to the age of eighteen who displayed a passion and talent for athletics, and finally; The Tunnel Trust. This oddly named charity, whose work was the support and rehabilitation of petty criminals into functional, productive citizens, was to provide Gideon with the final piece in the jigsaw puzzle that was his sexuality. It was occasional contact with the ex-cons given a helping hand by The Tunnel Trust that awakened in Gideon an appetite for rough trade.

Occasionally, the Board of The Tunnel Trust would invite a guest speaker who would share his 'journey' from a life of small time crime and semi-frequent bouts of sadistic violence, to a new life as a dry cleaner, a parking attendant or garbage collector. The simple narrative theatre of these testimonials moved him, but more than that, while recounting their stories of bad luck, poverty, poor choices, criminal enterprise and salvation, at some point the redeemed would catch Gideon's stare and immediately recognise his need and hunger for them. Far from being deprived, downtrodden, passive recipients of charity and goodwill, Gideon felt that their innate sense of his desire made them powerful agents of sexual provocation.

As they spoke, he would catalogue their eyes, hair colour, their lips and hands, their arms and the trim of their sideburns, moustaches and beards only to reanimate them in vivid fantasies of prolonged submission and dominance and eventual sexual release. These impulses were to become the primary characteristics of his homosexual repertoire for the rest of his life.

Just like his mother's numbing faith in the Church, Gideon's sexual appetite for abjection, punishment, and obedience gave him comfort and a consoling understanding of his place in the world. He replaced the sacrament of bread and wine with flesh and semen, enacting his own Stations of the Cross in elaborate ordeals of sexual servitude and debasement, acting out his faith in public toilets, Soho backrooms and the occasional paid tryst in cheap, poorly lit hotel rooms.

Tasha alone would remain his confessor and confidant. She would listen patiently when he spoke in guarded terms about his sexual adventurism. She occasionally met the rough boys that Gideon was involved with, John and Pete and Gavin. She would marvel at how shy he became in their presence, how he would defer to them, consider their opinions, laughing at their dreary jokes, Adam and Simon and Robbie. It all came to an abrupt halt in 1977 during the Queen's Silver Jubilee celebrations. She held his hand as he trembled, bleeding and broken in the severe glare of Westminster Hospital Emergency after a savage beating by skinheads left him unconscious on the cold tiled floor of a Piccadilly public toilet, an event that left him in fear and celibate for almost two decades, through the years of the pitiless terror of AIDS, when he would quietly mourn casual lovers as he received news of their illnesses and deaths, Tony and Chris and Martin, and on, and on.

She sat with him when they buried first his mother who was silenced by a massive stroke while attending the Chelsea Flower Show in 1989, and then his father from prostate cancer in 1997, crying in a fog of morphine for his son. He would ramble for hours speaking as if he was back on the campaign hustings in 1956, *'My England is Your England!'*, he would declaim and then go on to mumble about Holm Oaks, heathlands and Avalon. He lay, hollowed out by cancer, tearfully sorry for his public shames and secret harms, *'Draw the curtains, Pip! The Sun!'* he screamed to his dead wife one morning, his reddened eyes straining to open wider, staring blankly at Gideon in surprise – he was suddenly dead.

For his part Gideon remained steadfastly loyal to Tasha. He consoled her through her father's suicide, when he gassed himself at sixty-three and her subsequent discovery that he had been diagnosed as a paranoid schizophrenic when he was in his twenties, her two abortions and a miscarriage, two divorces – both writers, Jeremy, a violently abusive Welsh poet and then Giles, an amphetamine addicted post-structuralist from Leeds – more than one flirtation with alcoholism, and one dismally unsuccessful attempt at lesbianism that left her with a black eye and a restraining order.

Eventually, she bought a roomy flat in Bloomsbury and she and Gideon developed a habit of meeting every Thursday for dinner in his spacious kitchen at Harvest Place. By that stage, Tasha considered Gideon's wealth as a slight embarrassment that was never discussed. After the death of his father and the formidable complexity of his inheritance was finally understood, Gideon extended the monies available to the Bannerman Prize in perpetuity, and in 2002 invited Tasha to act as Chair of the prize, managing the yearly invitations to make up the judging panel, overseeing the drawing up of the longlist, the subsequent shortlist, and ultimately the prize itself. Tasha understood next to nothing about the mechanics of the Bannerman fortune. Certainly Gideon's money was a solid fact to her but the movement of money, its malleable dynamism, the fluctuations of the markets, its incremental sensitivity to global calm or unrest was vaguely sinister to her and she remained wilful in her ignorance of it.

It was at one of their regular Thursday evening dinners that Tasha was introduced to Yuri Kuznetsov.

Summer, nine years ago. The large, tiled kitchen of Harvest Place was bathed in the soft yellow light of the fading day. Cooking had become Gideon's latest enthusiasm. He loved the formulaic nature of the processes, the selection of dishes, the measurement of ingredients and the calibration of time and temperature, the almost predictable results. His housekeeper, a sullen Ukrainian who went by the name of Yulia tolerated him in her kitchen but would absent herself when he decided to cook and would only return once Gideon had finished to ensure that he had cleaned to her satisfaction. Yulia would also clear out every Thursday evening at precisely the moment Tasha arrived.

A lamp burned brightly on a broad bench by the stove. The sound system in the kitchen was tuned to a Radio 3 program of symphonic music. Tasha sat at the wide oak kitchen table drinking a glass of Austrian riesling reading a battered cookbook as Gideon peered into an odd collection of copper bowls filled with a variety of chopped vegetables, ground spices and gleaming pink chicken thighs. Tasha slid her glasses over the bridge of her nose, looking closer at the recipe.

'Well, it says here that you're supposed to have marinated the chicken in the yoghurt mixture first – and for some hours.'

Gideon poured himself another glass of wine. 'Yes. I understand that, but you see, I hate yoghurt, and you know that.'

'But Giddy, it's the recipe, and in any case, surely the cooking would get rid of the yoghurty taste of the yoghurt in the marinade – who did you say was joining us? You know I hate surprises.'

Gideon put his head into the fridge. 'Do you think we could substitute sour cream for the yoghurt?'

Tasha slammed the cookbook shut. 'Sour cream? Are you completely mad? Stop being stupid. *Who is coming to dinner?*' She said, spacing out her words for emphasis.

Before Gideon could answer, Yulia appeared in the kitchen doorway. Ignoring Tasha she looked at Gideon, her icy grey eyes held concern coupled with an expression of fear that was at odds with her usual stony, glum demeanour.

'What is it, Yulia?' Gideon asked.

'Is visitor,' she said, staring at the floor.

Gideon brightened. 'Ah! Yuri's here.'

Yulia continued examining the tiles on the floor. 'He doesn't tell the name.'

At that moment, Yuri Kuznetsov stood behind Yulia, placing both hands on her shoulders grinning broadly at Gideon. He inclined his head down to Yulia's ear and spoke some words to her in Ukrainian. Yulia appeared completely disoriented by this, shifting her weight in her flat shoes from one foot to the other. She looked imploringly to Tasha before shrugging Yuri's hands from her shoulders.

'Thank you, Mr Gideon,' she said in an oddly formal way. As she turned to leave she hissed something inaudible to Yuri, also in

Ukrainian, which prompted a funny, hiccupping chuckle from him as he crossed the kitchen floor to embrace Gideon. Tasha took a long sip of her wine, her eyes widening as she peered over her glass.

The man was short Tasha thought, no more than 5' 6" or 7", stocky in build with thick black hair that was cropped close to his head and smooth, pale skin that appeared almost hairless. He was wearing tight red shorts with white stripes that ran down the sides and a sleeveless black t-shirt with the words, *Just Do It!* printed across it in white, blue running shoes that looked new, long black socks and a duffel bag slung over his shoulder. His body was decorated with multiple tattoos, all drawn with the same blue-black ink. Some looked like highly skilled illustrations, while others had the naive simplicity of poorly rendered hand-drawings. Tasha saw stars, roses, crosses, a skull, a bear, a church, angels, two guns, a snake and a knife.

Dropping his duffel bag to the floor Yuri hugged Gideon, who was holding a wooden spoon, leaning up to kiss him on the mouth two or three times. Yuri pulled away still holding him.

'Ah, Myshka!' Yuri purred. Raising his eyebrows, Gideon looked over at Tasha.

'Yuri, this is my dearest friend, Tasha. Tasha Moubray.'

Yuri turned to look at her, inclining his head to one side and smiling as if greeting a lost acquaintance, his arms spread wide, his palms open.

'Ah! Dearest friend! Yes! Natashka, Gideon speaks of nothing else.' Tasha held out her hand, which Yuri took in his, kissing her whitened knuckle, all the while maintaining his gaze on her with sharp eyes of ultramarine faceted with jade.

'Oh, I doubt that very much. I'm pleased to meet you,' said Tasha smiling thinly, looking from Yuri to Gideon and back again. Sensing trouble, a little too cheerfully Gideon offered, 'Yuri's just come from training at the gym. Yes. He's quite the fitness fanatic. He's tried taking me along, of course I'm hopeless.'

'Well, I suppose you've never really expressed an interest in physical training Giddy, have you?' said Tasha.

Yuri gave Tasha the slightest wink. 'He just need a good instruction, eh, Myshka?'

Gideon grinned stupidly, looking at the spoon in his hands. 'Quite. Isn't it sweet, Tasha? He calls me Myshka, it means –'

'Little mouse,' she said flatly.

'Yes, of course you'd know. Yuri, Tasha here reads Russian novels – in Russian,' he added with a note of incredulity.

Yuri looked at Tasha.

'Ah, beauty and brain.'

Tasha felt slightly nauseous, she straightened in her chair.

'And where did you two meet?' she asked.

The two men began explaining simultaneously, they broke off, laughed a little and started again, simultaneously.

'Why don't you tell me, Yuri, I'm so *curious*,' she said, smiling brightly. Yuri looked to Gideon who nervously opened the cookbook on the table and pretended to be looking at a recipe for cheesecake.

'Gideon's charity. Tunnel Trust. Working with ex-prisoners. We have similar program in Novosibirsk and we meet, Gideon and I, as part of information exchange.' Yuri put his hand on Gideon's shoulder, Gideon looked down at Yuri and fleetingly at Tasha before looking at a diagram in the cookbook on how to pit cherries.

'We find we have so much in common. So much to talk about and explore. Particular in the subject of prisoner outreach and social determinant of rehabilitation.' Yuri's accent thickened around these words, extending the vowels, proudly offering the phrase to Tasha as a kind of proof of his credibility. As he spoke Tasha appraised Yuri's body. It became impossible not to look at his tattoos, the most extraordinary of which was positioned at the top of his sternum, at the base of his broad neck. It was an all-seeing eye with radiating striations that ran across his shoulders and down his chest.

'So, you are based in Novosibirsk then?' she asked.

'Yes. For time being. I also have business interest in Turkey. Import and manufacture.' None of this was calming Tasha's sense of dread.

'You really do have the most remarkable collection of tattoos,' she observed.

There was something sitting behind Yuri's gaze as he stared at Tasha in her blue linen frock and cream silk blouse. He looked at her with an easy, attractive confidence that she was certain could effortlessly become darker.

'Ah, my tattoos. Natashka. Yes, they are my foolishness.' He gestured to indicate a five-pointed star etched into his neck in deep blue ink. 'When I was youth I did many foolish things.'

Looking up from the cookbook, Gideon attempted to insert himself into the conversation. 'Tasha, did you know that Yuri's surname, Kuznetsov, it means blacksmith in Russian?'

'Of course. Yes, blacksmith,' Tasha said tapping her finger on the side of her glass.

'Of course you did! Yuri, this woman knows everything!'

Yuri beamed. 'Ah hah! Natashka, *you are know-it-all! It is truth!*'

'Truth?' Tasha leaned forward.

'Yes!' Yuri added, 'A truth *universally acknowledge* – like they say.' His eyes appeared to be gauging how he was connecting with her.

'They do say something like that,' she said.

'Let me get you a glass, Yuri,' Gideon said kissing him lightly on the cheek.

'Thank you, Myshka.' Yuri and Gideon shared a secret little smile that neatly excluded Tasha. It sent a message along with their ease with each other that this relationship had been well-established but somehow never mentioned in her many conversations with Gideon over the last few months. Certainly more established than a few meetings about social determinants and prisoner outreach. She held a small sip of riesling in her mouth, she felt it warming on her tongue. Gideon poured Yuri a drink.

There was a momentary pause before Tasha said, holding her glass to her chest with both hands, 'You said Yuri, that your tattoos were youthful foolishness. I expect we've all done foolish things when we were young. I wonder, tell me, when did you get your last tattoo?'

Yuri's grin remained fixed, as was his gaze on a single strand of Tasha's grey hair as it hooked the base of her neck. She could feel, distinctly, the steady thrum of her heart beating inside her blouse. Suddenly the music began to swell on the radio. Gideon decided to intervene.

'Let's turn down this bloody noise.'

'It's not noise, Giddy,' Tasha said.

'No, Myshka, is Shostakovich. Seven symphony,' Yuri offered surprisingly. Tasha once again stole a glance at Yuri's all-seeing eye.

'Well, whoever it is, we are going to have to start this or we'll be eating at bloody midnight.'

Yuri lightened. 'Yes! Cooking. When I arrive, I interrupt you both. Sorry.'

Tasha slumped slightly in her chair, pushing her feet out in front of her; with some interest she regarded her right index fingernail and its chipped maroon nail polish. She looked over at Gideon who would not meet her gaze.

'Oh, that's all right Yuri,' she said. 'I believe when you arrived our topic was sour cream.'

Could it have been nine years ago? It must have been, Gideon thought. His feet began to feel cold but he was not moved to put his shoes on or to adjust the heating. Nine years ago. Tasha and Yuri.

He switched a lamp on and its warm light spread in a pool around him, illuminating the McBean portrait of his mother from another time. He looked down at the open pages of *The Guardian*, *The Times* and *The Daily Mail* spread out on the table before him. He found himself staring down at the patterns the words made on the page, the pictures, the pull quotes and the headlines. Almost involuntarily, his eyes picked up the thread of one of the articles.

Sex, Snakes, God and a Whippet, Has the Bannerman Prize Lost the Plot?

Carol Peyton

Sometimes arts journalism is a very dangerous profession. We may not report on war zones, national disasters or terrorism but there can be moments when you feel as if you are taking your life into your own hands. A simple question can leave you feeling endangered, like you are about to be cut down, blown to bits, snuffed into silence, but more of that later.

A book of pastiche 18th century pornography by first-time author, Isobel Dalby's *Her C**t* and a narrative derived almost entirely from text messages, Julian Adagoke's, *The Broken Tooth Upstairs* will compete with two-time Bannerman Prize-winner Martin Gillray's twenty-second novel, *The Clava*

Cairn, set on an isolated island north of Wales for this year's coveted prize.

In addition to those three novels the other three that make up the six books in this year's shortlist include:

Australian author Catherine Adler's savage critique of colonialism, *Commonwealth Bastard,* a book that examines the legacy of colonialism through the eyes of a schoolteacher who spirals into mental illness after lunching with the Queen during her first visit to Australia in 1954.

In the closest thing this year's shortlist has to a bestselling success, Alex Kosco's, *Foreign Bodies,* includes elements of espionage, intrigue, international diplomacy and state-sanctioned killing in a page-turner that has already been optioned by the BBC. Weirdly, it also includes a homemade antidote for potentially fatal snake bites that I've yet to put to the test!

And finally, with a lightness of touch and elegant poetic prose, Kai Noguchi describes a watercolourist's train journey through the Danish hinterland with vivid, almost cinematic immediacy in, *The Illustrated Danish Tree.*

Author and social theorist Natasha Moubray, the Chairwoman of the Bannerman Prize Foundation and daughter of the late novelist Allan Moubray, who will act as the chair of the panel of judges, said the books this year represented the best of an extraordinary range of submitted fiction. 'Each of these novels has been the subject of debate, analysis and at times intense but respectful argument.' Moubray said. 'They represent beautifully accomplished new voices as well as established authors, in some cases pushing our understanding of what a novel can be.'

It is this last point that has observers particularly puzzled over this year's selection. Always known for its eclectic mix of styles and form, this year's Bannerman shortlist appears to have set a new benchmark for what readers might consider 'a good read'.

From the knotty theological arguments in Martin Gillray's, *The Clava Cairn* and the subtle poetic prose of Kai Noguchi's, *The Illustrated Danish Tree* to the starkly confronting, bald pornography of Isobel Dalby's, *Her C**t,* and the frankly difficult task of following a relationship breakup by wading through 783 text messages (some of which deal with who will get custody of the family whippet, Misty) that comprise Julian Agadoke's, *The Broken Tooth Upstairs* – to some, the list may represent a challenge.

It is here, dear reader, that your intrepid arts correspondent wandered into an area peppered with land mines as my conversation with the formidable Natasha Moubray continued. Having a reputation for shredding arts journalists, I broached the topic of this year's shortlist with Ms Moubray with great trepidation.

I started with a general question, did she think about how the finalists might be received by the public when considering the works to be shortlisted? There was a pause of some seconds. 'Might be received by whom?' was the clipped reply. I swallowed and stepped on the first detonator. 'Well, you know, the public, the, reading public?' There ensued a silence where I had hoped we had been disconnected, but it turns out she was just drawing breath. 'What an absurd suggestion. *The public? The public!* Do you imagine that our work on the panel is to sit there in a lather of anxiety over the fickle interests of who we might think of as the *'public'* – this last adjective spat into my ear causing my face to redden hotly. A little dazed, I went on, 'Okay, well then what were your chief considerations when assessing the books? Was it form? Was it language? Structure?'

'I'm not certain that you understand the function of a prize like the Bannerman. Our job is to discern excellence. It really isn't that difficult a concept to grasp – the only consideration, the only question in our minds is this; *Is this great writing?* Full stop. All good writing is formally rigorous, the language is true and its structure serves both the narrative and the overall intention of the author. These are amongst our considerations. The function of the prize is to reward and draw attention to excellence.' I attempted to interrupt, but Ms Moubray was warming to her topic. 'We believe in the novel, we believe that the novel is one of the great remaining forms where written words can demonstrate their elasticity, their subversive qualities, their power to move people, and expand their vision of the world, more so than tweets, blogs, text messages, or (another pause) *newspaper articles.'*

Boom!

I concluded our chat with what seemed to me an innocuous question regarding inclusion in the Bannerman Prize and the need to reflect diversity in the works under consideration. Natasha Moubray was having none of it. 'I am speaking to you about literature. The topic of our conversation is the shortlist, if you have no further questions regarding the shortlist, if you have no further questions regarding literature, I have no interest in talking to you about anything else.' And with that

Ms Moubray hung up By then my bloodied body was being pecked at by blackbirds.

It will be just under three months until the winner is announced on 7 November at the Royal Society of Arts. My wounds might just about have healed by then.

The gears on the skeleton clock began to grind and whir again, and Gideon looked up to his reflection in the mirror, waiting for the little bells to toll five. This time his reflection revealed to him a greying man, unknown to himself, lost in his own house. Tasha's voice came to him across five decades, 'You have tiny ears, they're pretty.'

In the last moments of the afternoon the streets had come alive with the prospect of night. Great blades of amber from the retreating sun shone into the city, glinting off the river, bathing the air in a solid light that, to Gideon's mind, was the only material proof of grace, present for just ten short minutes shining on buildings, trees, parks, bridges, paths, and people before giving way to the luminous dark of the evening.

It had been a crowded day for Gideon. The Bannerman Prize shortlist had been announced. The six shortlisted books were sitting in a neat stack on the mantle. Before the day was over, Gideon Bannerman needed to write down some words of his own to Tasha Moubray, before he put his shoes on and walked downstairs, leaving Harvest Place for the last time.

HER C**T
Isobel Dalby (Red Pen Press) 420pp
The short but eventful life of Nell Balldock, a
celebrated bawd in 18th Century London who loved,
brawled, argued and intrigued with the demi-monde
of Covent Garden, imagined as a post-feminist
pastiche of romance fiction.

10.17 am, 380 Coldharbour Lane, Brixton SW9 8LQ

It was too late now of course, but Isobel knew that the dress was
going to be a problem. It was velvet and the colour of dried blood,
printed with overblown pink roses and emerald green leaves, it hung
on the back of the door of the bedsit, its beautiful sheeny lustre
reflected on the grubby cream paint of the walls. There was no getting
away from it though, the dress was going to be a very big problem.

That morning she had woken in the tiny flat she shared with her
girlfriend – she was not prepared to call Saskia her 'partner' – to the
insistent dull buzz of her phone as it vibrated on silent on the floor by
her bed amongst some discarded socks, a green woollen cardigan and
a pair of torn Nike track pants.

Isobel stretched and yawned, pushing her hair from her brow.

She looked up at the ceiling and the familiar, persistent black mould stain that was almost the exact shape of Italy. She rolled over, face down, looking over the edge of the bed at the phone, the illuminated screen read 'Mum'. She looked at it a moment and considered not answering. Although she was only sixty-seven-years-old, Isobel's mother, Pam had become increasingly dependent on her daughter of late in ways that were unexpected and confusing. Their bond had never been strong, and that was only partially explained by the fact that Pam had abandoned Isobel to be raised by Pam's sister Janet in a tiny terrace house in Burslem one week after Isobel was born. Recently, Pam had been working through a number of 'personal issues' with her gym instructor and life coach, Marita, and had come to the realisation that she had needed to put 'space' between herself and her newborn at the time of her birth, in order to become the best version of Pam that she could possibly be. The faddish selfishness of this logic did not allow that Pam may have actually suffered from post-partum depression or post-traumatic stress from the birth itself. No, in Marita's retrospective reading of events, baby Isobel was an inconvenience who would have impeded the personal growth of a creative, independent fire sign like Pam, and she agreed with Pam that the child was ultimately better off cared for by her aunty Janet. In this, and in this only, Pam and Marita were correct.

Pam and Janet's story had the classic symmetry of a fairy tale. Janet, older than Pam by five years, was generally regarded as a kind, large-boned, lantern-jawed girl with a petite mouth cushioned by overlarge florid cheeks and small, deep-set, green eyes that turned up into a squint when she smiled or laughed. By contrast, since she was a toddler, her sister Pamela was always thought of as a great beauty, with golden yellow hair that seemed to hold sunlight, large saucer-like blue eyes that appeared to be at once wise and innocent, complemented by translucent skin that responded to light and temperature in spectacular hues of cream, pink, deep red and subtle shades of mauve. The two sisters were orphaned in their late adolescence when their parents, Ted and Ena, were both killed in a freak accident that saw them electrocuted as Ted was attempting to fix a toaster using a knife as a screwdriver. Ena turned from the sink to see her husband's shuddering convulsions, coming to his aid she was punched to the wall by the current coursing through him, killing her instantly. Just as her grandparents and her parents had before her, Janet worked in the Royal Doulton porcelain factory on Nile Street, they in manufacture and she in accounts. She had been there barely a year when her parents died, leaving her to care for Pam. Their friends from the factory gathered in the tiny sitting room of their house after the funeral and solemnly offered Janet the gift of a new Sunbeam toaster. She held it in her hands unable to speak, unable to fully understand the anger the gift had given rise to. She thanked her well-intentioned co-workers and her parents' friends and walked into the kitchen. Standing at the sink, her fists clenched, her knuckles white, her mouth agape, too angry for tears. She drank a full glass of water before asking everyone to leave. After they had gone, Janet put the unopened toaster in the cupboard under the sink where it remained until, on the tenth anniversary of her parents' death, she finally threw it away.

Although Janet loved her sister dearly and essentially raised her from the age of thirteen, she understood Pam's physical beauty carried with it its own set of disadvantages, limitations and jeopardies that needed to be understood and negotiated with care to traverse adolescence with as little peril as possible. But in the unrelenting commotion of an orphaned puberty, Pam would hear none of Janet's advice or follow any of her directives. She drank with her friends down by the canal, she smoked, she had her nose pierced and threatened to get a tattoo once she'd saved the money. She wore so much make-up she resembled a trashy urban geisha with a school uniform that was hitched so high it bounced over her barely covered bottom as she walked the streets of Burslem to school. In the absence of their parents, Janet became the target of all Pam's frustrations, loathing, pettiness and self-serving manipulations. Within the scattershot confusions of her teenage years the one deeply held focus of Pam Dalby was her resentment for her sister Janet. Janet who she thought to be a fat, ungainly, ugly embarrassment, barely worth her pity. As for Janet, she refused to accommodate Pam with reciprocal aversion; quite the opposite, she remained loyal to her sister and attempted to cater to her needs when they were reasonable. She willingly put up with screaming fits, slamming doors and threats of physical violence for the simple reason that, as Janet saw it, now that her parents were gone, and largely out of respect to them, it was her task to care for her sister, at least until she had decided who she wanted to be and what she wanted to do. Janet also knew that she held a contrasting advantage over her sister's turbulent nature; she was clearly aware of her place in the world, and she was perfectly content to occupy it unremarkably. For her part, as Pam got older and grew to adjust to the burden of her beauty, she was faced with the troublesome prospect of her future.

Pam Dalby might have been described as a 'free spirit' were it not for the fact that her restlessness, her rages, her transient passions and intermittent cruelties masked a terrifying void in herself that troubled her life with poor choices, lost opportunities and the deeply hidden, fretful truth that she could never be responsible for her actions or herself. All of this was disguised by an unshakeable, paradoxical belief in herself as destined for some obscure distinction or greatness that she could never quite define. She felt she could have been a great dancer, but her feet seemed too big and she had no inherent sense of rhythm or physical grace. Her passion shifted to art, but that evaporated after a few months of Saturday drawing classes at a local church hall, where hands and feet remained stubbornly beyond her limited skills of draughtsmanship. Then there were the thoughtful months when she considered writing as an outlet for her unfocused creative energies but finally concluded, after many abortive paragraphs, some no longer than single sentences of seven or nine words, that life in Burslem was too boring to record, even as fiction.

At thirty-five, Pam began singing in a Blondie cover band called, Peroxide Dream, imitating Debbie Harry's narrow vocal range in a passably fake New York drawl. It was in Peroxide Dream that she found a modest measure of success playing clubs, pubs and draughty halls throughout the north in a battered, mustard-coloured Kombi van that was variously called the touring bus, the dressing room or the *Hotel Deluxe* depending on their circumstances.

In the claustrophobic world of the band, Pam found love. First with Tariq, the painfully thin bass player with hazel eyes and a moustache that drooped over his top lip, tickling Pam's ear as he mumbled words of love to her in bad hotels or on the foam mattress in the back of the van huddled against the cold. Then with Brian, the stocky Scottish drummer with freckles and oversized pink ears who insisted on being called 'Kit'. Kit, who would gently drum his fingers on her stomach after sex, quietly humming songs like 'London Calling' from The Clash or The Stranglers 'Golden Brown'.

The gap of time between Pam breaking off with Tariq and her declaration of affection for Kit was an afternoon and an evening that included a brief but violent interlude in the car park of the *Blue Rainbow Hotel* in Manchester. There was screaming, punches, kicking and an ungainly rotating headlock that resulted in the bloodied trio of Pam, Tariq and Kit crying in a huddle as five bored teenagers and two young women holding infants looked on. The following morning, as weak sunlight shone through a narrow crack of sheer, gauzy terylene curtains onto the nicotine stained walls of room 704, Pam blinked awake between the soundly sleeping, occasionally snoring, naked bodies of both Tariq and Kit.

In the hermetically sealed world of the band, the trio maintained this affectionate arrangement for the last three months of what was to become the farewell tour of Peroxide Dream. Less than a year later, Pam found herself giving birth as a single mother in an overheated maternity ward at Stoke City General Hospital while Janet, who had accompanied her for the birth, slept soundly on a blue vinyl bench in the glare of the waiting room twenty yards down the hall.

Through a drug-induced haze of exhaustion and release Pam looked down at the tightly swaddled, damp startled face of her daughter as she craned her tiny neck, twisting her face away from the light. Pam held out her finger to touch the baby's little pink, flexing fist, no bigger than a raspberry, as her minute hand opened and her tiny fingers gripped the tip of Pam's forefinger. Looking down at the child, she began to sob. Habituated to the emotional extremes of childbirth, Gwen, Pam's sturdy West Indian midwife stood with a green plastic clipboard completing details on a form.

'Now, tiny baby girl came to you at five pounds three ounces … fingers and toes … lovely head of black curls … ' she broke off as she scribbled on the form. Pam looked up from the face of her newborn daughter, her voice gravelled and thick with tears.

'What are they doing now? What happens now?'

Gwen kept writing, 'Oh my darling, nurse is just stitching up a little tear. You did so well! Now my sweetheart, the father? Who should I say? Will he be coming?' At that moment Janet appeared in the doorway, newly awoke and breathless.

'Oh Pammie! Sugar! Look what you've done,' she walked carefully to the foot of the bed.

'The father?' Gwen insisted, her biro poised. 'What is the name of your daughter's father?' Pam looked again at her baby. Her little crumpled face seemed to contort into a twist as her tiny tongue explored her mouth and lips. Pam shook her head and immediately felt a wave of nausea. Having her sister by her side brought on more sobs. 'He's not coming,' Janet addressed Gwen directly, 'The whereabouts of the father is unknown at this time,' surprising herself with her formality. Gwen looked back at her form.

'Unknown then,' Gwen intoned slowly as she wrote.

Pam tried to concentrate on the tiny furrows that were her baby's closed eyes as her own again blurred with tears. Janet stroked her hair.

'But she's beautiful Pammie! You did good, shug. C'mon now, stop crying.'

Overcome with exhaustion, Pam's head felt like an enormous weight on the pillow. Every time she blinked another hot rivulet coursed down her face. She was unable to stop it. Janet misunderstood. She believed her sister's tears were of joy and relief, but they were not. They were tears of sadness and fear. She looked down at the little stranger in her arms and was overwhelmed and confused by her feelings of uncertainty and panic. As she saw it, the shape of her future did not include a purple faced baby girl.

'What are you going to call this beautiful child?' Gwen asked, grinning at the sisters, tapping her pen on the side of her clipboard.

Pam looked at Janet, the massive effort of the birth and her sobbing overtook her with a drowsy heaviness that pulled her toward sleep. Somewhere, far-off, many floors below and streets away she could hear the ringing of a bell, it's regular, unhurried peal suggesting it tolled to mark time rather than dread.

'Jan,' she said, thickly, 'It's a bell, do you hear? It's a bell …' Her voice trailed off, she closed her eyes as Janet took up the baby, looking down at her she said, 'Isobel. That's what your mum has named you. Darling, Isobel.'

The following week Pam left her baby in the care of her sister in the house they had been raised in, embarking on a life of itinerant employment and unstable lodging, never moving beyond a fifty-mile radius of Burslem. She would visit bringing elaborate, expensive gifts for Isobel, treating her more like a beloved niece than the daughter she had given up in worry, pain and tears on a warm August afternoon in 1990. These periodic visits confused the young Isobel. Although she was raised in the full knowledge that Pam was her mother, it never became clear to her why she couldn't live with her and Auntie Janet, she was simply told that her mum had to go away to work. Pam would always arrive perfectly made up and slightly overdressed, drenched in the heavy scent of Elizabeth Arden's Sunflowers, it was a veneer of glamour taken from advertisements she'd see in *Vanity Fair* and *Tatler*. But over the course of a few hours the illusion would begin to wobble. Inevitably, amongst the gifts, the kisses, the hugs and the grinning questions about friends or school came the sobbing tears of her mother, her puffy eyes, streaked mascara and the frightening mystery of adult grief that only seemed to subside some hours after Pam had left, as the new toys stood idle and the tissue paper and cellophane had been flattened out and neatly folded away in a kitchen drawer.

Just as Pam's life was an unfocused shambles, Janet's sensibility was steadfast, stoic and resolute. Her parenting of Isobel was characterised by order, love, consideration and care. She was her guardian in every good sense of that word. She instilled in her a contempt for lying, a love of learning and books and a healthy suspicion of the motives of others. From infancy, Janet encouraged Isobel's reading and writing, giving her a chunky pink diary with a plastic cover decorated with butterflies and a unicorn, that could be locked with a tiny gold key. Her first entry, aged seven, late in the summer of 1997 simply read, 'It rained today. The dog next door was barking. Princess Diana is dead.'

As Isobel grew Janet could clearly see she was her mother's daughter. She was a beautiful child with blonde hair and blue eyes that were sharp and attentive. Janet recognised that she was sensitive, smart, she was quick, sometimes wilful, and Janet sensed she had the capacity – just like Pam – to be trouble. But for all that there were some distinct and peculiar differences that set Isobel apart from the haphazard sensibility of her mother.

The first was her curiosity about reading. Janet had never been able to throw away any of her parents' things, rather she stored them in battered cardboard boxes under the stairs. It was here that Isobel discovered a small collection of Mills & Boon romance novels that had belonged to her grandmother. Janet saw no harm in Isobel leafing through them, only realising that she was actually reading them one rainy midwinter Sunday afternoon as she was ironing in the humid sitting room of their terrace house as the television flickered a documentary entitled, *'Wallis Simpson: The Dark Duchess'*. Isobel looked up from the browned paperback edition of the *Winds of Enchantment*, holding her place on the page with a finger.

'What does *heaving* mean?' she asked, her brow creasing. Janet kept ironing in steady strokes.

'What do you mean, love?'

Isobel considered the page and read aloud, halting over the words. ''He reached behind her, his dark eyes glowing with love. He pulled gently at the blue ribbon around her hair, and her red tresses bounced over her shoulders and across her heaving bosom.' What's *heaving?*' On the television, jittery black and white footage showed Edward and Mrs Simpson on their wedding day, all smiles for the camera, in a gown by Mainbocher on the steps of a chateau in France. Janet looked down at the pleats she was ironing and thought about the question for a moment.

'Well, heaving … hmm … heaving, it means that she was out of breath, like this.' She put her hand on her chest and breathed deeply once or twice. They both laughed at this, then Janet asked, 'Do you know what *tresses* are?'

Without hesitation Isobel replied, 'Yes, I do. Tresses is hair, like *Rapunzel.*'

'Very good, love.' Isobel went back to her reading. Janet looked past her niece sitting on the couch and saw an image of the vulpine Duchess of Windsor sharing a joke with a group of Nazis, before going back to the steady work of her ironing.

Janet also noticed that Isobel was content with her own company. Unlike her mother, whose desperate yearnings meant she had the need to fill her life with noise, drama and distractions, Isobel could spend long hours in her room, writing in her diary, reading, or just looking out the window at the shifting sky, or down at the ribbon of grey pavements that bordered the crowded streets of Burslem. She was not a troubled or lonely child. Her solitude was not about introspection or shyness. She was unique among her small circle of friends and acquaintances in that she enjoyed the process of thinking. Time spent alone was not time wasted. She thought about her Auntie Janet and her boyfriend, Doug, who would stay at the house from time to time. She thought about her mother and what she did in the intervals between visits, the life she had after each tearful goodbye. She could close her eyes and remember, vividly, her make-up and her perfume.

She thought of all the silly women and girls described in the battered and dog-eared paperbacks her grandmother had left. She thought about her best friend, Lynda Otley, who lived four doors down, who was described at school as slow, dim-witted and thick. Lynda, who could talk for hours about *Pop Idol,* lip gloss and boy totty. Lynda, who Isobel loved for her uncomplicated idea of herself and her future – her dream of leaving school and working in Boots behind the cosmetics counter. All this she would record in her diary, and when that was filled, she would start to write in exercise books, describing in minute detail everything that she saw and considered.

She made her way through all the Mills & Boon titles in the torn cardboard box under the stairs, *The Faraway Bride, The Spanish Interlude, Flame of Fate, The Dilemma of Mavis,* and more. By the time she was twelve, between the sad fantasies of her mother and the florid confections of Mills & Boon, she was poised to enter puberty well versed in the fiction of romance.

It was at this time, as oestrogen coursed through her body and the daily interrogations of her appearance in the small rectangular mirror in the bathroom became more complex, that Isobel tried her own hand at fiction. For inspiration, she looked no further than the sitting room, crowded with her grandparents' scratched, mismatched furniture and an oversized television. There in the hypnotic glow of TV shows like *Coronation Street, Prime Suspect* or *Big Brother,* Isobel looked at the walls of the room, hung with pictures of her grandparents and their children. Her grandparents on their wedding day, her grandfather in a square shouldered black suit, his hair combed into a glossy Brylcreemed slick accurately parted to one side, her grandmother in a tightly waisted white lace dress, hemmed demurely below the knee, her hair garlanded in white flowers topped with a gauzy scrunch of white tulle pushed back over her shoulder, flecked with confetti. Then there were the pictures of her aunt and her mother. One of Janet in her school uniform taken in 1972, her cooperative joyless smile dimpling her cheeks, reflecting the ordeal of the portrait. Then there were four pictures of her mother. There was Pam dressed as a fairy on her sixth birthday, Pam dressed as a bumble bee for a school concert, one of Janet holding Pam like an oversized chubby doll, her face on the verge of erupting into sobs and finally, a school portrait of Pam, her school tie carelessly pulled to one side, her hair tangled into an unruly topknot against the same background of mottled greenery that her sister was photographed in front of, but without any sense of an accommodating smile for the camera, rather, her heavily lidded and mascaraed eyes held the lens with an expression of numbed boredom and mild resentment.

Underneath those family portraits, collected over a lifetime of work at the Royal Doulton factory, her grandparents had gathered a precious collection of porcelain figurines crafted in the timeless banality of fake Regency. Carefully arranged on the mantelpiece there was a selection of nine 'ladies' who all wore generous dresses that billowed out from their delicate waists in a variety of insipid shades of green, pink, crimson and blue, their little faces delicately painted and glazed with rosebud lips and lightly rouged cheeks. One or two carried baskets, one sat on a little bench accompanied by a lively terrier. In addition, there were three other figures; a gentleman sitting on a tree stump in a white wig and knee breeches smoking a pipe, an old man in buckled shoes and an apron holding a jug and an unexpected androgynous oriental genie with a skullcap, bushy eyebrows and a drooping handlebar moustache. This crowded group of uniformly ugly ornaments were to be the cast of characters in Isobel Dalby's first fiction, a fourteen-page handwritten story entitled *Blood on the Mantle*.

The plot of Isobel's story concerned the brutal murder of one of the lady figurines – Sarah-Jane, whose body had been found tumbled from the mantelpiece, laying on the hearth by the gas fire, her throat cut, her head almost severed, her dress torn from her and the head of a single pink rose stuffed into her mouth. Everyone left standing on the mantle were suspects, and they all had their motives to snuff out the life of Sarah-Jane. Jealousy, hatred, unrequited love (from both the men and the women), deep familial secrets and the momentary violence of a crime of passion all found their way into Isobel's unexpected prose.

What surprised Janet when she read *Blood on the Mantle* was the clarity of Isobel's writing and the detailed way she had drawn her characters. The annoying and ill-fated Sarah-Jane was described as 'a manicured and perfumed beauty whose insincere smile was over-used.' There was jealous, quick-tempered Margaret who wore men's boots under her dress, whose 'face would often brighten into hatred' and the knee-breeched dandy, Lord Appleton, 'whose wig was always askew, with a wit as slack as his jaw'. Then there was the strange genie, Raj, who was only visible to Lynn, the 'deaf-mute girl sitting on the tiny bench with her frisky terrier, Smudge, pawing at her knees for attention'.

The bloody story concluded on the lime green acrylic shag-pile mat in front of the gas heater, imagined by Isobel as a rain-sodden heath with all the ornaments surrounding Rose, a petite figure in a pinafore whose delicate eyes peered over a plain white fan. Rose was revealed to be not only the murderer of Sarah-Jane but her downcast half-sister, ridiculed for her stutter and her missing teeth that she took great pains to hide from the world. Isobel drew *Blood on the Mantle* to a close with these words:

> *Rose threw her fan to the ground, and instead of asking forgiveness for herself, she looked to heaven, crying out, 'G,G,G, God f,f,f,f, forgive Sarah-Jane!' The crowd looked on in shock and horror. Her guilt had made her feverishly hot as the clouds above her moved together, darkening the sky. Rose looked up again at the welcoming rain as it soaked her hair and her dress, the weight of it pulling her into the mud and the gathering puddles surrounding her. The silence was broken only by Smudge, who barked sharply three times and was then quiet. – The End.*

Janet sat at the kitchen table holding a cup of tea. She finished the story and kept staring at the words on the last page. Her immediate thoughts were not about Isobel, or her story, but of her sister, Pam, and the endless flatteries and encouragements offered to her beautiful sister. How Pam's belief in her own future of untrammelled possibilities and potential had led her to sing Blondie covers in sticky carpeted clubs throughout the north for money that barely kept her alive. A life of empty adventures that left her with a child she couldn't raise and unrelenting regret. Although Janet was aware of the new narrative around children and their capacity to achieve anything if they were just encouraged to believe in themselves, she didn't trust it. Her sister's self-belief struck her as little more than self-delusion and fantasy fuelled by the corrosive persuasion of others. Janet looked up from the page and placed it carefully on top of the others, she smiled at Isobel.

'That's a good story, Belle. I loved that the genie stole the dead girl's dress. Poor old Rose, eh?'

Isobel grinned back at her aunt. 'Really, Auntie Jan? You really liked it?'

'I did.' Janet stood and emptied her cup into the sink. 'Now, let's get a move on. Come and help me with your tea.'

Isobel kept writing. She graduated from Mills & Boon, and at the suggestion of her aunt she started to read great authors from the past. She thought about the worlds created by Jane Austen, Emily Brontë and George Eliot, the worlds of *Mansfield Park, Wuthering Heights* and *Romola*. She loved taking apart the long, knotty sentences in these books and thought about the hands that wrote them and the women that had imagined them. It was not yet fully formed in her young mind, but Isobel sensed that in these words and sentences, the stories and the books, there was a way of understanding people, ordering your world and living away and beyond the grey and dirty streets of Burslem.

Through her adolescence, Isobel became increasingly restive about the patterns of her life. Her time at Endon High was punctuated with the customary teenage rites of passage. Secret episodes of smoking and drinking with Lynda that left her dizzy and hungover. Her first kiss was shared with Barry Moffatt, a tall ungainly boy of her own age who had a port wine stain birthmark in the vague shape of a heart on his cheek, who could be seen constantly flicking his fringe of dirty blond hair from his eyes. It was beside the bike shed on a cold, windy afternoon, that he gently took her hand as they embraced and made her rub his erection through his school trousers. She panicked slightly when for the first time she experienced the odd sensation of a boy moaning with pleasure into her mouth. She pushed him away laughing, when he tried to put his hand under her skirt. Some days afterwards Isobel became an instant schoolyard celebrity when Barry, standing with three of his friends, accused her loudly of being 'a cock teasing slag.' She was standing with Lynda who whispered in her ear 'Leave it, Belle', but she pulled away from her friend, Lynda could see that Isobel's eyes were calm as they narrowed slightly. Isobel turned away and walked up to Barry Moffatt, shrugged off her backpack, and head-butted him to the ground.

Her first crush was a black girl one year ahead of her, Beth Driscoll who was tall, athletic and long-limbed with bleached yellow hair that was carelessly streaked with black regrowth, whose full lips and perfect smile were flawed by a rakishly bent front tooth that Isobel adored. At sixteen, Beth had a voice that carried a deep, mannish rasp that Isobel imagined would vibrate through her entire body when she spoke or laughed. Isobel was content to admire Beth from afar until one afternoon she walked up to the bus stop after school and found her sitting, distractedly chipping burgundy polish off her thumbnail. She was wearing Adidas track pants and trainers and an oversized red pullover, she'd pushed the sleeves up to her elbows, a denim jacket was tied around her waist. Isobel carefully sat at the end of the bench, her body pulsed with excitement and dread. She noticed that Beth wore a chunky gold bangle made in a pattern of interlocking 'G's. She could hear its gentle clink as Beth moved her hands. Isobel looked from the bangle to Beth and found herself saying, 'That's a lovely bangle.' Beth looked up at her and smiled with one side of her mouth.

'Thank you, darlin'. Yeah, it's good innit?' Beth held out her arm regarding the jewellery, before dropping it into her lap.

'It's Gucci, y'know?' Her one-sided smile then turned downward as if to express doubt. Then Beth Driscoll did something that was to live in Isobel's memory forever. She winked at her. Then she added, 'Well, he *said* it was Gucci, you know what I mean?' Isobel had barely enough time to nod in agreement, smiling nervously, when the bus squealed to a stop beside them, the doors opening in a mechanised gasp. Beth got on and Isobel remained, in a state of shock, exhausted by the ordeal of this brief exchange, as the bus drove on down the road.

Sometimes, before she climbed into bed, Isobel would turn her light off and stand by the open curtains of her window, closing her eyes, she would chant Beth's name to the darkened rooftops and chimneys of Burslem, summoning her to life in her imagination. *Beth, Beth, Beth, Beth,* she would whisper, as each little puff of breath left a tiny cloud of fog on the cold glass before diminishing to nothing.

Nothing would come of Isobel's devotion to Beth Driscoll, and it didn't matter. For Isobel, Beth represented a sleek, elegant and mysterious alternative to the sloppy fumbling boys who were drawn to her. Out of curiosity, weeks after the head-butting incident Isobel allowed Barry Moffatt to have sex with her. She cooperated mechanically in a process that she found unbelievably boring, gross and painful. Was this seriously the off-stage climax of all those Mills & Boon romances she'd studied? This hot breath? This groaning? This insistent tongue? This uncomfortable hot jet of ejaculate? When it was over she thanked Barry, not with a kiss but with a high five and a playful slap across his acned cheek. Walking home, she wondered if this was what Beth had needed to do to be compensated with a shiny gold bangle. Just like her writing, Beth was a secret Isobel could keep that offered her deliverance from the deadening pattern of school and a life bordered by grey footpaths, sneering boys and dull routine.

As their adolescence drew to a close, the lives of Isobel and her good friend Lynda began to diverge. Lynda went on to realise her dream and, inadvertently, provided Isobel with a vivid example of what her future might be like if she were to stay in Burslem. Four months after leaving Endon High, Lynda Otley was behind the counter at Boots in Scotia Road, Tunstall. It was in Scotia Road that she busied herself dusting cellophane-wrapped boxes of Calvin Klein and Giorgio Armani scent, slavishly wiping down her glass-topped counters and advising customers in foundation, rouge, acrylic nails and eyebrow pencils. As the months of her employment dragged on though, by degrees, Lynda came to the stony realisation that life behind the counter was not all glamour. Eventually the endless hours of boredom she endured in the fluorescent box of the pharmacy induced a kind of mania in her that, in turn, led to months of petty theft. Firstly, of small items like false eyelashes and nail varnish, but then on to larger things she neither wanted or needed like the 'Express-

And-Go Breast Milk Starter Kit' and boxes of incontinence pads. Eventually, she began to pocket money from the till and although this would ultimately lead to the end of her career at Boots, she was unable to stop. Each theft instantly erased her boredom, quickening through her like bright, transient exhilarations that became addictive. She became lost in the invisible glamour of being a thief. *'I'm a thief'*, she would say to herself as she waited with strangers for the bus, and it filled her with a secret happiness. She would brazenly look up, smiling at the security camera mounted in the ceiling as she opened the cash register, scooping up a few pounds at a time.

Finally, as she knew it must, the day of reckoning came for Lynda Otley. It was a rainy Wednesday afternoon, she was found in the storeroom fellating a courier called Vikram who was delivering a consignment of Dr Scholl corn removers when an unconcerned policewoman stood in the doorway.

'Would you be, Lynda Otley?' she asked as the radio mic on her shoulder crackled with some indecipherable sounds. Lynda looked up from her labour, but it was Vikram who finally spoke.

'Ere! Um … excuse us, we're nearly done 'ere.'

The policewoman gave Vikram a wry smile as his drooping erection waved in front of Lynda's face.

'Get up love, you're going to have to come with me.'

In her final year at school, studying for her A-levels in history, English and geography Isobel started to see some odd changes in the rhythm of her life at home. She noticed that her aunt Janet would be home in the afternoon, having not gone to work, she tired often and would ask Isobel to prepare their dinner, and then just pick at it in front of the television before going to bed. Isobel became confused by her aunt's moody, snappish behaviour until one afternoon, late in May, tearfully she told her beloved niece that she had been diagnosed with stage four cervical cancer.

'It's not good, Belle, but you need to know.' She said, stroking Isobel's hand. Isobel stared ahead at a football calendar pinned to the wall and a picture of English Defender Ledley King expertly balancing a ball on his knee. It became impossible for her to process this information. Cancer was bad, she knew that, but what could *stage four* mean? Janet's words repeated in her head, *'It's not good, Belle'.* They sat in silence as Isobel looked down at the carpet and the shape of her aunt's toes in her green slippers, the soft blue vein that ran across the top of her foot. She looked up at the photograph above the mantle of Janet in her school uniform, then Janet holding Pam as a baby and her eyes pricked and blurred with tears. She began to sob as her aunt took her in her arms.

'Come on, Belle.' She hugged Isobel's shoulders and looked into her eyes. 'There's a lot to do, love. Let's have a cup of tea.'

That was May. By late December Janet Dalby was dead. In early September of the following year, Isobel and her mother stood in the sitting room of the house they had both been raised in. After Janet's death Pam had decided to move back to Burslem. Now she slept in her sister's old room, the room her parents had slept in. All morning Isobel busied herself packing. She had been given a place to study creative writing at South Bank University in London and for at least the first term she would be living in the halls of residence. Her mother, dressed in leopard print leggings and an oversized t-shirt that commemorated something called *Big Fun Run Manchester,* had aimlessly followed Isobel around all morning as she readied herself to leave. When she wasn't staring at the tiny screen on her phone tapping out text messages, she was sighing loudly. Finally, as Isobel waited for her taxi, there were no more distractions and mother and daughter were forced to be together in the silence of the house, and the memory of Janet. Isobel sensed her presence everywhere, in the small rooms, the curtains and the windows, the stairs and the furniture. She was quiet for a moment, staring at her suitcase and her backpack and then attempted to break the spell by talking of mundane practicalities.

'So, I'll be in New Kent Road, I think I already told you that – near Elephant and Castle.' There was no response from Pam as she stared glassily at the family portraits over the mantle.

'I'll text you when I get in – probably after five.' Her mother continued to ignore her. She moved slowly until she stood with her back to Isobel in front of the gas fire looking up at the pictures on the wall. The Royal Doulton figurines set out in a tidy row on the mantle, neatly dusted before her.

'Your Auntie Janet sat with me when Mum and Dad went, it were just there, in the kitchen.' She distractedly pointed to the floor behind her. Isobel felt slightly sick. She stood and listened.

'Your Auntie Janet sat with me when you were born. She named you, she did … she called you Isobel …' Pam's voice trailed off, her last words barely whispered. She put her mobile phone down on the mantle beside the figurine of Sarah-Jane, her hands gripping the little white shelf as she stared at Janet's school portrait. She whispered to the picture.

'Janet … my darling … my dearest darling, darling …' Then in one violent, shocking gesture she swept all the ornaments on the mantle across the room and onto the floor. Some smashed against the wall, others fell to pieces on the green shag-pile mat. Isobel gasped, unable to speak, her mother cried out in a howl of hollowed out grief.

'What the fuck am I going to do here? Eh? Just tell me that!' Her knees slowly folding underneath her as she collapsed, sobbing amongst the broken pieces of coloured porcelain. Isobel's mouth was open, she noticed that her hands were trembling, she felt cold inside her rust coloured wool overcoat. In less than ten seconds, her mother had exorcised the ghost of her sister. Isobel realised that her sense of her beloved aunt had fled that place, now it was just a sitting room littered with smashed ornaments. She walked the few steps to her mother and knelt by the hearth. She saw that the figurine of Rose had shattered and a single shard, her arm, elbow and head had come away in one piece, her tiny hand still holding her fan. She picked up the broken fragment of porcelain and placed it carefully in her pocket. She took a deep breath and spoke with direct clarity to Pam as she whimpered into the wall, leaning against the grille of the gas fire.

'*What the fuck are you going to do here?*' Isobel said, she paused, her anger, which seemed to be beating through her head from the back of her skull, pulsed through her hair to her brow and eyes giving her a deliberate calm. She tried to form more words, but there was too much to say. She needed to talk about how she felt that she had been abandoned by her mother, about the strangeness of her occasional visits and attention, her indifferent cruelty to her sister, her sense of her mother's terrifying loneliness and need, the weirdness of living in this house with her now without Janet, and her mother's testy insistence on being called 'Mum', even though she was not much more than a stranger to her daughter. But none of this could be spoken by her now. Not today.

'*What the fuck are you going to do here?*' Isobel repeated again, she went on, spacing the sentence for clarity, articulating each word carefully. 'Well, you can start, by clearing up this lot.' She waited a moment, and then went to touch her mother's shoulder as her crying began to subside when she heard the blare of the taxi's horn outside.

'Okay, I'm off.' Her mother remained crouched on the floor. As she took up her case and backpack she called out, 'I'll call you later.' She paused and then added the word, 'Mum.' And with that she slammed the door on her life in Burslem.

The phone on the floor stopped ringing. There was an interval of less than fifteen seconds and then the two short buzzes that indicated a message. Isobel sighed. Now she would have to call her back. She lay for a moment listening to a plane far-off in the sky. She knew there were things she had to do today and she tried to remember. She had to pay some bills. Saskia had left six hundred pounds with her to pay a number of accounts that were overdue. Saskia had lost her wallet three weeks ago and had been negotiating with the bank for the renewal of her various cards and had become reliant on Isobel to manage their finances, but she was aware that this carried with it a degree of risk. One of the first things Saskia discovered about Isobel very early in their relationship was that she was extremely relaxed about money. On one of their first dates Isobel had insisted on taking Saskia to *The River Café* where she spent one hundred and sixty pounds on food and wine only to discover after she had paid the bill that in fact, that was the last of her cash for the next four days.

They had met two years earlier at a party when Isobel was six weeks from completing her degree at the South Bank University. They were in a crowded, humid flat in Lewisham shared by two students from Isobel's class, Tim Holman and Vihan Bindal, who had somehow made it to the final year of their course in creative writing without producing anything written, or at least anything Isobel had seen. Tim had been rumoured to be writing a book about a group of National Gallery floor polishers who decide to steal Titian's *Bacchus and Ariadne* during the time of Margaret Thatcher's government, and Vihan was working on a series of linked short stories about immigrant workers in low paid service jobs in hotels all over London. They talked often of these projects, the research around them and the characters they were creating, but Isobel had not seen, or heard a word of their writing. They both worked as part-time porters at University Hospital in Lewisham, and they had invited a rowdy bunch of orderlies and nurses to the party along with a few people from the University. Isobel was introduced to Saskia by a drunken Tim who stood by the kitchen sink pouring and spilling tequila into plastic cups.

'*Belle!*' he shouted over some vintage Joy Division. 'This is *Saskia!* She's an emergency.' Isobel took her plastic cup from Tim, laughing.

'Hi, I'm Isobel, Belle, you're an emergency?' Saskia tapped her plastic cup against Isobel's, smiling. 'No. I'm not *an* emergency, I'm a nurse *in* emergency, emergency at the hospital.' Tim gulped down a slug of tequila, gasping.

'You should have a chat to Belle here, she's writing a dirty book. I can't lie. It's fucking *brilliant!*' Saskia held out her cup for more tequila, Isobel took a sip and felt the clear spirit sting her tongue.

'Okay. So I'm going to ignore you Tim – *loud* Tim.' Isobel said, shaking her head, she smiled at Saskia, who leaned toward her.

'Hi Belle, so, you're writing a book?' She said.

'Tim's lying.' Isobel shouted into Saskia's ear over the music. 'It's not brilliant, and it's *not dirty,*' said with emphasis for Tim, 'and it's not finished – well, it's nearly finished.'

Saskia was holding her plastic cup in her hand, she reached over and hooked the sleeve of Isobel's cardigan with two free fingers.

'Let's sit somewhere quiet and you can tell me all about your not brilliant, not finished but nearly finished, but *not dirty* book.'

They made their way to the small balcony of the flat and were immediately chilled by the cold night air. *'Fuck man!* It's fucking freezing!' Saskia said as she lit a cigarette, clutching her plastic cup of tequila close to the side of her face. A string of fairy lights blinked on and off irregularly, looped across and around some dead and dying pot plants. Already, between the two of them there seemed to be a soft but discernible current that they were both aware of but were not yet willing to acknowledge. In the corner of the balcony there was a wicker basket where, surprisingly, there lay curled up a silver greyhound who looked up forlornly at the women as Saskia closed the glass door on the noise of the party.

'Oh hello love, who are you?' Saskia said to the dog as it swung its neck upward.

'That's Daphne. Tim said she came with the flat. He said she's very old, and very deaf apparently.'

Saskia laughed. 'Lucky Daphne not to have to put up with listening to Tim!' She crouched down beside the dog and gently stroked one of her thin velvet ears between her fingers. Daphne slotted her perfectly chiselled nose between her paws neatly folded underneath her, her worried eyes still looking up at the two women.

'So, you work in emergency. That must be full on.' Saskia stood and took a sip of tequila.

'It was when I started – I've been there nearly four years now. In the beginning it fucked with my head a bit. But now I think I've sorted out a way to deal with it.' She laughed a little. 'I'm not sure I'll do it forever, but for now it's good.' She pulled her jacket together at the front and folded her arms, she sipped again from her cup. 'And what about you? You've written a book?'

'Yeah, okay, yes, my book. Well, I've nearly finished it – I started writing it three years ago when I first started the course at South Bank, I really wasn't sure it was going to go anywhere, but now I'm nearly done.' Isobel looked down to the street below. There was a knot of boys standing around a lamppost watching something on a phone, a moment passed and they erupted into laughter. Saskia leaned on the ledge of the balcony, her chin resting in the heel of her palm.

'So, what's it about, your book?' she said, straightening with a slight adjustment to her shoulders.

Isobel drew a deep breath, she looked at Saskia, not surrounded by others now, she could see her clearly. Not much shorter than herself, in blue jeans, a bulky green turtleneck pullover and a black jacket, thick, shiny red shoulder-length hair and pale skin reddened by the cold. Isobel noticed that she had icy, light-blue eyes, alert and attentive and slightly terrifying. She was standing by Daphne who now appeared to be asleep at her feet, she held her plastic cup in one hand and a cigarette in the other. Isobel saw she wore a thin gold ring on her little finger set with a small red stone.

'Can I have a drag?' Isobel asked. Casually Saskia handed her the cigarette, Isobel didn't put it to her lips immediately. For a moment she looked through the glass door of the balcony hung with orange net curtains to the crowd of people in the tiny sitting room, then she looked back at Saskia. She began tentatively, 'Well, it's really about women, but it's slightly complicated.'

'Oh dear, *slightly complicated* women, go on then, I'm all ears, but you're going to have to give me back that fag.'

Isobel talked to Saskia about her Aunt Janet and her mother and her life in Burslem, about Lynda Otley and Beth Driscoll and Barry Moffatt and how writing had been like a key to the bigger world outside her tiny town. Saskia laughed easily as Isobel described the plot of *Blood on the Mantle* and her self-schooling in literature from Mills & Boon to the Brontës. She talked about her love of writing from the past with its complex plotting, vivid characters and dense, intricate prose. How it had led her to set her story in London in 1770 and to create a character that would not be out of place in the fiction of Thackeray and Defoe, a woman who was equal parts Moll Flanders, Becky Sharp and Fanny Hill with a hint of Scary Spice, a chancer, a streetwise slut who understood her place in the world and sought to upend it. She explained to her how she'd started writing it as an exercise in form and style to see if she could convincingly create that world and make her heroine, Nell Balldock, come alive. She said that she'd written almost 140,000 words that described Nell's rise and fall over a tumultuous decade in the life of eighteenth century Covent Garden.

'Oh god! You can tell me to shut up, listen to me banging on!' Isobel looked into her now empty cup. Saskia fiddled idly with a button on her jacket. She considered Isobel for a moment.

'So why does Tim think it's a dirty book then?' she asked.

Isobel rolled her eyes. 'Oh, he thinks that any book that has sex in it is dirty. And to make matters worse, it's been written by a girl. I mean, there is sex in my book, but I think it's totally justified.' She thought for a moment before adding, 'I'd say it's *earned.*' She said it carefully as if she was examining the word, immediately regretting it, sensing that Saskia was aware of her embarrassment she went on, 'He's just completely misunderstood it, that's all.' She added, 'He's so bloody lazy, I mean, he's great but I'm amazed he's made it to final year.'

Saskia's head was cocked slightly to one side. 'And what's it called then, your book?'

Isobel shrugged, smiling. *'Her Cunt. The Life and Times of Nell Balldock.'* There was only a moment before they both laughed. Saskia knocked Daphne's basket with her foot causing the dog to wake with a start and a slight yelp. She looked up from her bed, craning her long neck in an elegant arc and began licking Saskia's hand with her warm tongue.

At some point Tim yanked the glass door of the balcony open. He was shirtless, his hairless, white chest, wide drunk eyes and open mouth gave him the appearance of an oversized boy, his fingers hooked around the neck of a bottle of lager. He seemed slightly out of breath.

'We were just saying that, um … we're going to go on to Marko's place – he's got some stuff …' Both Isobel and Saskia looked at him before Isobel asked, 'What stuff? Who's Marko?' Tim laughed about something that was said behind him, something Isobel and Saskia couldn't hear. Tim twisted his head around to yell into the room. 'Shut the fuck up!' he turned back to the girls. 'Y'know, *stuff* man … what the fuck are you doing out here anyway?'

Saskia and Isobel looked at one another, standing close, side by side, shoulder to shoulder, then they looked back at Tim.

'We're enjoying your party,' said Saskia. Tim's broad grin

threatened to turn into a giggle. 'Now, why don't you bugger off?' Saskia said. Still holding his beer Tim pointed at Saskia. 'You Cow! She's like this at work! Don't let her spike your drink, Belle!' And with that he slammed the door shut, joining the others in the overheated sitting room. Isobel thought it must be very late. She'd started working at Caffé Nero in Paternoster Square, and her shift began at 7 am. In the distance, the sky above the lights of the city was glowing a dull green signalling the coming morning. They huddled together against the cold, still holding their empty cups. The wind picked up and threw strands of Isobel's hair across Saskia's face. 'God! It's so cold my heart is racing.' She took Isobel's hand and placed it across her chest. Isobel could feel the steady rhythm of Saskia's heartbeat. 'It feels like it's getting louder,' she said. She shut her eyes, her hand remained on Saskia's warm breastbone. Saskia's fingers combed through Isobel's hair, gently holding the back of her head. She kissed her, at first lightly on the mouth, whispering, 'My heart feels *louder?* And this coming from a *writer?*' They shared a laughing kiss before Saskia added, 'Idiot.' Drawing her other arm around Isobel's waist, pulling her closer.

Five weeks later, Isobel moved into Saskia's bedsit on Coldharbour Lane and it was in this tiny flat that the deeper intimacies of their relationship were navigated. They had fallen in love, and now they had to learn each other, the things they held in common, and the oppositions that made up their life together. They preferred beer to wine and baths to showers and found that they could lose hours in front of the television watching re-runs of *Antiques Roadshow* or *Spooks*. They were fans of cooking shows and would watch Rick, Nigella and Jamie whip up dinners and desserts that neither of them would ever cook. Saskia once remarked that Nigella's kitchen looked bigger than their entire flat. There were differences though as well, and the most significant of them was reading. When Isobel arrived, she discovered that Saskia had one book in her bedsit, a copy of *The Da Vinci Code* with a torn cover which sat on top of the fridge with junk mail and take-away menus from a range of local cafes and restaurants. The afternoon she moved in, Isobel stood in the kitchenette holding the book.

'*Dan Brown*, really?'

Saskia was finishing a bag of crisps, she licked her fingers. 'Oh, don't bother with that. It's rubbish. The movie's much better.'

Isobel looked at the last page to be dog-eared. 'You only got to page sixty-seven. Although you are right about one thing. It is rubbish, and I'm now discovering that your taste in movies is as bad as your taste in books.' She grinned as she popped the top from a Corona.

'Ha! Just like my taste in women. I've got no time Belle, by the time I get home – I'm knackered.' She reached for the beer, 'I'll have some of that, love.'

It was not long after Isobel graduated that a small portion of her novel was published by an online literary magazine called *Cut & Paste*. The excerpt, which was the first chapter of her book, prompted Rachel Nevelson from Red Pen, a small independent publishing house in Cambridge to email her, 'Congratulations on your piece in *Cut & Paste*, I'm intrigued, I would be very interested in reading the manuscript. Could we meet?' Isobel emailed a copy of the book to Rachel and they met two weeks later in the cramped office of Red Pen which seemed to be housed in the conservatory of Rachel's house on the outskirts of Cambridge. She was surprised to see that the publisher was young, in her mid-thirties, a single mother raising a two-year-old and managing Red Pen with her ex-partner, a barrister called Michael. They had published three titles and were on the lookout for new work when Rachel spotted Isobel's piece. She sat opposite Rachel in her study, amongst stacks of books, cardboard boxes, a bowl of dead tulips in brackish water, an oversized Apple computer screen and a printer that whirred into life from time to time during their meeting.

Rachel looked at Isobel, she said nothing for a moment and then, very deliberately she put her glasses on saying, 'I finished your book, and I loved it. I could not put it down.' Isobel felt empty in her stomach and slightly terrified.

'Thank you. That is very kind.' She clasped her hands on her lap. Then Rachel took a single page from a large stack of paper beside her on the desk and began to read from it. Isobel's mouth became dry as she realised she was reading the first words of her novel.

'Nell Balldock. She was born and she died. She lived between two mysteries. The womb and the sod. Between two darknesses she had a life of dirt and joy, of promises and lies, of riches and penury, of pain and hope.

'After the mother who sold her, after the prince who tore her virtue, after the clergy who beat her, after the captain who robbed her, after the child who was lost to her, after the actor who loved her, after the soldier who raped her, after the physician who murdered her, her body in its tinselled finery was lowered into the frozen ground to sleep for good. After her grave was sealed, the life of Covent Garden slowly assumed its clockwise rotation once again, and continued to spin forward.

But the thud of her coffin in the winter earth caused a shift in the axis of the tiny world, barely noticed at first, and yet changed forever – once and for all. Consider, dear reader, the brief life of Nell Balldock.'

'There's work to do here Isobel, but I think your book is beautiful and we'd love to publish it.'

Isobel laughed loudly at Rachel, and then she covered her mouth. 'Oh, I am sorry. That was unexpected, I'm so, so, sorry.' Rachel took her glasses off and held them in her hand, she leaned forward on her desk. 'That's okay, don't worry. It's fine. Do you need to think about it? Do you need some time? Do you have an agent I should contact?'

'No,' Isobel said immediately. 'No, I don't need to think about it, I don't need some time, and an agent? No, I don't have an agent.' There was a pause. 'There is one thing though.'

'Yes?' Rachel said. Isobel leaned forward. 'I'm not changing the title. I've called my book *Her Cunt,* and I want to keep that title.' Now it was Rachel's turn to laugh. 'Oh, I don't want to change *that.* That title will move books!'

That was fourteen months ago. The book had been published the following year to excellent reviews, *The Guardian* said it was, 'a post-modern bawdy romp that bares its teeth and tears at your heart.' *The New Statesman* wrote that it was, 'feminist pornography with an important and sharp axe to grind', and *The Times* enthused, '*Her C**t* is a debut of lyric maturity and gutter language that transcends pastiche to achieve a poetic truth. Looking to the past, Isobel Dalby has written a modern classic.' The book sold 532 copies.

Isobel's phone buzzed again. 'Oh my fucking god! Mum!' She sat up in bed and swiped the phone to answer. 'Mum! Yes. Hiya.' Her mother seemed out of breath. 'Oh god, Belle! You've won a prize.

Darling! You clever girl, you've won something! It's in the paper – it's on the news!'

'What? Calm down, what do you mean? I've won something?' She was immediately suspicious. In the five years since she shut the front door in Burslem, her mother had tried to pursue various passions she was convinced could 'change her life'. These included song-writing, and when that proved a dead end, poetry, when that yielded nothing but frustration she enrolled in a speech and drama course for older 'artists', her latest foray was an adult learning course on fashion design where, at least for the last eleven months, she felt she'd, 'really found' her 'voice'. Each empty ambition filled Isobel with anger and a vague concern. Her mother went on. 'It's on the news – the Bannerman Prize, you've won it, love!' Isobel put her phone on speaker and saw that she had nine missed calls and seventeen text messages, six from Rachel Nevelson, the last one just as urgent as the rest – 'CALL ME IMMEDIATELY!' She sat up in the bed and felt giddy.

'Mum! Shut up, okay? I have got to go I'll call you later, okay?' There was a silence as Isobel imagined her mother at the other end, taking in these words as if they were instructions.

'Yes, love. Belle?' she said with genuine urgency in her voice.

'What?' She said as she scrolled through other messages, one from Tim, 'Who's a clever little bitch then? Belle! WOW!' and Vihan, 'OMFG!!! Belle you are a star luv! Let's get legless!'

'Meet me after lunch darling, I'll text you where I'll be. Oh my darling girl. Okay?'

'Yes, okay I'll see you later.' There were more messages of congratulation but she was most concerned about Rachel and her six urgent messages to call her. She was still giddy, she felt a vague sense of pins and needles in her fingers. She dialled Rachel who answered almost immediately.

'Oh Isobel! Fan-tastic news isn't it?'

She was still sitting on the bed, she raked through her hair, pulling it away from the side of her face. 'Oh, yeah, I don't really know, my mum called and said I'd won the Bannerman Prize, that it was on the news?' Isobel could hear Rachel's throaty laugh.

'Oh, bless. No you haven't *won* the Bannerman Prize – not yet anyway. You've been shortlisted! Isobel! The longlist was one thing, but nothing's guaranteed, this is the next hurdle. This is great news!' There was a silence as Isobel attempted to take this in. Her face seemed very still, she stared ahead and heard herself say, 'Oh-kay'.

'It's more than *okay*, Belle. I've been on the phone all morning – and why don't you answer your phone by the way? We're printing a third edition, I mean, we still have nearly two thousand copies left, but now that you've been shortlisted – everyone wants more stock. Look, there's a number of things I've lined up for you, the BBC called, they want to interview you along with a few of the other shortlisted authors next week, then there's a panel discussion with all the authors who can make it at the Cadogan Hall on the 15th, *The Guardian, The Standard* and *The Times Literary Supplement* have all called for interviews with you – The TLS are sending a photographer as well. Belle, this is amazing, not only for you but for Red Pen. Congratulations darling, this is just brilliant! Did you ever imagine?'

Isobel felt hot. She kept trying to focus. It was like being on the verge of being drunk. She'd never really thought that she'd be shortlisted. She felt that in some ways it would be a relief not to be. She had thought being longlisted was a fluke.

She was lightheaded, a thin film of sweat broke out across her brow and upper lip. She found herself concentrating on the folds of an orange towelling dressing gown hanging on the back of the door, a discarded pair of jeans were splayed on the floor by a set of drawers.

Downstairs on the street she could hear the steady beep of a van or truck reversing. Rachel's voice sounded tiny and metallic on the phone.

'Belle, are you still there? Did you get all that?' Isobel snapped to attention. 'Rachel, yes. Yes, I'm here. I'm just a bit blown away really. Sorry I didn't answer earlier, I had a late shift last night at the café.' She had been working at a place called Cha-Cha in Acre Lane. 'Who else, I mean, who else is on the shortlist?'

'Oh, Kai Noguchi, Julian Adagoke, Jane Adler, you're the youngest person on the list Belle, you're the youngest person ever to be shortlisted – it's just fantastic – Martin Gillray is there, Belle – you're on the same list as Martin Gillray!'

Isobel remembered ploughing through a couple of Gillray's novels as part of her course at South Bank. The books were dense, difficult and full of symbolism and allusions that she didn't fully comprehend. She remembered having to read some sentences three times to wring out the meaning. She was aware of his reputation but thought his prose was as unwelcoming, cold and unapproachable as the author was reputed to be.

'Oh really? I think his stuff is so boring.' She sensed the slightest panic in Rachel's laugh. 'Oh well Belle, we'll need to keep that to ourselves. He's being considered for the Nobel Prize, love. Anyway, there's a rumour that he's going to ask to be removed from the list, and of course he's won it twice before, but darling who cares? You're on the list and I couldn't be more thrilled. Can we meet tomorrow so we can plan your schedule for the next few weeks?'

'Yes, I think I could be there at five, I'm working during the day.'

'Well, hopefully, soon, you can leave that job Belle. I'm going to email you with all the details of this, but let's talk tomorrow. Oh Belle, I'm just so happy for you, for us!'

Rachel was gone. Isobel looked down at her phone and the screensaver picture of herself and Saskia taken last year during a brief summer holiday in Madrid, both peering over their sunglasses sipping large glasses of sangria. Her conversation with Rachel lasted less than ten minutes. Fifteen minutes ago she was a writer wiping down tables in a café in Acre Lane. Now she was a recognised author, a writer who had been longlisted and now shortlisted for the Bannerman Prize along with the likes of Kai Noguchi, Julian Adagoke, Jane Adler and Martin Gillray. She looked up, at that moment, the sun came out and brightened the untidy room with a watery, temporary light that just as quickly retreated. She felt an unfocused sense of urgency. She started moving around the room, tidying up clothes. She pulled the covers across the bed and then recovered her phone from beneath them. She needed to call Saskia, but she knew that she couldn't come to the phone if she was on shift. She decided to text her instead, Hey Darlin' amazing news – I made the Bannerman Shortlist!!! – love you xxx. Logically she knew she should be as thrilled as Rachel, but as she moved about the tiny bedsit, randomly tidying and pulling on clothes, the one tangible sensation she felt that pulsed in tandem with her suddenly very present heartbeat, the feeling she was just unable to shake, was wild, blind panic.

Her mother had texted her to meet at the Starbucks in Conduit Street. As part of her course, Pam had to review high profile fashion outlets as a way of studying brand management, to this end she was going to visit Vivienne Westwood down the street from the coffee franchise.

Isobel had arrived a few minutes early. She ordered a latte and sat by the window, watching the crowd move down Regent Street toward the tube station at Oxford Circus. She carried a copy of the newspaper with the article by Carol Peyton describing her book as 'bald pornography', she'd rolled the paper into a tight hot tube that had left newsprint on her palm. There were pieces in *The Times* and *The Standard* and in *The New Statesman* online that wrote about Isobel as part of the Bannerman shortlist. She'd finally spoken to Saskia at lunchtime.

'Belly! That's amazing! So okay, what does that mean? Can I leave work now? Can I become a kept woman?' Isobel could feel the subtle, warm thrum of a headache beginning as she spoke.

'Er ... no. Put it this way, I'll be back at the café tomorrow steaming my face off at the coffee machine, darlin'.'

'So that's the secret to your youthful glow. Let's go out tonight Belle – we'll celebrate my love – hey and don't forget to pay those bills, lovely. I left you the money. I've got to go, I love you!' The feeling of unfocused dread that had clouded her thoughts since Rachel's call settled round her now like a hard, unyielding anxiety. She had read all the articles reporting on the shortlist and cringed every time she read her name. When her book was published, for the most part, she had enjoyed reading the reviews. It was exciting to her that her work was being seriously considered by critics who had scrutinised her work, who had understood and appreciated it. But the Bannerman Prize for Literature was different. She was staggered when she was longlisted and thrilled as well because she knew that she would never be shortlisted, that didn't happen to girls from Burslem who graduated from the South Bank University. She thought that once the shortlist was announced life could settle down, she might even start to write something new. But it was too late for that now. Suddenly she had been pitched against five other authors, and her book, her precious work that had taken four years to research and write was now an item in a fiercely contested internationally recognised competition.

Vihan had texted her that Ladbrokes were putting her chances of winning at 20 to 1, 'Not great odds Belle, but I'm going to put a tenner on you – each way!' There had clearly been reaction to the list in blogs and comments posted online, each post authored by people who only wanted to be known by odd little nicknames. Isobel read them grimly. Some were flattering. Candlewick wrote, 'At last, some fresh blood for the Bannerman. Isobel Dalby's remarkably assured debut should give privileged old white farts like Gillray a run. I vote Dalby!' Others were dismissively hostile. Betty the Goblin wrote, 'Her C**t is this year's modish, mildly disgusting, frequently boring rubbish entry. I think Ms Dalby ought to pursue a career in television writing, something more attuned to her disposable talent. Tosh!' And then there was the plainly confusing. HarrowWing wrote, 'Reading Isobel Dalby's book was like looking at a dead sparrow in a shoebox.' None of this made her feel any less overwhelmed.

She arranged to meet her mother at three, but she had been sitting in the Starbucks window now for forty-five minutes, her elbow bent at the counter, her fist in her cheek, she was checking the time again on her phone when she was startled by a rap on the window. It was Pam, squinting in the sunlight. She wore an oversized pair of sunglasses on her head, she held a bunch of keys in her hand, she was yelling at Isobel through the glass.

'Hey! My clever girl! Hiya!' She waved with the keys in her hand, Isobel could hear their soft jangle through the glass. Her brow furrowed. She couldn't work out why her mother was calling to her from outside, as if she'd been quarantined. Pam then pointed to the entrance to indicate that she would come inside, Isobel nodded. She rested her forehead in her palm, her mouth was slightly opened as she twisted her head to see her mother's entrance. Pam was wearing red tartan leggings and a white t-shirt cropped above her waist printed with the words, 'Everyone Should Be A Feminist' under a large sleeveless Afghan overcoat that looked a little grubby at the front. She carried a macramé tote bag slung over her right shoulder, on her feet she wore chunky sandals that made a clacking sound as she walked, extending her thin arms to greet her daughter.

'Oh my Belle! You genius girl! You've done it, my love!' She pulled Isobel to her, giving her a kiss on the cheek that felt warm and moist, she pulled back, holding her daughter at arm's length. Isobel had always had an uncomfortable physical relationship with her mother. When she was a child, during her occasional visits, Pam would smother her with kisses and hugs that Isobel would struggle to be released from. As she got older their occasional physical contact of greeting or goodbye became more formal, but Isobel noticed that the older Pam had become, the more she had insisted on public displays of affection that she felt deeply ambivalent about. She smiled weakly. Her mother's brittle hair had been dyed a honey yellow that had grown grey at the roots, it was randomly streaked with red as well. Her apricot lipstick glistened in the tiny vertical lines that bordered her mouth, there were two smudges of kohl above her eyes and two delicately incised eyebrow arcs drawn on her forehead, her body had been sponged with orange tanning liquid that seemed to be applied unevenly. Isobel had the impression that her mother had attempted to render the youthful, vivid Pam, on the surface of Pam's sixty-seven-year-old face, and that the illusion stubbornly would not take. Recently her mother had tried a succession of extreme diets and food fads in an effort to 'tone' her body. She had become thin and wiry.

She'd taken to wearing girl sized track pants and leggings coupled with crop tops that revealed her tiny wizened stomach that carried three worrisome horizontal creases punctuated in the middle by a ruby naval stud, that would only occasionally be glimpsed when she stretched into a yawn or laughed suddenly, before disappearing again into her dark, tea coloured skin.

'Oh Mum, sit down. I haven't done anything, I haven't won anything – I'm on the shortlist that's all, do you even know what that means? I'm not going to win it.'

Pam swung her bag onto the counter and began rifling through a stack of newspapers, she pulled them all out and slapped them on the counter. 'I do know what it means my darling – you are in all these papers! One man called you a *curious talent'*, bloody cheek!' Isobel looked on as her mother began opening some of the pages.

'Mum, don't. Do you have to? It's so awful. And where have you been? I've been sat here for nearly an hour – you said three o'clock.'

'Oh, I'm sorry my love, is it really nearly four? Oh my god! The time just got away from me.'

Pam hugged Isobel close again, rubbing her back vigorously, her mother's body felt fragile and shivery. Isobel leaned into the thick bushy wool of her mother's coat, it had the faintest scent of old rags. Suddenly tears filled her eyes, tears splashed onto her hands as she clasped them around Pam's shoulders. She pulled away, wiping her cheeks with her hands. Her mother looked slightly affronted, she looked around, making a lightning scan of the coffee shop.

'Here Belle, what's all this then?'

'Look at me! This is mental. I'm not a bloody child.' Suddenly she laughed, then her laughter subsided into a gentle groan. She felt at once light, giddy, and dreadful. She looked at the startled appearance of her mother and thought this was how she must feel all the time.

Pam dabbed at Isobel's cheek with a balled-up Kleenex that her daughter pushed away. She caught her breath and looked out of the window, she saw three women crossing the street wearing niqabs, heavily loaded with shopping bags from Harvey Nichols, M&S and Topshop.

'Oh I don't know. I *should* be happy, and I am but I just think ...' She trailed off for a moment, she looked down at her hands in her lap. She started to speak again, almost to herself. 'I mean, I'm in the paper, *in all these papers,* and do you know what? I'm going on the BBC next week.' Her mother covered her surprised mouth with her hands. 'Oh Belle!' She said through her fingers.

'I'm up against five other authors, most of them I've never heard of ...' She paused to sort her thoughts into sentences, then she began to speak again, slowly. '... and, I don't know ... I just can't help feeling that this is all so ...' She looked at her mother's expectant face and then the word dropped into her mouth. *'Temporary.'* This she felt was the right word. In saying it she was struck with the realisation that her stress and anxiety about the prize was linked to her mother's talentless serial failures, her hungry need, and her empty longing for a life of creative distinction. A hot wave washed over her that felt like guilt. She looked at the paper on the counter open to the page where the shortlist was published, 'Sex, Snakes, God and a Whippet, Has the Bannerman Lost the Plot?' She didn't blink for a moment, her lips were slightly parted, she looked back at her mother. In her mind, four words beat out a steady rhythm that pulsed from deep in her gut to her fingertips, painfully repeating over and over; *'you-are-a-fake'.*

Pam's head jolted back slightly in a gesture of theatrical shock, looking at her daughter, her eyes seemed to harden. She took both Isobel's hands in hers, Isobel saw that there was writing scrawled across her mother's hands in Biro, possibly some numbers, and there was a collection of coloured elastic bands around her left wrist.

'*Temporary?* Oh no, my love. I'm not having this. *Temporary?* This prize is going to set you up for life!' Isobel laughed emptily, looking up at the ceiling, raking through her hair with her fingers. 'You are joking, aren't you, Mum?'

'I am *not* joking Isobel. You know your Auntie Janet would be so proud of you, but Belle, you also know, you are your *mother's daughter.* You're amazing you are.' Her hands squeezed Isobel's in a tighter grip. 'You and I, we're like peas in a pod. We've got *dreams,* Belle, we have. My darling. Don't you see? In so many ways, you're just like me, my sweetheart.'

'*Dreams,*' Isobel repeated evenly, staring at her mother.

It was suddenly painful to think of Janet and the ordered life she'd made to raise Isobel, the care she'd taken, the unfussy, dependable way she was loved by her aunt all through her mother's prolonged absences. She realised too that all the complicated ways she felt about her mother, the hate, the irritation, the embarrassment and the pain, all amounted to love in the end, that she was deeply and fundamentally bonded to this woman forever, for better *and* for worse. She retrieved her hands from Pam's grasp. She'd had nothing to eat all day but a piece of toast, a cup of tea and half a cup of coffee that now sat cold on the counter beside her. She looked back at Pam as if she'd just taken in the words her mother had said to her.

'I'm *just like you? Really?* Are you *really* telling me that?' She shook her head and sighed, suddenly exhausted. 'Oh my fucking god,

Mum, I hope not.' Pam looked blankly at her daughter, there was the briefest pause.

'Belle, love, would you like another coffee?'

Isobel gathered up her newspapers and stood up. Along with everything else, she now felt shamed for her cruelty. 'C'mon, Let's go.'

Pam led the way down Conduit Street the short distance from Starbucks to the pink neon sign of Vivienne Westwood. When they entered the store, Pam called out a bright 'Hiya!' to a bored young Japanese man who momentarily looked up from a laptop computer on a glass counter, before staring back at the screen. Isobel never ventured into stores like this. The clothes were hung in two or three orderly rows, there didn't seem to be much on the shelves, but the items that were displayed were lit as if they were exhibits in a museum. She saw a beautiful shirt embroidered with flowers and insects that was priced at 350 euros, there was a little red handbag for 600 euros and a pair of high heels with pilgrim buckles for 780. All these price tags were like signifiers to a life she would never know, each figure neatly reinforced her exclusion. She made her way past objects that were carefully arranged and precisely folded to the back of the store, and that's when she saw the dress.

It was displayed on a mannequin wearing a World War II gas mask. It was blood red and had the dull sheen of old velvet. Isobel held the fabric on the sleeve between her fingers, it was heavy and rich and its hue changed depending on the angle of the light. It was printed with full blown roses and emerald green leaves that seemed to twine and grow around the hem, the bodice and the long sleeves that sat below the wrist, over the hands. It was artfully twisted at the throat and fell in an elegant line below the knee. Isobel thought it was possibly the most beautiful dress she had ever seen. She could hear her mother at the counter.

'Excuse me. Hello there. I was wondering if you could tell me something about the um … marketing strategy of the shop here. You see, I'm doing a course …' The Japanese man cut her off, waving his finger at her.

'No, no, no. We have no marketing – just what you can see.'

Pam struggled on. 'No. Well, yes, you see, you have a *website* … and then you have this er … *shop.*' She gestured around her as if the man could not understand English or perhaps didn't fully comprehend where he was. He looked at Pam, disturbed.

'The *website*, Madame?' he asked.

'Yes, the website, um … look, do you have any more information at all?' The man smiled thinly, staring at Pam's grubby coat and the elastic bands on her wrist.

'Information, we don't have. This is Vivienne Westwood.' Pam was about to go on but Isobel cut in standing by the mannequin.

'This dress,' Isobel said.

The troubled store attendant looked from Pam to Isobel as if he was being assaulted from multiple directions.

'That's my daughter,' Pam explained proudly. The assistant's brow creased further as he spoke to Isobel.

'I'm sorry?'

Isobel walked toward the counter. 'Don't be sorry. I want to try on that red dress.'

'She's going to win a big prize!' Pam offered. The young man was now convinced that these two women were insane. He would humour them until he could alert security.

'This dress, it's called Johanna, it's designed by Andreas

Kronthaler,' he said very quickly.

'Oh Belle, that's Vivienne Westwood's husband and design partner,' Pam added.

'I don't care who designed it. I want to wear it. I'm a medium.'

The Japanese man couldn't be sure if she was referring to her size in dresses or some psychic ability she believed she possessed. He nodded, repeating the word *'medium'* as he made his way to a rack of dresses at the back of the store. He took a gown from the rack and bought it to Isobel. She felt its softness and its luxurious weight, the smooth lining, cold to the touch. Pam walked over and stood beside her daughter.

'It's beautiful, Belle, it looks like it was made for you love, doesn't it?'

The man ushered her into a change room that was mirrored on three sides. She quickly undressed. For a moment she looked at herself standing in her underwear, the hard halogen light gouged deep shadows under her eyes and her collarbone, it shone on the slight pouch of her belly. She held the dress in front of her, unzipped the back and stood into it, pulling it on, pushing her arms through the sleeves and over her shoulders. She looked again in the mirrors, at the hundreds of Isobel's reflected there. The Johanna dress fit her perfectly. It gave her an air of serene beauty and untroubled intelligence. This, she thought is what a serious writer might wear, a serious writer might be photographed in this dress for *The Times Literary Supplement*. She smoothed the fabric across her stomach, tracing the outline of the rose pattern with her finger. For the first time since this morning and her mother's frantic message about the prize, she felt an even calm around her. The price tag hung from the sleeve at her wrist, 830 euros, marked down to 415 on sale. It was hers.

She emerged from the fitting room and walked directly to the counter, the dress over her arm. Pam was standing by the Japanese man. Isobel didn't look at him.

'I'm taking this. I'm paying cash. You do take cash here at Vivienne Westwood, don't you?'

She pulled out the notes that Saskia had left her for the bills and laughed a little as the man counted out the money.

It was 7.30, and Isobel was back in Brixton. It was too late now, of course but she knew the dress was going to be a big problem. She lay on the bed looking at the garment hanging on the back of the door. She noticed that the dress had taken on a deep maroon shade, its roses and leaves acidly luminous in the evening light. She heard the familiar tread of Saskia on the stairs, her key in the lock. The door opened and she stood at the foot of the bed laughing at her girlfriend propped up on the pillows.

'Belly! My gorgeous, sexy, clever wife!' She dropped her bag and leaned down to kiss Isobel, hugging her warmly around the shoulders. 'How was your crazy mum?' she asked. 'Oh she thinks I'm going to be bigger than J.K. Rowling.' Isobel grinned.

Saskia laughed. 'Right. I s'pose dinner's on you then.' They lay in the quiet for a moment with the hum of the traffic outside and orange beams of light angling through the net curtains of their window. Saskia turned her head to nuzzle into Isobel's shoulder, it was then she noticed the dress where it hung on the back of the door. She was startled, as if a spectral disembodied stranger suddenly conjured to life had been looking at them the whole time.

'Here, Belle, what's that dress then?'

7.30 pm, Harvest Place, Kensington SW7 5

For a long twenty minutes Tasha Moubray just stood on the pavement, looking at the darkened windows of Gideon Bannerman's family home. From where she stood she could see that the large black door to the house was ajar. She had always trusted her intuition and her intuition was saying do not walk up those steps, do not go inside that house. Middle-aged professionals streamed past on the path ignoring her, just another elderly woman with bad knees and a walking stick. A beautiful young woman who Tasha assumed to be a nanny pushed a pram down the street. She took a deep breath, filling her mouth and lungs with chilled air and lowered her head as she walked up the steps and pushed the heavy door open.

'Giddy?' She called out, although she knew that the house was empty. She walked over the black and white marble chequerboard floor to the foot of the stairs and called again.

'Gideon? Hello?' There was a hollow coldness to the sound of her voice that made Tasha more apprehensive. She steadied herself on the black iron bannister and climbed the stairs to the first floor landing. Uselessly she called out again, 'Giddy, it's me.' She was merely calling to reassure herself. There was a bitterness to the cold that made her think of films about haunted houses, about women in peril looking terrified up into empty stairwells. She made her way to the doorway of the beautifully proportioned sitting room on the second floor. There was a dirty teacup set on the mantle next to six hardback editions of the shortlisted books for this year's prize, random bits of paper littered the hearth, some torn up, some screwed into tight balls.

A worn and tatty wingback chair had been pushed into the far corner by the fireplace, on its seat sat a lamp, its torn yellow shade set at an angle that made a theatrical, warm pool of light on the floor and the rug. Next to the lamp, on the chair was a bright, white rectangular envelope. Tasha looked up at her ghostly reflection in the mirror hanging over the mantle. She felt not quite in her own body as she walked across the large room, each step she took seemed to be propelling her heavily into an awful, sickening present.

She stood by the chair a moment and noticed that some of the horsehair stuffing was working its way out of the armrests on both sides. She lifted the lamp carefully and placed it on the floor near the hearth. She could see in the scattered bits of paper on the floor some notes, mostly crossed out, she made out the words, *this is what you mean to me,* in the torn corner of one piece.

She took up the envelope on the chair and sat, holding it gingerly by the corners, as if it were evidence that needed to be preserved in a mystery. She looked inside, but there was nothing there. She turned it over and looked at the scrawl of handwriting across the front, in an almost continuous, almost illegible line of blue ink it read, *Tasha.*

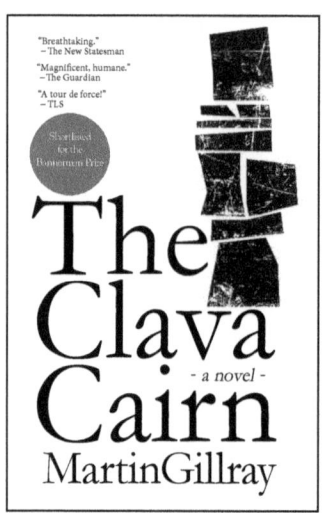

THE CLAVA CAIRN
Martin Gillray (Quadri Press) 380pp
Life on a remote island north-west of Wales is
disrupted when a stranger appears bearing a
surprising message from God.

9.45 pm, Kensington Police Station W8 6EQ

Tasha Moubray sat patiently beside an intoxicated Sikh with a
bloodied nose and shirt that had been torn open, who only appeared to
be sleeping. At odd intervals he would attempt to make conversation
with Tasha, sitting rigidly upright with her walking stick planted on
the floor before her, her eyes fixed, staring straight ahead.

'Do something real!' the man suddenly exclaimed, twisting
his head to give Tasha a quizzical, sideways glance. She made no
response.

'*Do something real!*' he repeated, his voice raised to almost a shout.
This attracted the attention of Sharon Webster, the duty sergeant who
had given Tasha forms to fill out when she arrived and had instructed
her to wait, someone would be with her shortly – that was two hours

ago. Sharon leaned over her counter to speak sternly to the man, she pointed at him with a ball-point pen.

'Now *Kevin*, Mr Dhariwal, I'm going to ask you to please be quiet, okay? Don't be bothering people, otherwise I'm going to have to organise to have you put somewhere quiet to wait for your son. Do you *understand, Kevin?'* Sharon repeated for emphasis.

'Do something real!' Kevin replied thickly, he then went on. 'Become a police officer and do a job that matters!' It was then that Sharon realised that he was reading a recruitment poster taped to the front of the counter. Her wide smile broke into a little laugh.

'I shall take that very good advice on board Kevin, thank you. Now please shut it. I hope he's not bothering you, madam.'

Tasha looked up at Sharon. 'No. He isn't particularly. How much longer do you think I shall have to wait?'

Sharon flicked her wrist, looking at her watch. 'It shouldn't be too much longer. I'll just check for you.'

And with that she disappeared. For a moment there was silence, then Kevin spoke again, solemnly regarding his grubby Nike trainers. 'Do something real!'

Tasha stared down at the brochure that she had already read four times since she arrived, published by the UK Missing Persons Bureau, 'Has someone you know gone missing?' Full of practical questions, it detailed a process that she feared would be pointless.

A heavy door to the left of Tasha opened as Sharon appeared at the counter again. 'Miss Moubray? This is Sergeant Timewell, Don, he will look after you now.' She was taken down a bright corridor to a small room furnished with a table and four chairs. She sat opposite Sergeant Timewell, thickset, she thought he could be in his fifties, his silver hair was razored close to his pink scalp. He had large, kind eyes and long, brown eyelashes that Tasha suspected might be artificially coloured, she also noticed that at some stage in his life, both his earlobes had been pierced.

'Now, Natasha is it?' He had the forms that she had completed clipped to a black folder in front of him.

'Yes, that's right, Natasha Moubray.' She watched his fingers as he scanned the pages. 'I understand that this all might be very distressing for you, but please be assured that we will do everything we can to locate your friend. Now, you've indicated here that Mr Bannerman is married, have you spoken to his wife? Does she have any idea where he might have gone?'

'That's husband. Mr Bannerman is married to a man. A Russian national who goes by the name of Yuri Kuznetsov. I believe, at this time Mr Kuznetsov may be in Turkey, but I couldn't be absolutely certain.'

Sergeant Timewell was making notes, he stopped, his pen poised. 'And have you contacted Mr Kuznetsov?'

'No. I have not. I don't have a current contact number for Mr Kuznetsov. I've not spoken to Mr Kuznetsov in over a year. He and Mr Bannerman are divorced.'

Timewell scribbled some more words. 'And you have tried contacting Mr Bannerman on his phone?'

Carefully spacing these words in a way that Tasha felt was practised, procedural. She bit the side of her lip. 'I have tried calling him every ten minutes since I came from his house, but my calls just go to his message bank.' There followed a full minute as Tasha listened to Sergeant Timewell's pen as it scratched out notes in his folder. He stopped and put his pen aside, he put his hands on the desk, folding his fingers together. He looked at Tasha with his head slightly inclined to the left, this also seemed practised.

'I've just got a couple of questions before you go, Miss Moubray. Has Mr Bannerman had any significant professional, family or relationship problems in the recent past?' Tasha put the brochure on missing persons on the table, then she placed her hands over it, one over the other.

'His family is dead, and his marriage is over, so I suppose you could consider those things as significant, but in Gideon's case, I think not. He actually doesn't have a profession, as such, he is a person of independent means. He's not on medication, he's not an alcoholic and he's not taking any drugs of dependence. He's not, to my knowledge depressed, he's had no history of self-harm – unless, of course, we count his marriage to Mr Kuznetsov, and there has been no significant change in his behaviour.' She took a deep breath, she kept her teeth clenched and breathed out evenly through her nose. 'Sergeant Timewell, I have known Mr Bannerman for over fifty years, I have no idea where he is. What I *do know* is that he was here on Tuesday, and he is gone today, and I would very much like to find him.'

Timewell hunched forward, resting his elbows on the desk. 'You consider his marriage an act of self-harm? In what way exactly?'

Tasha immediately recognised that she had slipped. There was a pause. 'Gideon believed that Yuri, was the love of his life, his soulmate – he and I did not see eye to eye on that.'

'How so?' Timewell asked.

'I consider Yuri Kuznetsov to be a very clever, thuggishly coarse, opportunist, in short, a leech. But that is just my opinion, and as I say, they have not seen each other, to my knowledge for over two years.'

Sergeant Timewell looked at Tasha's face, at her eyes and her closed mouth.

'And finally, he didn't call you, he didn't leave you a message of any kind, a note about where he was going?' Tasha returned his gaze, there was the most subtle hint of suspicion in the space between them. From off down the hall and through the closed doors she could hear Kevin Dhariwal's insistent words again, *'Do something real!'* The empty envelope Gideon had left her was in her bag on the floor, by her side. Apart from her name it had held nothing.

'No Sergeant Timewell, he did not. No message. No note. He left nothing.'

As if on cue, once she was outside, on the steps of the police station, her phone started buzzing. The evening was still and the street had been glazed with a thin film of rain. She rummaged around in her bag for a moment and retrieved her phone, the screen read, 'Martin Gillray'. She was at once relieved to be pulled into the world of books, the world of the prize. Attempting to sound normal, she answered the phone.

'Martin, hello!'

'Get me off your bloody list.' Do you hear? Take me off it!'

'Martin, it's so lovely to hear from you. Congratulations on being shortlisted – again!'

'Natasha?' There was a pause as Tasha listened to the rasp of Martin's breathing down the line. 'Natasha. *Take me off the list,* can you hear me? *I don't want it.'*

She hailed a cab on Earl's Court Road, holding the phone to her chest, she gave the driver her address.

'I'm sorry, Martin, you're breaking up – are you still on the coast? Do please give my love to Edith.' With that she ended the call, and sat with her phone in her hand, her eyes closed in the cool interior of the cab, as it made its way in the dark to her house.

He sat close to the light on his desk in his study, staring at the phone he habitually put on 'speaker' as the rain pelted against the window, he studied his face in the sharp reflection of the glass. 'Martin, it's so lovely to hear from you. Congratulations on being shortlisted – again!'

'Natasha?' He paused. His gnarled fist held a glass half-filled with whiskey. Am I that man staring back at me? *When did I become so old?* At eighty-one Martin Gillray's face had achieved the status of a national institution. It was a face that had none of the softened, bloodhound folds of Auden, the doughy puffiness of Burgess, or the deeply furrowed, expressionistic cross-hatching of a weathered Beckett. Martin Gillray's face had the appearance of being roughly hewn from solid planes of Welsh granite. His eyes were set deep in his head, coloured emerald-green flecked with gold, they had been described variously as hard, flinty, piercing, quick and sharp, although looking at his reflection in the window he decided they just looked tired.

'Natasha. *Take me off the list,* can you hear me? *I don't want it.*' The little screen of his phone had under-lit his face, making his reflection in the window even more ghoulish.

'I'm sorry, Martin, you're breaking up – are you still on the coast? Do please give my love to Edith.'

'*Natasha!*' But she had gone. His mouth was open, he stared at his phone a moment longer. He looked up at his reflection as the steady rain beat against the window, trickling down the glass in intricate, crisscrossed patterns. The sodden heads of the climbing roses that covered the wall outside his study nodded and threshed in the wind. His room was crowded with books and papers, it appeared to be in the process of being boxed up for removal or relocation. Some cardboard cartons on the floor were filled and wedged with papers, magazines and programmes from theatre or opera performances, but they were not to be moved – they had sat that way for years. Some had split open, random bits and pieces of paper were scattered across the floor, some seemed to be stained with splashes of tea or wine. Somewhere in the house the radio was on. He could hear, far-off, a discussion about the debilitating legacies of Brexit. He looked down at the papers on his desk, some strewn across the keyboard of his computer. The uppermost page was an email from his agent, Barbara Farrow. He'd already read this message twice that day, but with the distant sound of voices talking about markets and tariffs, he sat heavily in his chair and in a distracted way, read it again.

Martin –

I've tried to call you a number of times today – I have just now tried again – without success – please take your phone off silent! – congratulations on your Bannerman nod – I suspect I know your attitude on that matter – they're keen for you to go to the Cadogan Hall to meet with the other authors in a couple of weeks – I'm just letting you know they've asked – I know you won't consider going – for what it's worth, I think you should stay in the prize, I know you and Edith don't need the money – if you win you can give it away – to someone, that money represents a year to write – consider it Martin, you were poor once - I have a request from Dario at *The Times* – more of a favour really – he's asking that you complete the

Proust Questionnaire for the Sunday edition – published in two weeks' time – this will run alongside the feature piece on you that he's written – he told me that the interview went very well – until it didn't – he was only slightly terrified – you may be losing your touch! – he said to apologise to you again for bringing up the prospect of the Nobel – he thought you were going to hit him! – Please do not speak to Natasha until we've had the chance to talk – <u>please take your phone off silent!</u> – If I haven't spoken to you by Wednesday, I'm driving down there to do it myself – I invested in that new phone for you for <u>a reason</u> – specifically to *speak to you, to keep in touch* – semi-regularly – when the little screen lights up and you see the name *'Barbara F'* – <u>answer it</u> – then we can talk – then you can hang up – that's how communication works Martin – it's sort of a two-way thing – consider the Proust questions – it may make you seem less frosty to the great unwashed.
Barbara.

The wind shifted, and for a moment the rain lashed the windows from the other direction. Something above him in the attic space creaked. He looked down at the first question on the page from Barbara, 'What is your idea of perfect happiness?'

Edith appeared in the doorway. A year older than Martin and a full three inches taller, she leaned on the door jamb of her husband's study wearing grey tweed trousers, a green linen shirt and a knee-length coarse wool cardigan that she had pulled closed, folding her arms across her chest, a mug of tea in one hand and a pair of black framed spectacles in the other. Her unruly hair formed a silver halo surrounding her head from the light of two yellowed lampshades in the hall behind her. Their nervous, highly strung, chocolate Burmese, Wanda, crept around Edith's feet, nudging into her calves, arching her back and flicking her tail.

'Was that Barbara then? On the phone?' Martin looked at her silhouette in the doorway. 'Who?' he asked.

'Barbara. She's been trying to speak to you all day. She's been texting me, too. She tried me again about an hour ago.'

'No, it was Natasha.' He was still holding the printed email.

'Oh, okay.' Edith took another sip of her tea. 'How did she take it then? You pulling out.'

'She couldn't hear me, she said I was breaking up, she said hello.' He looked again at the page of questions.

'She what?' Edith moved away from the doorway, scooping up a bunch of newspapers from the seat of a low armchair and put them on the floor, she sat, crossed her legs and held her mug of tea with both hands close to her chest, the gentle steam warming her chin.

'She said hello to you, or no, she said, *give Edith my love.*'

She looked at him and said, 'Oh,' a sound that morphed into a wide yawn, once that was done, she scratched the side of her head with the arm of her glasses, saying, 'What's that you've got there?'

Martin opened his mouth to speak, his head shifted slightly as if to calibrate the precise degree of indignation he wanted in his voice before he spoke.

'This, is the Proust Questionnaire. After putting up with that idiot Dario the other week, asking endless moronic questions about my book, about all my books, now she has sent this bloody list of questions. She said his piece will be published in two weeks, but you know, Edith, it will just be the usual drivel. Do you know how it will go?'

'Actually – ' Edith leaned forward on the chair but was silenced as Martin continued, gesturing from time to time with his glass of whiskey.

'Martin Gillray, whose fourteenth novel, *The Clava Cairn* has just been shortlisted for the prestigious Bantamweight Prize for literature, greeted me in the rustic Devon home he shares with his wife, mathematician and scholar, Dame Edith Morley.' At this point he gestured to toast his wife who had now been joined, on the arm of her chair by Wanda who was staring blankly back at Martin. 'Gillray's new novel, dedicated to the memory of his son, the gifted poet Robert Gillray, argues not for the existence of God, but the necessity of God in a secular world. His difficult novels, blah, blah, blah ... then there'll be an observation or two about the untidy study, the mess of this room, the books on my desk, the shopping list of authors, Neruda, McEwan, White, Ondaatje, Murdoch and Hughes, then he'll describe the photographs on the wall of you, you and Robert, then that one of the three of us on that boat in Norway, then he'll draw attention to the solitary picture of Robert on my desk ... there will be talk of tragedy ... there will be words about loss ... '

Here Martin's voice trailed off. He looked at Edith and pointed to the picture with his whisky glass in his hand. For a moment the amber liquid wobbled and glinted deeply golden through the light of his desk lamp. The photograph had been taken twenty years earlier on a wet and blustery morning in Gateshead. Robert Gillray, the gifted young poet, son of the celebrated author and the esteemed mathematician stood on a hill in front of Antony Gormley's sculpture, the *Angel of the North*. Robert's arms are stretched out to echo the outstretched wings of the Angel, a wide grin has broken out across his face, his mouth slightly open, almost ready to laugh, his feet standing together, his blue backpack just visible over his shoulder. There is a bank of black cloud behind him, but the sun is shining on the wet grass of the hill. The recent rain has formed tiny droplets that cling to the shoulders of his red anorak, and a single strand of his dark hair is plastered across his forehead. Robert Gillray, vividly alive, standing on a hill, on a spring morning in Gateshead, April 1998.

Robert, whose first volume of poems entitled, *The story of the house, the tree, the bike and the dog* had been shortlisted for the T. S. Eliot Prize for Poetry. Robert who, three months after this photograph was taken, woke one morning to the summer sun, fashioned a noose from the towelling belt of his dressing gown and hanged himself from the closed door of his bedroom, a short poem to his parents' safety pinned to his t-shirt. Martin had found Robert on that terrible morning and for years had closed down around the subject of his son, never visiting his grave, and never entering his room, undisturbed since 1998. But during the last year, Edith had seen a change in her husband. One afternoon she noticed the door to Robert's room was open, when she looked inside she saw Martin sitting on the edge of their son's bed staring out the window to the garden beyond. She stood with her hand on the doorknob.

'Martin? What are you doing?' Without turning to his wife Martin replied.

'Did you know that there's a nasty draught that's coming in through this window? It's shut. But there must be a gap somewhere.' Edith joined him on the bed, still he didn't look at her. 'It can't be very pleasant, there's a real chill to it.'

She thought for a moment. 'I suppose we could get it seen to.' His gaze remained fixed, he spoke almost in a whisper. 'We should get it seen to. Poor boy.'

*   *   *   *

Since then he would sometimes refer to Robert in ways that demonstrated to Edith that their son had assumed a vibrant continual inner life in the mind of her husband. She had her memories of their son, but she felt that this was different. From infancy onward, their son had been afflicted by a psychosis that had been difficult to diagnose and almost wholly resistant to treatment. Deeply paranoid and prone to extreme, sometimes violent mood swings, both Edith and Martin tried everything at their disposal to care for him. She remembered his keening cries on his bed for hours, inconsolable over a totally imagined terror, falling into a deep sleep of rattled exhaustion afterwards, his body trembling, shuddering in unconsciousness like some febrile animal. She remembered his repeated threats of violence to herself and to Martin, and on at least two occasions where he had held a knife to her throat, railing in his madness at the 'fucking pig who had given birth' to him.

There was the time he went walking with his father and calmly said as they sat on a deserted, windy beach not far from home, that he knew that his parents were spying on him for the government and unless they stopped, he would have to kill them both. He spoke calmly as he sat pinching a piece of seagrass between his fingers, gently pulling it apart. 'It's nothing personal, Dad – you probably didn't expect me to find out, but there we are – we each have our responsibilities.' Martin had sat beside him, listening to this, unable to respond. Every time his son's illness articulated yet another obscenity, Martin was left with the familiar sensation of a heavy stone bearing down on his chest, leaving him dumb with fear, not for himself or Edith, but for his child's future.

But then finally there were the almost three years of calm, where clozapine and regular psychiatric care was able to give Robert a sense of balance and order in the world. It was during this time that he wrote the seventy-two poems that would ultimately be published as his first and only volume of poetry. He had even allowed his father to edit the collection and had dedicated the book to, *Martin and Edith, who made me.* It was months after the publication of his book when a cautious confidence and an even temperament allowed Robert to give readings of his work and move in the world as others did, with managed emotions, of sadness and joys that didn't threaten his frail, newly found, chemically controlled equilibrium. Finally, Martin and Edith felt that they had been rewarded for their perseverance with his illness by a loving son who was talented, productive and hopeful, if still painfully shy and prone to solitude. He'd started a tentative relationship with a Swedish poet called Lovisa Eklund whose steady hand held the camera and took the picture of the smiling Robert in Gateshead that April morning. But the cruelties and terrors of Robert's illness had not disappeared, they lay in wait until they could claim him, the last poem he wrote, pinned to his t-shirt, simply read,

Goodbye my now, forever,
Your tiny bud, now froze.
The winter robin's song
Unheard by the blackened stars.
The multitude of silent weapons in your eyes
Are trained on this soft target.
Claim your victory, here hangs
the dead sun, unfurl the flag,
Hear it snap in the pitiless bright, shiny wind.

Sorry Mum, Sorry Dad - speak soon. Love, Robert.

*   *   *   *

Edith could tell that the drink was blurring her husband's thoughts. She knew that when he began this monologue about Dario and Barbara and the prize he'd have had no way of knowing that it would lead him to that rain sodden hill in Gateshead with their grinning boy. She sat on her chair, staring at the back of Wanda's head, her soft ears flicking, as the steady rain beat against the windows of the study. Martin turned from the picture of his son, looking at Edith, his brow deeply furrowed.

'Well, I'm pulling the pin, Edie. You know that.'

'I do, Martin. I do know that.' Wanda's head twitched into a sudden sneeze, she recovered with a shake of her head and began methodically kneading her claws into the arm of the chair.

'In your interview with Dario, did you talk about Robert?' Edith asked carefully. Martin considered his glass for a moment. Finally he said, 'It looks like this rain has set in.'

Martin and Edith had been married for fifty-four years. They had grown into a way of communicating with each other through a complex series of non-sequiturs, monosyllables, silences and disconnected sentences that carried with them their own intimate logic. A typical exchange would run along these lines,

'Have you seen my green scarf?'

A silence.

'I thought we might have a leg tonight.'

'It was hanging on the back door.'

'There's still some chicken left, but I was thinking about that for lunch if you'd like.'

'Eh?'

'Just now, I was thinking.'

Another silence. A drawer in the kitchen is opened. The sound of cutlery. The drawer is shut.

'I was wearing it yesterday in the garden. I hung it over that chair I think, I'm sure I did. Have you read that thing about Cameron?'

'Or perhaps some soup.'

'What a coward.'

Martin was still holding the print-out of Barbara's email. He looked at Edith. 'What am I meant to do with this?'

What was left of her tea had now become cold, she looked at the pale skin across its surface. 'That's the questionnaire, yes?'

Martin looked again at the piece of paper as if it contained something deeply offensive.

'The what?' He said.

'*The Proust Questionnaire* that Barbara sent you, from *The Times*, they want your answers to go with the article. Dario's article.'

Martin looked again at the email. He looked back at Edith.

'Really?'

'Yes, darling. You just told me.'

He turned away from her. He put the paper on his keyboard.

'The first question reads, *What do you most dislike about your appearance?* – Edith, really? Utter garbage.'

She had noticed this as well, over the course of the last few months, since his book had been published, he would repeat stories, sometimes within an interval of less than an hour, the same story, with no recollection that he had recounted the same set of events – with slight variations just before. Edith's discipline was mathematics, and her life had been concerned with patterns of meaning that rendered experience with more than logic, explanation and sense. Mathematics to Edith held the key to the elegant grace of the world. Her entire career had been concerned with showing the relationship between mathematics and all forms of artistic expression. She had written books on the complex mathematical structures discerned in works by artists as diverse as Leonardo, Mozart, Beethoven, Diaghilev, Shakespeare, Jackson Pollock, Bridget Riley and Sir Christopher Wren. She'd been awarded both the Fields and Christopher Zeeman Medals for mathematics, and in 2004, she was awarded an OBE for services to science, education and the arts. But over time, she had become acutely aware of the limitations of her discipline. No theory or algorithm known to her could have untangled the troubled pathways of her son's brain, and recently, with a growing sense of dread she had come to understand that she had begun lose the familiar patterns of Martin. His predictable, discernible logic and habitual behaviours had, over time, begun to scramble. She'd noticed moments of intense anger over trivial things that would immediately subside, his sleep was unusually disordered, and she'd seen that his walking sometimes would become unsteady, like the gait of someone who was drunk. There had been significant changes in the ways he understood what was happening around him and how events from their past were suddenly and disturbingly woven into the present. And more recently, there was his habit of spending late afternoons in Robert's room, sitting on the edge of his bed in silence, looking out to the garden beyond.

Edith put her mug onto the floor beside her chair. She stood, she stroked the back of Wanda's head with her thumb. She went to Martin at the desk, putting her hand on his shoulder.

'Here, give it to me.' He handed her the email. She read a few lines. 'You really should answer Barbara's calls, Martin. It's not fair on her.' He looked at her blankly, there was a short silence.

'I do see what you mean about these questions though, *What is your idea of perfect happiness?'* She laughed a little. 'Do they not allow that perfect happiness might, by necessity, carry its own minute imperfections?' He looked at her with a faint grin. He took up, and held four of her knotted, arthritic fingers, looking down at them. 'You know, I always loved it when – just now and then ...' he paused and fluttered his fingers over hers as if her were conjuring a magic trick. 'When you used to paint your fingernails.' He laughed, a short, breathy laugh before kissing each of her fingertips. She stood looking down at his head, his white hair and the delicate, pink skin of his scalp.

Painted fingernails. Edith couldn't be sure who her husband was talking about, it could have been any one of a number of women over the last sixty years. His serial infidelities, which began not long after Robert was born, fit a depressingly regular pattern. All his conquests needed to admire his work, they needed to fall in love with the man in the jacket photographs of his books with his green eyes and his Easter Island profile. They had to believe the critical raves about his work printed on those books, as if praise for his prose would somehow be transmuted to the man himself. 'Visionary', 'thrillingly authentic', 'blindingly transcendent' and 'a seer for our times', his literary capital lent him a potency that was irresistible to some. First, he would feign indifference to their attentions, before an intense sexual interlude would commence that could last for weeks or months, before he would abruptly end the affair, the lying and the deception, the empty promises and the savoury regrets. Each episode ending with the realisation that he loved Edith, and that she was all he ever needed, until the next time.

First there was Claire, the serious, overly polite editor of his fourth novel who insisted on lengthy afternoon meetings in her London flat. Then Kyra, the Phd Student from Amsterdam who abandoned her thesis on the metaphysical symbolism found in the fiction of Martin Gillray, once their six-month affair had ended. There was Jess, the book publicist who could recite whole passages of Martin's prose by heart, who said that she would always love him, even though their midweek trysts at her studio flat in Peckham came to an end after five short weeks. Then there was Rachel, and Marjorie and Laura and Melanie. Finally there was Jelena Petrovic, a Serbian academic and translator who fucked Martin for a year in the same room of the *Hotel Moskva* in Belgrade, whenever he would visit, doing research for his ninth novel, *The Broken River*, set just before the commencement of World War I. Jelena, who, after their relationship had run its course, caused a minor publishing scandal by writing a book that documented their affair through three hundred and twenty six dreary pages entitled, *Hotel Moskva, Room 403, My Year With M.* Edith was caught off guard by the book, which Martin had wilfully ignored, but when a *News of the World* journalist asked her what she thought of the intimate, and at times sexually explicit memoir, she simply said, 'Oh, I have a sort of unwritten policy, not to read books with three titles.' Martin only heard from Jelena once more, a year after the publication of her book he received a postcard from Belgrade, on the back she had written,

> *Martin, I'm teaching a course at the University now, it's called* The Fiction of Martin Gillray, *something about the clear truth of that title appealed to me. you were never really here, and we were never really together. Good luck, Jelena.*

For three months he used the postcard as a bookmark before throwing it away. For her own part, Edith found infidelities a distracting waste of time and energy, she preferred to focus on raising Robert, and her work, and the domestic life she shared with Martin. She had never been particularly troubled by his affairs, they had angered her at first, but she eventually put them down to a juvenile part of his nature that would always remain self-obsessed, coupled with his relentless vanity, which she found vaguely heroic in a man who was not, by any conventional definition, handsome or attractive.

Jelena and all the others, the painted fingernails Martin was admiring could have belonged to any of these women, but Edith knew it could never have been her.

In the time when they were still undergraduate virgins at Cambridge, he had teased her about her habit of biting her nails. They had stood at *The Eagle,* Martin twenty-one, Edith twenty-two holding pots of cider in the smoky interior of the pub, when he spontaneously took her hand in his, gently stroking her fingers as he looked down at them, her saw that her nails were bitten to the quick. She immediately withdrew them, her face reddened.

'Oh don't, Martin, I know it's stupid. It's just a silly habit.'

He was smiling at her. 'Edith, why does a nice girl from Bexhill-on-Sea need to tear at her nails?'

She ignored his question, smiling at him as she sipped her cider. He liked her, but he felt that, at times she was difficult to read. She was serious, and very smart. She knew about things that he had no understanding of, abstract calculation and logic, Hindu-Arabic numeral systems and Islamic mathematics, Euclid and Pythagoras, she read Ancient Greek and Latin. She also knew about things he understood quite well, things that he loved. She talked to him about the structure of Wuthering Heights and Mansfield Park, about Ted Hughes and Eliot and Beckett, she had LPs by Stockhausen, Shostakovich, Dave Brubeck and Petula Clark. Her hair held a coppery sheen and she had large black, scary eyes that seemed to look into him. She had an easy, relaxed laugh and he loved the casual way she'd playfully slap his shoulder when she thought he was being funny or stupid. She seemed to him at once completely open and unaffected, but he could also tell, in the quiet, thoughtful way she would sometimes look at him, listening to him speak, that there was a current that ran through her that was deeply private and unknowable to him. He felt, in his third year at Cambridge, completely distracted by her, with no real sense of how she felt about him. Only once, in the eighteen months he had known her, had she broken through the casual defensive ways in which they interacted with each other to show how she might really feel about him.

It was when his first story was published in *Varsity*, the student newspaper. Entitled 'The Carriage', it consisted of the interior monologues of nine individuals on a train, travelling from Cambridge to Ely. The last monologue coming from a twelfth-century stone mason working on the west tower of Ely Cathedral.

'Look at these tired, dirty hands. How might I keep cutting stone with these torn, bent fingers in the cold? In the chill of this wind. To what purpose? To what earthly purpose? To what end? God is not a building. And now, see? He brings the snow.'

She'd stopped him outside the Wren Library, she was pulling her hair away from her face in the breeze. 'Martin, I read your story.' She was looking at him incredulously, as if she had just discovered he had an extraordinary skill he was trying to keep secret. 'Oh right. Yes, okay.' '*Martin!*' She said in an odd, emphatic way. 'It was *fantastic!*

You are a wonderful writer.' Then she did something surprising. She hugged him. He was caught off balance and tried to hug her back, but by then she had released him. He felt awkward and embarrassed. 'Thanks. But, you can't *know* that, on the basis of one story in a student newspaper, you know, that I'm a wonderful writer, surely.' She looked at him in a quizzical way for a moment, as if she were making some inner, intuitive calculation. Then she said, 'No. I suppose you're right. It was presumptuous of me. After all, I'm sure there are going to be many opportunities for you to disappoint me in the future.' He laughed, but he wasn't really sure why. 'Yes, I expect so, quite.'

Some days he pretended he didn't care about her at all. He'd get lost in his work and forget about her for minutes at a time. Then, unbidden, an image would flash into his brain, the way she'd casually raise her skirt slightly to scratch her knee mid-conversation, or her mouth as she laughed, or the memory of her terrible, tuneless voice, half singing, half humming to Roy Orbison's 'Running Scared'. He'd then have to stop and enter a detailed fantasia about her pale skin, the shape of her breasts under her Fair Isle cardigan, her hair and her naked body, her nakedness under him. There were moments when he'd feel an impotent rage against Edith and the power she seemed to hold over him, a rage that would quickly subside as he began to think about what he'd say to her the next time they saw each other. These competing emotions led his small circle of friends to consider him moody and arrogant. But when he was with Edith, he tried to be another kind of Martin, a witty, relaxed and happy young man. When they were together, she would often regard him with a wry half-smile that indicated to him that she hadn't been taken in. It was a smile that told him that it might be safe to be himself with her, that she would patiently wait until he trusted her.

That finally happened as they stood, leaning against the wall, drinking their cider, in the stuffy confines of *The Eagle* during Lent term, February 1962. He was fingering a button on his blazer as he held his mug trying not to appear nervous.

'No, really Edie, why do you do it? Bite your nails? It's odd, yes?' Her eyelids fluttered quickly and he saw that she had rolled her eyes.

'Oh, I don't know, *The Bomb? Pollution? Starvation?*' She sighed, 'All right, if you must know, I worry that Brenda Lee won't make it to number one on *Pick of the Pops.*' She drank some more of her cider and felt slightly nauseated by its warm sweetness. His face broke into a wide happy grin.

'I had no idea that your feelings about Brenda Lee ran so deep.' She looked over at the crowded huddle of men at the bar. 'Please don't tell anyone Martin, it's not a secret I share with many people.' He reached out and touched her shoulder. 'Cross my heart.' His finger traced a little cross on his green pullover. He saw that her expression seemed to shift, as if she was thinking about something far away from this pub, far away from him. She swirled the last of her cider around in the bottom of her glass.

'Anyway, I don't,' she said

'Don't what?' He asked.

'I don't bite my nails because ... *Oh God,* can we stop talking about my *bloody fingernails?*' She laughed. There was a brief pause, then Martin listened very carefully as these words came out of his mouth.

'Why not come back to mine? We could listen to some music?'

Her eyes shifted to him, she folded her arms. 'Some music?'

Suddenly he felt exposed, a wave of heat ran through him.

'Well, yeah, sure, I thought we could ...' She placed her glass on a nearby table and swung the strap of her bag onto her shoulder. She leaned forward and kissed him softly on the mouth, then she stood back and looked at him again.

'Music sounds lovely. Let's go then.'

In his room that afternoon, to the scratchy sound of Helen Shapiro singing 'Walking In My Dreams' on Martin's transistor radio, they undressed each other clumsily. She left his socks on, he managed to remove her bra and pull off her underwear, but left her box-pleated tartan skirt on, hitched around her waist. Afterwards, in the early evening, laying on the floor in the dull glow of the amber bars of the radiator, his head lay on her warm stomach as it gently rose and fell, her hand stroking his hair. She could feel his warm breath as he said, almost in a whisper, 'Thank you, Edith.' Suddenly, he felt a laugh run through her body. 'There's really no need to thank me Martin, it was a team effort after all.' Then they both laughed. Some minutes passed, then he said, 'I think It's really brave of you to take me on.' His ear rest in the little valley of her naval. 'Take you on? Hang on a minute,' she playfully grabbed his hair in her fist, 'I thought we were just listening to music.' He kissed her stomach, then his voice became serious again. 'You know, Edie ...' He twisted his head to look up at her face. 'I'm never going to leave you.' She thought for a moment, 'Okay, and you want me to *stop* biting my nails?'

Now she looked down at that same head, pink and lightly freckled, almost sixty years later. She put Barbara's email back on his keyboard, she bent forward and kissed him. 'I'm off darling, time for bed. Don't be up too long.' Edith left him then. Wanda followed in her wake, her tail snapping in and out of curvy question marks as she went. Martin leaned over and pushed a button on the side of his computer, turning his screen off. He suddenly noticed that the rain, that had maintained a steady thrum on the roof and windows for much of the night, had abruptly stopped. Far-off, somewhere in the house, he could hear Edith, a tap was running. It stopped. A door was closed. When had she left? He wondered. He could see outside, fat drops of rainwater dripping down from the eaves of their thatched roof, falling like silent points of light.

His eyes shifted again to Robert smiling on the green hill. He remembered a time, long before his illness descended around him like a toxic fog, when his son was a child, how they would play together with bows and arrows, teaching him the names of plants and birds, bluebells and juniper, crows, robins and red kites. He remembered holding his child's fragile, sleek limbs as he taught him to swim, drying his eyes after the pain of a bee sting, hearing his pure, child's voice singing 'Twinkle, Twinkle Little Star', dressed in a white pillow-slip, doubling as an angel's smock, making the sound of that lullaby a sacred thing to him, feeling his boy's sudden heaviness as he fell asleep, his head cradled into Martin's shoulder. Then there was Robert's last poem, *Your tiny bud, now froze.*

He remembered how, in the weeks after his death, he was not made numb by the experience, that would have been welcome. Rather, grief magnified the world for Martin and made being alive in it almost intolerable. He felt assaulted by the light of the day, the movement of the clouds across the sky and the wind, sound was alive to him in ways that made him yearn for silence, then the silence, when it came, held its own terrors. People became grotesque to him. His head held no answers, he had no words to console Edith in her uncomprehending sadness. For years after, he replayed the moment of releasing his son's body from where it hung on the door frame. The horror of his lolling tongue, his eyes and the rank smell of shit. He could feel the weight of Robert as his lifeless body slumped into his arms, laying him carefully down on the carpet of his room. He shut the door and lay on the floor beside his boy, stroking his cold face with the knuckles of his fingers, his own mouth gaping in a silent scream as his eyes pooled with tears. It was some time before he noticed the note pinned to his t-shirt, *speak soon, love Robert.*

But in recent times, Martin imagined how the story of that terrible July morning could be changed. One Sunday evening he happened upon the ITV series, *24 Hours in A&E.* As he watched, he became obsessively engaged in the small and large dramas occurring in the accident and emergency department of St George's Hospital, London. The cuts, the falls, the car accidents, the heart flutters and the unexplained numbness travelling down the left side, all resolved over a twenty-four hour period, edited and packaged as an hour of weekend diversion. Watching the show, it seems to Martin that everyone is cared for with simple kindness, professionalism and sympathy. Looking at Robert's photograph again, the mechanics of the fantasy whir into motion once more.

He is on the floor with Robert's unconscious body, he cuts the towelling belt from around his neck as his fingers frantically dial 999. *'It's my boy, there's been an accident, please come quickly.'* As the air ambulance is sent, Martin takes up Robert's hand, it's warm, there is a pulse in his bruised neck, his pale face has a blue cast, but his eyelids appear to flutter in slight movement. Then the fiction moves to the A&E department where, after fourteen hours of speedy but efficient care, a Tamil doctor, who Martin has named Khushal, finally gives Robert the all clear. *'There has been some damage to the larynx, it's best if he doesn't speak for now, you understand.'* Martin and Edith are then led in to see their troubled boy, bruised and exhausted, but miraculously alive. Edith rakes her son's hair from his forehead and kisses him. Martin takes his hand and Robert squeezes his fingers reassuringly. In the fantasy Martin holds up the note Robert had pinned to his t-shirt. *'Here son, you say Sorry Mum, Sorry Dad, but don't be sorry Robbie, your poem wasn't that bad.'* Then the frozen, televised tableau would gradually fall apart and Martin would be left desperately trying to piece memories of his son back together, but all his considerable powers of imagination fall short of conjuring him back to life.

The roof creaked once more, as if this would be its last accommodation of the storm this night. Martin thought that in a cheap fiction, this creaking house would be a sign that their beloved long-dead son was still amongst them. A ghost. Martin longed for that consolation. When he was a boy he read with rapt attention, stories of the afterlife. Accounts of headless horsemen, or strangled princes and poisoned kings, of rustling spectres rising from the dead, ships, mansions, lakes and towers holding unquiet shades, drifting beyond life and death. Stories of haunted, anguished children visited by the dead, claimed by the dead to remain children forever, tethered to the dead. Now at eighty-one he was lost. His grip on the present becoming weak, he waited for a visitation, a sign or a message from Robert, his gifted boy. He rubbed his tired eyes with the heel of his palms and realised he'd been crying.

Barbara's stupid questions lay on the keyboard. 'If you could change one thing about yourself, what would it be?' 'What is your favourite journey?' He took up the page and tore it into thirty-two tiny squares and let them flutter to the floor around him.

He drained the last of his whiskey, leaning back in his chair he closed his eyes for a moment, pushing his glasses to the top of his head. When he opened his eyes again, he looked down at his watch and saw that it was 3.15 am. He was cold, and his body felt thick with exhaustion. He stood and stretched, there was a pain that ran from his shoulder to behind his neck, he yawned. He looked around him at the tiny pieces of torn paper on the floor. He pinched the bridge of his nose, pulling his glasses down from the top of his head, he put them on. He stood, he leaned against the doorframe of his study, looking down the darkened hallway to the closed door of the bedroom. He wanted air. He walked downstairs, he opened the back door and walked into the garden. He smiled at the spray of rainwater as he kicked through the long grass of the unkempt lawn. The wet leaves of the trees that surrounded him glittered in the cold. He walked to the middle of the garden and looked back at the house in the night, his breath a vapour of fog in the sharp air. Five darkened twelve-paned window frames set into the white limewash wall, the black rectangle of the kitchen door left ajar. The cold was now in his clothes and he began to shiver. He pushed his fists into the pockets of his corduroy trousers. His feet were cold in his shoes. He looked up at the sky, he could see no stars. Heavy clouds of black and silver overhead gradually drew apart to reveal a blurry sliver of white moon. He closed his eyes and hugged himself, even his eyelids were cold. He wanted to be freed from the heaviness of his body. He tried to shut out the noise in his head. Natasha and the Bannerman Prize, her voice on the phone, 'You're breaking up', the sinister new black phone Barbara had bought him to keep in touch, 'What is your idea of perfect happiness?' Edith, Edith and Robert, Robert and the Angel of the North, holding his lifeless hand on his bedroom floor, speak soon, Love Robert. He took a deep breath into his chest, and the smell of the clean, cold garden was drawn into him. He seemed momentarily revived. Almost in thanks, he closed his eyes again.

'What is your favourite journey?' That was the next thought that drifted into his head. With his eyes still closed and his feet almost frozen to the ground, he thought about this question seriously for a moment.

The short walk across Fingle Bridge. Crossing that stone arch structure over the River Teign when Robert was twelve. They'd set out on a cloudy morning to hike to the North Moor. By eleven, the sun had come out and they'd stopped to rest at one of the triangular cutwaters on the bridge to look down at the river as it washed below them. Robert wore a green backpack and a denim jacket. They were both leaning over the edge looking down at the smoothed, mossy stones under the water. 'How old do you think this bridge is, Dad?' Martin looked at the ledge and the ways the stone had been laid. 'I should think a few hundred years, what do you think?' Robert's chin resting on his thumb.

'Have you read *Frankenstein*, Dad?'

'I have, yep. A long time ago.'

'Do you think they will ever be able to do that?' Robert asked.

Martin looked at his son. 'What's that?'

'Do you think they will ever be able to make a creature out of other parts? New arms, new hands, new head?'

'No, no I don't.'

'Did you like *Frankenstein*, Dad?'

Martin straightened up, turning his back to the river. He tried to remember the book. 'Well, it was the first thing Mary Shelley ever wrote you know. I thought it was a pretty good first go.'

Robert looked down at the grasses as they waved in the flow of the water. 'I never want to go fishing again, it's cruel.' he said thoughtfully.

Crouching down, he picked up a stone. He turned back to the river and held it over the edge for a moment before watching it drop with a splash. They stood in silence for a few more minutes listening to the soft babble of the river. Robert turned to his father and pointed to the water below. 'There's a whole world down there, Dad.' Martin smiled and waited a moment before saying, 'Shall we push on then?' Robert smiled too, not looking at his father, 'Okay, let's go,' he said.

His eyes blinked open. The finest mist had begun to fall, it swirled around him in silver shawls in the frigid air. High up, somewhere in the trees he heard the song of a robin, as the light from Robert's room came on above him, leaving him standing on the grass in the cold, in a clearly defined amber rectangle, looking up, his mouth agape, tasting the rain as it fell.

11.30 am, Keppel Street Practice, Bloomsbury WC1E 6DP

'I'm not at all happy with these numbers, Natasha.' Tasha looked at the chart on the computer. Systolic 160, Diastolic 100. Jocelyn Owen, her doctor peered closer, tapping her glasses against the screen for emphasis.

'Not good?' Tasha asked.

Jocelyn looked away from the numbers and slumped back in her chair. She was wearing a mauve pullover that Tasha noticed was frayed at the neck and a Liberty print dress that looked too thin for the weather. She was three years younger than Tasha, and although she was almost completely bald, she still insisted on dyeing what was left of her hair, a brittle coppery orange. Together with her bright blue eyes, it gave her the appearance of a neglected Victorian doll.

Behind her desk was a framed print from the Royal Academy, *David Hockney, A Bigger Picture*. There was a collection of six glass paperweights from the Scottish Highlands lined up on her desk, next to a black phone showing three red lights that blinked intermittently. She leaned forward with her elbows on her knees. She wore a string of chunky green agate beads that she threaded through her fingers as she spoke.

'I'd like to say you're improving,' said Jocelyn.

Tasha looked back at her.

'Well then, why don't you just say, *Natasha, you're improving.* And then we can go to lunch.'

Jocelyn consulted some notes on her desk. 'Are you still taking the Coversyl? How do you find it?'

'How do I find it, Joss? Well generally, I look in my bag, and there it is, in a flattened and torn little box. When I remember, I push one or two out of the blister pack and swallow them.'

Jocelyn sat back with her hands in her lap. 'My good friend. You've got to take better care. You're in your seventies now, and your blood pressure is dangerously high. Consistently. What's going on? Are you taking any exercise? Do you walk? Are you stressed? Talk to me.'

Tasha thought of Harvest Place, three weeks ago with the front door ajar, of Gideon's envelope left for her on the shabby chair in the deserted upstairs sitting room, Sergeant Timewell's tedious questions and the missing person's brochure, 'Has someone you know gone missing?' The brochure that she kept with her, as if its creased, battered presence, with all its impersonal, procedural information might reassure her that a process was indeed in train to find Gideon, but that was a hope that dimmed with every passing day. Tomorrow the police would issue a press statement, appealing to the public for any information regarding the whereabouts of Gideon Bannerman. Far from comforting her, this part of the operation seemed to confirm for Tasha that he would be lost forever. His disappearance had begun to coalesce around her like a stony reality. Gideon's missing. Gideon's lost. Gideon's gone. And very soon she knew, he would remain in the past tense forever. *'Oh yes, well, we were very close, from childhood really, but he went missing, and he was never found.'* These sad thoughts angered her as she stared back at Jocelyn. The phone in her bag began to buzz, she thought it might be Timewell.

'Oh Joss, do forgive me, I'll need to take this.' Jocelyn rolled her eyes. Tasha looked at the phone, no caller I.D. 'Hello. Natasha Moubray speaking.'

'Natasha! How lovely to have caught you. It's Gordon Bennett.'

'Gordon?'

'Yes Gordon, Gordon Bennet, from Bromleys. The auction house? Do you remember? I suppose it's been a while.' Tasha remembered that Gordon Bennett was the unwelcome presence she'd always run into at gallery openings, the opera or charity events. He was a pale man, with suspiciously white, even teeth and dry skin that seemed to be constantly flaking away. His wife, a small Spanish woman called Irma, was always to be found at his side; Gideon once joked that she looked like a microscope. Tasha recalled that Irma's only contribution to shared conversations was to grin wanly and to intone, *'Yes, quite.'* from time to time, followed by a nervous laugh that was like a series of short coughs.

'Oh Gordon, yes. I'm awfully sorry, yes. How are you? How's Irma?' Tasha noticed Jocelyn moving her mouse on her desk and suddenly, instead of her blood pressure results, the screen was illuminated green with a game of *Patience.*

'I'm very well thank you, Natasha. Irma's fine, thank you for asking. I've actually called for a favour, I'm not sure if you'll be interested or have the time with your commitments to the prize, congratulations on the shortlist by the way, it's marvellous, so varied.'

Tasha watched as Jocelyn moved the digital cards around her screen. 'Thank you, Gordon. Now, this favour, I'm intrigued, please go on.'

'Okay. We've been offered a large collection of furniture, paintings and curios from the estate of Gideon Bannerman. It's really quite impressive, it all comes from Harvest Place, it includes a Bonnard, some Constable drawings, there's some Bulgari pieces, a –'

'There's really no need to tell me what it includes, Gordon, I'm a regular visitor to Gideon's home.' She felt a wave of heat run through her body. Her hand gripped the phone tightly. Her knuckles whitened. 'Can I just ask you Gordon, how this collection was consigned to Bromleys?'

'Yes, of course. It's all being offered through a shelf company, I'm assuming for reasons related to tax, it's Caxap Holdings, odd name, apparently it's Russian for –'

'Sugar,' said Tasha flatly.

'Yes. That's right. Well, the company is run by Gideon's partner, his er … *husband,* –'

'*Ex-husband,* yes, Yuri.'

'Oh yes, quite, Yuri Kuznetsov. Fascinating man. Anyway, I was thinking, I was aware that you had known the Bannermans' for decades, you were at Oxford with Gideon if I remember correctly.'

'Yes. That's right. We were at Oxford.' Tasha spoke these words quietly, almost to confirm for herself this simple fact from the past.

'Well, the staff here met yesterday to discuss the collection, and I thought it would be a wonderful idea to approach the esteemed

Natasha Moubray to write an essay for the catalogue, since you and Gideon are so close, and of course, you knew his parents when they were alive. I haven't been able to get on to Gideon, though I have left messages, but I thought I'd approach you first, strike while the iron is hot, so to speak, what do you think?'

Tasha remembered walking up the stairs of the empty house in Kensington, calling out for Gideon as she went. She remembered the night she met Yuri for the first time, his ridiculous tight red shorts and his illustrated body, '*Ah my tattoos, Natasha. Yes, they are my foolishness.*' She could sense Gordon's apprehension at the other end of the phone as she allowed the silence to become extended.

'Natasha? If it appeals as an idea, I was thinking perhaps three or four thousand words?'

Tasha thought for a moment more. Then she spoke, her tone was almost jovial. 'Gordon, normally with the shortlist being announced, I'm terribly busy. As you would appreciate, there's still so much work to be done with the judges before the winner is announced at the prize dinner, but I may be able to offer you something.'

'Really? Oh, how marvellous. I knew you'd be able to produce a really considered piece on the family and the collection, and the catalogue itself is going to be quite lavish, we're – '

'Oh, I have no doubt Gordon,' she straightened in her chair. 'I'd love to provide a context for the sale and I think I can set the tone by entitling my piece, *The Progress of a Slug; Yuri Kuznetsov and the Pageant of Greed,* what do you think?' But before Gordon could answer Tasha hung up.

'Venal prick.'

Jocelyn swivelled her chair around to face her friend, she smiled. 'I'm all played out here Tash, and I'm starving. Lunch then?'

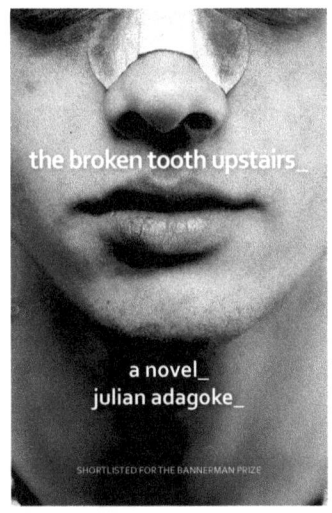

THE BROKEN TOOTH UPSTAIRS
Julian Agadoke (Corinthian) 526pp
Documented through two thousand and forty-seven
text messages over a period of fifteen months, Derek
Newcombe loses his wife Lydia, his Nigerian mistress,
Dara, his whippet Misty and finally, his mind. What
happened on the 11.25 tube to North Clapham?

6.41 pm, Hampstead Tube Station NW3 1QG

He couldn't breathe and he needed to pee. He crossed Hampstead
High Street when he emerged from the tube station into the cold
early evening. He'd pointed to a bunch of blue flowers at the flower
sellers at Oriel Place and was trying to concentrate on what he was
being told about forget-me-nots as he painfully tried to manage his
bladder. An elderly woman with a jumbled knot of grey hair that sat
asymmetrically on her head, skewered with two crisscrossed red
chopsticks, held a small posy up to Julian's face, so he could look at
the flowers at a closer range.

'Forget-me-nots, such a lovely name, so much nicer than scorpion
grass, as they're also known, they don't look like scorpions at all
really ...' The woman's voice trailed off, regarding the flowers

herself. Julian fumbled in his pocket for his puffer as he felt the inner constriction of his airway tighten his breathing into a rasp. He found it and put it to his mouth, sucking the salbutamol deep into his lungs.

'Oh dear. You're not allergic are you? Are you all right?' The woman was now holding the little bunch in both her hands, her soft blue eyes held an expression of genuine concern. He shook his head, still holding his puffer to his mouth. He desperately needed to piss and he could feel his phone vibrate in his pocket with another incoming message. He recovered.

'Oh no, no, no, I'm quite okay – thank you. Yes, I'll take them. Yes, thank you.'

'Okay. That's eight pounds thanks, love.'

He crossed the road again and continued walking down the street. He stood for a moment opposite Waterstones. The window display in the bookstore showed neat stacks of his new novel, *The Broken Tooth Upstairs* which had been recently rescued from middling sales and a generally indifferent public reception, by being longlisted and now shortlisted for the Bannerman Prize. Above of the books was a large poster reproduction of the cover – a close-up of a man's face, his nose plastered with a bloodied bandage. The poster was advertising a 'Reading, Q&A and a book signing with celebrated author, Julian Adagoke, tonight at 7.30'. He looked at his watch, he had forty-five minutes. He had to find a toilet. There, on the corner, the King William IV pub. He walked in clutching his flowers. He found the bathroom. He made it into a cubicle. With some effort he undid his trousers and leaned against the wall pissing noisily with relief at last. He took his phone out of his pocket. Fifteen messages from Nicola. He winced. He rubbed his palm across his forehead and noticed that he was sweating. He flushed the toilet, and with his trousers still undone, he sat on the seat, gently placed his flowers on the tiled floor and scrolled through the messages. He noticed that the first one was sent an hour ago.

17.40   Julian – I'm breaking my silence to give you fair warning – it's the ethical thing to do – oh, I'm sorry – ethics, fairness – you'll need to look those words up

17.41   Can I respectfully request that you NOT mention me in ANY of your appearances? Is that really too much to ask? Just talk about yourself – that's when you're happiest, then it doesn't matter how much you lie. PS – this text cannot be described as HARRASSMENT!

17.45   It isn't just that your book is so dishonest – we both know that it is – it's gimmicky, stupid, infantile and – as you're about to discover – libellous

17.55   I don't bloody care anymore – I just don't – Mark told me not to contact you but fuck that – you parasitic prick!

Julian paused for a moment, who was Mark?

18.01   And no – I've not been drinking – Mark says we have a VERY strong case

It was then that he remembered. Mark Poultney was Nicola's solicitor.

18.06   How dare you? It makes me sick to think that Miriam and all the others were right about you from the start – she told me not to trust you – she thinks you're a bastard

He continued to sweat. Miriam was Nicola's old housemate, but all the others? What others?

18.08   You ARE a bastard – I am NOT drinking

18.11   Fuck Mark's advice – I'm going to say this – you used me and our relationship – all the time you were betraying us with your scribble – scribble, scribble, scribble – that's all it is – shameful! The Bannerman? Are they having a laugh?

18.15   I really wasn't surprised when I heard you wanted mediation

18.16   OMFG! Mediation!!!???

18.17   Mediate my ARSE you bastard!

18.22   You've hurt me Julian

18.25   I want you to know that today I put your book in the fireplace – I opened it and made a little tent of the pages – then I set it alight

18.27   It took exactly 18 minutes and 17 seconds to burn to nothing

18.31   You've really hurt me Julian – bye for now XXXX

He heard himself say out loud, 'Oh my god.' He closed his eyes tightly, pinching the bridge of his nose. He whispered, 'Oh, Nicola … ' and the sound of her name turned into an elongated sigh, *'Oh, Nicola … '*

It was summer, four and a half years ago in the offices of his publisher that Julian was introduced to Nicola Galbraith, the publicist assigned to his eighth novel, *The Bone Garden*. The book was a gothic thriller about the trade in corpses, set in 1842, whose central character was Samuel Barnsley, an invention of Julian's, appointed as the first caretaker of Tower Hamlet's Cemetery, East London.

'Hello Julian, I'm Nicola. Nice to finally meet you.' She held out her hand as she stood in a partitioned work cubicle that was overcrowded with stacks of books and papers. It was decorated with postcards from holiday destinations – Cairo, Madrid, Berlin, Salonika – along with pictures of a variety of attractive young people embracing or drinking or both, some of them featuring Nicola. A single author adorned her wall of pictures. It was a black and white portrait of E. M. Forster in profile. Julian guessed it was taken when Forster was a young man at Oxford. There was an assortment of coloured Post-it notes stuck to the edges of her computer screen, most were illegible, but one large green one simply and ambiguously read, *Don't forget Tuesday!* Sitting down on a chair in the cramped space, Julian pointed to the note.

'What's happening Tuesday?'

Nicola looked at her computer and thought for a moment. 'Oh, do you know what? I've quite forgotten,' she said laughing. She appeared to be in her late twenties or early thirties with a broad, open face. Her youthful skin was lightly fuzzed and she appeared to wear no make-up. She had casually untidy brown hair with no discernible part and small ears, each studded with little red stones the colour of rubies. She wore black trousers and a crumpled red shirt polka-dotted with small white spots, three buttons were undone at the neck and Julian could see a fine gold chain that she wore underneath it. She'd pushed her sleeves up past her elbows and her arms were lightly tanned. Her dark brown eyes looked intelligent and inquisitive. During their conversation Julian quickly observed that she would fix him with those eyes and incline her head forward at a slight angle when she thought he was being evasive or unclear. She seemed immediately at ease, actively interested, but not in awe of either him or his writing.

'I quite liked your book,' she said, drumming a pencil on her thigh.

'Well, that's a ringing endorsement from the person responsible for promoting it to the world,' he said grinning. She grinned back at him and crossed her arms.

'In 1842 Samuel Barnsley is given the opportunity of a lifetime. Free board and lodgings and a modest wage to become the caretaker of the dead, in London's new Tower Hamlet's Cemetery. *The Bone Garden* explores loss, danger, love, class and loyalty in Victorian London. Julian Adagoke has made a world both terrible and beautiful, hard-bitten and transcendent. Here he demonstrates the mastery that has established him as one of this country's finest novelists. How's that?' Julian thought for a moment, looking at the chewed end of Nicola's pencil.

''Hard-bitten' is good, I like that. 'Transcendent' is a bit much though, don't you think?'

'Mr Adagoke –'

'It's Julian.'

'Mr Adagoke, the first book I worked on here was Sophie Caldwell's *The Hotel Paperback* – do you know it?' Julian rolled his eyes, Nicola continued.

'Quite. It's 1984. Siobhan works in housekeeping at the Grand Brighton Hotel at the time of the Conservative Party Conference. One fateful night in October she is called to Mrs Thatcher's suite, and before her shift is over, half the hotel will be destroyed by an IRA bomb and Siobhan's life will be changed forever. Sophie Caldwell's finely tuned, acutely observed novel is a profoundly moving examination of the price of truth and the need to make the world anew amidst hate and destruction.

'Now, five months after I wrote that description for the flyleaf of the book, I was at a party where I met a boring man who had no idea I worked in publishing, I think I told him I was a veterinary assistant anyway, he started talking about 'this marvellous book he'd just finished called '*The Hotel Paperback*, you really must read it', he said. I asked him what it was about and he thought for a moment and then he said, 'the writing, it's so finely tuned, it's really acutely observed, I suppose, ultimately it's about the price of truth, yes, that's how I'd describe it.' Do you see my point, Mr Adagoke?'

'Please call me Julian. Um … I suppose your point might be, it's best to lie to people about what you do if you don't want to go home with them?' he offered.

'You've written a good book, probably a great book, and it's my job to market it. *The Hotel Paperback* sold thirty-five thousand copies in its first month.' Her mouth immediately made an insincere tight-lipped smile.

'That book,' Julian said pausing for effect, 'was pretentious drivel, by a Thatcherite apologist. Sophie Caldwell can't write for toffee.' He thought for a moment. 'And wasn't there a vague worry that some of it was plagiarised?'

Nicola was still smiling. 'There were some, er … issues. With regard to your assessment of the writing, that's one opinion. I couldn't possibly comment, only to say that it gave me thirty-five thousand reasons to be cheerful.' She leaned forward, her elbows on her knees. 'The point of what I'm doing here is to provide people with a vague description. We've got to establish a tone for your book, offer up a couple of emotive triggers like 'mastery' and 'transcendence' that are generally concordant with your place in the market, your brand, if you like. Do you know what I mean?'

'*Brand?* I don't have a brand. What nonsense,' he said.

'You *do* have a brand Julian. You're associated with intelligence, insight, a slight edginess. Your readers are generally the left-leaning, socially aware, quasi-intellectual types who subscribe to *The Guardian* and *The London Review of Books*. On their bookshelves they have McEwan, Amis, Barnes, Gillray, Rushdie, Mantel, there might be a Murdoch somewhere that they've never finished. They favour Ken Loach over Mike Leigh, but they'll watch both.' Without breaking her stride she looked briefly up at the ceiling as if she were picking these facts out of the air. 'They're members of the Tate, the National Theatre and the Royal Court. They're very concerned about the climate and they used to donate to Oxfam, but now it's Save the Children. They're for refugees and they know that Black Lives Matter. They holiday in Scotland, the Lakes District, Umbria or the Languedoc, they're indifferent about the monarchy, but they loved the Queen, even if they're not sure about Charles. If they don't *actually live* in London, they all complain that London isn't what it was. They're fierce remainers who hate *Love Island* but never miss *Antiques Roadshow* or an episode of *Fake or Fortune.'*

He'd noticed she'd called him Julian for the first time, he could feel his neck blushing red. *'Fake or Fortune?'* He said, spacing out the words for emphasis.

Nicola leaned forward, she lowered her voice to a conspiratorial whisper. 'They secretly think that Fiona Bruce and Phillip Mould are brain-box totty.'

'That is fucking ridiculous, and frankly, offensive,' he managed to say.

'I know, *Phillip Mould?* What *are* they thinking? But really, Julian, who are we to argue?' A slow grin broke out across his face. Nicola smiled back at him, she drummed her pencil on her thigh saying 'Shall we crack on then?'

Julian remembered little of the conversation that was about promotion or marketing, but he observed during the course of their exchange that Nicola would say funny, mysterious things that intrigued him. 'I tried writing fiction once. *God!* It was so *depressing;* I couldn't get out of bed for two weeks. Poetry was worse.' He saw that she had a bruise on her forearm that was the shape of a thumbprint, she noticed him looking at it. 'Oh that. My advice to you is *not* to go drinking with Swedish backpackers in Sicily, Mr Adagoke.' 'Noted,' he replied. 'Have you visited Stromboli, Julian? I think you'd love it. You know, it has an *active* volcano?'

At various times during their two-hour meeting he'd felt annoyed, angry, frustrated, patronised, irritated and amused. He stood to leave, saying, 'Thank you, Nicola, this has been all very interesting. I've never had my brand dissected in detail, I feel slightly violated.'

'Only slightly?' she replied, looking at him evenly.

Then he surprised himself by adding, 'Perhaps you'd fancy getting a drink sometime?' She reached for her bag and slung the strap over her shoulder saying, 'We're going to the Chesham Arms.'

'What, now?' he said.

'Yes.' She switched off her computer and grabbed her mobile phone. 'And you're paying, Mr Adagoke.'

That evening at the Chesham Arms lasted for six hours. From the moment she walked into the pub, Nicola seemed in charge. Julian noticed that she knew all the staff behind the bar, she introduced him to them, and he immediately forgot their names. She was handed a Guinness without asking, and Julian had no way of knowing when he ordered, 'Just the one,' glass of New Zealand sauvignon blanc, that before the night was over he'd empty almost two bottles of it.

Over the course of the evening, Julian discovered that Nicola had an ease with intimate disclosures that he found warmly attractive. She talked; about her mother and father in Weymouth who were both retired schoolteachers, about the scandal of her father embarking on a short-lived infidelity with a student teacher called, Gail Yardley, who had been befriended by the family. About her mother's discovery of the affair, about angry silences and unexplained tears at the breakfast table, of smashed crockery and slamming doors. About how, eventually their marriage was reconstructed to accommodate resentment, hurt, betrayal and disappointment. How her parents now travelled the world volunteering for the Red Cross. She talked about her brother, Ross, who was gay and worked for the NHS in Islington and her ex-boyfriend, Alec Sala, a Romanian medical student who had recently cut off all contact with Nicola. Again, described by her with one of those elliptical, incomplete, puzzle sentences that were threaded through her conversation.

'If you're being *repeatedly* buggered by a Romanian, Julian, don't keep going back for more in the hope that *eventually* he'll flip you over – run a mile!' This after at least seven pots of Guinness, she added, 'Do you fancy a pizza? I'm starved. They do a great mushroom and ham here.'

She talked about studying art history and visual culture at Exeter University, about her unhappiness there, of endless course-hopping and a succession of terrible boyfriends. She described the enemies she made – 'Never call someone who thinks of themselves as a post-structuralist, a bullshitting wanker. You'll find that post-structuralists, by and large, don't really *have* a sense of humour. That doesn't mean that they're not bullshitting wankers, it just means that they're humourless bullshitting wankers.' She'd surprised herself by graduating with a first for a thesis entitled, 'Love, Hatred, Class and

Social Intercourse in the Fiction of E. M. Forster and Jane Austen.'

'That sounds fascinating.'

'It's really not. I managed to say one or two interesting things, but it's actually rubbish.'

'Well, you managed a *first.*'

'I suppose that's not all that surprising. I was a mouthy feminist writing about Jane Austen and one of this country's most distinguished gay authors, they wouldn't dare *not* give me a first,' she said before draining another glass of beer.

'So, what you're telling me is that you *were* a mouthy feminist?'

'Oh, for fuck's sake shut it, Julian!' she laughed.

She explained how she'd drifted into the world of publishing via a brief stint in advertising working for, as she described it cryptically, 'Satan and Satan.' Here she paused. Surrounded by empty glasses she put her elbows on the table and raked the fingers of both hands through her hair. She stared down at the random bits of pizza crust that were left on the plate in front of her.

'I have a confession to make, Mr Adagoke.'

Julian poured himself some more wine. 'I'm afraid it's too late to tell me that you work as a veterinary assistant Ms Galbraith – I know what you do for a living.'

She leaned forward on the table, her chin in her palm held her head at an angle. 'I've actually read every one of your novels, some more than once. *The Clarence Road Fire* is one of my favourite books, I read it at least once a year.'

'My first book? Are you serious? Really? I'm very flattered. Thank you.'

Nicola continued to speak, but her voice had none of the protective veneer of cynicism that surrounded other things she said. She spoke with a direct simplicity that Julian found oddly moving.

'I think it's beautiful. The character of Sandy, the descriptions you write of being a student painter, her involvement in the bomb protests, and that terrible relationship she has, and the hideous abortion. Writing it all in her voice was such a great idea, and her voice is *perfect,* it's *uncanny.* I love how you made London in 1965 seem so dreary, not swinging at all but hard and cruel. It felt real. She's amazing. An amazing creation.'

As she was speaking, Julian struggled to remember the details of his first book, the wine was fogging his memory.

'Thank you Nicola, I'm so glad you liked it, and you know, it's sold more than thirty-five thousand copies.' He winked at her.

'Oh, now you've spoilt it by *winking.* Don't wink. It's vulgar, and it makes you look like a perv.' She took a big gulp of Guinness and added, 'Anyway, it's such a shame that the film version was such crap. Film people seem so weird to me.'

'I suppose film people can be weird, but then, so can book people.' He grinned.

She winked at him and laughed, 'You're not wrong, Mr Adagoke.'

It was midnight when they left the pub. The minute he was outside, Julian realised how drunk he was, he actually felt giddy. In contrast, Nicola seemed completely unaffected by six hours of steady drinking. As they made their way down Isabella Road, she took his arm as they walked, she huddled a little closer to his side.

'It's got a bit chilly,' she said.

'I don't find it cold at all.' For no particular reason, he was smiling. She stopped as they reached the corner and turned to face him.

'Thank you, Julian, it was lovely spending some time with you.'

The lights of the traffic in the street were reflected in her eyes, they glittered. He offered her his hand to shake, she looked at it and took it, pulling him close to her. She kissed him lightly on the side of his face, their lips touched briefly. She looked at him closely for slightly too long he thought, he felt flushed and exposed.

'This isn't happening,' she said. Then she kissed him again.

''*This isn't happening?*' You could have fooled me,' was all he could think of to say. He wanted to kiss her again, but she had hailed a cab to take her home.

'Well maybe you're easily fooled, Mr Adagoke.' She squeezed his arm in a way that indicated that there would be no more kissing. 'Goodnight, Julian.' For many minutes afterwards, he watched as the taillights of her taxi retreated into the night.

He marked the official commencement of their relationship with a text message he received the following morning as he lay in bed with a dry mouth and a throbbing head. It contained two simple words.

7.47:   Hello you

They worked together steadily over the next few months. Initially Julian kept making excuses to drop into the office, or to call her. Part of this was practical. There were endless details concerning the release of his book, which publications and critics to send it to, the interviews he was willing to do, radio, podcasts, print and video. Then in the months that followed after the book was out, they fell into a habit of eating dinner together once or twice a week. He realised it was more than the fact that he enjoyed her company. To the extent that he understood his emotions – and there were some terrifying gaps in that understanding – he knew that he was attracted to her. Although, it was not at all clear how she felt about him. Apart from admiring his first novel in that conversation at the Chesham Arms, she never talked about his writing or referred to his other books. Rather, she would talk about her work promoting other authors, some of whom she actively loathed. She would update him on sales of *The Bone Garden,* which sold over seven thousand copies the day it was released, or she'd talk about her flatmate, Miriam, who she was delighted to inform Julian, did not approve of the friendship she had struck up with him.

'Miriam thinks you're to be avoided. She thinks you're suspicious,' Nicola said, at once betraying a confidence and sharing a secret that she believed, at the time to be a harmless warning from an overly cautious friend. They were at Julie's bar in Holland Park. She was drinking a pilsner, Julian distractedly stirred the ice in his white Negroni.

'Suspicious? Based on?' He asked.

'Wikipedia.'

His brow creased. 'Seriously, Nicola?' She took her phone from her bag and tapped the screen.

'Julian Kenneth Adagoke, born 17 April, 1972 is an English novelist and screenwriter. He has written eight novels. His first book, *The Clarence Road Fire,* was shortlisted for both the Booker and the Bannerman prizes for literature and was turned into an award-winning film. He wrote the screenplays for two further film adaptations of his work, *The Island of Sorrow* in 2004, a fictional account of the aftermath of the Brixton riots that took place in 1981, and *Intimate Histories* in 2009 which was nominated for the Academy Award for best screen adaptation. His most recent novel is the historical thriller, *The Bone Garden.*

'Mr Adagoke is a Fellow of the Royal Society of Literature and is the recipient of the Costa Book Award, The James Tait Black Memorial Prize and the WH Smith Literary Award.

'Adagoke has been romantically linked with a number of women including Lady Willa Darmody, daughter of the 6th Earl of Suffolk, BBC newsreader and commentator Elizabeth Downey, the model and fashion designer Alexa Chung, and conservative party hopeful, Gina Field. Mr Adagoke has been engaged twice, in 2001 to self-help author and entrepreneur Lucy Aldridge and in 2011 to film editor Marcia Haldon who described Mr Adagoke in an interview in *The Times* as, 'A thorough disgrace to his sex.' The acrimonious split from Ms Haldon led to an out of court settlement. Mr Adagoke lives in South London.'

'I'd steer clear of him if I were you. Sounds definitely off,' he said.

'Quote, "A thorough disgrace to his sex." Unquote.' Nicola put her phone on the table, face down.

'Well, while you're so busy avoiding me would you like another glass of pilsner? I'm certainly having another Negroni, then perhaps we could order a bite.'

Nicola looked at the sudsy pattern on the side of her beer glass. 'I probably shouldn't have said anything. You'll think less of Miriam now.'

'Slightly less.' He squinted as if to get a sharper focus on a far-off object. 'But then, I never thought much of her in the first place, that's the price of gossip, I suppose.' He sat back in his chair, his glass in his hand, looking at Nicola. 'I've met her what? Once? Twice? and all she knows of me she's gleaned from one dubious secondary source.' There was a brief pause where they listened to the sounds of the others at the bar.

'Did you really go out with Alexa Chung?'

'Do you hear yourself, asking stupid questions?'

He consciously tried to suppress his growing irritation. A subtle moment of concern clouded her eyes. He sensed that she may have stumbled into a new knowledge of him.

'I was just curious. She's very lovely.' She said quietly.

'I have never met Alexa Chung. And just for the record, I think she's beautiful, charming and funny and I'm confident that she would not be the least bit interested in me. Now, if you have no further questions, I have two for you.'

'Yes?'

'Will you agree to never read to me from Wikipedia again?'

Nicola laughed, she understood by the deliberate, even tone of his question that she had hurt him. 'Agreed. And your second question?'

That night, almost casually she agreed to go home with him.

The following morning she sat up in bed on the first floor of his large house in Perrymead Street, Fulham, as he handed her a steaming cup of tea.

'Thank you.' She could hear jazz music floating around the house, coming from another room downstairs. 'What's that music?'

'It's Ornette Coleman.'

'God, what an awful noise.' She hugged her knees. She was looking at a large framed picture of a sleeping whippet on the wall. 'That's a beautiful drawing.'

'It's an etching. Freud, Eli the whippet.'

'She looks so peaceful, she could be dead.'

'Really? You think so? Actually, a lot of Freud's subjects are asleep. I suppose it kept them still. I do love the shape of that dog though. The way her paws fold in like that.'

Nicola stared at the picture. 'Do you know, I've never slept with someone from work before?' She looked back at him. 'It's sort of a rule I have.'

'I'm not from your work.' He was wearing blue boxer shorts printed with a pattern of tiny white anchors. He walked over to the bay window facing the bed and yanked the drapes open revealing a weak morning light and a plane tree with bright green leaves the size of an open palm waving in the breeze.

'You're not from my work?' she said.

He sat on the edge of the bed with one foot on the floor, his other leg bent. He was unaware that the fly of his shorts gaped open. Her smiling mouth sipped her tea.

'No, I'm more of a client you looked after, I suppose.'

'A *client?*' She laughed and rubbed her nose. She looked at the tangle of her discarded bra on the floor. 'Well, if you're a *client,* then that makes it much, much worse.' He leaned over and they kissed.

'I don't think it makes it much, much worse, unless of course you expect me to pay you for last night.' She playfully slapped him on the arm. 'It's alright, Ms Galbraith, I'm not going to make a complaint against you,' he said, kissing her stomach.

'No, but I might.'

'Really?'

'Tea and no toast? You're in serious trouble, Mr Adagoke.' They kissed again. Three months later, Nicola moved in with him.

If Julian had believed in portents, he would have understood the afternoon that Nicola arrived with her bags of clothes and her boxes of books, that their relationship would end, and that it would end badly. It began simply enough, with a postcard in an ugly gilt frame.

Nicola was kneeling on the floor folding pullovers in the bedroom when Julian noticed the little picture on the windowsill facing the bed.

'So, this is a framed postcard.' He spoke in a purposeful tone, as if he were itemising evidence of some kind. She looked over at him as he slumped into a blue armchair, one of a pair he had proudly announced when she first visited the house, were designed by Carl-Johan Boman. She'd given him a look at the time that indicated that she didn't know or care who Carl-Johan Boman was.

'Yes, it's Constable actually, *Weymouth Bay.*' Julian took up the frame and held it delicately between his two forefingers. The postcard showed an overcast beach at low tide, two deft smudges revealed themselves to be a couple walking on the sand, in a flick of pink and white paint the woman's dress is seen blowing in the wind coming off the jade water.

'This is an odd thing.' He noticed that some of the gilt had chipped away from the corners of the frame. 'It's the kind of thing you put on a corkboard or a fridge with a magnet souvenir of Toledo or the Scottish Highlands.' She'd become aware of the flirtatiously cruel ways in which they'd often talk, and how this was cloudily linked to the sex they shared. But she also sensed, correctly, that flirtatious cruelty could very easily flip into real cruelty in an instant.

'You think so, do you? Do you not remember it? It was on my bedside table back at the flat in Kenninghall Road. Did you never notice?'

'I did not,' he lied. 'I suppose I was noticing other things.' His mouth pushed up into a one-sided grin.

'Constable painted that sketch when he was on his honeymoon in 1816. My grandmother bought it for me on an outing to the V&A when I was ten.'

'How sweet. Looks like a pretty glum honeymoon though.' He replaced it carefully on the windowsill. 'We should find a spot for it.'

'Actually, I've found a spot for it. I'd like it to stay there.' She stood with a bundle of jumpers and walked out of the room. The wind shifted about the branches of the trees outside and the sun coming into the room moved the shadows around. And for a minute or so, Julian was left alone staring at the newlyweds on that saturated, gloomy beach, walking away into their future.

In the beginning there was love, consideration, sex and affection. Theirs was such a polite and sexually charged seduction, played out by two people who looked and talked just like Nicola and Julian. They were witty, intelligent, clear-eyed and successful. They cut a stylish silhouette in the pages of *The Times*, *The Guardian* and *Tatler*. She was characterised as a millennial bohemian professional who had a sharp opinion on most things, whose slightly shabby clothes always looked elegant on her tall, gangly frame. He was older. His face, although once boyishly handsome had matured in his mid-forties. He looked appealingly worn and a little rakish. In the beginning, whenever they were together there was an air of sexual availability and playfulness between them that they weren't prepared to admit, or just couldn't comprehend, could not possibly be sustained over time. Over time, the real Nicola and Julian did things to each other that were inconsiderate, petty, insensitive or just plain hurtful. Things that no amount of playful sex could paper over.

There was Phoebe, the unwelcome whippet puppy Nicola bought as a surprise birthday present. Phoebe who chewed the armrest of one of Julian's beloved Carl-Johan Bowman armchairs down to the stuffing and who nervously barked at Julian and pissed on the floor regularly whenever their paths crossed in the house.

For her part, Nicola made the fatal error of confusing Julian's work with Julian the man. His prose was characterised by a precise examination of human emotions and frailties, of descriptive passages that held the resonant depth of poetry. She couldn't understand how someone who could describe the effects of sunlight through the fine veins of a tulip petal, or the delicate scent of a sleeping baby's head being like warm vanilla bread, could be the same person who would sulk about losing a pair of green socks, or get testy if he couldn't find just the right pair of Nike trainers in his size.

Then there was the matter of Dora. Two years after the publication of *The Bone Garden*, a Polish version of the book was being translated by an academic from Edinburgh University called, Dora Morrell. Nicola met Dora only once, at a party for the premiere of the film version of the novel. She and Julian stood with six or seven others in a stuffy foyer in Leicester Square drinking terrible wine with Geoffrey Rush, who'd starred in the film. She remembered Dora as a woman in her forties with glamourous streaks of grey in her black hair, laughing too loudly at the actor's anecdotes and jokes and touching his arm, exclaiming, 'Oh, that's priceless, Geoffrey! That's just *too funny!*'

Nicola and Julian both slumped in the back seat of a cab back to Perrymead Street in a cloud of depressed disappointment at the terrible film which neither of them could bring themselves to talk about. Staring out of the window at the people and the traffic and the lights of the city, Nicola realised she was tipsy, maybe a little more than that, perhaps she was drunk.

Lately, she'd thought that one strategy to deal with Julian's increasing moodiness would be to make herself small, disappear a bit in his presence, then somehow the storm could be weathered without her unknowingly making things worse. But an instinctive part of her hated that way of thinking and actively rebelled against it. She felt his distance from her, his silences and indifference seemed designed to provoke a confrontation that he was too weak to declare openly himself. She was drunk. She wanted to drink more. She pretended to yawn. Still staring out of the window, with some effort she made her voice light.

'Who was that fucking dreadful woman pawing at Geoffrey in that way?' Julian was looking down at his phone, she thought he might be tapping out a text message or scrolling through the news. He cleared his throat as if he was surprised that she's spoken, he didn't look at her.

'That fucking dreadful woman is Dora Morrell. She's translating the book into Polish.' There was a silence, then he added, 'I think she's lovely.' Nicola smiled, feeling the heat of tears welling in her eyes. She bounced her head lightly on her headrest and rolled the word 'lovely' around her mouth for the rest of the trip home.

Nicola gauged that the affair with Dora lasted just over four months. There were the phone calls from his study with the door shut. She couldn't work out what he was saying, but she could discern by the pattern of his voice, his tone and his laughter, he was being intimate and warm. She remembered that he sounded that way when they first met. Then there were the regular, essential trips to Edinburgh, where he would phone at the last minute to say that he would be staying over and would be back in the morning. There were the condoms she found in his shaving bag, and an antique edition of George Eliot's *Romola*, which Dora was stupid enough to inscribe with, 'To Julian, for Tuesday with love from D.' The arrangement between them must have shifted after four months because Julian announced one weekend that he would not be going to Edinburgh anymore. He needed to concentrate on his new book. Nicola laughed at him openly when he eventually told her that the book was about the impossibility of intimate relations in the modern world. She concluded that he had decided to stop seeing Dora, or maybe he was meeting her somewhere in London, but by that stage it meant nothing to her.

One Monday afternoon she sat in his kitchen with a large tumbler of red wine. She'd grown tired of being angry with him and finally, she'd grown tired of him. He'd been upstairs in his study writing all afternoon. He walked into the kitchen without acknowledging her. He stood with his back to Nicola as he filled the kettle. She didn't look at him, she talked to her hands as they rotated her glass on the table.

'I thought I'd write you a letter today,' she said. He would not turn to face her.

'And what would you have written in that letter to me?'

She thought for a moment. Phoebe was asleep at her feet, her warm head nuzzled into her instep. She started to speak, slowly, deliberately.

'I would have started by saying how grateful I was that we'd met and how happy I'd been living here with you. I'd have mentioned that I was glad that we came together working on your book and how that book would always remind me of that time. I would tell you that I believed that our relationship was founded on mutual understanding and trust. And that I thought that I could see things in you that others didn't, that you were sometimes misunderstood and that you were able to see past my insecurities and occasional flakiness. I thought that you saw special things in me that no one else was aware of. That you weren't like the terrible young men I was usually drawn to. You were different. I'd tell you that in that regard I was right, you were different, you were actually much worse.' He took two cups from the cupboard and set them down on the bench, he pulled two teabags from a box by the toaster and dropped them into the cups.

'I'd go on to say that I regret not understanding you more, of trying to but failing really, failing in the long run. I regret thinking that things would just work out, but they don't do they? And they haven't. I regret thinking that because I'm younger than you, that you'd love me for that and understand me for it, but you don't, I don't think. Finally, I don't think that you care about that at all. I'd write that I regret being so naïve that I believed that you considered me your equal, but I was never that. Never, really. How could Nicola Galbraith, publicist, meet Julian Adagoke, novelist on equal terms? You pretended that we were equal, then you encouraged me to believe it, until you decided that we weren't, then you decided to … *shed me.* I'd let you know that I feel like a ghost in this house now. You ought to be very sorry, ashamed really, that your cruelty allowed that to happen while I was still under this roof.' He'd turned to look at her. He was leaning against the sink staring at the back of her head as she sat at the table. He could see her hands and the half-inch of wine left in her glass.

'I'd go on to tell you that I judge you poorly for lying to me. For shutting me out and not having the sensitivity to see that I'd risked a lot to move in with you, that the end of this would mean that I would need to start again and that that's hard and painful. It's not nothing. I'm sorry that for at least the next few years, people are going to ask me what you're like, then I'll have to think of you. I know that no one is going to ask you anything about me.' The kettle whistled. She heard Julian filling the cups with boiling water. He pulled a drawer open and rummaged around for a spoon. He took some milk from the fridge.

'I'd write that I judge you very badly over your deceit and weakness in relation to Dora – I'd let you know clearly that I don't judge Dora at all, that I genuinely feel sad for her, and for me, especially for me, and finally for you because this is going to happen again and again and again.'

She heard the clink of the spoon in the cups. He set one cup down in front of Nicola, scraping a chair back to sit in front of her at the table, he clasped his hot cup in his hands. She was grateful for the wine, it had given her a clarity and a reckless bravery. Her tone changed from her imagined letter, now she spoke to him directly.

'It will happen again, but it won't be happening with me. Not anymore.' She drained her glass and put it back on the table. He considered his cup.

'I don't really know what this is all about.'

'Oh, my darling man. You really don't, do you?'

'What do you want me to say?'

She shifted in her chair and looked down at Phoebe who had woken with a noisy yawn.

'Nothing.' She turned to face him. 'At this stage, nothing at all.' They sat for a moment in silence, then Julian got up from the table.

'Don't let that tea stand, Nicola. It'll go cold.' Then he walked upstairs. For almost all of the next day Julian was away from the house, in the city discussing some new chapters he had submitted to his editor. By the time he returned home, almost every trace of Nicola Galbraith was gone from Perrymead Street.

It was now just after 7 pm. It was colder. He pulled his jacket around him and hunched down into it, his little bunch of forget-me-nots sticking out of his pocket. He made his way toward the amber glow of Waterstones as the slow evening traffic moved along the street. He felt a shiver go through him. Nicola's text messages had unnerved him. He hoped that she was alright, but mostly he hoped that she would just go away. *Go away, go away, go away* is what he found himself repeating in his head as Beau Fuller, the publicist for his new book emerged from the small crowd milling about the doors to the bookstore.

'Julian! Hi! You made it, hahaha, do you want to come through? It's a great turnout.' Beau had the habit of laughing nervously whenever they met. Julian had tried a variety of methods to put Beau at ease, but nothing seemed to work. Now he just affected a slightly annoyed and distracted demeanour whenever they had to speak.

'Hello Beau, is Janet here?' Janet Fraser was hosting the evening for Waterstones. She and Julian had met at the University of East Anglia, where she had tutored him in creative writing for ten months, until he dropped out. At the time she considered him a poor student who was self-consciously withdrawn and who could not adhere to any kind of deadline. He would drop into her office unannounced and talk to her about his life, about his Nigerian grandparents and his father's aspiration for him to become a dentist. Sometimes he talked about James Baldwin, Maya Angelou, Martin Amis, Ian McEwan and literature more generally, but she never believed that he had the capacity to write any of his own. She found him intelligent, sensitive and mildly arrogant, but she thought him too timid, finally, to ever actually produce anything. The afternoon he left he went to see her to let her know that he wouldn't be returning. He wanted to thank her for her patience with him. She'd asked him what he planned to do and he looked at her seriously, taking some moments to answer. 'I'm going to write of course.' This, she felt was unlikely. A year and a half later he sent her an advance copy of *The Clarence Road Fire.* When she opened it she was shocked to see that the book was dedicated to her, *To Janet, for her guidance.* They stayed in contact. She was now in her seventies and retired from the university. For the last five years she had hosted a weekly books podcast concentrating on classics of English literature called *Between the Covers* for BBC4 that Julian had appeared on from time to time.

Beau looked momentarily confused. 'Oh, Janet! Haha, yes I think she's upstairs in the café. I'll let her know that you're here.' Julian stood with his back against one of the bookshelves looking at the mainly middle-aged and elderly crowd. No one seemed to recognise him. The photograph they had used to advertise the evening, the same one that was on the back cover of his novel, was at least five years old. His close-cropped hair had greyed slightly at the temples, and his features had slackened in the intervening period. He saw that tables of books had been moved to the side of the store and there were already about thirty to forty people seated in front of two chairs and a small table with a carafe of water and two glasses.

'Hello again!' Julian looked down to see the woman who had sold him the flowers. She'd adjusted the chopsticks in her hair to sit more centrally, and she wore an oversized charcoal tweed coat with a badge on the lapel that read, 'Bollocks to Brexit'.

'Do you know when this is starting?' she said.

'Seven-thirty, I think.'

'Oh good, in a few minutes!' She stood beside him nodding to someone in the crowd she had recognised, she waved in a hurried motion mouthing, *Hello.* 'Yes, I'm not really a fan of his stuff at all. I've just popped in to get warm, it looked like rain outside. They do this quite regularly, you know. They had Anne Enright here last month, did you see her? She was marvellous.'

Beau appeared, breathless. 'I tracked her down.'

'Julian, how are you?' Janet kissed him on the cheek.

'Good Janet. It's lovely to see you. These are for you.' He handed her the flowers, her hands, heavily roped with blue veins clutched the posy close to her chest.

'Oh thank you, scorpion grass, aren't they sweet!' Beau was standing between them awkwardly. 'I think they're keen for us to get going.'

As they sat in their chairs, Janet said, almost offhandedly, 'Isn't it odd about Gideon Bannerman?' He only managed to say, 'What?' before she took up her microphone and addressed the crowd.

'Hello everyone. I think we shall get started. My name is Janet Fraser and I'd like to welcome you to this evening's discussion and Q&A with Julian Adagoke. Julian burst onto the literary scene, I'd say fully formed with his much-acclaimed debut novel, *The Clarence Road Fire* which was shortlisted for both the Booker and the Bannerman prizes for literature and turned into a highly successful, award-winning film. Since then Julian has written numerous novels and screenplays and his ninth novel, *The Broken Tooth Upstairs* has recently been shortlisted for the Bannerman Prize for Literature. It's with some concern that we note that the Metropolitan Police just this evening have issued a missing persons appeal for Gideon Bannerman who, it's understood was last seen two weeks ago. This is obviously a matter of some serious concern, and I'm sure I speak for everyone when I say I hope Mr Bannerman, this champion of literature is found safe and sound, and very soon too. I'm sure he would want us to proceed in discussing and celebrating one of this year's most interesting shortlisted books and its author. Join me in welcoming, Julian Adagoke.' There was a generous round of applause as Julian adjusted his pose in the chair.

'Now Julian, your last book, *The Bone Garden,* which was turned into an acclaimed film –'

'Oh let's not mention the film, Janet.' There was some laughter at this.

'Okay, well, *The Bone Garden*, the *novel* took us into the dirtied, corrupted heart of Victorian London on the brink of the industrial revolution. It was part thriller, part social history and part revenge tragedy. You constructed that world so completely it read like contemporary nineteenth-century reportage. Now your ever-restless creativity has delivered us *The Broken Tooth Upstairs* – an epistolary novel entirely comprised of telephone text messages, something that could only have been conceived in this way in the twenty-first century. For those of you who haven't read it, the story describes the complete trajectory of a relationship between Phillip, a highly celebrated and respected journalist and Gemma, an arts graduate from Portsmouth, from their first meeting, until the end of their union, some eighteen months later, and Phillip's subsequent mental breakdown on the tube to North Clapham. Other characters are part of this story, there's Abigail, the hypercritical best friend to Gemma, there's Dara, a Nigerian tele-journalist working for Al Jazeera with whom Phillip has an affair, and then there's Misty, the whippet hound given to Phillip by Gemma, a puppy who emerges as a very important figure late into the plot. The novel starts with a simple greeting, 'Hello you!' and as the story progresses it runs the gamut of emotions, from lust, joy, excitement, love, familiarity, indifference, boredom, anger, disgust, contempt and finally sadness. It's complex, it's tragic, it's voyeuristic, multi-layered and above all, intensely human. My first question to you Julian, is why did you want to write this story, the story of an intimate relationship, in this particular way?'

The event was unremarkable. Until the end. After more discussion, a couple of readings from the book and some odd questions from the audience Janet was wrapping things up. She sat forward in her chair, holding Julian's novel in her hands.

'Before we finish, could I just ask you to read from the last few pages of the novel. It's no plot spoiler to say that the relationship between Phillip and Gemma ends badly, but that's not the point, I think. I believe that the real achievement of this book is that in spite of the fact that the communication between these people is truncated by the very technology that enables it, and that it is littered with misunderstandings and lost opportunities, somehow the humanity of these people is preserved and burns through the seemingly endless messaging. If you would Julian, could you read one of Gemma's final messages to Phillip?'

'Yes, I'd be happy to. As Janet said, this comes toward the end of the novel, it's not quite their last exchange, but it is near the end.' He took the book from Janet, relaxed back into his chair and began to read.

'I'm texting you this because I want you to have it – so that it's set down and it won't be lost – of course you could delete it – and in that way delete me from your life but what we shared was real and you can't erase it – so let these words stand – I believed that our relationship was founded on mutual understanding and trust – I thought that I could see things in you that others didn't – that you were sometimes misunderstood and that you were able to see past my insecurities and occasional flakiness – I thought that you saw special things in me that no one else was aware of – that you weren't like the terrible young men I was usually drawn to – you were different – in that regard I was right – you were different – you were actually much worse – I'm sorry I never really understood you – I suppose I thought what we had was strong enough that things would just work out – but things don't just work out do they? Our connection was so strong I didn't believe – when it started to happen – that you could just lose interest in me – it was slow and subtle and cruel because you never once acknowledged it – and then it was complete – you just shed me – it was as if I wasn't there anymore – like I was some spooky presence you were living with – a hazy memory – you'll think this is because of your shabby weekends with Dara but you'd be wrong – I actually like Dara and I feel sorry for her but mostly I feel sorry for myself – and sorry for you because this is going to happen again Phillip – just not with me.'

'Phillip replies, I don't understand any of this – what do you want me to say?

'Nothing – at this stage, nothing at all.'

Janet smiled at Julian, then turned toward the audience. 'And that's where we'll leave them, Julian is going to sign some books now, but please join me in thanking him for spending this time with us.'

More applause. Some people stood, shrugging into coats, adjusting scarves and hats. A loose line of about fifteen people stood to get books signed. Julian was well practised at this. He enjoyed meeting readers but tonight something was off. Nicola's messages had triggered in him the now worrisome, familiar feeling that he was somehow little more than a lucky fraud. He thought notions of a 'mid-life crisis' were stupid. He was fifty-two, he was hardly going to live to be a hundred and four, but something in him had changed. It was as if Nicola had left him with a sobering virus that had seeded into every hidden corner of his self. He watched as Beau made his way down the queue, affixing

Post-it notes to the covers of each book to be signed, with the names written in large block letters. Julian managed to suppress his anxiety by making himself smile, and by finding something brief to say to each person as they held out their books to be signed.

There was Owen with the untidy grey hair and a bandage across one ear. 'Thank you for the talk. *The Clarence Road Fire* is one of my favourite films.'

'Didn't they do a great job?'

Beth, who wore an alpaca poncho and who held five other well-thumbed novels for Julian to sign. 'I hated what they did to *The Bone Garden,* the film I mean. Who does Geoffrey Rush think he is?'

'I really couldn't tell you, Beth,' he said, handing her back a battered copy of Zadie Smith's *White Teeth* that had made it into her pile.

Tall, serious Heather with the dangly amber earrings and the long scarf looped loosely around her neck, leaning in, lowering her voice to a whisper. 'You know, I got dumped by text once. I ended up in therapy for two years. I've only now just gotten over it. I'm stronger now.'

'Oh, I'm so pleased for you.'

Tightly wound Marion in the aqua leggings and the red puffer jacket. 'I'm buying this for my sister. Her name's Christabel. She's at Cambridge doing gender. Do you think she'll like it?'

'Here's hoping, eh?'

Muscular Imari in a herringbone three-piece suit. Gripping Julian's hand tightly so his knuckles compressed, cracking painfully. 'Mr Julian Adagoke, brother, your novel *Intimate Histories* is the story of my life.'

'Really? I'm so glad you connected with it.'

'I hated it.' Adding mysteriously, 'It was too soon, *too soon!* I'm going to give this one a go – don't disappoint me!'

'I've done my best.'

The final person was heavy set with a glassy faraway look in her eyes, wearing a pleated tartan skirt and a long cardigan. Julian had the vague idea that he recognised her, but couldn't quite place how or why. As she approached with a hardback copy of the book, she held it before her, horizontally as if it were a little tea tray. She walked directly to him, but when she was about three feet away she stumbled. She tripped forward and the book slid out of her hands in a straight line to Julian's face as he sat in the chair.

There would have been less than a second between the book leaving the hands of the woman, and the spine of the hardback hitting his nose. In that split second, before the impact, and the blinding white-hot pain, the blood, and the shattered maxillary and nasal bones, Julian experienced the momentary relief and mini-joy of remembering who the woman in front of him was. He even managed a half-formed look of rehearsed, delighted surprise, just before the book smacked him in the face. A little heavier, and a little greyer, it was Miriam, Nicola's old flatmate and confidante. From that evening forward she would insist that it was an accident. She would say that she barely knew Mr Adagoke and that she certainly bore him no ill will. Even the security footage from the store showed that Miriam appeared to trip.

His sinuses never really fully recovered. For years afterward, at odd times when he would breathe he would hear the tiniest whistle deep in his nasal cavity. All sorts of shames and regrets were contained in that little sound that he could never quite get out of his head.

7.30 pm, Kensington Police Station W8 6EQ

After the ordeal of the television cameras and the public appeal for information, Tasha was ushered into another anonymous room at the police station. She thought there must be hundreds of rooms like this all over the country. Cheap blue tables, plastic chairs, a whiteboard and fluorescent lighting. Rooms where all the troubles, sorrows and griefs of people were known. She hadn't been able to shake Detective Sergeant Donald Timewell, if anything, given she had returned to the station a number of times over the course of the last few weeks, he had annoyingly affected a kind of familiarity with her that she sought to repel at every turn. He was joined tonight by two other detectives, a young woman with thick-framed glasses and thin brown hair whose head seemed to be on a permanent tilt to the left until, half an hour into this meeting she suddenly tilted it to the right at precisely the opposite angle. Tasha thought it must be a habit of concentration formed years ago when this woman was a child. She was with a middle-aged man who looked like he had just walked off the set of *Silent Witness* or *Taggart.* Overweight, pale and worn, with tiny, kind eyes set in a deep furrow under his brow. Tasha immediately understood that these people were a different rank to Timewell, but she didn't know how. There were some random pieces of paper on the table that the sergeant scooped up as they entered.

'Now, Miss Moubray, Natasha, would you like some tea? Coffee?' He motioned to a chair.

'No, thank you.' She sat at the table as the others faced her.

'Right then. This is Zoe Gardiner. She's a forensic accountant from the Special Crimes Unit, and this is Chief Inspector Peter Dreyer who is part of the team here at Kensington.' Zoe Gardiner smiled at Tasha as she took an iPad from her bag and opened it. Inspector Dreyer kept a steady eye on Tasha as he started to speak.

'I read from the reports that have been lodged, that over the course of the investigation into Mr Bannerman's disappearance, you've voiced concerns about his husband, his ex-husband as it turns out, Yuri Kuznetsov, and I'd like to assure you that we have taken those concerns very seriously.' He had a large blue bound notebook in front of him which he opened and referred to from time to time. 'Before I pass over to Miss Gardiner, I'd like to let you know where we're up to with that line of enquiry, the one related to Mr Kuznetsov.' Despite the cold brightness of the light, Tasha felt that there was a shabby gloom dormant in the room. She felt slightly anxious and jumpy. The thought dropped into her head that this is what it must feel like just before psychiatric professionals announce that you are going to be sectioned. *Now we don't want any trouble, this is for your own good.* She wilfully shook this off.

'What have you found out about, Yuri?'

'Well, you had said that you thought he was in Turkey.'

'To the best of my knowledge, that's where he was, yes.'

'You were right. He is in Turkey. Our team has been in touch with him and he is just as concerned about where Mr Bannerman might be as you are. He has even offered to post a reward for information that might lead to him being found.' He waited to see what effect this news would have on Tasha. She stared back at him. She waited.

'We have had a look at Mr Kuznetsov's movements and dealings over the past year and that has led us to rule him out as a person of interest in this enquiry.'

'His movements and dealings?'

'Yes. He's been very cooperative. He's been domiciled in Turkey for the past year, that's where his business is headquartered. He has travelled regularly to Russia, Belgrade, Poland and the Ukraine, but he has not entered the UK in that time.' Tasha sat heavily in her chair, her walking stick was leaning against her side. She felt tired and hollow, exhausted by her anger, induced by being patronised by well-meaning professionals.

'Are you sure you wouldn't like a drink? Some water perhaps?' Timewell asked.

'I'm quite sure, thank you. Just out of interest. How much money has Yuri offered to put up as a reward?'

Dreyer looked down at his notes. 'Fifty thousand pounds.'

'I see.'

Dreyer took three fuzzy CCTV images from his folder and laid them out neatly in front of Tasha. It was unmistakable. They were of Gideon. She could feel her heart beating, she could feel her pulse reddening her face.

'These are the last CCTV images we have of Mr Bannerman.' He tapped each picture as he spoke. 'He walks down Old Brompton Road. He goes into a Pret a Manger and buys a ham and salad sandwich and a can of Coca-Cola – we know this from his credit card record – he leaves his credit card in the machine at the Pret and then, here he is walking into South Kensington tube station. His credit card was used again later that night, but this was picked up as fraudulent – some headphones and trainers and there was an attempt to draw some cash, the card was retained at a cash point in Covent Garden. There has been no activity recorded on any of his accounts since that evening.'

Tasha was lost in the blurry images of her friend. The familiar beige overcoat, the maroon cashmere scarf and his thinning grey hair, blown untidy in the breeze. She could see the fingers of his left hand pulling his coat together at the front. Dreyer looked at Tasha staring at the pictures.

'Would you like to take a break? Are you okay Ms Moubray?'

'I'm perfectly fine thank you.'

'Okay, well please let us know if you would like to stop at any time. Now, Zoe?'

'Miss Moubray, I know this must be upsetting so I'll keep this as brief as possible. Are you aware at all how Mr Bannerman's finances were arranged?'

Tasha crossed her arms. 'I really don't at all. I know there is a trust connected to the Bannerman Prize, and that that has been in place since the beginning, in the fifties, but apart from that, I have no idea at all.'

Zoe looped her hair behind her ears as she consulted her iPad. 'Well, it was all rather complicated. Mr Bannerman has a number of London properties, the house in Princes Gate, Harvest Place, and other commercial properties, then there's a house in Suffolk and a large parcel of land attached to that, and an extensive share portfolio and of course, the trust that finances the Bannerman Prize. His general holdings, together with cash and assets, amount to approximately one hundred and eighty million pounds.'

'You see, I have no idea of any of that. Gideon and I had no cause to discuss money or his affairs at all.'

Dreyer turned a page of his notebook. 'According to records, Mr Bannerman divorced Mr Kuznetsov two and a half years ago.'

'Yes, that's correct. They are no longer together.'

Zoe looked back at her screen. 'So, you would have no way of knowing that eighteen months ago, almost a year after their divorce that Mr Bannerman signed control of his holdings to Mr Kuznetsov through his company, it's called ...' She scrolled down her screen. Tasha's mouth was completely dry, with some effort she managed to speak.

'Caxap Holdings,' she said.

'Yes. That's it. You know about this?' Zoe asked.

'Only that Caxap Holdings consigned the contents of Harvest

Place to Bromleys for an auction in a few weeks. Forgive me, but can anything be *done* about this?'

Timewell slumped back in his chair and looked to Dreyer to deliver the bad news. 'It's all completely legal. There are emails to his lawyers that prove that this is all in accordance with the express wishes of Mr Bannerman.'

'We have copies of everything,' Timewell added. Tasha refused to look at him. She realised that each time they met, her hatred of him gathered new subtleties.

'So, just so that I'm clear here. What you're telling me is that Gideon, a full year after he was finally rid of Yuri Kuznetsov, signed his entire holdings over to Yuri Kuznetsov to be controlled by Yuri Kuznetsov through the Caxap company. And does Caxap also control the trust for the prize?' Tasha was aware of the stupidity of the question as she asked it.

Zoe looked up from her screen. 'Yes. According to the records, Caxap controls every aspect of Mr Bannerman's portfolios. But the trust for the Bannerman Prize is protected in the arrangement. It will continue. There have been regular quarterly deposits into Mr Bannerman's account since this arrangement has been in place. It's in the form of a percentage payment, an allowance if you like.'

'An allowance with no control.' Tasha said.

Peter Dreyer leaned forward on the table. 'Mr Bannerman ceded control to Mr Kuznetsov. He signed the documents. It was entirely his arrangement.'

Tasha ignored Dreyer and spoke directly to Zoe. 'What percentage is the allowance payment to Mr Bannerman as part of this *arrangement?*'

'Well, from what I can see, it appears to be two per cent.'

Tasha put her hand to her forehead. She felt cold, and there was an ache of hunger in her stomach. She decided to speak calmly, she knew that her voice could betray no anger.

'So, Gideon Bannerman goes missing four weeks ago. As far as we know, he has no money and his last known meal was a ham and salad sandwich and a can of soft drink. We now find that for the last eighteen months his ex-husband has been controlling his estate and allowing him a monthly pittance. My question is, does anyone in this room consider that these events might be *related?*' She looked to the three of them. Dreyer responded.

'I suppose my question to you, Ms Moubray, is in what way would they be related? There is no advantage to Mr Kuznetsov in the disappearance of Mr Bannerman. Mr Kuznetsov already has the advantage established. Notarised. Signed and legal. By Mr Bannerman's own hand.'

'Can I ask where the two per cent allowance goes if Gideon is never found?'

'After seven years, if there is no evidence that Mr Bannerman is still alive then that two per cent, estimated currently to be in the order of three hundred and sixty thousand pounds per annum, would go back to the estate under the control of Mr Kuznetsov, there being no will that we have found that would determine otherwise,' said Zoe.

There was a full minute where no one said anything. Dreyer then spoke. His tone was warmer.

'We know how difficult this is. We are following every credible lead. We have the full cooperation of Mr Kuznetsov, and you of course Ms Moubray. We will continue to take every appropriate and proportionate action to find your friend, until such time that we do find him, or find out what has happened to him.'

Tasha looked to each person in the room. She looked at the folders on the table, then she focused on Timewell's name badge. She desperately needed food and drink and a place far from this room. She rose to her feet, speaking almost to herself. 'Yes I know, *I know*. I've been hearing those words for weeks now. How can a man wander the streets, buy a sandwich and a drink and then be swallowed by London, never to be seen or heard from again? Can you please tell me that?'

Dreyer stood. 'Before you go, I think you need to consider at least one more possibility.'

'Gideon would never harm himself. I know that much, detective.'

He held the door for her. 'Perhaps not. But you must understand that he may not want to be found, by you or by anyone. You need to remember that as an adult, Mr Bannerman has a legal right to disappear.'

'Thank you. I am aware of that, Mr Dreyer. And you need to remember that I have a legal right to your assistance in finding him.'

11.45 pm, Tavistock Square WC 1H 9RD

She paces the wet pavement that borders Tavistock Square. She is near home, but she doesn't want to go home. She has eaten a bowl of pasta and drunk five glasses of red wine. She stops. She leans on the iron railings that enclose the square. She is beyond exhaustion. '*He may not want to be found. By you or by anyone.*' The alcohol has left her feeling light, almost transparent as her hands grip the metal bars of the fence. The trees and the bushes are wet with rain, tiny drops shimmer and fall to the ground. A gentle sprinkle on her head and face as a breeze moves around the square. She knows these gardens well. She's walked these paths for over fifty years. She knows its hedges and trees, the hawthorns, field maples and plum trees. She sees the bronze of Gandhi solemnly sitting in the lotus position on top of his pedestal of Portland stone in the middle of the square. Then the little bust of Virginia Woolf on the far side of the garden. Both are telling her the same thing. The wet paths and the green velvet grass and the bare spindles of the cherry blossom planted for the dead at Hiroshima are telling her too.

'*You will never see Gideon Bannerman again.*
Never.
He doesn't want to be found.
By you or by anyone.'

She waits. A young woman in a black hijab and a scruffy tan trench coat passes her, she looks at the old woman holding the cane with concern and then she looks away, then walks on to stand and wait at the bus stop.

She doesn't remember walking home, putting her key in the lock or making her way to her bed. She sleeps. She dreams of Gideon at fourteen. Her new friend in his new, stiffened evening clothes, her in an apricot frilly dress and diamante ladybird hair clips. Far-off there is music, there is a crowd and laughter. He looks at her, and through her and he says, *I wish you wouldn't call me Gideon Bannerman all the time. It seems like you're blaming me for something.*

She sees the tattoos etched into Yuri's flesh, the crosses, the skulls, the snakes, the guns, the bear and a knife, then she sees his black eyes. And then she wakes in the white light of the morning and remembers none of it.

COMMONWEALTH BASTARD

Catherine Adler (New Holland) 508pp
April Holman, a young schoolteacher is chosen to
have lunch with Her Majesty Queen Elizabeth during
her first Commonwealth Tour to Australia in 1954.
That afternoon meeting will ultimately leave April
without a home, without a family and finally, without
a country.

2 pm, Broadcasting House, BBC, Portland Place W1A 1AA

'This is the BBC. Hello and welcome to *Bookmarks*, my name is
Yvonne Larwell. This week we hear from Australian writer Catherine
Adler whose new novel, *Commonwealth Bastard* has been shortlisted
for this year's Bannerman Prize. The book examines the troubled
legacy of colonialism, cultural displacement and British cultural
dominance through the eyes of April Holman, a young English
teacher who is chosen, from over a thousand other candidates, to have
lunch with Queen Elizabeth during her first visit to Australia in 1954.
This is the story of a set of historical fictions reinforced as historical
facts and the price that is paid when cultures are erased.

The story begins at lunch on board the Royal Yacht *Gothic*, during
a stifling afternoon on Sydney Harbour, and I wonder Catherine, if

you could read for us from the opening pages of your book?' Catherine adjusted her glasses slightly.

'It was the whitest skin she'd ever seen. Somehow, her pictures in magazines showed her to be pink, but she wasn't pink at all. April decided that her skin was paler than that, she felt finally, that it had the polished sheen of ivory. Her Majesty first appeared to her as a silhouette, standing in the dining saloon, backlit by a window overlooking the sparkle of the harbour. Her tiny frame standing in a beautifully cut Norman Hartnell floral chiffon that floated around her knees. She wore no make-up, or none that April could discern apart from some crimson lipstick so artfully applied that it didn't appear to move during the three courses of lunch, or the coffee or the drinks that were served before and after the meal.

'April stood, as did the other guests, the generals, the admirals, a famous swimmer and a jockey, all waiting for the Queen to take her seat at the table. As the strange vision sat, she took up her napkin from beside her plate and set it on her lap. These brief seconds allowed April to look at the Queen in an unguarded way. Yes, it was the Queen and yet, at the same time it was not. She was alive. Less than five feet from her. Her Majesty's face was broad and smiling. The tiny pearl earrings she wore matched the double rope of pearls around her neck. Her eyes were a shock. There was a hardness about their blue dazzle as they shifted about the table. April opened her handbag, looking for nothing, terrified that the Queen would speak to her. She'd studied the protocol document that she'd been sent weeks beforehand. In it, the Queen was referred to as 'Elizabeth the Second, by the Grace of God of the United Kingdom of Great Britain and Northern Ireland and Her other Realms and Territories. Queen, Head of the Commonwealth, Defender of the Faith.' April snapped her handbag shut and looked up to find that the impossible face, framed with perfectly coiffed auburn hair was actually looking directly at her. Her heart jumped. Her mouth was dry and her eyes widened. At that point the Queen opened her mouth, and the sound of her voice broke the spell.

'At last we're sitting down. I'm ravenous. Gin always sharpens one's appetite, I find,' she said in a flat nasal whine. April's lips parted, but there was no sound. She swallowed. Finally, she was able to speak.

'Your Majesty ...'

'Oh no, you've done that bit, when you were presented, do you remember? Now it's just 'ma'am' as in 'ham'. You're Miss Holman aren't you? April, is it?'

'Yes ma'am, that's right.' April was startled that she'd remembered her name.

'I'm so pleased to meet you. I know a May and a June, and now an April. How *awfully* funny.' April managed to smile. A heavy china plate was set down before the Queen by a member of the Royal household wearing white gloves.

'Ah! Smoked salmon. Oh yummy, do tuck in.'

April lifted her fork, it was the heaviest cutlery she'd ever held. She cut a portion of the pink flesh and put it into her mouth and was only mildly surprised on this astonishing afternoon to find that the fish was chilled. She noticed that the Queen ate quickly. She'd finished her salmon while April was barely halfway through hers. The Queen's plate was cleared, and so was April's unfinished entrée along with all the other plates at the table in readiness for the next course.

'I understand that you and I are the same age, twenty-seven!' Each clipped sentence the Queen spoke seemed to conclude with a bright ambiguous exclamation mark. It was either an invitation to shut up or an invitation to further conversation. April considered the latter course, carefully.

'That's right ma'am, I'm twenty-seven.'

'And an English teacher. Remarkable. You're awfully lucky to live in such a beautiful climate. I was telling my husband only this morning how very like Malta it is. Lovely and warm. Have you been?'

'To Malta? No ma'am, I haven't. I've never actually left New South Wales. But yes, you're right, it is very warm at the moment.' April felt a single trickle of sweat run from her underarm to her elbow.

'I expect I shall see more of Australia than you have. In sixty days I'm visiting fifty-eight towns.'

'That is a lot.'

The Queen sat back in her chair, smoothing out the napkin on her lap. 'This country has achieved so much in less than two hundred years. With industry, infrastructure and culture. Prince Phillip and I were at the ballet last night and saw the *Corroboree,* all the dancers dressed up as aborigines performing a native dance. It was marvellous. So evocative. Have you seen it?' April could feel beads of sweat breaking out across her brow as she replied.

'Er, no ma'am, I haven't seen it.' There was a brief pause

as the Queen turned toward the open doors at the end of the saloon where the staff had emerged with the food. April heard herself saying, 'Actually Ma'am, the culture in Australia is much older than two hundred years – it goes back thousands and thousands of years. Before time was even recorded.'

The Queen was staring back at her with the slightest smile. Her eyes were still. The icy blue, amethyst and cerulean of her irises seemed engaged in some inner calculation. Another plate was set in front of her. Her gaze remained steady, her head did not move.

'Ah April, *Tournedos Rossini,* look at this lovely red meat!' The Queen took up her knife. 'Now, weren't you saying something interesting about *time?* Remind me.' What followed was the noisy clatter of silverware on china.'

'Thank you, Catherine, and congratulations on being shortlisted for the Bannerman. I think even in those opening passages we can sense the unease in your story and the idea that things might not go well for April, your young protagonist. But I suppose nothing really prepares the reader for her journey into madness and the savage critique of the Commonwealth and what England has come to symbolise in Australia that follows. Why do you think that this story is important to tell now?'

It was a simple enough question, but Catherine took a moment to answer. She'd been awake for fifty hours. Her body had gone beyond exhaustion to inhabit another space entirely. Her take on the world was no longer a solid thing. Everything around her seemed to be insubstantial. Her psyche was mangled by the compound effects of sleep deprivation, chronic jet lag and menopause. She'd boarded the plane in Melbourne, resigned to the twenty-six hour journey across the world. Never a good sleeper, she hadn't slept at all the night before she left, and even though she'd never managed to sleep on a plane in the past, she entertained a fantasy that she'd sleep soundly on the flight. She'd packed Valium, temazepam and Julian Adagoke's *The Broken Tooth Upstairs,* a novel that simultaneously annoyed and bored her. She'd known Julian for years – they'd struck up a casual friendship after repeatedly meeting at book fairs and literary festivals. She would be meeting him in London, but on this flight she hoped the book would put her to sleep, as it had done every time she attempted to read it. So far, she'd made it to page twenty-three.

But once she was seated by the window in the cabin she read an article in *The Times Literary Supplement* about the Bannerman shortlist and decided that nearly every book listed was better than her own and that she had no chance of winning. Her book was described as, 'A disquieting account of identity theft, not of an individual but of a nation.'

There were tiny thumbnail pictures of the authors to accompany the article. Catherine's own, taken some six years ago made her look deceptively cheerful. In the photograph her mouth had twisted into a cheeky upturned grin and her blonde bob, now almost entirely grey and shedding at an alarming rate, shone in the sunshine. Her eyebrows were slightly raised, and her pale green eyes looked intelligent and lively. She knew some of her fellow long-listed authors and their own pictures looked like carefully manicured fibs as well. There was Martin Gillray looking benevolent against a stone wall, the debut novelist Isobel Dalby looked like an uncooperative adolescent, and Julian's picture must have been at least a decade old. She stuffed the magazine into the seat pocket and crossed the globe watching a succession of films that bled into each other in the manufactured twilight of the cabin. Idly she'd scribbled the titles on her boarding pass, but as she stood woozily in the lounge of Dubai airport during the stopover she couldn't recall seeing one of them. Had she really watched *The English Patient, Out of Africa, The Talented Mr. Ripley, Shadow of a Doubt, La Dolce Vita, Last Tango in Paris* on the in-flight classics channel, together with two episodes of *Breaking Bad*? She remembered sobbing fat ridiculous tears at one point but she couldn't remember why.

Sitting in the lounge, nibbling at a pile of pickled vegetables and sipping warm orange juice, she saw on the oversized television mounted on the wall a news item from CNN, the headline running across the bottom of the screen reading, 'HEIR TO BANNERMAN MILLIONS IS MISSING'. The sound was off but the video showed a group of people at a long table, it looked like Natasha Moubray was speaking, there was an inset picture of Gideon Bannerman on the screen. Before she could properly focus on it, the piece was over, replaced by footage of a tennis match. By the time her flight was called she believed that she had imagined it.

She reboarded the flight at 3 am in a mechanised daze. She endured the rest of the journey eating the dreadful food, staring out of the window down at the undulating folds of the mountains and the occasional distant glitter of cities and towns. Long journeys always inspired fantasies of catastrophe in her. She imagined being sucked out of the aluminium and plastic cabin, the shock of the cold, her freefall flight through ice crystals and the deafening rush of the winds in her head. She was hot, she was cold, and she wondered where her body would be kept if she died in her seat. She imagined her sister, Thea, who had a family and a life in London being notified by the police. How her grief would immediately be turned to stoic practicalities. *'Catherine? Dead? Where is she?'* She imagined her sister identifying her body in these black leggings, compression socks and oversized mustard-coloured dress. She'd hold her cold hand and say, *'Yes, that's Catherine, that's her, my sister. Is there a form I need to sign?'* The drone of the engines combined with her exhaustion, scrambled memories of herself and her sister and their life together.

Catherine was born seven years after her sister. Her mother always described her grinningly as a 'happy accident', a 'joyous mistake', a 'beloved miracle'. As for Thea, even at seven years old, as she peered into the bassinet at the pink, glowing bundle that was her baby sister, she felt a kind of glum resignation. Just as she was leaving infancy and entering childhood with all its newly minted uncertainties, excitements and mysteries, she was faced with Catherine. Swaddled in a woolly rug, her tiny legs kicking, her fists punching the air, her small, glassy eyes blinking attentively at her, shining with the freshness of a perpetual rival.

Their father drifted away from the family when Thea reached her teens. At fifty-five years old, at a time when some men start to dye their hair, wear chunky silver neck chains and gain comfort from expensive soul mates half their age, their father developed a passion for beekeeping and retired to the southern coast of Tasmania.

Their mother had been a runner-up Miss Australia in 1960. During the competition she was asked what personal achievement made her most proud, she flashed a dazzling smile and replied, 'My hair!' She barely seemed to register her husband's departure, settling into a life of mild resentments, bitterness and competitive amateur golf. Thea and Catherine grew up experiencing a kind of benign neglect from their parents. Their age difference made shared interests difficult. So, it wasn't until Thea was in her early twenties and Catherine in her teens that they began to share the secret lives of sisters. They painted each other's faces, shared confidences about their changed bodies and charted each other's attachments.

A Polaroid was taken at this time at a swimming pool in suburban Brighton. The photograph's deeply etched colours show Catherine and Thea together, their angular shoulders stippled with goosebumps, hunched forward so their shining faces can get closer to the camera. Both are wearing stringy orange bikini tops and thin silver chains around their necks from which dangle zodiac symbols, Aries for Catherine, Aquarius for Thea. Their wet hair is plastered across their brows. The children they were are still present in their expressions. Thea's mouth is open in a sunshine smile, Catherine's tight-lipped sly grin and sideways shadowy glance shows she's smart and a little shy.

Another picture, taken eighteen months later at a barbeque to celebrate Thea's graduation from medical school tells a different story. In the photograph Catherine is quite close to the camera, her face dominates the frame. Unsmiling, her mouth, in a tight grin clamps a cigarette, more as a defiant joke than as a habit this sunny afternoon. Several strands of her light blonde hair are swept across her face by the breeze, her nose is lightly freckled, her green eyes stare straight ahead with the confident gaze of someone with a hungry curiosity about the world and how it works. Behind her, Thea has raised two fingers in a peace sign, in her other hand she is holding a half glass of beer in a gesture of cheer. Her expression has almost shifted into a wink. She stands about two or three feet behind her sister with Catherine in the foreground in sharp focus and her sister, an assembly of soft blurry shapes behind her. Eighteen months separate these photographs. Eighteen months of regret, happiness, trauma and knowing.

There was the panic of Catherine's late period the previous June. Thea's casually violent boyfriend, Neil, who threatened, and then made a half-hearted attempt at suicide when she left him. Their mother's shocking four-month affair with Terry Gaskill, an accountant from the golf club with a reptile grin who only ever referred to them as 'the terrors'. Their mother's good friend, Patricia Hamley, two doors down, who waved her children off to school one Friday morning before gassing herself in the kitchen. The police, the ambulance, the family gone. There was the favourite red dress of Thea's, borrowed by Catherine and returned with no explanation, torn at the waist with a stiffened patch of dried vomit on the hem. The two of them lying side by side on the grass in the backyard in the heat of summer, their eyes closed, both singing every word of Fleetwood Mac's 'Landslide' as it played on the transistor radio. The awful sadness of the jars of Boxwood honey sent home to them by their father. Their terrible arguments, and silences, the relief of forgiveness. Hating each other. Loving each other. Bound to each other forever.

She switched the reading light on and opened Julian's book. The words danced about the creamy paper so she shut it again and turned the light off. Every two hours she moved about the darkened interior of the plane. She stood looking at her fellow travellers with shock at the intimacy of watching them sleep, some huddled down, some with gaping mouths and eye masks. She went to the toilet and stared at the woman in the mirror. Her soft pink skin, her hollowed eyes and her hair like an odd collection of grey rags on her head. She went back to her seat and looked at the fuzzy screen on the seatback. She became hypnotised by a documentary about a whaling ship in Japan called the *Oriental Bluebird*. She imagined herself as the beleaguered whale targeted by explosive harpoons from the ship. As the whalers dragged the dying animal onto the boat, awash in the red drenching blood she began to cry again. She switched it off and shut her eyes. Every now and again, folded into her seat in the least uncomfortable position, she managed to find little pockets of happiness.

She knew it was sleep deprivation and The Change but every minute as the aircraft seemed at once motionless in the air while at the same time speeding across the sky, she was overcome with relief. She was glad to be away from her tiny cell-like office on the University of Melbourne campus where she was expected to be Professor of Anthropology and Novelist, Catherine Adler. She was glad to be away from staff politics and passive-aggressive millennial students. She was happy not to be speaking to Ivan, her ex-husband of twenty-three years who failed to find happiness with Rowena, the twenty-six-year-old travel consultant he left her for. Associate Professor Ivan Finch, who now wanted to 'catch up' regularly even though, awkwardly, they both taught in the same faculty. Ivan who would hold her hand in a tight, needy grip, staring into her eyes saying 'Where did we lose our way?'

She was overjoyed to be thousands of kilometres away from Jin-Joo, her withdrawn Korean PhD student whose thesis on 'The Gendered Dimensions of Local Foreign Interactions in Truckstops from Mumbai to Kangakumari', Catherine found almost completely incomprehensible. Most of all she was happiest to be away from her half-renovated kitchen and Tomek, the Polish plumber she had begun to have sex with three months ago as a way of treating herself for the publication of her new book.

Tomek, ten years younger than Catherine with a bald head, some mysterious scars, a soft, downy round beer belly and a hungry appetite for oral sex that she found exceptional. Tomek, who she took out to dinner, immediately knowing it was a mistake as he eyed the waiting staff suspiciously, spending most of the evening unwinding the entire plot of *Game of Thrones* for her. Tomek, who, as she tugged his underwear off the first time they fucked in her hallway, miraculously produced a small tube of lube, winking at her, whispering, 'This might help.' Tomek, who'd given her flowers and beer and chewing gum. Tomek, who excitedly promised to show her 'the *real* Krakow'. Tomek, who wanted to spend more time with her even though her porcelain double Belfast sink was still on the floor by her back door, sealed in bubble wrap. Tomek, who 'sexted' her with aubergines, peaches and lolling tongue emojis and pictures of his meaty penis with the accompanying text, 'my gift for your beautiful cunt'. Tomek, who said that her kitchen would be finished by the time she returned, promising to fuck her on the newly installed Caesarstone benchtops.

High over the mountains of Albania in a startling flood of emotion, she believed that she could love Tomek and they could have a happy life together. Then somewhere over Bergamo, she dismissed any further contact with him as ridiculous. Interred within the deadening hum of the engines she was glad that every second pulled her further and further away to the other side of the world.

She landed at Heathrow, collected her luggage and took the train to King's Cross. It was cold but clear. She had a sudden rush of euphoria at the morning sun on the red bricks of St Pancras station, a euphoria that evaporated by the time she checked into her serviced apartment in Whidborne Street. She sat on the bed and phoned Thea to say that she'd arrived safely, but her call went straight to message. She sighed as she realised, once again, that the edges of her sister's familiar Australian accent had been worn away by over thirty years in North

London. She spent half an hour under a hot shower and brushed her teeth so vigorously that she drew blood from her gums. Now, hours later, fortified by three coffees and a paper cup of fruit salad from Waitrose she sat in the studios of the BBC, the exhausted and frayed Catherine hiding inside Catherine Adler, Australian novelist, shortlisted for the Bannerman Prize for Literature. The illuminated clock on the wall read 2.40, she'd just managed to read the opening pages of her book and Yvonne Larwell was looking at her across the black console of the studio asking her a question.

'Why do you think that this story is important to tell now?'

Could she articulate to Yvonne that the book came out of her feelings of dislocation, of non-being, not only in her own country, but in her life? From the growing sense, now in her fifties that she'd been flung into a world of uncertainty, ambiguity and barely hidden hostilities? That right at this very moment she was experiencing a panic-stricken need for escape?

Catherine shifted her head to one side and addressed Yvonne directly. She felt if she concentrated on her face she could suppress the wave of nausea that threatened to envelop her.

'I suppose I wanted to write about what happens when the culture of the country that you live in is filtered through the reality of another one, in this case England. For me, in all the critique of the British colonial experiment, the questions surrounding culture are the most important ones. I wanted to look at what survives in a culture infused with secrets and lies. Where the lies are an indelible part of the fabric of our own culture, part of the pattern of who we are. As to your question, why is this story important to tell now? I have no idea at all. All I know is that it's important for me to tell, for it to be told and known.'

In her altered state Catherine was aware that she was listening to herself as she spoke. She looked across the console at Yvonne. How old was she? She wondered. She guessed that she was somewhere in her late thirties. Catherine imagined that she was an arts graduate whose degree was in English or worse, media. She hoped in her exhausted delirium that she wouldn't wander into anger during the course of their conversation.

'You say 'a culture infused with secrets and lies', what do you mean by that specifically?'

'Well, if you're an Australian, you live in a country whose head of state lives on the other side of the world. I was raised singing 'God Save the Queen', with portraits of the Queen everywhere. We were schooled in English stories, reading English books, English poetry, living in a system of parliamentary democracy that's English. We watched English television and sang English songs, the Queen was on our biscuit tins, our tea towels and our teacups, etched into our pounds, shillings and pence. When I was at school I was told lies about the settlement of my country, secrets were kept about the brutal, violent, chauvinistic, criminal history of my country. This history is now known of course, but I wanted to lend my voice to examine the past and what it means for the present.' She took a sip of water and noticed that her palms were sweating, the back of her neck prickled with perspiration. Yvonne looked down, referring to some notes in front of her.

'Speaking of the past and what it means for the present, it's a fact, isn't it, that the Bannerman fortune originated in the sugar trade and the profit from slave labour in the eighteenth century. Do you think that there is any tension in the position you take in this book and being shortlisted for a prize with the Bannerman name attached to it?'

'The benefits of the colonial experiment are woven into the fabric of this country, into society, into its institutions – even the BBC, I'd venture to suggest – I hope my book does something to shed light on that. I think my inclusion in this particular prize is subversive in that sense – that's why I'm participating. That's why I'm here.'

'Of course Queen Elizabeth was a much revered monarch, and it's clear in your book that you're not taking issue with her per se, but the institution itself. Is that right?'

'That is correct. The institution itself and what it represents. Queen Elizabeth the Second, King Charles the Third, William the whatever, it really makes no difference.'

'It's fair to say, isn't it Catherine, that the book has been met with what you could call a lively critical debate back in Australia. *The Sydney Morning Herald,* although acknowledging the quality of the writing, has described *Commonwealth Bastard* as 'an unforgiving narrative of dislocation and mental illness. A sad book that demands of readers that they take a side. Adler suggests that we live nowhere and that we have nowhere to go.' *The Australian Book Review* called the novel 'a speculative anti-Australian fantasy', and 'a betrayal of – your – intellectual and artistic reputation.' How do you respond?'

'I don't respond, and I don't need to. I would agree however, that the book is an unforgiving narrative; when I wrote it I was not in a forgiving mood. As for it being a betrayal of my, what is it? "My intellectual and artistic reputation?" Well, that's not for me to betray. My reputation, such as it is, is manufactured outside of myself and if a book like *Commonwealth Bastard* can betray it, then I say bring it on, really.'

'You began your career as an academic in anthropology, turning to fiction when you were thirty-four. You've written eight novels on subjects as diverse as incest between a mother and son in *The Day Bed* to the politics surrounding the climate change crisis in *The Penguin Manifesto*, which was shortlisted for the Miles Franklin Award and both the Booker and the Bannerman prizes for literature. But *Commonwealth Bastard* is the first book you've written that's entirely set in the past and it's really the first time that you've tackled Australian culture head-on in fiction. Was it a particular challenge?'

'Each book is a challenge in its own way. The particular challenge of this book is that I was writing about something that I experience every day – it is very direct. So much of Australian culture is framed by a very particular view of our past. Our culture is made up of these very corrosive and infantilising nostalgias that have served to erase and distort our history and our place in the world and England is a very big part of that, actually the Queen in my book is literally the embodiment of that.'

'How so?' Yvonne's question held the slightest hint of hostility.

'Because she had the gig. Because she was the figurehead of a system of imperialist expansion, exploitation and subjugation. You might argue that all that's over now, but it's the *legacy* that's enduring. You just have to look at history to see that colonialism has hardly been an experience that generally resulted in fellowship or common good. In Australia, we got by for decades on the mere 'idea' of the Queen. She was a smile, gloves and a set of pearls. But like all illusions, the closer you get, the less concrete it all becomes. Actually, today, the whole enterprise of the monarchy and what it represents is in my opinion, a toxic fantasy that just crumbles when you subject it to anything like close scrutiny.'

'So, what do you say to those critics like Leslie Palfreyman in *The Times* who has said of your book that it is just a 'hysterical and histrionic appeal for a republic?''

'I would say that I'm not *appealing* for anything. Not a thing. What I am doing through fiction is describing a series of events to underline the fact that culturally, socially, politically, ethically and morally, being part of the Commonwealth has come at a significant cost, a cost that won't be fully reckoned until the day we take the first fragile, faltering steps as a republic. But I probably need to add that many Australians approach that day with both a sense of inherent destiny, and terror.'

Because she had no other way to respond, Yvonne was heard to say, 'Fascinating.' Then she added, 'Catherine, just to conclude, could you read for us a passage from late in the book, nearly ten years after that first fateful lunch with the Queen where we meet a very changed April Holman sitting in the grounds of a psychiatric hospital in Sydney?'

'It would be my very great pleasure.'

"What was she like? What was she really like?" April sat on the wooden bench as the hot December sun beat down on her head. Her dirty feet were gently prickled by the coarse grass of the lawn. *What was she like?* The question rang in her head like a constant bell. Many years ago, she'd shared lunch with Her Majesty on her yacht during another hot afternoon. '*What was she really like?*' The question had been asked so many times and by so many people that finally for April its subject had shifted and blurred. Now she understood the question to be as much about herself as Elizabeth.

What was she like? She was thought to be overly sensitive, she was given to moods, to rages, she was prone to wander off, she was not quite right. That was before the hot baths, being strapped into water for hours. Then there were the clamps on her temples that sent volts through her head like lightning in a cloudy sky. That delivered her to calm. To peace. To a quiet chair, a cup of tea and a biscuit. The last of her blood bled out of her.

She sat under the plane trees in the garden and considered all the gifts of Elizabeth. The starlings, the blackbirds, the goldfinches, and the sparrows, the rabbits, the foxes, the rats and the mice, the sugar, rope and shackle.

God save our gracious Queen

Long live our noble Queen

Her friend Elizabeth stared down at April from every wall of Callan Park. She wore a beautiful pale blue satin dress, there were sapphires studded around her throat and a diamond-encrusted tiara crowned her head, her liquid eyes watched over April every day and every night. She looked down at her dirty, torn nails against her calico smock and brought her fingers to her dry and peeling lips.

She needed to be tidied. Elizabeth was coming back. She may even be floating on the harbour right now. April needed to greet her old friend. There was so much to talk about, so much to tell her.'

Yvonne beamed over the console. 'Catherine Adler, thank you so much for talking to us today. Catherine's book, *Commonwealth Bastard* is published by New Holland Press and is shortlisted for the Bannerman Prize, the winner is announced on the tenth of November. Good luck to you, and thank you once again.

And we leave you today on a note of concern. Listeners may

not be aware that the news is reporting that Gideon Bannerman is missing. Gideon of course, is the son of the late Adrian Bannerman, the man who set up the Bannerman Prize. Gideon Bannerman was last seen at a London tube station three weeks ago. The police have made an appeal to the public for anyone with any knowledge of his whereabouts to come forward. Our thoughts are with those close to him, and of course, we hope for his speedy and safe return.'

It was 4 pm and the day had darkened in the late autumn afternoon. Catherine swung her legs out of the cab and stood on the pavement at the entrance to the National Portrait Gallery. The fresh cold air revived her and for the first time since her early morning arrival, she felt happy to be in London. During her interview with Yvonne, Thea had left a message telling her sister to meet her at the tearoom of the Gallery where she worked as a volunteer guide. 'I'll be a few minutes late – order a coffee and a cake'.

She wandered into the gift shop and stared blankly at a wall of postcard portraits. She picked out a random selection that she would use as bookmarks. She was still shaky and her choice of cards seemed to her an insightful barometer of her state of mind. Sir Joseph Banks, Lucian Freud, Twiggy, Jane Austen, Germaine Greer and Johnny Rotten. She made her way downstairs to the café and was accosted by a beautiful young girl with red hair that fell in ringlets about her shoulders. Her name tag identified her as Anjelica. She wore a black apron and a white t-shirt with the short sleeves rolled up over her shoulders. There was a tattoo on her left arm of a disembodied hand holding a single rose while her right shoulder bore a heavy-handed rendering of a skull wearing a top hat, a cigarette between its teeth, and a single line of inky smoke snaking its way under her sleeve. A dark haired boy, Karim, identically dressed leaned against a glass cabinet of cakes and sandwiches, stared at Anjelica as she spoke to Catherine.

'Hi. What would you like, ma'am?' Her voice was low and smoky with an indeterminate eastern European accent.

'Oh, um … ' Catherine was momentarily stumped by the question. 'Oh, okay, I'd like a cup of tea, thanks. A cup of English breakfast tea and a raspberry friand. Thank you.' Her fingers pinched at the cards in her wallet.

'You can sit. We will bring to you.'

She chose a table against the wall that gave her a view of the entrance, she would see Thea approaching when she came.

Catherine had been coming to London for over three decades, often visiting more than once in a single year but there was never any question that she would stay with her sister. Thea's large Victorian home in Brockley was a busy place with three grown children, boyfriends, girlfriends and dogs together with her newly retired husband Lyle Owen, a career executive from the pharmaceutical industry who, Catherine believed was the most consistently boring human being she had ever met. Thea had been working in public health when she met Lyle at an infectious diseases conference in Geneva in 1987. Before she introduced Catherine to him she described Lyle to her as 'unusual, surprising', as someone who was 'unexpected', unlike anyone she had gone out with before.

The night Catherine met him they dined at Boulestin in Covent Garden. The two sisters arrived first and were seated when Lyle appeared, smoking. He made a small performance of kissing Thea for perhaps too long on the lips before he sat down. 'I'm so sorry I'm a few minutes late,' his eyes appeared to twitch as he looked at his watch, 'It's just now gone half seven.' He had been squeezed into a light blue suit that had a subtle sheen, his navy and yellow striped tie was knotted snugly around his neck but the most powerful thing that Catherine noticed about Lyle was his cologne. At once astringent and sweet it seemed to carry its own corona of heat radiating from his florid pink skin. She instinctively moved her chair to position herself as far away from him as possible within the confines of the situation and the small round table.

He took his place, running his fingers through his thick greying hair saying, 'Oh, it's so lovely to meet you finally, Thea has given me one of your books to read, haven't you my darling?' He gave his fiancé's fingers a conspiratorial squeeze, the sapphire that was set in the centre of her engagement ring glinted in the light. 'Yes, the one about the mother and the son, I plan to read it. It's so interesting that you're a writer *and* an academic. I heard Jeffrey Archer speak at a conference dinner once, *fascinating* man, but I really don't get that much time to read novels, I'm up to my neck in research, really, all the time, and then there's Thea of course and all the plans for the wedding, but I'm leaving all that up to her, she's so creative, aren't you darling, not at all my strong suit.' His fingers went through his hair once more and he continued talking as he was handed the menu. 'Oh this looks wonderful, did you know, Catherine Adler,' he leaned on his elbow, his face suddenly close to hers, her eyes slightly watering, 'that this is the most expensive restaurant in London? It really is top drawer, and I want you to order anything you want, anything at all. This is my treat!'

In less than two minutes Thea understood that Catherine hated Lyle. She spent the rest of the evening attempting to smooth out the conversation, tactfully interrupting or contributing when she could, to give her sister a subtle context for Lyle's nervous crassness. Late in the evening, after too much wine had been drunk, to navigate the exhausting dinner, Lyle struck a match to light another cigarette, turning his attention to his fiancé.

'Do you know Catherine, your sister is the first Australian I've actually got on with?'

'Oh Lyle, really,' a wearied Thea said, her mouth pulled up into a half grin, attempted to interrupt him.

'No, really my sweet, it's true. We met at this dinner in Geneva and we just *connected*.' He snapped his fingers for emphasis. 'You remember darling, *Infectious Diseases, Advances and New Modalities: 1987.*' He lowered his head slightly, looking up at Catherine under his hooded eyes. 'It's a fascinating field, we have a number of products in development, but really, with Thea, it was like meeting an old friend, we just talked for hours, or you'll probably say *I talked* for hours darling,' there was more table top hand squeezing at this point, 'but we just hit it off, really. We were like two peas in a pod. That was last year, now the family's given this fantastic woman the seal of approval, we're snug.' Catherine stared down at her fingers, rotating the base of her wine glass.

'I was wondering when we might get to have the opportunity of approving you, Lyle?' Her eyes were like still points as she smiled at him. Thea's stomach was wound into a tight knot, she tried ignoring her sister. Lyle motioned to the waiter for the bill with a gesture of scribbling something on his palm.

'Well, I'm hoping that's a given of course. It's all go from my point of view. I really feel like the luckiest man in the world. I'm over the moon,' he said as he pushed his chair out. 'I'm just off to the loo.' And with that he was gone. There was a heavy silence as the sisters looked at each other. The waiter arrived and set the bill down on the table. Finally, Thea spoke.

'Wasn't the octopus amazing?'

'Thea, you cannot be serious.'

'Oh look, he's nervous. He wants to impress you. He said to me he's hopeless with arty types. You could try, Cate. You could attempt to make this a bit easier.'

'*Arty?*' Catherine snorted. 'You can do better, he's an oaf.'

Leaning forward, Thea lowered her voice to a hiss. 'Just stop being so fucking judgemental. He doesn't have to meet your lofty standards, he's marrying *me*. I love him Cate, he is funny and sensitive and caring, do you understand that? Don't you see it will be so boring if we're one of those families where you loathe your sister's husband? *Please.*' Her eyes were brimming with tears.

'Oh give it time Thee, I don't know him well enough to actually loathe him yet, but I have to say, the signs are very encouraging.'

She picked up the bill from its little plate and unfolded it. 'Three hundred and sixty-two pounds.' She said, rolling the words around in her mouth. She put the bill back on the plate. 'You know he's going to mention it don't you? And then he'll talk about the tip.'

At that moment Lyle joined them again and Catherine experienced another wave of powerful scent. Her brow furrowed as she wondered if he actually carried a little bottle of it with him, applying more in the toilet. She decided to breathe through her mouth. He leaned over and kissed Thea on the cheek.

'All right, darling? What a wonderful dinner, this has been really fantastic, very enjoyable.' Catherine could see that Lyle was already drafting the memory of tonight's meeting in his mind. He took up the bill. 'And all for under four hundred pounds, amazing.' He took his wallet out of his jacket. 'And I'm going to leave them with something to let them know just how much we *really* loved it.'

*   *   *   *

'Catie!' She was startled awake. She had no sense of it, but she must have fallen asleep briefly as she sat and waited.

'Cate! Here you are.' Thea called out as she approached. Catherine saw that she was a little heavier than the last time she'd seen her, dressed in navy blue trousers, a white shirt and a navy jacket with an identity badge affixed to the lapel. She was moving with a slight limp. Catherine stood to hug her, not wanting to show in her expression that she felt that her older sister was suddenly old.

'What have you done? Why are you limping?' Karim arrived and set down the tea and cake.

'Oh, Kas darling, this is my sister, Catherine, she's come from Australia to visit.'

'Ah, really? Australia. Wow. Okay.' Now that she wasn't just another anonymous middle-aged woman ordering tea, Karim allowed her to see his beautiful smile. Thea lowered her voice to a stage whisper. 'Now, darling. Could you get me a glass of sparkling rosé?'

'Of course.' He turned to Catherine, 'And anything else for you?'

She stared down at her teacup. 'Actually, I think I'll have a glass of rosé too, thank you.'

Catherine noticed there was a faded hue of mauve growing out of Thea's grey fringe as she sat heavily opposite her.

'Are you sure you're okay? It looks painful.'

'It's just a sprain, I did it at lunchtime. It'll be fine. I'm normally gone by now but tonight we're opening this new exhibition, *Tudors, Teddy Boys and Beyond – Costume in Portraiture 1500 – 2020,* so we're open another two hours.' Thea pinched the edge of Catherine's cake breaking off a piece, she popped it in her mouth. The almost deserted café echoed with a laughing conversation between Karim and Anjelica.

'Your hair's purple.'

Thea touched a few strands of her fringe. 'Oh yes, Marina did this. She said, 'Mum, this will really suit you, and of course, it didn't. It was a bit of fun, that's all, it's nearly all gone. Oh, there's a few things to catch you up on – one of them is that Marina has decided that she hates being called Marina and from now on we've got to call her Albertine.'

'Albertine?'

'Yes. Last year she tried out Giselle for a few months, but then she let that go.'

'But what's wrong with Marina?'

'Well, I did ask at the time but I was told that Marina was not who she was. I'm not asking again. At eighteen she can call herself whatever she wants. You know, ever since we took her to that psychologist who assured us that she wasn't on the spectrum she's been on the lookout to distinguish herself in some other way. Now she's Albertine.'

'Darling girl. Better you than me.' Catherine said as Karim arrived with the rosé.

'Enjoy!' Automatically they raised their glasses. 'Cheers!' Thea broke off another piece of cake. 'Don't let me eat all of this, Cate.'

'You can have it. I ordered it and now I don't want it.'

'Oh thanks. Twisting my ankle meant that I didn't get very far at lunchtime.' She broke the cake in half.

'I'm so tired, Thee. I barely know what day it is. This is London isn't it?'

'It is London. How was your flight? How did it go at the BBC? Mum hates your book by the way.' She smiled.

'Mum hates all my books, and just like all the rest, she hasn't read this one. Someone at the golf club asked her, 'Why does your daughter hate the Royal family?' That put an end to that. She's got them all,

Thee, all lined up on a shelf. None of them opened. Not one, not once.' Thea watched a line of bubbles as they made their way to the top of her glass in a gentle arc.

'Poor Mum. I quit medicine and you write books. We're useless to her. Have you spoken to her lately?'

'Two weeks ago? Three? She's fine.' The rosé was flooding Catherine's exhausted body with emotion. She tried to stop it by talking. 'You said that there were a few things to catch up on – you mean apart from *Albertine?*'

'I'm so glad you're here Cate, I really am. It's so good to see you. It's so unfair that you won't go on Facebook, we could catch up all the time then.' Catherine laughed a little, shaking her head. There was something else. She knew Thea was stalling.

'Facebook is an evil waste of time. Now, what is it? What do you want to tell me?' Thea drank down half her rosé in one gulp. Her steady eyes were looking back at her sister, trying to read her.

'Well, I wanted to wait until we were face-to-face, it's so funny, now you're here it's suddenly so hard to say. But you should know that I've decided to leave Lyle.'

There was a moment, then Catherine exploded into laughter, cupping both hands to her mouth, her eyes crinkled up into little brackets. 'Oh Thea!' There was a loud scrape as she pushed her chair out. She hugged her sister, kissing her on the cheek.

'How long have you been married to him? Thirty-two years is it? Well, you certainly take your time mulling things over.' She sat back down.

'Oh Cate, it's been terribly hard. I knew it would seem like nothing to you.'

'Thea, it's not *nothing,* not at all.'

'He's good Cate, you never really understood that, but he is. It's just that over the last few years, he's changed. No. That's not quite right. The real truth is that he *and I* have changed.'

'I know he's good. A good person, I just never thought —'

'No. Let me finish. I've been thinking about how to talk to you about all this for months. You're the one who's good with words, just be patient with me.'

'Sorry, I'm sorry Thee.' She took another mouthful of rosé and allowed its bubbles to dance in her mouth before she swallowed.

'You'll laugh, I know, you always said I was so careful all the time. Never took chances, how I'd never rock the boat. It's true. I married Dad, I married my father. That's really the truth of it. It all sounds so boringly conventional. It's just that really, the point of it is that no one in the family really *needs* me anymore. The kids aren't kids anymore, they have their own lives and Lyle and I …' Here she trailed off as if she was ordering something in her mind. 'Well, for the last few years Lyle and I have really just been ignoring each other.' She laughed. 'When I realised that, I thought, oh okay, that's all right, he's someone to be with in the house, sharing meals, watching telly, holidays and so on. There was no nonsense, no rows, everything just sort of, faded away. But you *can live* like that you know, exist anyway. I thought about it a lot, I had a lot of time to think about it. But Cate, it just isn't enough, or to put it more accurately, you don't realise it isn't enough until you meet someone else who gives you an idea that life can be filled with joy instead of just passing the time. I'm listening to myself and I'm realising how bloody conventional this story is. How fucking predictable it all is.'

'Someone else?'

'Someone else. Alex. A security guard here at the gallery.' Thea waited, trying to gauge her sister's reaction.

'Oh Thea, bugger convention. Predictability. This is your life you're talking about. I mean, yes, marriages end, look at me and Ivan. You've been a fantastic wife and mother. Three children, all stable, well-adjusted young adults. Okay, they might want to change their names from time to time but Thea, you deserve to be happy. I'm glad for you, I really am.' A large tear streaked down Thea's face. Catherine took her hand in hers across the table. 'So, Alex. Tell me about Alex.'

'Oh Cate, it's so good to *talk to you,* you just have to come *more often,* you know we never see each other.' She took a deep breath and dabbed at her eyes with a handkerchief. 'Okay. Alex. I've known Alex for about three years, but really, more as friends. But then, towards the end of last year we started going for a drink after work and we just got to know each other better. Oh Cate, I've never laughed so much, but more than that, we've just got so much in common. We're the same age – three weeks apart. We both stopped liking music after 1989, we love the same films. Old books! I've finally found someone who loves Graham Greene as much as I do! And we both love working here. We share stories at the end of the day, about Americans who ask where they can find that picture of the Queen who got her head cut off – *they really ask that.* Or random Japanese girls who ask me where Ed Sheeran is – I know it probably doesn't sound like it, but it is such fun. Since I've met Alex, I've found someone I can *share* things with. I had no idea how important that really was. I know you'll laugh at me Cate but at sixty, I'm in love again. It's bloody amazing. Scary amazing.'

'Oh darling, Thee. I am just so happy to hear this, I really am.' Thea squeezed her sister's hands.

'Even just talking about Alex makes me happy. I can't wait for you to meet her. Oh Cate, she's just perfect.'

'Her?'

'Yes, she's ...' At that point Catherine saw a middle-aged woman approach the table. She was wearing the black uniform of a security guard. On her shirt she wore two little badges, one was a picture of James Baldwin, the other a portrait of Virginia Woolf, underneath it read, 'Arrange whatever pieces come your way'. Her hair was piled high in dreadlocks on her head with the occasional coloured bead threaded through it. A thin green leather braid circled her wrist and it was only at that moment that Catherine realised that Thea was wearing a matching one. The woman greeted Thea by touching her on the shoulder.

'Here you are. You hobbled down here did you? Having a sneaky one before the opening.' She looked over at Catherine. 'Hello there. I'm Alex.' To Catherine, Alex's face seemed to glow in the light of the café. Her perfect skin was the colour of black tea, and her large liquid eyes swallowed her as she took her in.

'I'm so pleased to meet you.' Catherine went to shake her hand but was pulled into a gentle embrace.

'Thea cannot stop talking about you, you're quite the star of the family it seems. I'm reading your new book, it's *fantastic!* What a story, and shortlisted for the Bannerman too, congratulations.'

'Oh, thank you, yes, so far so good. Fingers crossed, so far only a few people really hate it.'

Alex shook her head. 'It's a book of ideas. If you're not offending someone, you're not doing your job, surely.'

'Oh Cate does a very good job when it comes to offence, it's one of her particular talents.' They laughed.

'Thanks very much! Thea tells me that you've worked here for three years.'

'Yeah, that's right. I came here from Marks and Sparks. I'd done twelve years there, can you believe it? I got tired of shoplifters and the poor homeless who I had to ask to leave all the time. I needed a change. I love it here, it's much calmer.' She and Thea shared a look. Catherine was making multiple adjustments in her brain, assembling a picture of her older sister and the woman in the security uniform who was sitting across from her at the table.

'Alex is in Hackney, not too far away. I stay over at hers a few nights a week.'

'My daughter, Poppy was with me up until last year but she's gone off, she's at Manchester University studying psychology. Did you just arrive this morning, Thea was telling me? You must be shattered.'

'It comes in waves, I'm really okay. I was just saying to Thea how happy I was to hear about you, and how you met here.'

Alex clasped her fingers together on the table in front of her. 'It was totally unexpected. Out of the blue really. I'd given up. Websites, crazy people. I just couldn't be bothered anymore. But then, we just seemed to click, didn't we?'

'We just ended up spending so much time together. Here, then after work, in the end Cate, there just didn't seem much point in going home.' Both Thea and Alex laughed at this.

'Are you going to be here long, this visit?' Alex asked.

'Three weeks, I go back next month.'

'Oh, then we'll see a bit of you then. I can't wait to visit Melbourne, I've never been as far as Australia.' Alex looked at Thea. 'We're coming at Christmas.' Catherine was now convinced that she'd stumbled into someone else's life for ten minutes.

'Oh really? Fantastic. We'll be able to show you around. Thea, have you spoken to Mum?'

'Not in so many words. Not yet. I wanted to speak to you first.'

'Wonderful.' Catherine was convinced that this was the right word. She stared at her untouched pot of tea. She put her hand around it and found that it was only vaguely warm now.

'Cate, why don't the three of us get something to eat after the opening? I know you're tired, but you should eat.'

'That would be great. Yes. I'd love to. Somewhere close though.' She went to stand and gather her things to leave. She craved some fresh air, a glass of water and some time alone. She saw that Alex and Thea were also standing, Alex was saying something about pizza.

Then there was nothing. Catherine was weightless now. Through a blur of speed she could see the plane as it flew off far away from her through the clouds. She was falling, thousands of feet per second through the night sky. She's suddenly joined by Tomek. Naked Tomek who takes both her hands like a free falling parachute duo. Pulling her face to his, there is only time for one brief kiss. He yells to her, '*Krakow! Here we come!*' before pushing away, both thumbs up, tumbling into the dark. Her mouth opens but her scream is ripped away by the winds. The yielding clouds, nothing more than mists parting for her, each second a terrible, greater falling as her tender, fragile body hurtles down to the velvet earth. Then with a jolt she's on the Japanese whaler, the *Oriental Bluebird*. She is standing next to Virginia Woolf, starboard side, as twenty-five thousand pounds of gleaming minke whale is hauled up the deck. Immediately a crew of efficient whalers begin to cut into the smooth black flesh. Catherine is only mildly surprised to hear Virginia directing their work in fluent Japanese. Virginia has her back to her. She can see the icy salt wind blowing strands of her greying hair free of the tight bun at the nape of her neck. During a break in the work, amidst the carnage of hacked meat and organs, she offers Catherine a rolled cigarette. It would be rude to refuse. They stand at the railing. She looks down at Virginia's brogues and stockings splashed with blood and water. Her droopy brown eyes regard Catherine with suspicion. *'I'm stronger than all of them.'* She's looking inside the dead whale now, at the purple ribbons of its gullet. *'That's my burden, and my peril.'* It's not clear to Catherine if she's referring to her strength or the whale, she's too awed to ask. Virginia's arm gestures at the torn animal as she turns to Catherine, shouting, *'Arrange whatever pieces come your way!'*

She never felt the floor as she collapsed, but as she lay on its cool surface, her eyes opened and she saw Alex and Thea looming over her, above them the faces of Anjelica and Karim were looking down with concern. Pins and needles bounced around her cheeks and forehead, down her arms and fingers. Alex placed one warm hand on her chest, the other hand held her wrist, she felt her pulse beating under Alex's fingers. Catherine heard the comforting burr of her low voice as she spoke to her.

'Here you are! Back with us. You're with friends, Catherine. I think someone needs a good feed and an early night.'

1.40 am, Argyle Square WC1H 8AS

Tasha's leg had been troubling her all evening with a twinging pain, but now as she drank from her third glass of whiskey the discomfort began to soften. In the inventory of her body's quirks and soreness this pain in her thigh was new. A dull muscular ache that would sharpen from time to time and then subside. She sat in the dark in front of her computer screen sorting through emails that needed attention, and others she could trash. Since Gideon's disappearance had become public her inbox had been glutted with correspondence from concerned colleagues, friends and acquaintances all offering their thoughts or asking how they might help. Some pre-emptively referred to Gideon in the past tense. Jane Pope, an editor at the *New Statesman*, wrote:

> Poor Gideon, you know, I never really got close to him. I thought that he was an easy man to warm to – difficult to know. I suppose I found him to be essentially characterless, a blank. Still, he was your friend and I'm sorry he's gone.

There was Eric Norris, her editor at Jonathan Cape.

> Bad news about Gideon. It's so hard with old friends, isn't it? Funny though, in the end, all that money meant nothing did it? I still need that introduction for your collected essays Tasha, we discussed two thousand words.

Then there were the emails from the Bannerman judges. Over the years, Tasha had worked with a succession of public intellectuals, artists, journalists and academics in her capacity as occasional chair of the judging panel. This year's judges included author and Cambridge Professor of Old and Middle English, Esther Greaves; Samira Prasanna, one of the nation's finest poets; literary journalist and novelist, David Kemble; Professor of Economics and social commentator, Douglas Budgell; and acclaimed actress and occasional columnist, Cynthia Blakemore. Tasha had thought to kick off the deliberation process regarding the shortlisted novels by asking each judge to nominate one book they felt warranted the prize. First, there was Esther Greaves.

Tasha, why are we being asked to do this so early? I wasn't going to reply, but if this is to get the conversation started I think *The Clava Cairn* and *The Illustrated Danish Tree* have to be serious contenders. The book of porn by Dalby is young junk. And I think on the evidence of *The Broken Tooth Upstairs* that Julian Adagoke must be having a breakdown of some sort. I think of *Foreign Bodies* as just faux Ondaatje. As you know I argued not to have them on the longlist or the shortlist, but then here we are. Any news of G? – Thanks, Esther

Samira Prasanna wrote,

At the moment I would submit *The Illustrated Danish Tree*. The prose is so concentrated it leaves you heady. No doubt others will have their thoughts. Samira.

David Kemble's argumentative email prosecuted the case for a number of novels that failed to make the shortlist before concluding,

If I had to nominate one book then I'd argue for *Commonwealth Bastard* or *Her C**t*. It's a toss-up. I'd have to put *Foreign Bodies* and *The Danish Tree* in there as well. Kemble.

Douglas Budgell curtly replied to Tasha's request,

Greetings T. *The Illustrated Danish Tree*. DB.

Cynthia Blakemore wrote,

Dearest Natasha, you have been in my thoughts often since I heard the news of Gideon Bannerman's disappearance. I know you must feel his absence most acutely. Can we ever really know anyone? As to the task at hand, I think I would choose *The Illustrated Danish Tree* or *Foreign Bodies* to be awarded, but who can say? Yesterday I thought it should be

The Clava Cairn, and this morning, *Her C**t,* such a fresh, new voice and a woman to boot ... and of course *The Broken Tooth Upstairs* is both hilarious and moving, thinking of you, Cyn X.

So, this was only partly helpful. On the evidence of these emails, Tasha saw that she would easily be able to knock *Foreign Bodies* out of contention. She had hated the book but finally agreed for it to be shortlisted as a concession to David Kemble's impassioned arguments about 'popular, readable fiction'. *Foreign Bodies* would go, she would see to it. Then she could turn her attention to steering the discussions, the horse-trading and compromises of choosing this year's winner. She drank some more whisky as a new email was delivered to her inbox. Who would be sending emails at 2 am? It was from Detective Sergeant Inspector Donald Timewell.

Dear Ms Moubray,

Just thought I'd drop you a line to let you know that since the public appeal, we have been flooded with suspected sightings of Mr Bannerman. Someone thought they had seen him in an off-licence in Inverness, another person thought they saw him at an exhibition of Aztec artefacts at the British Museum, someone else thought they saw him loitering on the banks of the Thames down by Blackfriars Bridge. This is quite common. Almost none of these potential sightings bear further investigation. We did follow up one lead that turned out to be a mildly dementing osteopath from South Riding who had left his wife after forty years of marriage. He was found at a Holiday Inn near the Corn Exchange in Leeds. To be fair, when he was found I could see the resemblance but then, Mr Bannerman is a white male in his seventies. I expect he looks like a lot of people. Our search continues. I will keep you informed.

I thought you might like to know that I and my better half suggested *The Broken Tooth Upstairs* for our book club and it went down a treat! Julian Adagoke gets our vote!

Oh by the way, you're probably already aware but Yuri Kuznetsov has told us that he will be in London from the 18th for two weeks. He has advised us that his UK address will be Harvest Place, Mr Bannerman's house in Kensington, but you probably know that already.

All the best. DSI Don Timewell.

Tasha hunched forward, closer to the screen. She read the last three sentences of the email five times before pouring herself another drink.

THE ILLUSTRATED DANISH TREE
Kai Noguchi (Linnet House) 180pp
Poetry, song, a philosopher's riddle, a night train
journey from Copenhagen to Amsterdam and a
life-changing encounter with a stranger as a famed
watercolourist works on an illustrated catalogue of
Danish flora.

4 pm, Ole Lynggaard, Fine Jewellery, Østergarde 4, Copenhagen

She took it from its black leather case and set it down on its own
blue velvet cushion. She had introduced herself as Lisanne D'Souza
when he had enquired about the ring. They were sitting opposite each
other in comfortable green leather chairs. A low table, almost entirely
covered with a beige suede pad, separated them. She rotated the blue
cushion so he could look at the piece from every angle as she spoke.

'This piece, it is called 'Winter Frost'. It has been designed by
Charlotte Lynggaard.' Lisanne gave Kai a moment to take this in
before continuing in perfect English that held the soft rhythms and
accents of her native Portuguese.

'You see the form is created to appear like a sprig from a young
tree that has been twisted into the shape of a ring, as perhaps a lover

would do.' There was another pause. Kai looked at her and smiled. He guessed that she was probably in her late twenties. Her eyebrows were sculpted into the shape of two elegant scimitars above clear brown eyes so dark they could have been black. Her hair, pulled back smoothly from her brow, secured into a thick ponytail that swung between her shoulder blades as she moved. She wore no jewellery that he could see. The thin, tapered fingers of her small hands pointed to the ring.

'You will see now, the leaves spreading out from the tiny branches are white gold encrusted with diamonds, beautifully placed to suggest the frozen dew. You see? The facets of colour in the stones?'

Kai knew that this was all rehearsed, but he didn't care. Nothing about Lisanne was pressured or hurried. Her classically tailored clothes, her posture and the way she inclined her head to him as she spoke suggested that she could talk in this gentle, considered way for hours about this particular Charlotte Lynggaard ring. They were both here to appreciate the beauty of its conception and the craft of its making. The idea of the cost of such an object seemed to be a far-off vulgarity, not of their concern.

'Here, you see the perfect pavé diamonds giving lustre to the larger stones. There are one hundred and twenty-one diamonds in total here.' Another pause. 'Exquisite, no?'

Kai moved to the edge of his chair and leaned over the piece on the table. 'It is very beautiful.' He looked from the ring to Lisanne, his brow creased upwards. 'And the cost?'

There was the slightest calibration to hardness from the dreamy, curatorial tone that Lisanne had employed to describe the ring as she said, 'This piece is valued at ten thousand, one hundred and fifteen euros.' She raised her eyebrows slightly, almost playfully to suggest that the very idea of money was a joke that they could both share. He noticed that almost concealed beneath the sleeve of her cream silk shirt, she had an infinity symbol tattooed on the underside of her wrist. He took the ring between his thumb and forefinger and passed it to her.

'Please, if you would. That would be lovely.' He reached into his jacket pocket and took out his wallet.

'Certainly, sir.' She carefully positioned the ring in its small black case and then tied a black ribbon around the box. Her voice became lighter.

'If you don't mind me asking, is it a gift?'

'I don't mind you asking at all. Yes, it is a gift.' He handed Lisanne his credit card. She again pulled another hidden drawer from below the table and took out a small card reader. She looked at his credit card for a moment, and then back at him, her mouth opened.

'Oh, wait, no – you're *Kai Noguchi?* You're not the novelist Kai Noguchi, the poet, are you?' The even gloss of Lisanne's professional demeanour evaporated in seconds.

'Yes, I am the novelist and poet Kai Noguchi, I'm afraid.'

Her fingertips went to her lips. 'Oh god. Oh, really? Oh Okay. I *love* your book, *The Train to Cornwall,* and the *film!* And *The Chelsea Marriage,* and your *poems* – just beautiful. My God! It's really you! Are you staying in Copenhagen for long?'

'No. Actually I leave this evening. I'm taking the train to Amsterdam.'

'Oh, excuse me, I'm sorry. It's just – and now you're nominated for the Bannerman Prize, I read online.' She flapped a hand in Kai's direction in an involuntary gesture to clear the air between them of her embarrassment. 'Oh, I'm sorry …'

'No, not at all.' He said. He had been trying not to think about the Bannerman Prize. He had been longlisted, then shortlisted twice before, losing both times. His immediate reaction on hearing that he was in contention was an involuntary pulse of excitement, followed quickly by the inevitable comparisons with the other authors, at least one of which he'd never heard of and hadn't got around to reading.

'And I saw in the news that Mr Bannerman is missing.' Lisanne's brows knitted together in an expression of concern.

'Yes, I saw that,' he said.

'It is worrying, no?'

Kai remembered meeting Gideon Bannerman only once and was now struggling to remember exactly what he looked like.

'Oh, I'm sure he'll turn up. If he comes in here, just point him in the direction of England.'

She laughed, shaking her head. 'Do you know? I've actually memorised whole poems from your collection, *The Basement Studio*. I just love them. Would you mind, just a moment?' She got up and went through a door. His body slumped slightly, he hoped she wasn't going to ask for a selfie. In less than a minute she returned holding a crisp new hardback edition of his book, *The Illustrated Danish Tree*. She opened it to the title page.

'Would you mind? Could I ask you to sign it for me - *To Lisanne?*' Kai noticed that as she held out the book to him, her hands were trembling.

He'd flown from London to Copenhagen that morning. He'd wandered the streets of the city in the afternoon, enjoying the luxury of having no plan, no one to call and no one to meet. He'd bought a millefiori paperweight in an antique shop on Sundkaj, he'd eaten tortellini at Rufino Osteria and on an impulse, he'd walked into Ole Lynggaard where he'd found Lisanne and 'Winter Frost'. He'd now taken his seat by the window in the dimming early evening light and waited for the train to depart. With his oxblood leather satchel at his feet, he folded his arms across his chest and felt the ring case in his jacket pocket like a secret joy. Tomorrow Alida would meet him in Amsterdam. Tomorrow he would give her the ring.

A month ago his agent, Theodore Glazer had called to say that *The Sunday Times* were willing to pay Kai to take the train from Copenhagen to Amsterdam. They wanted him to write a piece describing the journey as a tie-in to the publication of his new novel, whose entire one hundred and eighty pages described the very same journey, taken by night in 1932 by his fictitious protagonist, the watercolourist, Emile Blum. Although he had initially agreed, he had meant to get out of this task. But as the weeks went by after publication and all his promotional obligations stacked up, he kept putting off making the call until finally it was too late to reasonably refuse.

But as the train began to pull out of the station he was struck by the realisation that he would write nothing for *The Sunday Times*. As the landscape began to thread past him, the suburbs, the yellow lights of evening coming on in kitchens and living rooms, he saw glimpses of people sitting at tables, watching television, walking down streets. Then the scene shifted to the countryside. The wind farms, waterways and fields, the industrial parks and the petrol stations, and the rapid mesh of green and black as trees rushed past the window. He was glad to be on the train. Tomorrow he would see Alida. Tomorrow they would have breakfast. His mind began to settle into the drift and rhythm of the journey. Here it was warm. Here he was sheltered. His mind was clear. As the train made its way he began to doze, listening to the soft racketing of the tracks through towns and cities, travelling from Copenhagen to Amsterdam.

Roskilde

The house in Keighley that Kai was raised in was built in 1643. Over the course of hundreds of years the house had been partially burnt out, demolished, remodelled and extended. Part of the eccentricity of the main house was the construction of five small belltowers ornately designed from black Yorkshire stone that stood high above the heavy oak and iron front door. It was thought that the bells' five-note peal was a secret message to Catholics in the seventeenth century, but this had never been verified. Now, and for as long as anyone could remember, the house was known as Five Bells.

Kai grew up surrounded by heavy dark furniture and hundreds of objects he was forbidden to touch. Ancient paintings scabbed and layered in filthy varnish, pewter plates and cups, Delftware, stuffed dead animals and birds and faded, moth-eaten tapestries. Years after his grandparents had died and Five Bells had been left to him along with the entire Goldsmith estate and holdings, worth some many millions of pounds, he discovered that most of the contents of the house were worth next to nothing. However, Five Bells did hold one treasure. A drawing by Hans Holbein the Younger. It was a study for his 1542 *Portrait of a Gentleman with a Falcon* drawn in red and white chalk. The drawing was almost hidden in his grandfather's study, hanging on a patch of wall between leather bound books and manuscripts that were never opened. The man and his falcon in the drawing had stared out of their niche in the bookcase at people for hundreds of years. Whenever Kai caught sight of them he would stop still. With their patient, even gaze, these creatures from another time carried the knowledge that people at Five Bells lived, and died, but that they had remained, and would remain staring calmly between the mouldering books forever. Whenever he found himself in that room, Kai made every effort not to look at the picture. He didn't fully understand why, as a grown man when he gifted the house to the nation to cover the inheritance tax, the Holbein drawing was the only thing he kept. Five Bells had belonged to his grandparents and was where his mother, the painter Laura Goldsmith returned to after giving birth to him in 1978. Kai's father, the classical pianist Shiro Noguchi only visited the house twice, once when he was on a tour that coincided with Kai's fifth birthday, and then four years later to attend Laura Goldsmith's funeral.

Nyborg

Laura's hair was the colour of rusted metal, it grew in coarse thick frizzy curls and her eyes were a vivid, translucent green. Her neck was delicate and her head was unusually round with a high forehead that was prone to freckles. These were the features that everyone who met her remembered. Her pale skin would often flush in irregular red patches depending on her mood or the circumstances she found herself in. She was withdrawn but not shy. Even to her parents, she was something of a riddle.

On her eighth birthday, Laura was given a pony she named Margot that she fed with apples, carrots, bunches of hay and wet grass. When asked by her mother why she never rode Margot, she explained patiently, 'I could never get on Margot's back Mummy, she's my sister.' One wet Easter she sat down to lunch with her parents and, after some moments her mother asked, 'Where is Justine?' Laura's only friend from school had come to stay for the holidays, they had been playing a game and Laura had tied Justine up and gagged her, just as she had seen in an episode of the police drama *Z-Cars*. But she had quite forgotten about her when she came down to lunch. When Justine was finally found and untied Laura couldn't understand why she wouldn't stop screaming, or why her father grabbed her and shook her so violently that her eyes seemed to wobble in her head and her teeth bit into her tongue, yelling at her, 'Look at what you've done, you horrible, *horrible* child!'

She loved drawing, but both her parents were puzzled by the mountainous, romantic, windswept landscapes she drew, always depicting Laura, her mother and father (sometimes she would include Margot) with their backs to the viewer, perched on various rocky outcrops looking out at the dangerous weather and terrain. 'Why do you always draw us like that, darling?' her father asked once as Laura lay on the floor hunched over a picture of the family, standing together on a high cliff by the sea, about to be engulfed by an enormous wave. Without looking up, Laura continued to scratch at the paper with a piece of mauve chalk saying, 'Because that's where we're going, Daddy.'

Snoghøj

At nineteen Laura was accepted into the Slade School of Fine Art to study painting. She decided to live in the lower floor of her parent's London home in Chelsea. The roomy basement housed the kitchen, the servant's quarters and a dining room that backed on to its own walled terrace garden. It was this room that Laura converted into a studio space. More than twenty years after her death, among piles and piles of discarded drawings and paintings, Kai found some fragments of a long-forgotten journal of sorts that his mother had kept in the first few months of being at the Slade School. In it she recorded her impressions, sometimes accompanied by small line drawings of her fellow students. Each entry was headed with a day underlined, but no date.

Tuesday. Nerves. Horrible morning. A boy called Jacob Arcuri asked me for coffee. He talked about Joseph Beuys – how much he loved his work – I lied and said how much I loved it too. Such a liar – shaming. Let's hope for a better 1970!

Wednesday. I love drawing. I could draw all day. I was all afternoon with charcoal, the sound of it sweeping down the paper. Calming. Like sleep.

Monday. Elke Baumann came for tea today after school. She talked about *The Female Eunuch* and performance art. I regretted her coming, but once she was here there really wasn't much I could do about it. She drank seven cups of instant coffee and smoked all afternoon. She went on and on about how we must fight for those without power. I had not the foggiest idea what she was talking about. She said when she met me she thought I was so posh – so English. She's odd. It probably has something to do with her being German. She wouldn't shut up about the size of our house. I thought she'd never leave. Before she went, she said I was 'cool!' I suppose there's a first time for everything.

Thursday. Keith Fenton (painting tutor) asked me to explain why I painted rooms with no people in them. He asked me this with everyone else in the room. It was so quiet in the studio with everyone painting. I blushed. He made it worse by saying,

'You've gone red. Are you all right?' I lied and said I was all right thank you, just a bit hot. Brian Eastgate (action painter) came over to me and said not to worry, that everyone knew that Keith was a talentless cunt. I wanted to die.

Tuesday. Today we all went for Italian in Gower Street after a grisly painting assessment. Brian and Jacob drank too much and ended up yelling at each other about something (Jackson Pollock? Sean Scully?) Elke got a bit drunk on cider and told me and Sharon Coulsen that she'd had an abortion. It's probably true. I don't like her. A gloomy boy (Ben Hardy) who has ignored me for weeks gave me a lovely drawing of a fox. An awful girl from Margate (Jessica Sharpe) said stay away from that one – he's trouble. I went home at 9 and had a bath with candles.

Friday. Today Mum and Dad came down to visit. I showed them some drawings and two paintings that were nearly finished. She sat in the corner looking out at the garden saying, 'We'll have to get those roses cut back', then she told me she thought I was wearing too much eyeliner. He said 'How can you possibly work with all that smell of turpentine?' They're leaving on Sunday.

Tuesday. Watched Elke do her 'performance art' piece this afternoon. I didn't know what to think. It had something to do with Cambodia. There were bloodied t-towels that she pegged on a string, while she chanted some numbers. Then she came up to each of us who were watching and looked at us as if she was hypnotised or something. You weren't allowed to talk. Then she took all her clothes off and pointed a plastic gun at her stomach. I got very bored. I think Elke is such a fake, an idiot. No one clapped at the end. I imagined Mum and Dad watching it – they'd be so livid.

Monday. Ben came over tonight. His face was bruised and he'd cut his arm. He said he'd fallen over. Five stitches wrapped up in a grubby bandage. He brought over a bottle of Black Tower. We talked and talked. He told me he doesn't trust anyone at the school. He said they look down on him because he's from Manchester. He said I was different – innocent in a way, of course I was so embarrassed. He has a glass syringe and a needle – he showed me – he told me he has to carry it with him always because he is a diabetic. It was in a black box. It all looked very medical, and a bit sinister. I burned incense and we listened to Joni Mitchell and Van Morrison. We sang along to *Big Yellow Taxi* but the only words we could both remember were the chorus. Before he left we lay down on the divan and stared up at the shadowy patterns on the ceiling in silence for ages. When he got up to leave my arm had gone to sleep.

Wednesday. Met Ben in Soho. We went to see a film – *Deep End* with Jane Asher. Ben said afterward that I look like her – she died in a swimming pool at the end of the film. Sometimes I think he's such a mystery. He came back to mine and we smoked some grass listening to Bartók. His hair smelled like roasted peanuts. Funny. We fell asleep.

Friday. It's the end of term. Ben gave me a portrait he'd painted of me. I didn't know how to respond – my eyes look like wide dark stains – still, I love it. We went to Marlborough Fine

Art in Mayfair and saw the most beautiful painting of a horse done by Lucian Freud. I cried, it was so lovely. Right there, in the gallery, Ben kissed me and said, 'You mean everything to me'. It was overwhelming. He's coming to Five Bells for a week. Fingers crossed everyone gets on!

The last entry was accompanied by a scratchy line drawing of a naked young man with a cigarette in his mouth, unshaven with tousled hair sitting on the edge of a bed with a cup in his hand.

<u>Sunday.</u> Had a dreadful row with B. He'd taken seventeen pounds from my bag. It was horrible. At first he laughed at me and said he couldn't believe I was accusing him of theft. Then he said he couldn't understand why I was so angry – it was only money. It means nothing. He said I was so bourgeois. He said you're just like you're parents. He accused me of not backing him up during the disaster stay at Five Bells – it was hateful. I said I couldn't care less about the money – all he had to do was to ask if he wanted money – I didn't care. He bruised me. Then he showed me, wrapped up in his duffel coat a bottle of claret – he said, 'I bought this for us.' What could I do? We both cried and cried and he said – 'No one understands me like you'. When he'd gone Mrs Kempson came down and told me that some of Daddy's wine had gone missing and that if this kept up she was going to have to tell him. I begged her not to. Now I don't know what to think. Ben has a good heart. I know that. I love him. I know that too. Tuesday we're going to Scotland. We need to get away.

Lunderskov

The carriage was almost empty. A young couple slept three rows from Kai. A girl across from him was scrolling through photographs on her phone. He leaned his head against the window as rain began to streak and bead on the glass outside. There is no indication in the sometimes banal entries of his mother's journal of how the Scottish holiday went. There was no written record either of the Thursday afternoon, two months after they returned, when Ben slid a needle into the pale blue vein in the crook of Laura's elbow and gently pushed the plunger of his glass syringe into her arm. She watched that first time as a tiny ribbon of blood danced around inside the glass vial with Ben caressing her face, saying 'I wanted to be the one to share this with you'. He gifted her a glass syringe that became one of her treasures. Whenever she looked at it she would remember his expression of loving, gentle concentration as he examined her arms for sturdy veins to inject. Of course Ben never was a diabetic. He stole from her and lied to her and cried in her arms for forgiveness.

The last time they met in her basement studio she had refused to give him forty pounds so he punched her in the eye, before wishing her luck as he walked out of her life leaving her sobbing on the floor staring down at the carpet. Ten months later in a cold room in a Glasgow squat, he wrote half a letter to her that she would never receive. He called her his soulmate and wrote,

'I think of you when I wake up and every night before I sleep, then I see you in dreams – I fucked this I know – I remember us in your studio last winter, you read Eliot to me, something about the short bright days, and frost and fire. I keep trying to draw you – it's hopeless, nothing captures your light. Your eyes always saw me.'

Before finishing the letter he curled up on his dirty mattress and injected a last, lethal dose into a collapsing vein behind his thumb.

Frøslev

None of this was known to Kai. He had cried when he discovered his mother's diary, staring down at the words on the paper as if he might be able to conjure her from the dead. He studied her looping cursive hand and tried to imagine himself with her as she wrote these simple descriptions down, but she escaped him. His memories of her were few but vivid. He remembered the formal way she addressed his father the one time he came to visit them. The way she took the book his father had bought him as a present, *A Field Guide to British Birds,* and held it tightly to her chest. The way she knelt next to him wearing a green wool dress, pointing to the tall Japanese stranger saying, 'Say hello, Kai. This is your Daddy', then as Shiro Noguchi knelt to join them, how the man kissed Kai's forehead, cupping his five-year-old head with his warm, elegant hands. He remembered one Christmas at Five Bells playing a game with his mother where they both lay on the floor amongst the presents underneath the large tree, decorated with tinsel, lights and glass ornaments looking up through the dark crisscrossed branches. When they heard his grandparents approaching his mother brought her finger to her lips, hugging him close saying 'Shhh! We're hiding from the enemy!'

Jübek

Laura met Shiro Noguchi in 1977, three years after she graduated from the Slade School as a mediocre figurative painter with a deeply secretive addiction to heroin. She sold work occasionally to her parents' friends and acquaintances but the bulk of the drawings and paintings that she exhibited would end up being sent back to the Chelsea house where they crowded out her studio space, and found their way to the deserted rooms upstairs.

In the summer of 1977, Laura had a small painting accepted into a group show at the Whitechapel Gallery entitled, *Contemporary Figures 77.* It was a picture of her empty studio with two chairs in the foreground and canvasses stacked up against the walls. At first glance there appeared to be no figures in the painting at all, then off to one side, in the corner of the room Laura had painted a photograph, pinned to the wall of her mother and father taken on their wedding day in 1941, their faces just two light grey smudges rendered with her thumb, set against a dark background.

The evening of the opening was balmy and humid and Laura had spent most of it in her ankle-length Biba print dress smiling vacantly and pretending to be interested in the paintings on the walls. She hadn't wanted to attend, never knowing quite how to respond when people asked her about her pictures. At the last minute, on impulse she'd decided to go, a decision she was now regretting. She had positioned herself with a glass of Moselle as far away from her own work as she could. She was with Harriet Copeland in front of a large canvas of two naked men standing in a green meadow under an overcast sky with an Irish wolfhound sitting at their feet. Harriet had completed the work just two days before the show was to be hung and Laura could smell the heady mix of spirits and oil paint coming off the canvas. She was trying to concentrate on what Harriet was saying, something about the Slade – but she was finding the crowd and the noise distracting, then Harriet said something that immediately focused Laura's attention.

'Of course, they were expecting a painting from Ben Hardy, but then nothing turned up. Someone told me he was living in Edinburgh in a commune. You two were quite close weren't you? Do you hear from him much?' Laura's neck and chest began to flush in patchy red splotches as she sipped her warm wine. Without looking at her, she moved close to Harriet so that she could speak directly into her ear.

'Actually, I've not seen Ben, or heard from him for years now – not since college. We lost touch.' Harriet saw someone she knew in the crowd and waved at them, mouthing 'hello!' Then she turned to Laura, 'Such a talented painter, but I found him so moody, anyway, let's hope he's enjoying life in the ashram, or whatever.'

Laura felt a tap on her shoulder. She turned to see Avis Preston, an old friend of her parents who worked for the Corporation of London, and who was burdened throughout life with an uncanny resemblance to the Princess Margaret. Avis was comically overdressed for the opening in a gown of many layers of tangerine chiffon and an emerald choker, her slightly blurry lipstick had been bravely matched with her dress. Avis's face had broken out in a light sweat and her mouth was pulled up into a crazed rictus of excitement that exposed a number of gold fillings in her uneven teeth. She clasped Laura's forearm, while her other hand, holding a glass of wine and a cigarette in a short black holder, indicated the man standing by her side.

'Laura, darling! *Wonderful* show, aren't you *clever?* Sorry to interrupt. Have you met Mr Noguchi? Shiro Noguchi? This is the daughter of my oldest friends, this is Laura Goldsmith, and she's a *marvellous* painter. I spoke to your mother yesterday, I think it was yesterday, and she said that they're coming to see the show next week, when the fuss has all died down. Laura has work in this exhibition Shiro, I think her picture is over there, somewhere.' Avis motioned with her arm across the crowded room. Shiro took

Laura's hand. She was aware of her sweaty palms.

'I am pleased to meet you,' he said.

'Mr Noguchi, this is my friend Harriet. This is Harriet's painting.' Before Shiro had a chance to respond Avis raised her voice to almost a shout.

'Shiro is here to give some concerts at the Albert Hall – it's so *exciting*. He's just released a series of LPs – Beethoven sonatas – so *accomplished*.' Avis raised a hand to her throat and smiled, basking in her proximity to the famous musician. Laura found she also had to raise her voice to be heard.

'Yes. Congratulations. I have some of your records at home – the *Goldberg Variations* – they're wonderful.'

Shiro bowed his head slightly. 'Thank you. Your exhibition is so interesting.' He gestured at Harriet's painting. 'This painting is such an interesting painting.' By then Harriet had begun another conversation and had moved a few feet away.

'You *must* show Mr Noguchi your own work, Laura – it's *so original*.' Avis was then distracted by an extremely elderly woman who wobbled into view, wearing bright diamond earrings and a silver fox fur stole. '*Oh Marjorie …!*' Shiro leaned in close to speak to Laura, she felt his breath on her neck. 'Please. Show me your work. I would be very interested to see it. I would love to see it, please?' Laura recognised that this was less about a curiosity for her work and more a bid for freedom, she took his hand.

They threaded their way through the crowded galley to the other side of the room where Laura's painting hung. Shiro stood in front of the modest canvas for many minutes. Laura became aware of others in the gallery staring at him as he leaned in close to the depiction of her parents. His long fingers were clasped in front of him in a gesture of concentration and she noticed that his black curly hair was shot through with strands of white. He was older than her, she guessed that he must be in his early forties. She stood beside him wanting to leave. Finally he spoke. 'It's just no good,' he said, shaking his head. Laura laughed. She actually thought this reaction was a step up from *'interesting'*.

'Okay. Yes. I see that. What an interesting response. Thank you,' she said.

'Ah no! No, no, no …' She could see that he was embarrassed. 'No, I'm sorry. No. It's just no good. When it comes to painting, the only thing I know, is that I know nothing about painting.'

She couldn't be sure that he wasn't joking, she laughed again. 'It's funny you should say that. I feel exactly the same way, most of the time. Let's get out of here, shall we?'

Neumünster

The affair of Laura Goldsmith and Shiro Noguchi lasted eleven days. She took him to the National Gallery, the Tate and the Serpentine. They walked together in Kensington Gardens. She saw him perform at the Albert Hall and he sat for her in her studio. She did a large drawing of him sitting with a straight back in a leather chair smoking and drinking whiskey. The almost formal arrangement of artist and model allowed Laura an unpressured, intimate examination of her subject as he spoke in imperfect English about his life. He talked about the rigours of travelling almost ten months of the year, about his apartment in Paris, his favourite cities, Leipzig and Florence. He told her about his sister, Akari, who was a violin teacher in Tokyo. He casually mentioned that he was engaged to be married to a lawyer called Jennifer Arnault who was currently working in Chicago.

As she worked Laura got a sense of Shiro Noguchi outside the spoken story of his life. She drew his head slightly too large for his body. She described the planes of his face, his deep brow and dark, quick eyes, the soft hair of his attempted moustache, his lips and his long fingers. She played the recording of his *Goldberg Variations* and smiled as she noticed his fingers unconsciously tapping out the notes on his knee. They were listening to Variation 22 when she asked him if music had always come easily to him. He shifted his pose slightly and looked at her.

'Was painting always easy for you?'

Laura looked at the charcoal in her hand and at her blackened fingers. 'Okay, yes. A stupid question. I'm sorry.'

'This music is not easy. That is a mistake to think it is easy.'

'It just seems so effortless when you play.' He leaned forward in the armchair and listened carefully to his piano.

'This is hard. For this music, you need tears. You need to feel –' He paused, searching for the right word. 'You need to know *pain*.' He said simply, spreading his fingers across his chest. The track finished and there was a moment of silence.

'Come and see,' she said, standing back from her easel. He came and stood behind her. He didn't laugh, as most people did when they saw their portraits. He put a warm hand on her shoulder, still holding his whisky glass.

'Look at my head, it's so awful.'

'Do you not like it?' He took her hands and looked down at her dirty palms.

'I think it's perfect. Thank you for your drawing.'

A week later, Shiro Noguchi left London for Madrid, and unknown to both of them, Laura was pregnant with Kai.

Hamburg

Kai was born in May 1978. Five years later he met his father for the first time. Nine years later his mother was dead. Her mother's immediate thought was suicide, but Laura had no intention of killing herself. The day she died Kai was at Five Bells with his grandparents and Laura was in her studio in London. She was happy. She had found a way to salvage a friendship with Shiro once his shock and anger of not being told of her pregnancy or Kai's birth subsided. She explained that once she became aware that she was pregnant, she never considered termination. Her baby was one of those events in her life, like going to art school, or loving Ben Hardy, or meeting Shiro, that she felt were part of her destiny, that she was unwilling to change. Shiro was touched that she had given the baby a Japanese name, and his own surname. 'He needs to know that you are his father. I don't want or need anything from you, only that.'

Bremen

It was a cold November evening. The radio was on. Laura could hear the comforting tones of the BBC Shipping Forecast. The sharpness in the air made her breath mist as she stood at the open doors to the garden. *There are warnings of gales in Thames, Dover, Wight, Portland and Plymouth.*

She'd been working all day on a painting of a lamb, and she felt it was going well. Her style had developed since the days at the Slade. She no longer painted in broad strokes that showed the rough texture of the paint. Now her work was all about detail. She'd laboured all afternoon rendering the fine texture of new wool on the lamb's head. Before finishing for the day she'd decided to paint the animal's eyes so that the lamb could watch her as she worked. As she touched some white and cobalt to indicate a reflection of light in each iris, she stood back from the canvas. 'Well, hello there.' She smiled as she realised she'd given the lamb Kai's eyes, with their dark simple innocence. She was happy.

As soon as she discovered that she was pregnant, and for a time after the birth of Kai when she was breastfeeding there were long intervals without heroin. After he began to walk her use was occasional but steady. She loved the rush to her senses. The euphoria that began as a deep flooding relief, radiating out from within, to the ends of her fingers, to the air and the world around her.

On this November evening it's been a year or longer since the last time she used. She never thought of Ben much anymore but tonight, as she snaps open the case that holds her syringe, his fate in the Glasgow squat unknown to her, she wonders if he has found happiness. Did he marry, have children? She imagines meeting him again, now, years later, she wonders how they would be together again after their lives apart. The vein is found easily. She rubs the inside of her elbow and feels the warmth of her body in the chill of the night. She pushes the plunger down with slow deliberation.

Then she floats. She lies back down on the rug. She can hear laughter, distant voices. And the radio, *A complex area of low pressure will persist around the Norwegian Sea and Southern Scandinavia.*

She wants to stand up. She needs to get back to her painting. The tiny feet of the lamb need work, she needs to paint the blades of young grass shooting up from the dark earth, the gentle shadows on the ground angling away from the lamb as she silently stands on the ground. *A low off south-west Iceland is expected to deepen a little as it trucks east to be near the wash by Saturday midday.*

She is happy. The flood and drag of the drug pulls Laura down into sleep. A sleep that will stop her breath. She rests her open palms on her stomach. She stares up at the eggshell white ceiling where she had once lain with Ben years before looking up at the shadows from the trees outside. *Land's End. Occasional rain, fog patches. Later moderate or good.*

It's late now. She'll pick up her brushes again in the morning.

Diepholz

Kai looked at his watch. It was 4 am. The soft, continuous rhythm of the train had lulled him into sleep. That same rocking motion had just woken him. The couple that had been sleeping a few rows from him were now standing in the aisle. The girl, who Kai thought could be no more than twenty, raised her arms above her head to stretch, her boyfriend held her hips and kissed her exposed stomach, she laughed shaking her yellow hair from her eyes, they hugged. The girl to his left, across the aisle, had bunched up her backpack and was sleeping soundly, her mouth slightly open.

His mouth was dry. He was thirsty. He felt tired and uncomfortable in his clothes. He stretched his legs under the seat in front of him and crossed his arms, the ring case in his jacket pocket pushed against his ribs. He shifted in his seat. He looked out of the window but mainly saw his exhausted reflection in the black glass. Looking down at his phone, he saw that there were two messages from Alida, one of them was a photograph. For the last ten months she had been working at the Rijksmuseum in the conservation department on the restoration of a picture by an unknown eighteenth-century artist, depicting the abduction of Psyche by Zephyrus. For months she'd been painstakingly removing centuries of varnish, dirt and grime.

The picture that she had sent him was a detail of the painting that showed a delicate ladybird on the ankle of the goddess. Her text message read, 'Look what I've uncovered with cotton buds after 300 years! We'll talk in the morning, see you then, X'. With his thumb and index finger Kai enlarged the picture and saw the intricate brushwork of the tiny insect against the pearlescent skin of Psyche. He tapped out a reply, 'On the train – I love your ladybird – but your ankles are better than Psyche's – tomorrow my love Xx'.

He'd known Alida Damico for two years. They'd met at a dinner organised by his Dutch publisher. She had admired his writing, but not effusively. He asked her about her work in restoration and she had answered his questions with knowledge and humour. They'd sat opposite each other. As the dinner progressed he realised he was paying close attention to details about her. Her hands and fingers as she gestured when she spoke, the small fan of fine lines around her green eyes as she laughed or smiled, the gentle scoop at the base of her throat and the shadow it made when she turned her head, her sleek, black hair, pulled casually back from her neck and held with a tortoiseshell clip, the tone of her unhurried voice and the coarse surprise of her sudden, open-mouthed laughter. Their intimacy was uncomplicated and unhurried, and they would lay for hours talking when their relationship began. She talked about her brother, Marco, a speech pathologist in Milan, her parents who remained fervent communists who had a villa in Sicily. And she told him the story of how she got the three-centimetre scar in the shape of a crescent moon just above her right eye. He told her about his mother and what he knew of his father. He told her about his work, how writing allowed him to create worlds, to go deep into himself and the secrets of others. He thought that she believed him. He liked her, then he loved her, and more than once, each day, he wondered how it would end.

Almelo

It is late October 1991. Kai is thirteen years old. He is at Five Bells, on autumn break from Ampleforth College in North Yorkshire where he is about to transition from Junior Boarder to Senior.

It is mid-morning on a cold, clear day. The watery blue of the sky is at odds with the sharp chill of the air. As he moves through the large kitchen, down the passage lined with framed drawings from his mother's childhood, the backdoor has been left ajar and he can feel the cold outside as a solid thing. He takes his red puffer jacket from the hook by the door and steps into his scuffed white Adidas trainers. He slings his grandfather's prized binoculars over his shoulder. He pockets a small notepad and his precious copy of *A Field Guide to British Birds* before placing the headphones of his Discman snugly over his ears, pressing 'play' as he pushes the door open. Instantly the world is made more vibrant as the crisp, percussive beats of Depeche Mode's 'Policy of Truth' pulse in his head.

Kai walks with purpose down a path beside a billowing paddock still speckled with yellow rattle and red clover. The path leads to his mother's grave in a family plot beside a small orchard. The trees are heavy with green Bramley apples, some pocked brown, some littered about the ground. Kai picks two that appear unblemished and places them carefully on his mother's granite headstone, 'Laura Jane Goldsmith, 1948 – 1987'. He lingers for a moment, and thinks about her middle name, a name unknown to him when she was alive. *Jane.* He mouths it in a whisper before looking back at the gables and chimneys of Five Bells. He closes his eyes for a moment, shivering inside his jacket.

He walks on, down a gentle slope to a stand of yew trees hemmed in by a smaller group of spindles, their bright red and orange leaves suddenly picked up by a breeze moving through the branches, sending them flying and twirling to the ground. As he walks away from the path, his trainers kick up the long grass, spraying flakes of frost and dew over his shins, up to his knees. Off, about twenty yards he sees what he thinks may be a redstart thrush gently bouncing on the lower bough of a Yew. He takes the heavy binoculars and in seconds, peering through the wobble of the lenses, he has found the bird, its head quickly swivels left, then right, then it flies off and up, into the tree. He drops to his knees and opens his *Field Guide,* inscribed to him by his father in Japanese characters that he has never understood. It's not a redstart, it's a robin. He makes a note on his pad, the bird, the time, the weather, and places a tick against it.

He stands and looks beyond the slope of the meadow into the shadowy trees of the forest. Five hundred acres of protected woodland bisected by the gentle bends of the river Aire.

He presses a button and Depeche Mode is silenced. He walks a few more paces and hears his trainers crunching down the frost as the grass of the meadow gives way to the floor of the wood. He sees a large broken bough rotting on the ground, nearby there are three beer cans, stamped and flattened near the blackened circle of a dead fire. He pulls the collar of his jacket closer, his breath now frigid puffs that disappear in an instant. For half an hour more he continues to walk deeper into the forest. He sees a tree sparrow, a song thrush and a chime of wrens. He has crouched down, noting two rooks when a figure emerges from behind a grove of sessile oaks surrounded by an odd grouping of blackthorn bushes.

'Hiya!'

Kai looks up. He sees a man, his face unshaven, he has a moustache. He might be twenty, he stands on a slight rise, he is large, stocky, and he seems out of breath. Incredibly, in this autumn chill, he is wearing khaki shorts and a black Hard Rock Café t-shirt. His arms are mottled red, but that could be the cold. Kai's mouth opens in surprise at the fact that the man is carrying a large bow in one hand with a leather quiver strapped and buckled over his shoulder and around his waist. He's now less than ten feet away. Kai's warm breath mists as the breeze shifts, bringing with it the sound of the river some way off in the distance. There is a moment when nothing is said, they both listen to the water, before the man speaks again.

'Hey, sorry, hiya!'

Kai remains crouched, his pen in his hand. *2 rooks, 11.43 am, clear sky.*

'Hello.'

The man doesn't move. 'Hey, yeah, I was just hiking. I saw you from over there.'

Kai says nothing. He moves from the crouching position and stands. He pockets his pad, he holds his pen.

'I'm Teddy. Are you hiking too?'

'I'm birdwatching …' he answers like it is a question in itself. He takes hold of his binoculars as a kind of proof. From time to time he has met other walkers in this wood. The usual acknowledgement is a nod. Usually nothing is said. The man moves a few paces closer, Kai notices a chunky black watch on his wrist.

'Great day for it.' The man says. They both look up at the sky, a ripple of light cloud has begun to move above the trees.

'Are you on your own?' The man hitches his thumbs into the pockets of his shorts.

'I am,' Kai says, then he adds, 'I live over there, not far from here.' He motions with his arm, behind him, he turns back to the man who points to his headphones.

'What are you listening to?'

Kai is unsure how to answer, suddenly embarrassed he looks down at his Discman.

'My dad, my father is a musician. It's one of his records.'

'Cool. What does he play?'

'Piano. Mainly piano, sometimes other things.'

'Would I know him? What's his name?'

There was another pause. The breeze picked up again. Kai combed his fringe from his brow with his fingers.

'That's a very big bow.' Kai points.

The man smiles at Kai. 'You like it? It's a recurve bow. Do you know what that is?' He hands the bow to Kai. He takes it with both hands, it's light and its fibreglass construction is smooth to the touch, warm where the man had held it.

'Have you ever used one before?' Kai shakes his head, he has looped two fingers around the bowstring, he feels it taut, immovable, like wire.

'Here, I'll show you, it's easy.' The man takes an arrow from his quiver and surrounds Kai with his arms. His big hands take Kai's hands in his. This close, Kai can feel the heat of his body. He carries a scent that Kai can't place, it's sweet, like chewing gum or toffee with a hint of cigarette. The man puts his own fingers between Kai's and as he pulls the string back, the arrow, a perfect right angle to the bow, Kai understands in his own body how strong this man is. His mouth is close to Kai's ear, he feels his hot breath, his voice a whisper.

'When I count to three, we both let go. Okay? One … Two … Three.' With a snap the arrow is loosed into the air and cracks into a stump thirty yards away. There is the sound of a bird's wings flapping somewhere.

Kai's face is pushed to the ground. There is no time to cry out. With his oversized fist, the man stuffs a hanky or some cloth into his mouth. Something animal in Kai has the pulse of his beating heart running through his limbs, behind his eyes and up into his head. He's going to die. Like a reflex his back twists, but the man pushes Kai's pelvis flat against the ground, yanking his track pants to his knees. His pounding heart, the sudden cold. When it comes, the pain is like nothing he could ever imagine. It's like being torn apart. It shoots through his legs, up into his stomach, with each thudding pound and shove, out through his arms and fingertips, hot like something molten. On the back of his head and neck he feels the hot gusts of the man's gasping breath. He is grunting something that Kai can't make out. It's 'fuck' and 'fuckhole' and 'filth' and other things that are noises, not words. Worse than the pain is the fear. He is going to die. How long would it take? Where is his father? Is his mother watching? Will she take his hand and lead him away? He looks at his helpless hand, still holding his pen, the sleeve of his red jacket dirtied with mud. He knows it's his fault. He knows that he is to blame. He set this shame in motion by saying, 'hello'.

There is a great heaving groan from the man, and then just his dead weight covering Kai, crushing him down. For moments nothing changes. Kai looks at the digital screen of the man's watch: 12:22. He can feel leaves and grass on the side of his head. He twists his neck, trying to turn, to apologise. He wants to say sorry. The stench of shit that drapes over him and the man from the occasional breeze is his own, and for that, he is sorry.

'Sorry.' Kai whispers.

With efficiency, the man stands, saying nothing. He walks away as if this is just another rest stop on a long autumn hike. Kai looks up and sees him retrieve his arrow from the stump, then he is gone.

Kai is left breathing, fouled and wet. He spits out the hanky. His mouth is full of the iron taste of blood, he has bitten into his tongue. It's now that he allows himself to cry hot tears from his body hollowed out by pain. Hot tears that run clear rivulets down his dirty hands and arms. He tries to pull himself up, but he can't. His legs are cold and one of his shoes has come off, his sock is sodden in the mud. Minutes pass before he dares to look up again. When he does, he sees a single jackdaw alight from a low branch to stand on the ground. Her quizzical head twitches from one side to the other, and back again, looking at the boy crying in the dirt.

Amersfoort

Dazed and ashen, Kai stumbled around, out of the forest and back to Five Bells. He saw no one as he went upstairs and locked himself in the bathroom. He put the plug in the bath. He turned on all the taps, undressed and rinsed his track pants in the sink. He vomited once into the toilet, then he stood in the rising steam and watched as the bath filled. Then he eased himself into the comforting heat of the water. His head was slightly bowed. There was a high-pitched ringing in his ears. His jaw was slack, his mouth gaped open. He watched his reflection ripple from time to time as single drops of water dripped from the tap. Eventually the bathwater became tepid, then it was cold. His toes gripped the chain attached to the plug and pulled it free. He watched as the water was being sucked out of the bath, his shoulders prickled with the cold. The thinnest thread of blood swayed out of him as he sat, looking down, hugging his knees to his chest.

He would try to make sense of it. From that day forward, unbidden, the memory of that morning in the forest would return. 12:22. The man's large, grabbing hands, his shorts and his t-shirt, his hot breath and his words, the shit and the dirt and the blood and the pain that shot through him like lightning – again and again.

He would try to make sense of it. Now, he carried a knife with him when he walked in the forest. Time and again he would return to the place where he met him. He would stare for long minutes at the stump where the arrow had found its mark. He remembers the man's arms around him and his voice, close to his ear, *'One … Two … Three!'* He'd look at the spot where he was pushed to the ground. He would kneel down and pointlessly stab his knife into the earth where he'd lain, then he'd wipe the blade clean of dirt with his fingers. He took his *Field Guide to British Birds* and burnt it at his mother's grave. He bashed the ashes to powder and ground them into the dirt. He no longer looked for birds, and, if they looked at him, he'd throw stones, or bang sticks to frighten them away in the chattering leaves of the trees.

He would try to make sense of it. In time, he would seek out the word in the big dictionary in his grandfather's study. 'Rape, [noun] the crime, typically committed by a man, of forcing another person to have sexual intercourse with the offender against their will.'

This explanation angered him. It described nothing of what had happened, nothing of how he felt, of what was inside him now. He tore the page from the dictionary and burnt it in the garden. In an exercise book, he wrote his own words. He wrote everything he could remember, but it wasn't enough. He burnt this as well. He would try again, he'd keep trying.

He would try to make sense of it. Together with the death of his mother and the absence of his father, the shame of that autumn morning was now folded into him. He would never speak of it, to anyone. He began to write. And, from the moment he began, he knew that every word he wrote was a vain attempt to pull himself up from the cold, muddied floor of the wood.

Amsterdam

Kai woke with a start. Somehow it was morning. From his bleary vantage he could see two cleaners had arrived at the end of the carriage. One noticed him slumped in his seat and raised his hand, smiling in a quiet greeting. Kai straightened up and stood. He gathered his satchel and looked at his phone. A message from Alida – 'I'm upstairs, by the piano X'.

The platform was a shock of cold after the overheated carriage. He walked tentatively, still shaking off sleep. He looked up at the curved expanse of the iron roof of the terminus. There was the echoing sound of station announcements, of arrivals and departures. He made his way past the red brick and granite columns of the concourse.

He heard the piano before he saw it. The tune was vaguely familiar to him, but for the moment he couldn't place it. He walked further on. He saw a squad of schoolchildren in yellow pullovers, a couple arguing in Italian, he saw a man holding the hand of a toddling child in a striped hoodie. Some people stood motionless holding paper cups of coffee, staring down at the screens of their phones. There were backpackers, commuters and bicycles and then he saw Alida. She had her back to him. She was watching the man at the piano. He was skinny, with a white mohawk and pink skin pocked with acne scars the texture of porridge. The tune suddenly fell into place for him, it was ABBA's 'Fernando'. He stood for a moment, looking at her. She wore an oversized grey jumper and black pants, her hair fell loosely down her back, a green leather bag was slung across her shoulder, one hand was by her side. There were two silver bangles at her wrist. He'd been awake less than ten minutes and his eyes, fresh from sleep, saw these details with a vivid intensity. He put his hand on her arm, she turned.

He smiled, saying, 'Can you hear the drums, Fernando?'

'Kai!' she said as she raised her arms to embrace him. For a moment he rested his head on her shoulder. He breathed deeply, her hair held her perfume. He kissed her neck before pulling apart, his hands held hers.

There was something wrong. Tears gathered in the corners of her eyes. She bowed her head, resting her forehead against his chest. His hand stroked her hair.

'Hey Liddy, what is this? What's the matter?' He had guessed that this would happen, but when, he didn't know. Now they were here. As he held her, he looked at the young man at the piano. 'Fernando' came to a crashing conclusion. There was a smattering of applause. The man bowed solemnly, before pounding out the opening bars of 'Knowing Me, Knowing You'.

He hugged her closer. He could feel the ring case through their clothes like a stone in his pocket. Whatever happened he would give her the ring anyway. A keepsake for their time together. Would she keep this sad reminder in its case in a drawer out of reach? Would she look at it and think of him? She looked up. Tears streaked her cheeks. She wiped her eyes with the back of her hand.

'I need to tell you something. I'm sorry. This is stupid. I'm crying.' She made the sound of a little laugh, she bought her fingers to her lips, her brow creased. His mouth felt hollow. He could feel the blood drain from his face.

Alida reached up and put her hand around the back of his head, he felt her gently grip him. He would remember this exchange for the rest of his life. He'd replay it again and again, and each time the moment would be made new. The echo of the concourse, her grey wool jumper and the soft clink of her silver bracelets as her arms moved to hold him, the terrible piano. He looked at her, her eyes as clear as rainwater. For a shuddering moment his mind jumped back to the forest. He could feel the man's arms surrounding him as they held the arrow taut. *'One … Two … Three …'*

She spoke to him directly, her voice thick with crying.

'Mio caro, Kai. How can I tell you this … We are going to have a baby.' Her head was nodding as if to confirm this for herself.

For a moment he didn't react. Then he laughed out loud, holding her close. He rubbed her back, but it was more to console himself. He went to move but was surprised that he was unsteady on his feet. There was the arrow, there was the man's back as he retreated into the forest. It was the journey. It was the morning. Alida steadied him. Now he was crying. 'Thank you,' he said. 'Thank you,' he said again. Then he added, 'Let's get some breakfast.'

2 pm, Harvest Place, Kensington SW7 5

Carefully Tasha made her way up the six steps to arrive at the front door of Harvest Place. A sheet of white cloud covered the sky. There had been a brief shower at lunchtime, she picked up the fresh scent of rainwater on stone. The newly manicured box hedges on either side of the porch glittered with droplets of water. She had been coming to this house for over fifty years. One of the square marble tiles on the floor of the portico, to the left of the front door, had cracked into two neat triangles. It was an almost unconscious habit of hers to notice these shapes before she'd knock. But today, she saw the piece had been replaced with a tile that was almost, but not quite, the same tone as the others. There was something else. She saw above the door, mounted into the roof of the porch a sleek, black surveillance camera. She stared up into its glassy lens as she pressed the doorbell. She could hear its far-off ring within the house, and unexpectedly, the sound of a dog barking. Moments later, the heavy black door opened.

The woman standing in front of Tasha could have been anywhere between twenty and fifty. Her face had been augmented through subtle and mysterious processes. Tasha saw that she had the blank, generic appearance of people she sometimes saw on television, her face had the shorthand of a cartoon. Large blinking green eyes, smoothly rounded, moistened lips and shoulder length hair many shades of blonde. She appeared to be chewing something, from the repetitive motion of her jaw, Tasha assumed it was bubble gum. She was wearing a track-suit the colour of red wine and a tight white t-shirt with a red bus printed on it, underneath was the word 'LONDON'. She wore black trainers and she had looped a heavy leather strap around her hand that tethered a large spotted Great Dane, its big, boxy head pulled at her arm from time to time.

'My name is Natasha Moubray. I've come to speak to Mr Kuznetsov.' The dog barked once. The woman tugged on the lead, the dog's head was yanked against her thigh.

'Sasha! Nyet! I'm sorry for my dog. He must be with me. He is depressed. Anyway, please. My husband has been expecting you.' She made a sad, half smile.

'Your husband?'

'Yuri. Yes. He is coming. I am Anna.' She wore some gold rings on her fingers, there was a heavy gold bracelet around her wrist. She held out her hand to Tasha, as she did so, Yuri skipped down the central staircase. Tasha was shocked to see that he was practically unchanged from the man she'd met in Gideon's kitchen almost a decade ago. He wore an elegantly tailored suit of grey linen, his red shirt was open at the neck. She could see the five-pointed star etched into his flesh in blue ink. He was deeply tanned and the only hint of age that she could see was the phoney jet-black hue of his hair, betrayed by some strands of white that flecked his sideburns.

'*Natashka!* Many years since we met. How nice to see. Anouska, this is Natasha, Natasha Moubray, she's –' Here, Tasha cut Yuri off.

'I'm a very good friend of your husband's ex-husband, Gideon Bannerman. You may be aware that he is missing. This is his house. I'm actually very worried about Mr Bannerman, Anouska.'

Yuri looked directly at his wife, speaking to her in Russian. 'We'll go to the library. This will not take long. Bring us some tea.'

'Okay, I'll bring some cake as well.' Anouska said, turning to smile at Tasha. Tasha spoke to them both, also in Russian.

'Thank you, but I don't want any tea and I don't want any cake. Yuri, can we speak in private?'

'Of course Natasha, come.' Yuri replied, reverting back to English. He gestured with his arm up the stairs.

It had been seven weeks since she'd pushed the door open to find Gideon gone. Now the house was cold and heavy with the smell of fresh paint. The contents of the Harvest Place that she'd known had been removed, she assumed for the upcoming auction at Bromleys. Now the walls of the house were a bright, unforgiving white, newly hung with artwork that Tasha was vaguely aware of, that looked ill-advised in this house. At the top of the stairs was a painting of coloured dots, to the left, mounted on the wall, was a neon sign that read, 'My Heart is Torn' in a fluorescent white script. As she entered the library, she saw a canvas hung above the fireplace depicting what could have been a woman, floating in space, dripping in black and red paint. A large television tuned to BBC News was mounted into the facing wall. It showed cyclists rapidly descending a mountain road. The sound was off. All the books on the shelves had been removed and the soft, creamy yellow of the room had been replaced by the same hard white paint she saw through the rest of the house. There were empty cardboard cartons and sheets of crumpled plastic strewn about the floor. Yuri noticed Tasha taking all this in.

'Ah yes, the paintings. This, of course I leave to Anna. She is artist.' He waved his arm at the bookshelves. 'We have to organise so much from Turkey, you know. But is good to be back, for finishing touches, so important. She is even replacing books with other books – different colours. Crazy, no?' he said, smiling.

Tasha stood in the middle of the room. Disoriented by confusion, hatred and grief she knew she would need to steady herself. She decided to concentrate all her attention on Yuri. They needed to speak, then she would leave. He was leaning on a table of chrome and red marble she had never seen before. His head tilted slightly to one side, he was regarding her.

'Would you like to sit, Natasha?'

'No, I would not like to sit.' There was a moment when neither of them said anything. Tasha leaned into her walking stick, gripping it so tightly her hand began to ache. She was almost giddy with adrenaline.

'What are you doing here, Yuri?'

Still leaning on the table, facing Tasha, Yuri first crossed his legs, then his arms. Then he allowed himself another smile.

'I am enjoying London autumn. Is good to be back.'

She felt him looking at her. She felt his gaze seeing into her. Her aged body, the pain in her leg and hips, the occasional numbness in her left index finger and thumb. Her rheumy eyes and her failing hearing. The tiredness that bore down into her shoulders, the drumming, insistent beating of her heart. The torn lining in the right sleeve of her coat. The house keys in her pocket and the scribbled note reminding her to get detergent, garlic and toothpaste. She could have been naked before him. She didn't care. She almost laughed. She thought, this is what it must feel like to want to kill someone.

'You have been speaking to the police, no?' he asked.

'They told me about the arrangement that Gideon has made with you. They know that you have parted ways. Why has he done this? Where is he?'

Yuri's expression changed. He was picking through her words. 'Parted ways?'

'You are no longer close. You are no longer married.' Tasha's expression did not change, then she added, 'You are now married to someone else.'

'Anouska is old soul,' said Yuri, picking a piece of lint from his trousers.

'I don't need to know about her Yuri, in fact, I don't want to know about her. I just need to understand what you know of what has happened to Gideon.'

'Natasha, I too am concerned. I have made available reward. It was least I could do.'

'Yes. It was. The very least,' Tasha heard herself say evenly.

'This is what I know then, are you sure you will not sit?' he said.

'I am sure I will not sit. Go on.'

Yuri looked up at the ceiling, then he looked back at Tasha. 'I know we don't get on. I know you think me a fool – or criminal – or both. I know this. But let us be polite. Civilise. I know you are not stupid woman. From when we first met, I respect you. But you need to understand something about people like me and people like you.'

Tasha considered what he was saying. 'I never thought you were a fool.'

Yuri didn't seem to hear this. 'People like me have, like radar in the mind.' Here he tapped the side of his head. 'When we meet in the kitchen, years ago. Within a minute I know how you think of me. Why I am with Gideon. What I want. What I will do to get what I want. But Natashka, you don't know. You don't know me. I am dealing with people like you my whole life. People who think me scum. People who want me to leave. To go away. You think I am threat to Gideon. When I meet Gideon, do you understand what I see in him?'

'Opportunity?' Tasha offered.

'Kindness.' Here Yuri leaned his elbows forward on the table, his chin rest in his hands.

'All right then. You're no fool. You know how I feel about you. You claim to have known that since the first time we met, and you saw *kindness* in Gideon. How very *perceptive*. How very *sensitive* of you.' Here she paused and repeated the word, in an empty, bitter way. '*Kindness.*' He continued to look at her. 'And now, you've managed to monetise all that kindness – well done you. Yuri Kuznetsov has pulled himself up by his jock-strap and made a life for himself. You've got a thirty-room manor house in Kensington with modish junk on the walls that you don't care about and don't understand, a bubble-gum wife who's an artist no less, and a Great Dane called Sasha, for god's sake, *Sasha!* who suffers from *depression* – you really do have it all Yuri. Incidentally, I may have wanted you to leave, I certainly wanted you to go away, but I never thought you were scum. Yes, I thought you were a threat to Gideon, and to me, to be honest. Can I tell you that the only reason I'm meeting you today, is that I want to find my friend? I don't care about the money, I don't understand why or how all this has happened, you, here, in this freshly painted house. Why or how you're married now, to a woman. Why or how you managed to convince Gideon to sign all this over to you, do you understand? *I just don't care!* Yuri – please – I just want to find him. What you can't know is that it's not just because I care for him, not just because I love him as my dearest friend, he is my *history.* I won't let him go. I won't.'

There was silence. Yuri moved his tongue from one side of his mouth to the other.

'Natasha. I am not perfect man. I am very simple man. Gideon said he had plan – he asked me to do this for him. He signed everything. Just two things you must believe me. I love Gideon Bannerman. He made me happy, we were happy. And second thing, I don't know where he went, I don't know why he went. I don't know where he is. My hope is, he is safe. My hope is, he will return.' The simplicity of these words as Tasha heard them, as she saw him speak, made her believe that Yuri was telling the truth. She would not let him see her tears. Now on the television, a cyclist stood on a podium being sprayed with foaming champagne. At that moment there was a knock on the door of the empty library. Yuri remained seated.

'Voydite,' he said.

The door opened and Anouska appeared with Sasha by her side. 'Some tea. And some biscuit.' She set the tray down on the table in front of Yuri. There was silence except for the soft scratch of Sasha's claws on the broad polished wooden floor. Anouska took up the biscuits and turned to Tasha. As she did so, two of them slid off the plate. With a lunging, hunkering motion of his head and two laps of his enormous flat pink tongue, Sasha swallowed the biscuits whole. He then sat on the floor and grandly licked at his mouth and nose, his sad black expectant eyes all the while trained on Tasha.

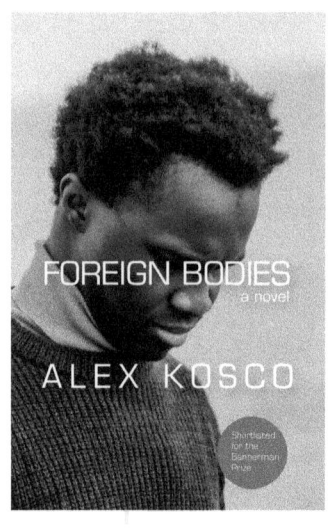

FOREIGN BODIES
Alex Kosco (Lowrey & Affleck) 398pp
The life of an ambitious foreign correspondent is put in mortal danger when he embarks on a perilous affair with the daughter of a Rwandan general during the Tutsi genocide.

11 am Cafebreria El Péndulo, Alesandro Dumas 81, Polanco, Mexico City

He looked at the crumpled pieces of notepaper he'd taken from his pocket. He'd arrived early. Half an hour. He'd told her he wasn't drinking and he'd estimated he could get in at least two before she arrived.

The morning was shaping up as a battle between Public Alex Kosco and Private Alex Kosco, and things were not looking good. There was Public Alex Kosco, bestselling author, whose literary thrillers had earned him comparisons with John le Carré and Graham Greene, whose work had spawned a cinematic franchise and whose latest book, *Foreign Bodies,* had so far sold over five million copies globally and had been translated into twenty languages.

And then there was Private Alex Kosco, who suffered from

a horribly debilitating but unfocused depression, whose wife occasionally threatened to leave him, and who was prone to sudden uncontrollable bouts of crying. He looked again at the paper, with words set down in his ordered script. His therapist had advised him that this would help.

'When you begin to feel overwhelmed, just make a list of the things in life that you're grateful for. Things that you love. Be very specific and detailed. Put your name at the top, then read through it. Then read through it again.' At the time Alex thought it all sounded a bit Oprah, and it added to his growing suspicion that Doctor Thorne – 'Please, call me Steve' – was little more than an expensive fake.

But the morning had started off poorly. Of course he wasn't going to drink but he'd lain in his bed at the Four Seasons listening to the rain that had begun sometime in the night, continuing its steady thrum into the early morning, with a familiar sense of blackening dread.

Long before he'd been diagnosed with depression he'd envisaged his condition as a cloud that hung over him. He knew this wasn't original, but it was real enough for him. This early morning he imagined his cloud as a velvet-dark cumulonimbus that was spreading mould spores over the ceiling, on the curtains and down the walls. He shut his eyes, as he lay naked in his troubled sheets. One hand across his chest, the other distractedly toying with his useless cock as imagined catastrophes played out in his head.

Someone close to him was going to die. His bed was a humid grave. He would be shot in the street by haphazard Mexican criminals. He would be publicly shamed for a forgotten transgression. He would be bundled into a black SUV off the street and kidnapped for a ransom his publisher or his agent or his wife would refuse to pay, leading to his decapitation in a corrugated iron chicken shack in Los Cabos. His headless body found dumped on a mountain of trash on the outskirts of the city. In his detailed and feverish imagining, seagulls pecked idly at the buttons of his bloodied shirt. A single tear ran down the side of his face and disappeared into the pillow.

He rolled over and took up the small pad on the side of the table imprinted with the spindly Four Seasons tree logo, and wrote his list.

Alex Kosco: Things I am grateful for, things that I love.
– Fifty-two years (not dead)
– New book (Foreign Bodies) – the hardback edition and the smell of vanilla in its creamy pages
– New book (FB) optioned by BBC
– New book (FB) longlisted and then shortlisted for the Bannerman Prize (both career firsts)
– Rosamund and our beautiful son Joshua
– Our farm in Norfolk – the pond and the ducks
– Women (generally)
– The romance of martinis
– Elgar – all of Elgar
– Cod fillet, bianco veloute & artichoke
– Ruth – my great ex-agent
– Ruth – my dear friend
– Sex with Ruth (once)
– Vodka
– The golden light that slants into my study at 8 pm on a summer evening
– Balmenach 30 Year Old Single Malt
– Our house in Highgate

He found himself staring at the words of the last entry – *Our house in Highgate.* He looked at the line until the words began to lose their meaning, turning into scribbles. He put the list down and drank three miniature bottles of vodka from the minibar and then walked into the bathroom. He tried not to see the appalling down-lit spectacle of his naked full-length reflection in the bevelled bathroom mirrors as he found the crushed box of paroxetine, his latest anti-depressant, and popped one into his mouth. He stood in the steamy shower for minute after minute, the hot water drumming on his head as the combination of alcohol and the molecules of the selective serotonin reuptake inhibitor coursed through his blood. When he turned off the taps, he rubbed his blinking eyes open. Now he would face the morning.

He dressed and left the hotel. The vodka had helped, but still the world around him seemed to be closing in. The rain had stopped. The freshened streets were alive in the thin, bright air. He'd read in the little pamphlet that was on his pillow when he arrived, 'Hola! Bienvenido!' that Mexico City was seven thousand three hundred feet above sea level, and that 'therefore the air can take some getting used to.' He thought that explained why, on his almost fifty-minute walk from the hotel to the café and bookshop, El Péndulo, he needed to stop from time to time to take some gasping breaths of air. It was either that, or the cancer that he knew would claim him sometime between fifty-two and death. Would it be his lungs? His oesophagus? Maybe his pancreas or prostate. He knew it was seeded deep inside and the tick, tick, tick of his life was just biding time before the metastasising cells flooded his system. It was cancer. He knew it. It was nonsense. He knew that too.

He would take his mind off his phantom illnesses by counting out the steps as he walked. Ten, twenty, thirty. Ten, twenty, thirty. The vodka had softened him, but he needed the rhythm of his steps on the pavement to quiet his blurry but persistent anxiety. It almost worked.

He had arrived in Mexico City on the eve of the Day of the Dead festivities, and from time to time as he walked he saw people dressed in skeleton t-shirts, with skull make-up, and skull masks, with papier-mâché skulls on sticks, with broad, stretched grins under sombreros. It occurred to him briefly that coming to a country that celebrates the dead so enthusiastically was perhaps not the best idea for a manic depressive. He shook that thought out of his head, the Day of the Dead was a celebration, after all, wasn't it? It was a cultural accommodation of mortality, it had nothing to do with him, or his black cloud. He walked on, ten, twenty, thirty.

His body was warm in his cornflower-coloured linen suit. By the time he turned into Alejandro Dumas, the sun was shining, the leafy, green trees that flanked the street sparkled with the recent rain. He stopped a hundred yards from the café. In the peaks and troughs of his depressive state, he was experiencing a now familiar sensation of transient, aggressive happiness. In his mind, a number of fireworks exploded, illuminating his joys. The world was beautiful! Just look at it! He was a successful author! His books had been made into films! His new book was going to be a series on the BBC! He was in Mexico City! He could do what he liked! He was shortlisted for a prestigious literary prize! He had a beautiful child who was now a beautiful young man of twenty-three, writing a PhD at Cambridge! A wife that loved him! Other women were attracted to him! He fucked who he wanted! He was staying at the Four Seasons, and he looked fucking great in his fucking cornflower-coloured linen suit!

The fireworks of his temporary euphoria had sputtered. Now, fat drops of rain fell on him from the branches above, one found its way to the top of his head and slid down his back. He steadied himself against a tree and looked down the street. He would catch his breath for a moment, then he thought that he could make it to the café. His phone buzzed in his suit jacket – 'Ruth.'

'Hiya!' she sounded bright.

'Hey,' he said, still leaning on the tree, his fingers feeling the bark.

'I'm just on my way. The flight was delayed in Los Angeles. I might be a few minutes late.'

' Oh, okay, right, fine.' He took a moment to catch his breath again. 'Yeah, okay, I'll see you when you get here then.'

There was a pause. 'Are you okay? You sound a bit, I don't know, you sound funny.'

'I'm fine. I'm really fine. I've just been on a long walk here from the hotel. It will be lovely to see you. Mexico City! Right?'

'Well, I've not seen much of it yet. Just the highway from the airport and now the hotel. I'll see you soon.'

He put his phone back in his pocket. He walked into El Péndulo. He wanted to look casual as he perused the shelves for his work. He found three of his previous novels and took them from the shelf. *Border Crossing, The Algerian Correspondent,* and his new book, *Foreign Bodies,* all translated into Spanish. He found a table and sat by the window and looked at the laminated menu. An orange juice, two tequila shots and a Smirnoff. That should do it. A young man in tight black trousers and a tight white t-shirt took his order. When he'd left Alex smiled and almost laughed when he realised that through the sound system in the café, Dusty Springfield was belting out 'I Just Don't Know What to Do with Myself.' He took the two little pages of notes of things he was grateful for, things that he loved, and twisted the paper into a tight twill and pushed it deep into the dirt of a pot plant by the window.

He would brunch with Ruth Matthews. They were both in Mexico City for a new writers festival, *Fronteras Ficticias*. He was to be a guest speaker on the ethics of using real political events in fiction, and Ruth was representing two other authors who were featured in the program. It had been three years since they last saw each other face-to-face. He'd left her when he was courted by Dominic Newell, a higher profile agent who was known for negotiating six and seven figure sums for his authors. It was after the boozy lunch when he told Ruth he was moving on that they had ended up at her flat, naked on the couch in the late afternoon light.

'Well, that was unexpected,' she said, her arm was resting on his chest, her fingers were stroking his hair.

'Yes. I thought this afternoon was about saying goodbye.' He realised that one of the top buttons of his shirt was still done up and he'd only taken one sock off.

'Oh, I think it's definitely about saying goodbye,' Ruth said. 'Never again. This can never happen again. I like Rosamund too much.'

'I'm rather fond of her myself.'

'Well, I should hope so.'

He shifted his position and suddenly became aware of his naked body. He pulled the tail of his shirt across his stomach. Sensing a shift in the mood Ruth sat forward, her elbows on her knees, cradling one hand in the palm of another she seemed to be staring at nothing. He noticed that she was twisting a black garnet ring on the index finger of her left hand.

'Why don't I make us a cup of tea? You can get dressed, then I can see you to the door, and we can say goodbye properly.'

'Okay. But I have to say, I quite liked our improper goodbye.'

*   *   *   *

Since that afternoon they maintained a friendly email correspondence as if the event on the couch had never happened. As if he hadn't watched as she walked away from him, naked across her open-plan sitting room to her kitchen, where she noisily filled the kettle. As if, in the archive of his erotic memory, he hadn't replayed the indelible sight of her hair, her shoulders, the calligraphic grace of the line of her spine and her perfect, abundant bum, rhythmically undulating away from him. A memory that was made all the more powerfully sexual in his mind as it was coupled with the sound of Ruth's voice saying, 'Never again.'

Three months ago they realised that they would be in Mexico City at the same time, and it was Ruth who had suggested they meet. She even invited him to visit the Frida Kahlo museum *La Casa Azul* with her, 'it would be fun'. He had sent back a one-word email reply – 'Yes!'

The waiter arrived with his order, setting out the glasses in a neat row. Alex downed the vodka in one shot. He then sipped the orange juice and emptied the tequila into the glass.

'Some food, señor?'

'Ah, yes please.' He quickly scanned the menu. 'The Omelette Juliette, I think.' He looked up cheerfully at the waiter. 'Thank you.'

It was then that his phone vibrated with an incoming message. The screen read 'Joshua' and he saw that it was a video. He tapped the message and his twenty-three-year-old son's face could be seen giggling as he adjusted the phone on a bench, it looked like the kitchen of his flat in Cambridge. He then went out of frame for a second or two, the camera was trained on a chair, he heard a brief, muffled, inaudible conversation and then Joshua reappeared and sat down. His son was naked and he was holding his erect cock, stroking it down to his balls. He remained seated. 'Come here, Crinkle,' he said, to someone Alex could not see. Then another naked man entered the frame and through a series of clearly well-practised manoeuvres he straddled Joshua, and they began kissing and fucking on the chair. Alex could see that the video had another 27 seconds to go. He watched his son grab the hair of the other man whose neck was seen to twist as Joshua kissed and bit him, all the while, they continued the rhythmic movement on the chair.

Alex was holding his phone but found he could not move his fingers to stop the images. He could hear the young men groaning with pleasure. From time to time during the short video, they made slight adjustments to their positions for deeper penetration. Alex stared dumbly at Crinkle's badly drawn tattoo of a Chinese dragon as it spiralled down his spine, animated by his movement. As the video counted down to the end, another blurry hand stopped the device recording, and it was over.

Alex looked up and felt an undertow of nausea rise in his stomach. He stood and moved briskly to the bathroom at the back of the café and vomited. He rinsed his mouth but still tasted acidic bile on his tongue and teeth. Then he vomited again. He rinsed his face. He looked into his reflection in the mottled mirror above the sink. Water ran down his face and dripped off his nose. His bloodshot, blue eyes looked startled. In less than a minute, his world had been tilted. He rested his hands on the edge of the sink and bent his head low. He couldn't look at his face again. He dabbed himself dry with paper towel, pushed his fingers through his hair and walked back to his table. He took three gulps of his drink and looked up, around the café. Over the sound system, Dusty's spooky mezzo-soprano was exploring 'The Windmills of Your Mind'. He looked down at his phone, at the first image of the video, Joshua's face in close-up, his twisted, boyish grin. Alex's finger hovered over the image. He looked up again. Four young people, three girls and a young man were at another table, slumped in their chairs, hypnotised by their phones. Next to them, an elderly couple wearing white tennis visors sat looking at the menu. He was panicked. No one could have seen what he'd seen, he put the phone down on the table and gripped his cold glass of orange juice and tequila.

So, his son was gay? His son was having gay sex in Cambridge with another young man called Crinkle? Who could possibly be called *Crinkle?* And who stopped the recording? There was someone else in the kitchen with them. So, this was a group sex thing? A gay group sex thing? And he had sent the video to Alex, but who was it intended for? It couldn't possibly have been for him. Who would he share such a thing with? Was it legal? Alex took a deep breath and felt himself sweating inside his cornflower linen suit. He would try not to cry. Not now. Joshua can't be gay. He had girlfriends. There was Allegra, the beautiful Italian undergraduate studying philosophy who had come to the house and had talked about Alex's novels admiringly. There was Sophie, the striking redhead who was a part-time model who was studying economics, and lately there had been Gabrielle, an older girl who was in the last year of medicine, who travelled with Joshua to Santorini during the summer, was it this year?

The insane proposition popped into Alex's head that he ought to call Gabrielle and explain that he was in Mexico City for a writers conference, but could he trouble her with a question that he desperately needed the answer to: 'Is Joshua Gay, do you think?' No. He would not do that. He could not do that, he didn't have Gabrielle's number. He certainly couldn't call Rosamund. This would be more evidence of his failure as a husband and a father, but maybe she already knew? Perhaps she had kept this secret from him so that it could be strategically weaponised at some later date. His eyes blurred and two tears ran down either side of his face. He quickly dabbed them away with a paper napkin. It wasn't the idea that Joshua was gay – okay, that was an adjustment, but okay, *fine*. It was the fact that he was now gay, *witnessed* by Alex. He had watched his son having sex – *actual gay sex* with another young man. In less than a minute Joshua, his son, had gone from a comforting remote presence, busy researching and writing his muddy PhD, '1603. Dreams Made Flesh; The Social Construction of the Virgin Queen', to a fully functioning homosexual adult. *Come here, Crinkle.* Crinkle. His mouth filled with saliva again. He steadied himself. He took another deep breath. Then another one. Suddenly the screen illuminated as a text appeared – 'Joshua.'

'Oh FUUUUCCCKKK!!!! Please tell me Dad that I did NOT just send you a vid! LOL – I mean Fuck! I can explain – if you have received a vid from me DELETE IT – DO NOT OPEN IT!'

Alex watched as his fingers found Rosamund's number and tapped it to call. In the seconds he had before she answered, he conjured Public Alex Kosco into being. He heard her voice slightly echoed, she'd put her phone on speaker.

'Hi, how are you?'

'Hi Roz, yeah I'm fine. I'm er, yeah, I'm fine, I was just calling to see how you were.'

'Really?'

'Yes, of course.'

'Okay. Thanks, yeah, I'm okay, listen, did you speak to the plumber about coming over in the morning? I got a message to say they'd be here at eight-thirty, but I've got that ceramics workshop all this week. Why would you get them to come tomorrow? You knew what I was doing.'

She didn't know. In the way that couples held knowledge about each other and their children, their personalities, their habits and their behaviour, their confidences and their secrets, Alex immediately understood that Rosamund knew nothing. There was nothing underneath the tone in her voice that indicated that she was aware that their beautiful son Joshua was now a practising homosexual and was buggering his boyfriend, Crinkle, in his kitchen in Cambridge. Still, he thought he'd test this assumption, gently.

'You haven't heard from Josh at all, have you?'

'Yesterday? Yes, it was yesterday. He was asking about Christmas, what we were doing. I think he wants to go to Scotland with some friends. Why?'

'Oh nothing, I was just wondering. Is he still with, oh God, what was her name, Gabrielle is it? Are they still together?' There was a silence.

'Oh for god's sake, Alex, he hasn't been with Gabrielle for over a year. You need to make more of an effort to keep up. Shame really, I liked her. Remember when she came over and the two of them cooked that amazing green curry thing? And studying to be a doctor too.'

'Really? Over a year, okay.'

'How's Mexico? How's the hotel?'

'Oh yeah, great. I'm just now sat in the most wonderful bookshop, café sort of place. I'm just about to meet Ruth for coffee, then the plan is that we'll go to Frida Kahlo's house.'

'Oh right, yes, I forgot that she'd be there. I wish I could have come, but as you know I've got this ceramics course, *which you've clearly forgotten about.*'

'Okay, look, I'll call the plumber, send me his number and I'll have it cancelled.'

'You don't need to bother. I've done that already. They're coming when you're back.' There was another silence. 'Are you all right, Alex? You don't normally call me to see how I am. You know how I am. Is something going on?'

'No, not at all. I'm fine.' There was no hint of panic, no tears in his voice. Public Alex Kosco was in control. 'I'm good, I just wanted to say hi.'

'Well, hi, and bye. I'm meeting some people from the course at six – we're having early dinner and then the cinema. Give Ruth my love, I expect I'll be seeing her at the prize dinner on Friday. We can talk tomorrow, enjoy Frida Kahlo, I've got to run, bye.'

'Bye.' But she was gone. Alex scrolled to Joshua's name on his phone. He called the number.

'Hello, you've called Josh – I can't take your call right now – leave a message.' Then a beep, but Alex could find nothing to say. He thought a moment longer.

'Hi Josh … Hey Joshie, I hope you're good. I did get a message from you, and I deleted your message – as instructed. This is all a bit mysterious. You'll have to tell me what it's all about. Talk soon.' He paused. 'Love you!' He felt a tap on his shoulder.

'Alex! Sorry I'm late.' It was Ruth, leaning down to kiss him on the cheek.

Alex stood. Could she see that he'd been crying? Could she tell that he'd just vomited? Did she know what was in his orange juice?

Did she somehow know his son was fucking a man called Crinkle in Cambridge? His Omelette Juliette arrived.

'Hi Ruth, would you like anything? Sorry, I went ahead and ordered something. I'm a bit famished.' They sat.

Ruth looked at the waiter, pulling her coat from her shoulders. She wore a black mohair pullover and a red cotton pleated skirt hemmed just below her knee.

'I'd like a double shot espresso, thank you.'

She took her fork and cut into his omelette. It had only been three years since he'd seen her, but she had changed. He'd remembered her that last afternoon they'd shared as a series of glimpses: the side of her face, her shoulders, the curve of her breast as it rested on her ribcage, the pattern of her hair as it fell about her shoulders, her back. But sitting opposite him now in the morning light, she was another person. She ruffled his hair playfully.

'Look at you going grey. Quite the distinguished author now.'

He smiled and shook his head. She was grey too, or at least he could see streaks of grey in her lemon-yellow hair that darkened at the roots. She'd fashioned two thin braids and pinned them across the top of her head, while longer, curved wisps of hair fell on either side of her face. There was a frosting on her lips of the palest pink, and her eyelashes held tiny particles of mascara, her black eyeliner was perfectly inscribed. The thing that hadn't changed was her eyes. They were jewel-like, precise and a terrifying ice-blue that sought out pretence, dishonesty and secrets. They had knowledge and wisdom, patience and anger. Her eyes were what people remembered of her. They made her a wonderful friend and a formidable enemy. She had a reputation for being blunt, honest and fearless, with a filthy sense of humour. She was only two years older than him, but he had always been slightly afraid of her. He felt that she knew more than him, not just about the publishing world, but the world in general. He'd always held the suspicion that she possibly knew more about him than he knew himself. More than once since he'd left her and her agency, Alex wished he hadn't.

'You know,' she said placing his knife and fork on his plate, 'I can't understand why I've never been here before.' Her coffee arrived.

'Me too. The air takes some getting used to.' He realised he was now quoting the hotel brochure, and he hoped that Ruth hadn't noticed that his features were being held in place by a delicate network of threads that were fraying. He avoided her eyes. She was stirring her coffee.

'I'm looking forward to seeing Frida's house. Although, if I'm honest, I'm not a huge fan of her painting,' she said.

'No?'

'No, not really. All that suffering. All those self-portraits. It's Frida, Frida, Frida! Didn't she get sick of it? I mean, she was sick, I know that but, oh I don't know, ignore me this is jetlag talking.'

She was looking at two of the girls sitting at the table opposite. They were holding a phone, taking a selfie, pasting on smiles for the shot. Then they repeated the action. Then there were frowns as they examined the pictures critically. Ruth giggled. 'I suppose she'd be right at home in this century as well.'

Alex laughed a little too. He took another gulp of his juice.

'Could I have a sip of that?' Ruth asked, she went to take the glass from him.

'Ah no, no you shouldn't Ruth, I'm just now getting over a cold.'

She pursed her lips together in a tight little smile.

'Okay.'

She leaned forward with her elbows on the table, resting her chin in her palm. Her eyes scanned his features. He dabbed at his mouth with his paper napkin, now scrunched up into a damp ball. He tried to pretend that he wasn't being scrutinised. It didn't work.

'Alex. What is going on with you? Are you going to tell me?'

He held her gaze for a moment, then he looked away. He knew he'd need to come up with something. He tried for a half-truth.

'I'm just a bit worried about Josh, to be honest.'

'Why?'

'Oh, you know, just a feeling I have. I haven't seen him for a few months, I've been so busy promoting the book, and the interest in the prize. I know practically nothing of his life in Cambridge, his friends and so forth. There's nothing the matter, really Ruth, seriously. Roz is looking forward to seeing you at the prize dinner.'

Ruth allowed him to change the subject. 'Yes, I'm looking forward to seeing her too. I'm not looking forward to the prize, it's such a fucking circus, and Gideon Bannerman doing his disappearing trick has rather derailed a lot of the publicity we'd normally get from the shortlist. I suppose his body will turn up sooner or later. Rich people aren't usually allowed to vanish into thin air. I'm not looking forward to the party. I hate parties, as you know. I've actually just signed one of your fellow short-listers.'

'Really? Who?'

'Isobel Dalby.'

'Oh god! Really?'

'Yes. Why *'really?'*'

'Isn't she just a lesbian with an asymmetrical bob?'

Ruth's brow creased, her eyes narrowed. 'What century are you living in? I've just managed to get her a fantastic deal with ITV for her to write a series from her book. *'Lesbian with an asymmetrical bob*'? Are you serious?'

'Oh, come on Ruth. Okay, all right. You've signed her. Well done. I couldn't finish her book. I'm sorry.'

'There's really no need to apologise to me Alex. I don't care what you think of her work. But do yourself a favour, and never use that term to describe her again. These days you'll get into a lot of trouble for it. I'm speaking as your ex-agent *and* your friend.'

'Okay. All right. Christ, Ruth, I was joking. Okay, it was a bad joke. Anyway, I think it's interesting that she's been shortlisted, I honestly do. She's new and it acknowledges her work.' He wasn't sure what he wanted to talk about, but he wanted to stop talking about Isobel Dalby.

'Work you couldn't finish. Oh Alex, you are funny. The shortlist acknowledges your work too – that's never happened before.'

'Yes. I suppose. I never thought that my work, my type of book, spies, politics, global upheaval, would ever be considered, much less shortlisted. I'd be surprised if I won.' This was a lie. Alex considered *Foreign Bodies* to be his best book, and ever since the shortlist had been announced he'd indulged in the fantasy of his acceptance speech.

'Oh *Alex*. You're not going to win, not in a shortlist that includes Martin Gillray and Kai Noguchi. No. I mean, there are some in the literary world, and beyond it, who think that mounting a work of fiction like yours that includes a romance within a frame of genocide is more than a little offensively tasteless. You'd know that if you read reviews. No, just enjoy the moment. I mean, I agree that books like yours don't generally get considered for these things, and if I'm really honest, I was surprised that you were longlisted, now shortlisted, but no, you're not going to win. And why should you care? You've never concerned yourself with prizes.' She leaned back in her chair and folded her arms across her chest.

'I remember years ago, in the beginning, we'd talk about what a farce the prizes were – they don't matter – it's *the work* that matters. I still think that. I remember you saying that prizes like the Booker and the Bannerman were just there to prop up sales for unpopular novelists. You'd say that every year when the lists were announced and you weren't on them. Again.' She laughed. 'Oh Alex, I can't quite believe that you're twisting your hanky in a knot about the Bannerman Prize. Getting all breathy and nervous about winning a crystal bauble. Is that what I can see behind your eyes?'

This was the Ruth that he remembered. There was no cruelty in her voice, and she would not consider for a moment that what she had said was offensive, and she probably wouldn't care if it was. He was still in the grip of the seismic shifts of his depression. And then there was Josh and Crinkle to consider, if only that video would stop playing in his head. Josh's smiling face, the kitchen, the chair. He loved Ruth as one of his oldest friends, she had believed in his work at a time when few did, she knew him well and he thought that she respected him, he knew she did. His anger was made more vivid for him by the realisation that what she had said was probably true. He would not win the prize. Even Public Alex Kosco lacked the performance skills to pretend that what she'd said hadn't hurt him.

'Could you not find it in your heart to lie to me to today? Okay, I don't write the kind of book that wins prizes. I don't play that game – and it is a game, make no mistake. It's a public cruelty. Tasteless? Offensive? Using that logic, *War and Peace* is nothing more than the work of an opportunistic hack. I write readable fiction that the TLS and the LRB couldn't give a toss about. But through some gross negligence, or an accidental permission, I am being considered for a prize alongside authors like Gillray and Noguchi and *fucking Julian Adagoke for fuck's sake.* That has *happened.* So I think it's not unreasonable to ask, to expect really, that my very good friend, my wonderful ex-agent and *one-time fuck,* could just take leave of her reputation for hard-nosed, intelligent, honest assessment and for once – *just once* – not feel that she had to make her opinion known, no matter the consequences, and lie through her teeth to her commercially successful and sometimes needy ex-client and friend, and say that he at least had a chance of winning, could you possibly see your way clear? Just this *once?*'

Ruth leaned forward and took his hand.

'Oh Alex, I have missed you, but I think we really ought to leave Tolstoy out of this, don't you?'

For a moment nothing was said. His head was fogged. It was the thin air of Mexico City, it was the paroxetine and the alcohol coursing through his blood, it was Josh and Crinkle in the kitchen and Ruth's hard assessments. He now felt clownish in his linen suit and all the efforts he'd made to keep the black cloud of his depression at bay, the tricks of confidence and his list of gratitude's, had come to nothing. He looked at Ruth again, his head shifted as if he was making some small internal adjustment. Then suddenly, uncontrollably Alex began to sob. At first he shielded his eyes from view, then gradually he hung his head as his body was racked with crying. After a few minutes the waiter came to the table and cleared Ruth's cup.

'Can I get you anything else?' He asked as if the sight of a middle-aged man sobbing at a table at Cafebreria El Péndulo was nothing exceptional.

'My friend is just very tired, you understand?' The waiter shrugged. 'Could I have another double shot espresso? And a glass of brandy please?'

The waiter nodded and left. Ruth gripped Alex's arm with her hand. He looked up at her, his eyes, hollowed out wells of tears. His face was streaked and the sleeve of his suit jacket was sodden. In a gesture of childish distress he raised his other arm and wiped his eyes with his sleeve.

'Sorry, Ruth.' This brought forth more tears. 'I think I'm a bit lost. I've been so busy and … and …' He laughed. 'I'm just having a moment.'

Ruth smiled. 'So it would seem.'

The waiter arrived and set down the coffee and the brandy. Ruth handed him the glass. Alex swallowed the drink in one gulp, he wiped his mouth with his hand. He took up his orange juice and drained that as well. The music changed again. The soundtrack to this awful morning now included Dusty's rendering of 'The Look of Love'. Alex was staring at his empty glass of juice.

'That had a double shot of tequila in it. Just so you know.'

'I think I might have known *something* like that was going on, darling.'

'Of course you did.' He leaned forward on the table and massaged his brow with his fingers. Then he cupped his chin with his hands and twisted around to look at Ruth.

'You know this isn't about the fucking prize, don't you?'

'Oh Alex, of course I do.'

He took a deep breath and exhaled.

'Fuck Dusty Springfield.'

They arrived at *La Casa Azul* just after one. It was only the middle of the day, but the rigours of the morning had left Alex heavy and tired. He would have liked to get a cab back to the hotel and curl up on the freshly made bed and sleep away the hours of the afternoon.

Instead he found himself following Ruth as they walked from room to room in the museum house of Frida Kahlo and her husband Diego Rivera.

He looked at the pictures on the walls and read the explanatory cards that described Frida's famous bus accident and the iron handrail that tore into her groin that was the catalyst for the world of pain that was her life. He learned about her two marriages to Diego and their bohemian sexual arrangements, her affairs with men and women, and even her tryst with Leon Trotsky just prior to his assassination in 1940.

He stood in Frida's bright yellow kitchen and suddenly thought there could be a book in that story. The assassins in the city planning the attack, first with guns, then with an ice pick, the famous communist exile and his charged sexual encounters with the broken painter, their political arguments, his murder and the life of the demi-monde of forties Mexico. For two or three exhilarating minutes he thought he could bring that story to life. But then he remembered Joshua again, and Cambridge and the kitchen chair and the notional novel evaporated.

He and Ruth stood beside Frida's four-poster bed that was so thin it could have been a coffin. There were some papier-maché skeletons mounted on the walls. Hand-crafted angels hung from the canopy of the bed and a mirror was mounted into it reflecting her shiny black death mask, placed on her pillow surrounded by a shawl embroidered with roses. Ruth leaned over and whispered in his ear.

'Apparently they put a different shawl on her every day.'

Alex didn't look at Ruth. His stomach felt light and he thought he might vomit again.

'Is that so? I think I'll go get some air. I'll see you in the garden.'

He left her and walked down the stone steps from the bedroom into the expansive enclosed courtyard garden. There was a large group of boys and girls, Alex thought that they couldn't be any older than five or six, being supervised by a young man with a black ponytail and a beard, Alex thought he was perhaps their teacher. He was stocky and wore denim overalls, leather sandals and a white t-shirt. There was a loose string of red beads around his left wrist. His forearm was decorated with a tattoo of a heart entwined by thorns and flowers. He had an open, happy face that smiled easily. Alex sat on one of the yellow chairs at the café and watched as the young man handed out white paper plates and crayons to each of the children, giving them loud instructions in Spanish. He heard the phrase, 'El Dia de los Muertos' spaced out for clarity, and he wondered how a teacher might explain the festival of the dead to children.

Pale grey cloud cover had moved across the city. The vivid lush greens in the garden cast no shadows, and the afternoon was becoming warm. Alex could see, off in the distant corner of the garden, against the electric blue walls, a life-size photographic portrait of Frida and Diego. He thought they looked like accomplished carnival performers. An overweight ringmaster and his tiny glamorous assistant. Alex could imagine Frida in tights, arms outstretched, standing balanced on a pony, skipping through hoops of fire. It didn't matter that her body had been gouged into, cut and incised to relieve her disability, or that she had been laced into constraining corsets and braces to correct her troubled spine. Her imperious, confident expression suggested that limitations were the concern of others, not hers. They stood, husband and wife, the tenured ghosts of *La Casa Azul,* looking across the distance of the courtyard regarding Alex Kosco, slumped in his crumpled suit.

Alex thought for a moment of his list of things he was grateful for, things that he loved. Was it too late to retrieve his notes from the dirt of the pot plant at *El Péndulo?* Was his situation worsened by this casual discarding of what was important to him? His depressive mind often worked in this way, ascribing meanings and outcomes to random acts. It was nonsense. He would speak at the conference tomorrow. He would attend the Bannerman Prize dinner on Friday. He would applaud and congratulate the winner. He would be a good husband. He would be a good father. He would speak to Joshua. He would maintain the lie that he hadn't seen the video. He would accept Crinkle, or whatever version of Crinkle his son ended up with. He took his phone from his pocket and deleted the offending message. He felt slightly better as the seed of fiction that he had never received the message in the first place began to germinate in his mind. He saw Ruth at the top of the steps leading to the garden, he couldn't be sure that she'd seen him. He would ask her where they might go for dinner. His nausea had subsided. He felt better. A little better. He would try to trust it.

There was general movement in the group of children now. They had each drawn skulls onto their paper plates and the young man was now cutting eye holes into them and fastening them to the faces of the boys and girls with string. One child had started to cry, and he crouched down by a fountain in the middle of the garden to console her with comforting words and a kiss on the forehead. Small groups of boys and girls broke off and started exploring the garden and playing on their own. There was a group of girls standing in a circle singing, some boys started a game of tag, running up and down the paved pathways of the garden, and one girl had started a game of hide and seek with around five or six others.

The children hid among the potted palms and trees and a couple found places behind chairs at the cafe. Alex watched as, one by one, the girl who was the seeker sought out the others, squealing with laughter as each was discovered. Until there was only one boy left to find.

She had drawn a particularly ferocious skull on her paper plate, its mouth gaped wide open with sharpened, pointy teeth. She was closing in on this last hidden child and Alex could see, in the way that her body moved, her tiptoeing steps, the moment when she knew exactly where he was, she could see his skinny legs, runners and socks partially obscured by a palm leaf by the fountain. Ruth was now in the garden too, and Alex saw her walking toward him.

The hiding child stood rigid, his fists clamped his paper plate death mask to his face in an effort to make himself magically invisible. The little girl searching for him was less than five steps away. Alex could see that the boy had sensed he was about to be caught, but there was nothing he could do. He watched as the child began to tremble, he seemed to be laughing inside his mask, willing the moment to happen, alive to the knowledge that he was about to be found.

7.43 pm, Royal Society of Arts, John Adam Street WC2N 6EZ

'I think it's fair to say that we've reached something of an impasse.'

With less than twenty minutes before they needed to have made their decision, Tasha surveyed the glum faces of her fellow judges in the Shipley Room at the Royal Society of Arts.

Esther Greaves, who had arrived at three in the afternoon wearing a man's dinner suit, was slumped in her chair with her arms crossed belligerently, her bow tie pulled loose, staring at a plateful of demolished sandwiches whose dry crusts were gently beginning to curl in the overheated room. Douglas Budgell was leaning on the table, his left hand supported his head, which was at an angle, looking down at random text messages on his phone. The actress Cynthia Blakemore was opening in Beckett's *Happy Days* at the Harold Pinter theatre in two weeks' time and had brought a well-thumbed and slightly grubby copy of the text with her to this last meeting. Tasha noticed her staring down at the cover of the play with a look of abject defeat. David Kemble was massaging his temples, staring at his dinner jacket hanging on a portable clothes rack standing against the opposite wall of the room, Cynthia's gown, an elaborate collection of layered and pleated blue and green silk panels hung next to it, sheathed in clear plastic. The poet, Samira Prasanna sat idly scribbling on a yellow quarto pad in front of her, seemingly oblivious to the others. In the corner of the page she had drawn two cats, one striped, one spotted. The six shortlisted novels were spread out on the large table along with notepads and discarded pieces of paper, some crumpled, some scattered and inscribed with scribbles.

In the silence, Tasha could hear the not-too-distant hum of the crowd who had gathered for the prize dinner in the Great Room, not twenty yards away. Everyone seated in that room at the circular tables, covered in white linen, set with china, glass and silverware would be aware that she and her fellow judges had not emerged. As chair of the panel, the fact that they had been discussing the six novels on the shortlist for nearly five hours and had failed to reach a decision on the winner weighed heavily on her. The cumulative exhaustion of the last ten weeks had bought her to this point. Yuri, Anouska, Sasha, Detective Timewell, the forensic accountants and the fuzzy images of Gideon's last appearance on the street with his can of soft drink and his sandwich crowded in on her thoughts in ways that left little room for anything else. She should have steered the meeting to her preferred author with subtlety, strategic accommodation and diplomacy, but it hadn't worked. Her heart wasn't in it, and she was only mildly surprised to realise that at that very moment she didn't care who was going to win. She wanted, more than anything, to go home to her darkened house. To forget this room, these people, retreat to her sitting room, to close her eyes, and forget.

They now had less than fifteen minutes to make a decision. She leaned forward on the table, lacing her fingers together she appeared to be examining her knuckles.

'It being just after a quarter to eight, I'm very much aware of the time. I'm going to paraphrase where we have got to in our almost five hours of deliberating. It is obvious that we all feel passionately about the books we all, individually, believe should win, but the time for consideration has passed. We need a resolution, and we will not arrive at a resolution if we remain dug into our positions, so to speak.

'The one thing we all appear to agree on is that Alex Kosco is out.' She picked up the copy of *Foreign Bodies* and took it off the table, setting it on the floor beside her chair.

'David, I know that you favour *The Broken Tooth Upstairs*, but I think that won't carry the day, ultimately.'

David straightened in his chair. 'Look, Natasha, it pushes the form, it's human, it's brave and uncompromising. I think it would be a worthy winner and would demonstrate that the Bannerman is moving forward.'

Esther snorted. 'Moving *forward*? To what exactly? *The Broken Tooth Upstairs* is a circus on top of a thimble – it is cheap *piffle*. It should never have been longlisted in the first place.'

Samira Prasanna looked consolingly at David as she picked at a cuticle on her left index finger. 'I was captivated by the book David, for the first seventy-three pages, but then it fell apart. I have now read that book four times, and on each occasion I have grown more unconvinced of Julian Adagoke's words, his intentions. I will not vote for it.'

Tasha took Julian's book off the table and placed it on top of *Foreign Bodies.* Before continuing.

'Now Esther, you still favour *The Clava Cairn* as the front-runner.'

'Yes. For the last time today, I am saying I support a book that holds a moral position, argues it passionately in prose that demonstrates that Martin Gillray is at the height of his powers.'

David smirked. 'I'm just now trying to see beyond the marketing speak of your argument here Esther. *The height of his powers?* You sound like a book jacket. He's not a magician, he's not some hypnotist, he's a national institution who's written a dense, unreadable book that should not be rewarded. If *The Clava Cairn* wins, the message that sends is that old white men are still at the helm. We'll be roasted.'

Esther looked to Tasha. 'I'm sorry Natasha, I was under the impression we were here to judge excellence in fiction. Now I understand that we are really engaged in sending messages. I'm sorry, but I did not agree to read over one hundred – often dreadful – novels to send messages. To whom? And to what purpose? *The Clava Cairn* is the best novel in the shortlist. It should win the prize. I'll say no more.'

Cynthia was staring at the last half inch of orange juice left in a carafe in the middle of the table, she spoke slowly, as if reading a pattern in the orange pulp left on the side of the glass.

'You know, Esther, I woke up this morning thinking as you do about *The Clava Cairn,* it really is such a human book, such a wise book isn't it?' She raised her eyebrows to emphasise the question, looking now directly at Esther. 'And yet, as the day has worn on I have really looked into my heart, and I don't think I can underwrite a decision that ignores the beauty of Kai Noguchi's novel.'

Douglas Budgell looked up from his phone screen. 'I agree. *The Illustrated Danish Tree* is perfect. Tone, theme and prose – perfectly resolved.'

Esther slammed her hand down on the table in a gesture of exasperation.

'For God's sake. *The Danish Tree* is decorative, it's thin. Each time I returned to it the book became more insubstantial in my mind. Yes, there are some touching passages, but it's the kind of inoffensive book you see pictured in bookcases in an Ikea catalogue.'

For a moment there was silence. Then Samira spoke.

'Can I ask? Is there a reason why we are not discussing the two women writers under consideration?'

Less than ten tense minutes later, they had arrived at a resolution. As if they had all had been stuck on a stalled train high in icy mountains, and were bonded by relief as the train began to chug forward, they all stood from the table, giddy and slightly shell-shocked. With the exception of Esther Greaves, who stood over Tasha at the table.

'This decision is a joke, and an abrogation of your responsibility to the prize. Quite frankly, I think you've completely buckled. I will not support this decision, not publicly, not tonight, or ever. If Gideon's disappearance was causing you so much grief that you felt that you couldn't give the prize the proper attention it deserved, I could have stepped in as chair, you only had to ask, and you know that. I thought you were stronger than this Tasha. What on earth can you be thinking?'

Tasha drew herself up into a gentle stretch that was like a small luxury after sitting for so long.

'What on earth can I be thinking? I'm hungry and a bit tired. And, in addition, I'm thinking I need a drink. I'm going to order the Bruno Giacosa Barolo Le Rocche del Falletto Riserva, I believe the 2000 is excellent.'

Esther's mouth remained open. She blinked three times before turning her back and walking out of the room.

BROMLEYS

HARVEST PLACE
Pictures, Furniture, Silver and Curios
from the Bannerman Estate

1.20 am, Argyle Square WC1H 8AS

As Tasha's cab turned into Argyle Square, she was reading an article posted online.

Giving It All Away! A Proto-Feminist Porno-Pastiche and a Commonwealth for the Insane – It's a Bannerman Prize Tie!

Carol Peyton

In a move that surprised many, not only at the Bannerman Prize dinner last night, but more generally across the publishing world, Isobel Dalby's debut novel, a sexually frank feminist reimagining of eighteenth-century Covent Garden, and Catherine Adler's savagely beautiful book on the debilitating legacy of British cultural imperialism, have both taken out this year's Bannerman Prize for Literature. Although the Booker Prize has, in the past, made tied judgements, on three occasions, this was the first time for the Bannerman.

The winning authors beat out two-time Bannerman Prize winner, Martin Gillray, best-selling first-time short-lister, Alex Kosco, and insider favourite, the poet and novelist Kai Noguchi in a decision that went right down to the wire according to the judges. Actress Cynthia Blakemore said after the announcement, 'We had been debating, discussing, and yes, you could say arguing for many hours, the time was ticking closer and closer to eight o'clock. But in the end, really, well … here we are.'

Academic Esther Greaves was a little more forthcoming and, it has to be said, a lot more unvarnished. 'I'm not happy with the outcome. I argued passionately for Martin Gillray. *The Clava Cairn* is a remarkable achievement from a novelist of insight, artistry and humanity, at the height of his powers – I want that to be on the record.'

Social commentator Douglas Budgell was perhaps the most sanguine of the judging panel, and the most prosaic. 'In the end, when art becomes a competition, somebody wins, and somebody loses.'

Quite.

Winner Isobel Dalby, who attended the dinner with her mother, and dedicated her win to her late aunt, appeared to be in shock after the announcement. 'I'm not believing this. Is this really happening? I live in a bedsit above an Ezy-Mart in Brixton! I wrote my book because I thought it was a story worth telling. I wanted to imagine a better life for women back then and a better life for women now. That's what I'm striving for in my work.' Her mother, standing beside her, was opened-mouthed in shock when Dalby added, 'I will be donating the money from this generous prize to Gingerbread, the charity for single parent families.'

Equally surprised was Australian author Catherine Adler. 'I'm still coming to terms with this. I did not expect to win, but I'm thrilled to share this prize with a debut novelist like Isobel, whose book was written with such authority, such heart, such invention, it's wonderful.' She also had something to say about her fellow authors who didn't win last night. 'Really, the field is strong, and any one of these books could have carried the day, *The Clava Cairn* is amazing, and I loved Kai Noguchi's book – I suppose tonight the real winner is literature – storytelling, and that's not a bad thing.' Ms Adler went on to say that she would be donating the full amount of her share of the prize to the Black Lives Matter Global Network Foundation. 'It's important for me to use the platform of the prize to draw attention to the continuing impacts of colonialism in the world, this money will go where it can be used for good.'

Before making the announcement, prize Chair Natasha Moubray paid a moving tribute to her lifelong friend and Bannerman Prize benefactor Gideon Bannerman who disappeared from his South Kensington home over two months ago.

'Over fifty years ago, I attended my first Bannerman Prize dinner. I was a fourteen-year-old spotty girl in an ugly frilly dress. My father had been shortlisted for the prize that year – and he didn't win. That night I met Gideon Bannerman and we talked about our lives up to that point, and our hopes for the future. Then we went home. Then our lives happened.' She raised a toast to the absent heir to the Bannerman fortune, and then made the surprise announcement of the joint winners.

Mr Bannerman is the subject of an ongoing missing persons investigation.

It was quiet in the square, but the night had snapped into a sudden cold that seemed to her all the more frigid for being still and cloudless. When she opened her door, she saw a brown parcel had been delivered through her letter-box and was now on the floor. She also noticed two dirty teacups on the third step of the stairs, sitting on a small stack of unopened mail and some discarded newspapers. She knelt carefully and picked up the parcel. It was weighty. She saw that it was from Bromleys, Bond Street. She walked into the kitchen and tore open the package. There were two things inside. A large catalogue entitled, *Harvest Place, Pictures, Furniture, Silver and Curios from the Bannerman Estate.* The cover photograph was the Adam Skeleton Clock that had stood on the mantle in Gideon's sitting room. Then there was another envelope. Inside was a note from Gordon Bennett:

'Dearest Natasha,

I hope you like the catalogue. I think it turned out rather well. We're all very happy with it and already there has been considerable interest in a number of lots. Time will tell!

I am also forwarding you a note that was addressed to you that we found between the covers of the book that is also enclosed. I conferred with Mr Kuznetsov and he advised us to pass it on to you.

Perhaps we will see you at the auction.

Warm regards, Gordon'

The enclosed book was From *Tropics to Table – The Genius of Sugar.*
Inside its cover was a single sheet of Harvest Place stationery folded twice.
Tasha opened it and saw a page of Gideon's twisty, cursive handwriting.

Tasha,

    *Don't worry, this isn't going to be one of those 'this is what
you mean to me letters', I know how much you would despise
that, and I wouldn't know how to write it anyway. But it seems
wrong to leave without explaining myself – in-as-much as I
can.*

    *I was always amazed at how you understood the poetic life
of people. The secrets of who they were. I could never see it
myself, but I understood it to be true enough, through you.
To me, it was like some magical power that you had. I always
thought it allowed you to be in the world in a brave, complete
way – to understand the nature of things. For better or for
worse, I never thought that I could do that, or more correctly
– Gideon Bannerman – could never have done that. But now,
don't laugh, I'm going to give it a go.*

    *I'm going to unlock the cage of Harvest Place and leave
the ghosts of my mother and my father, endlessly present in
the walls and the windows, the books and the pictures and the
clocks and the damned money.*

    *Think about it Tasha, what did they achieve? My mother
hated herself, drank most days, put on lipstick and looked in
the mirror. My father ran around in circles and went nowhere,
screaming on his deathbed for a fantasy England.*

    *I don't want to join them, and that's what will happen if I
stay – do you understand? They're waiting for me, here. That*

cannot be my story. I'm leaving all that for Yuri to sort. I know you think he was one of my biggest mistakes, but really, he was just part of the story. You see? I'm trying. Maybe I'll get better with practice.

You always said I had a gift for the obvious.

You and I are old now. We find ourselves, two old people still making our way in the world. In the time that is left to us, five years? A week? A day? Who knows? Whatever it is, I want to pull myself to the centre. I need to participate in the turbulent, shifting, messy, destabilising centre of things. I need to see what's there. Take my chances. I am going to change the way my story ends. Is it too late for a brave gesture? Let's hope not. You are my true friend. If anyone will understand this, it is you, and if you don't right now – I hope you will.

You will remember Tasha, you, who remembers everything, the first night we met at the prize dinner all those years ago, you said to me, you don't look like Gideon Bannerman. You told me I looked more like Neville Haddock. Who was Neville Haddock? You had already imagined a different life for me.

Wish me luck. Let's see how I go.

All my love, always, Giddy.

Her mouth was dry and her eyes were glassy. She stared at Gideon's handwritten words. Was this the note that was meant to be in the empty envelope she found at his house all those weeks ago when he vanished? How had it been misplaced? Did he mean to leave it for her and then had second thoughts?

For the past ten weeks she had searched for Gideon, she had petitioned for Gideon, and she had mourned him. Now she had found him, in these scattered words. She felt no better. She felt heavier, more drawn down into age. She couldn't be sure of what he hoped to find. In her exhaustion, his words swam about in her head. 'Turbulent', 'shifting', 'messy', 'destabilising'. Since he'd left, those words held a bitter, visceral reality for her. He was so much of her past. They were misfits together. She'd said to Yuri that Gideon was her 'history'. That was true for her. Now, this choice that he'd made, these words on this page, were also part of her story. She wondered for a moment what she ought to do. It was too late to call anyone. She would decide in the morning.

She left the note open on the bench and poured herself a whiskey. She began leafing through the catalogue. There was the Bonnard, a study of a woman at a table in front of an empty plate. A beautiful Paul Nash watercolour of a dark wood she couldn't remember ever seeing at the house. There was the photographic portrait of Philippa Bannerman, 'Silver gelatin print. Angus McBean, 1952'. A Cartier watch in the shape of a panther encrusted in sapphires. A Bulgari dragonfly in diamonds and emeralds and then, next to it, in a smaller photograph in the bottom right hand corner of the page, this item: 'Hair Clip. Gold plate. Six Diamante Ladybirds. Costume Jewellery, 1960'.

She remembered herself at fourteen, pushing that clip into her hair as she readied herself for her first Bannerman Prize dinner, poking her eyes awkwardly with the sticky mascara brush and trying to balance her blue eyeshadow evenly on both eyelids.

After her father had slapped her and dragged her away from the Royal Society for the Arts that night, she thought that her hairclip had been lost in the street, or in the taxi as she sobbed her way home. But somehow Gideon had found it and kept it.

Neville Haddock. Had she really called him Neville Haddock? In all the conversations she had had with him over the years, all of their shared stories, she marvelled that this had somehow snagged in his memory. Neville Haddock. If she had imagined a new life for him, it certainly wasn't this. Soon it would be winter. She hoped wherever he was now, and wherever he would be then, wherever he found himself, that Gideon Bannerman would be warm.

She finished her whiskey and stood. She felt the now familiar twinge of pain from her left knee to her hip, then it settled. The time was getting on now for two.

She walked to the window over the sink and ran some water in her glass. She was hungry, and her head sang with a buzzy weariness that made her feel light. Transparent. *In the time that is left to us, five years, a week, a day?*

She looked at the window and saw her ghost reflection, partly there, and partly not. She looked at the cubist zig-zag angles of the roofs around her, the chimney stacks, the satellite dishes and the aerials, the silhouettes of cranes and the low, green, acid light in her corner of the city. The lives that surrounded her. She flattened her palm on the glass, and felt the cold through the pane.

After a moment she took her hand away and saw the buckled yellowed rind of the crescent moon far-off in the clear, late autumn sky, and watched the ghostly, vaporous shape of her palm and fingers disappear.

Acknowledgements

Parts of this book were directly informed by a close reading of David Kynaston's exhaustive social history of post-war Britain, *Tales of a New Jerusalem*.

Thank you Ross Canadé for your detailed reading and careful attention. Thanks to Simon Ruth and Johann Ruth for their support in the completion of this book. Thanks to Jane Menelaus for our conversations, friendship and encouragement. Thanks to Deborah Walker who knows what we talk about when we talk about books.

Thanks to Kate Grenville for sharing her memories of being longlisted, and shortlisted for the Booker Prize and of her meeting with Queen Elizabeth. Thanks to David Marr for telling me war stories from the front lines of literary judging.

Thanks to David Hare, Christos Tsiolkas, and Andrea Goldsmith.

Thanks to everyone at The Faber Academy, Paul Kingsnorth, Tom Bromley, Alan Margolis, Katharine Ugeux-Lewis, CC Huang, Cathy Kirby, Jay Hargreaves, Dani Heywood-Lonsdale, Bex Cooper, Antonia Biggs, Elizabeth Le Vay, Troy Suarez, Rachel White, Nicole Adams and Isabelle Myers-Joseph. Particular thanks to Tim Farthing who provided feedback on the completed manuscript and Gordon Thompson for his incisive editing.

Thanks to James Griffin and Rachel Cook for their keen eyes, close reading and editing suggestions.

Thanks to Chris Anastassiades, Neil Armfield, Carol Boas, Bridget Haire, Val Kent, Dean Murphy, David Pottinger, Brian Pryke and Alia Dann Swift.